THRONE OF DARKNESS

AWAKENING THE LIGHTFORGED
BOOK 1

SPENCER RUSSELL SMITH

CONTENTS

GLOSSARY

*To Mrs. Simmons, who said she expected to see my books on the shelves
one day.*

BY SPENCER RUSSELL SMITH

Awakening The Lightforged
Throne of Darkness
Sanctuary
The Shattering
The Last Knight
Awakening the Lightforged (The Complete Trilogy)

Tales of Efruumani
Another Way (short story)
Music of the Lights (short story)
Cleareye (novella)

Visit my Website for Content Warnings

Get a FREE novella set in the world of this series—*Cleareye*— by signing up to my
mailing list at: www.spencerrussellsmith.com/freenovella or scan the QR code below:

There is a map included in this book, but if you want to see a full-color, high resolution
version to follow along with, you can find one on my website at:
https://www.spencerrussellsmith.com/art

A Brief Glossary of Auroramantic Abilities

Samjati Abilities

Violetnodes: sap heat from the air or produce ice
Aquanodes: manipulate existing ice or water
Greennodes: push and pull ice and water
Greynodes: enhance strength and durability
Clearnodes: enhance sensory perception
Opalnodes: flare other abilities
Orangenodes: see into the past
Yellownodes: manipulate luck, chance, coincidence
Rednodes: produce and manipulate darklight
Bluenodes: steal auroralight from others
Ambernodes: limited precognition
Blacknodes: hide uses of auroramancy

Natari Abilities

Violetnodes: produce heat, fire, and lightning
Aquanodes: manipulate existing fire or lava
Greennodes: push and pull volcanic rock and lava
Greynodes: enhance stamina and agility
Clearnodes: enhance sensory perception
Opalnodes: flare other abilities
Orangenodes: see into the past
Yellownodes: manipulate luck, chance, coincidence
Rednodes: produce and manipulate hardlight
Bluenodes: transfer auroralight to others
Ambernodes: limited precognition
Blacknodes: detect uses of auroramancy

Pre-Destruction Efruumani

Note: Globular Projection.

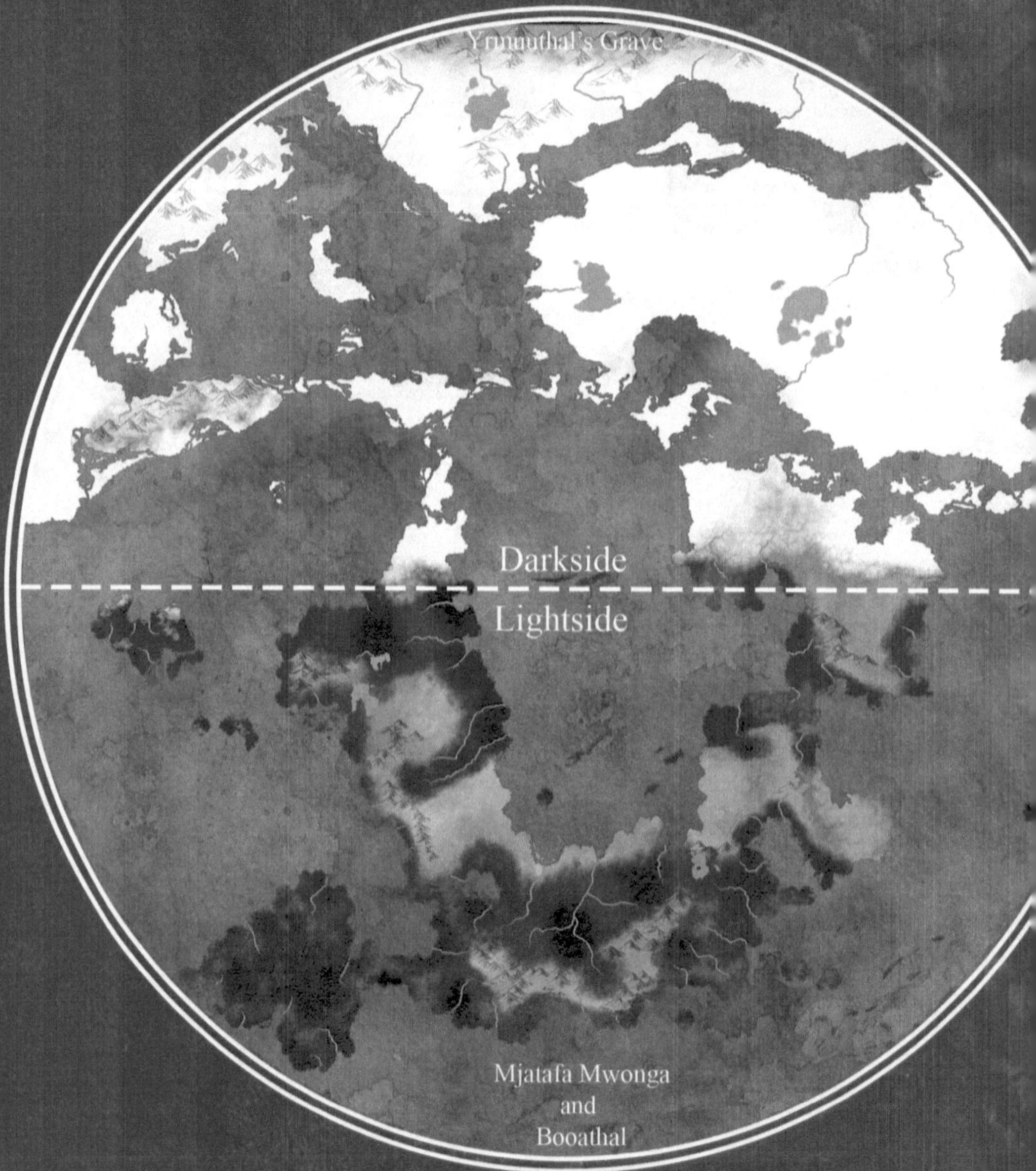

Planetary System Notes:

Satellite research of the Beyond has provided immesurable context for the Efruumani System. Our red-orange, volatile star ranks low in temperature and lifespan.

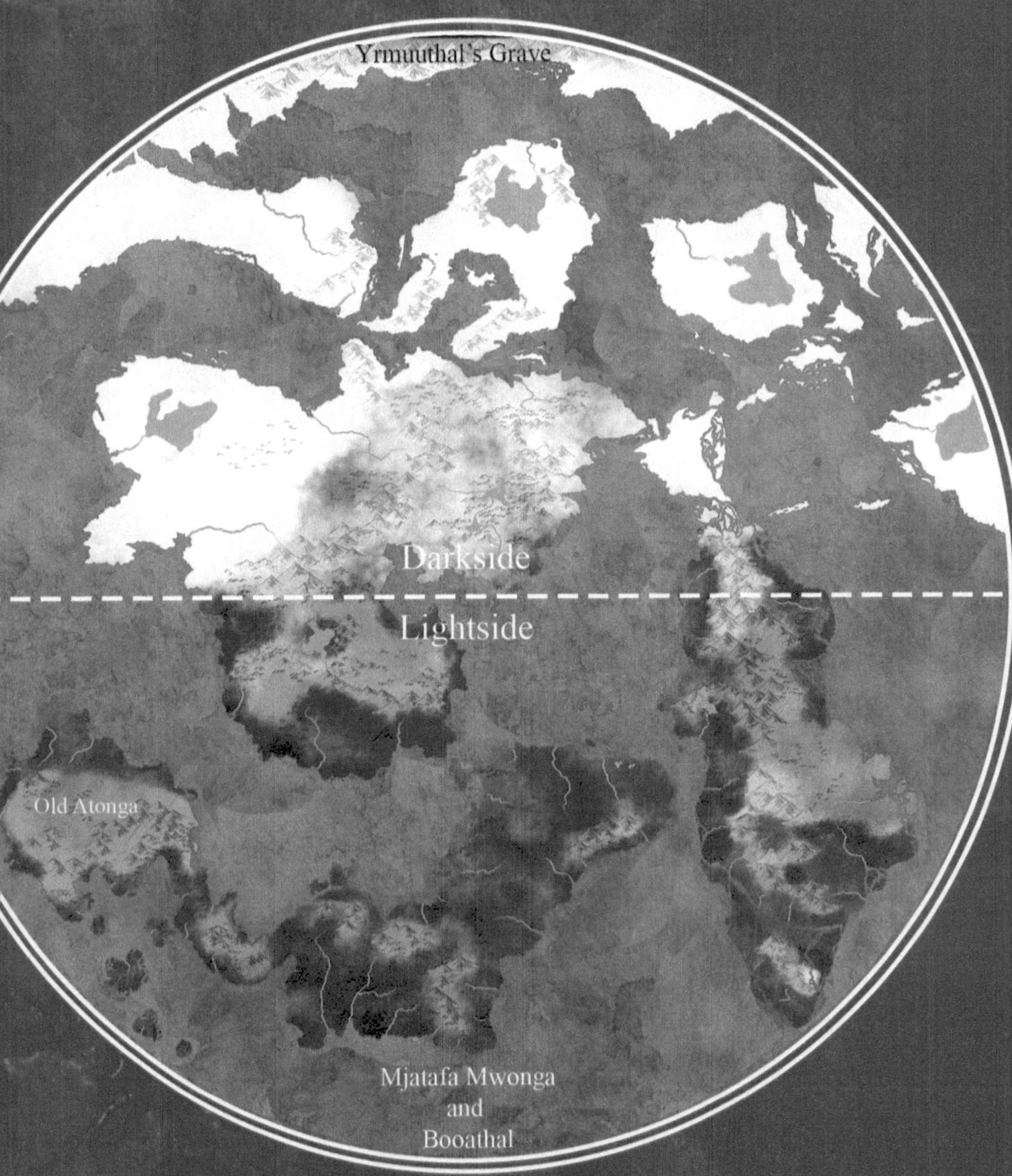

Efruumani appears to be a habitable moon of the gas giant, Myrskaan, rather than a planet in its own right. We were surprised to learn that Efruumani's tidally locked position in Myrskaan's Lagrange Point is unusual, and should be much less stable than it has been throughout our history. The Destruction of Yrmuunthal has made this painfully evident, and has spurred Mjatafa Mwonga's construction and the race to find a suitable home among the Beyond.

The Efruumani System
Myrskaan
Efruumani

Atjakuu

Notes on Pronunciation

Consonants

C: though not often used for names in this book, always has the value of *k*, never *s*

J: always has the value of *y* as in your, or yell

G: always has the sound of English *g* in get.

The apostrophe marks a glottal stop, which can be pronounced like an English double-consonant:

n'n for example, would be pronounced as the *nn* in *unnamed*, as opposed to *unaimed*.

Vowels

A: always has the value of *a* in *mark* or *kart*

AA: always has the value of *a* in *cake* or *tame*

AI: always has the value of *y* in *sky* or of *i* in *kite*

E: always has the value of *e* in *let* or *ten*

I: always has the value of *e* in *free* or *preen*

Y: always has the value of *i* in *kick* or *bid*

O: always has the value of *o* as in *okay* or *omen*

UU: always has the value of the *oo* or *ew* sounds as in *pool* or *stew*

If you want to hear how the names are pronounced, scan the code below for a TikTok where I go through the names in this book.

Prologue

Deathknight

C. 7 years, 2 months until projected Exodus Date.

C. 5 years, 1 month, 32 days, 28 hours since the Destruction of Yrmuunthal

The meeting was not going well.

Leaders of the six remaining factions of the Efruumani Union had gathered in secret to find a way off their dying world.

The idea of the meeting itself caused tension, but that had only grown since the faction leaders and their aides arrived. Everyone had removed their masks, which didn't bother Estingai, but it put her husband, Svemakuu, and the other Samjati on edge. It was a gesture of vulnerability and trust, reserved for family and loved ones. This was not a family.

Estingai, at least, could blame her nerves on the location: a cave far beneath the ground, connected to the surface by kilometers of dark, twisting tunnels and lava tubes.

She hated caves.

The meeting chamber contained no furnishings, no hooks for hanging lanterns, and no refreshments. Just the round, metal table they'd brought with them. The commanders stood around it in the center of the room, their aides a few steps behind. They wore clean and well-maintained clothing, if a bit worn, but Narvyk's coat was the closest any of them had to a uniform. Their armor and weapons were even more haphazard. Most were family heirlooms, or pieces scavenged or looted off the bodies of Imaia soldiers. Estingai and Svemakuu wore ensembles composed of all three.

In fact, the one thing unifying them was their lack of a uniform visual identity.

That and our desperation.

"We can't spare any more personnel to send to Darkside, Tepjo." Narvyk, head of the Ironpeak faction, rubbed his forehead between his antlers. He squeezed his golden eyes shut for a moment, broad shoulders bowed. "With the Imaia sending people there now and working on expanding their railway project, there's just too much risk."

"He's right," said Kogen. The Stormswind commander was like a younger, angrier version of Narvyk. Both men were solid, though even discounting his antlers, Kogen stood half-a-hand taller, with wider shoulders and a thicker chest. "Raids on supplies the Imaia ships to and from those locations, however—"

"We're not here to talk about lightless raids," Estingai grumbled under her breath.

Kogen stopped talking.

Estingai looked up to find all six commanders staring at her. She resisted the urge to bite her lip. This wasn't the first time she'd spoken her thoughts louder than intended.

"Reign in your Fireborn," Kogen said to Raima, the head of Frozen Phantom.

Estingai shut her mouth but did not drop her eyes. She met Kogen's dark gaze.

"Estingai," Raima warned.

She shifted her gaze to the wall behind the Stormswind commander. If the soft glow of Auroralight had been brighter, Estingai would have been able to see her reflection in it. Instead, the obsidian walls were black mirrors, the shimmering lights specters waiting just out of sight.

Estingai clenched her fists.

I hate caves. And tunnels. And lightless underground chambers.

Something brushed her gauntleted hand. Estingai glanced right, catching a faint grin from Svemakuu. She barely hid her smile. They wouldn't hold hands during a meeting like this, but if they stood close enough that their hands touched, so be it.

"What are they even doing here, Raima?" Tepjo grumbled. "I thought this meeting was leadership and a single aide each. To reduce the risk of word getting out, like last time."

The leader of the Icevein faction was a solid man with a slight paunch and just enough fat under his narrow chin to give him a round, ruddy face.

Estingai wondered, not for the first time, how Tepjo had claimed leadership of his faction. Most of those she knew that served under the man were hardy and hard-working. Tepjo seemed the type who would delegate any task he didn't enjoy or that wouldn't benefit him.

Vila, commander of Last Shadow, and the only faction leader that had worn full armor, snorted. "Why do you think, Tepjo?" Her voice dripped with contempt. "The Knights Reborn are all gone. Estingai and Svemakuu are the only Knights left who give us anything near the edge the Knights gave us against the Imaia. Our people—*all* of our people— see them as heroes. They deserve to be here."

Tepjo's jaw bunched. He looked about to speak.

"I also have good ideas now and then," Svemakuu said before the Icevein leader got the chance, "and Estingai's pretty good in a fight."

Tepjo and Kogen glared at Svemakuu, as did their aides.

He just grinned back. He did that a lot.

That dimpled grin and golden eyes got him out of as much trouble as they got him into.

They got him me.

After getting him in trouble with her first, of course. She'd nearly killed him.

Svemakuu was too handsome for his own good, even when he wasn't grinning. It got even worse when he grew facial hair—a neat beard that gave his angular jaw a silver trim. He kept his large, fan-like antlers in good condition, and his skin was just the right shade of light blue that it never affected the tint of the twelve colors of the glowing gemcrest atop his brow. At the moment, his face bore the dark tint of his blacknodes. As an Iceborn, that pair of biogems allowed him to conceal any use of Auroramancy by those at the table, should an Imaia piercer pass above looking for them.

Estingai kept the blacknodes of her own gemcrest bright too. As a Fireborn, she could sense nearby Auroramancy the way a piercer or seeker would, though her armored jacket concealed their light.

"Thank you, Svemakuu." Raima's tone was neutral, but she gave both of them pointed looks before turning back to the other commanders.

"I brought them, Tepjo, because if the Imaia somehow find out about this meeting, Estingai and Svemakuu are the only people that can take on multiple Lightforged."

They'd done that a few times, but Estingai hoped she never had to face one of those horrible creatures again.

"If we can get back to the purpose of this meeting?" said Narvyk. "Which, as Estingai pointed out, is not to discuss raids, but finding a way off this world. Mylora, do your people have any leads?"

The leader of Nightstone looked around the table, hesitated, then sighed. "I have, unfortunately, decided to end our efforts to preserve Efruumani with georaural technology. Even if we could find the correct techniques to hold the world locked between Myrskaan and the sun, or find enough biogems and spirits to create the amount of georaurals necessary, we would need to build structures in orbit for them to be of any use. The resources spent testing are too cost—"

Tepjo sniffed, cutting the woman off. "We should put those georaurals to work increasing the output of Icevein's lowlight farms and gardens. Bonde's death gave us the opportunity to lie low and let Atonga think they've broken us. As far as they're concerned, they eliminated the driving force behind our extremist elements. As long as Vila and her people can control themselves, Atonga will forget we exist. We can wait them out and reclaim Efruumani once they've left."

Vila glared at Tepjo, her voice as cold as Darkside's wastes. "Unfortunately, the rest of us don't have the luxury of an alternate reality, Icevein." She spat the last word.

Tepjo just shook his head and looked around them with an insufferable, patronizing grin.

Estingai's jaw bunched.

"You all seriously believe that Imaia propaganda?"

The leather of Estingai's gauntlets creaked as she clenched her fists.

"It's just a tool they used to scare people into their ranks and turn them against us," said Tepjo. "Now they just keep it up to—"

Estingai slammed her hands down on the table. "Propaganda? Are you really that stupid? The *oruu* are gone. I haven't seen a single spirit in over a cycle. Not to mark the passing of the hours, not to signal the auroras or holidays, not to dance with the flames of our fires. Darkside is near-uninhabitable without heating technology and regular supply shipments, even for former natives. The Imaia has rapidly lost farmland outside of *Mjatafa Mwonga* due to desertification. Do you really think the Imaia has somehow managed all of that as mere propaganda? You—"

"Estingai!" Raima's voice cracked like a whip.

Estingai snapped her mouth shut but did not break eye contact with the Icevein commander.

As she lifted her hands, Estingai felt the heat of the metal table through her leather gloves. She hid her chagrin, dimming the pair of violet biogems at her collarbone. She hadn't brightened them much, else she might have turned the table to slag.

"While Estingai spoke out of turn, her words ring true, Commander Tepjo." Raima looked around the table. "Even if the end of the world was Imaia propaganda, their efforts in building the city of Mjatafa Mwonga and their methods of fleeing to the stars have stripped Efruumani of resources. Their patrols keep us underground. Our hunting and foraging parties bring back less and less. Nearly half of our people cannot even walk in the sun without covering themselves. If you cannot agree that the world *is* ending, or at least work with us on that premise, you might as well leave now and see how well your lowlight farms serve Icevein once Efruumani hurtles into the sun."

Tepjo snorted, folding his arms. "You won't last long enough to escape Efruumani without the food from Icevein's farms."

The cavern's stuffy air grew thick with tension. Estingai primed her greynodes and violetnodes, ready to act at the first sign of violence.

Svemakuu barked a laugh.

Estingai jumped—as did a few of the commanders—and looked wide-eyed at her husband.

What in darkness...?

Then she caught a glint of something familiar in his eyes and relaxed a little.

"Something funny, Svemakuu?" Raima asked.

"Of course." He shot her a wide grin before looking to Tepjo, "I'm sorry that I'm the only one here that appreciates your humor, Commander Icevein."

"My humor?"

Svemakuu nodded. "That bit about the end of the world being Imaia propaganda. And threatening to deny us access to food. That was a joke, wasn't it?" He paused just long enough for Tepjo to open his mouth, then continued before the man could speak. "It must have been a joke. If it wasn't, that would mean that the friends I have among your people don't realize they're being led by someone who would see them dead through willful ignorance. It would mean you believe that our people who were lost stealing Imaia resources died for nothing. I'm sure you didn't mean to imply that. Or that you would withhold valuable supplies from your brothers and sisters in arms because you refuse to accept reality. Surely, Commander, you did not mean that."

Svemakuu's voice had lost all warmth or humor, his tone as dark as the cavern walls. He pinned Tepjo with an icy gaze as utter silence filled the room.

Estingai's husband was not a violent man. He had, however, little patience for those who would put their interests above those of the many. People like that brought out a darkness in him.

Everyone in the room had a shadow in them. Constant war, upheaval, and the end of the world did that to a person. But Svemakuu kept his darkness well-hidden.

Estingai had feared that would change when the God King killed Svemakuu's parents. But it had not. And none of the tragedy he'd seen in the cycles since had, either.

Somehow, her husband smiled. And that kept her doing the same.

Svemakuu's parents had taken in Estingai when she'd had no one else.

And now, they're gone, too.

His brother Koruuksi, and their adopted sister Uuchantuu were all they had left.

Estingai's chest grew tight even as Tepjo cleared his throat and laughed.

"You're right, of course, Iceborn Svemakuu." The Icevein commander forced a grin. "You're the only one here with a sense of humor." He looked around the table before continuing, "Can't a man joke about the end of the world?"

"My thoughts exactly." Svemakuu grinned.

"Hopefully, we can now get down to some more productive discussion." Tepjo cleared his throat again. "Icevein's farms are at your disposal. I can send farmers and horticulturists with seeds and saplings to your bases. I'm certain you all have a lot of underutilized space. Especially you, Vila, with those enormous caverns you keep your stolen ships in."

"That is very generous of you, Tepjo," Narvyk said, "and a good start to formalizing our alliance. Unfortunately, not all of our bases have enough water—or at least not enough easily accessible sources of water—to sustain more gardens than we already have."

"My engineers could help with that," Vila suggested. "There's not much raw copper left on this continent, but my people have found leftover tools and finery from the abandoned Atonga ruins that could be used for piping. We've even been able to just transplant some piping systems to our base. It's harder than field irrigation, but we've made it work."

Estingai nudged Svemakuu. *You're incredible,* she mouthed. *I love you,* he mouthed back.

The simple words she'd heard so many times still sent an amazing warmth through Estingai. Merely touching his gauntleted hand with her own didn't seem enough.

That's not what we're here for.

There would be plenty of time for the two of them alone when they returned to Wolfden.

The corner of Svemakuu's mouth twitched as though he knew what she was thinking. He usually did.

"Mylora," Kogen said, "I don't believe you'd finished telling us about your research."

The woman frowned. "We should be able to spare some georaurals for the rest of you. As I said, we've deemed preserving Efruumani no longer viable. With the Imaia leaving, perhaps we never should have considered it. Though they had been looking to the stars even before—" She paused, biting her lip and glancing around the table for a moment. "Before Yrmuunthal's destruction."

The room's mood dampened at that. Everyone had known Efruumani's two Aathal, the World Trees, were important. Just not *how* important.

Not until one was gone.

The trees had resisted the few attempts to harvest their leaves and wood such that most believed only a god could destroy them. Nobody had imagined that one of the gods would do just that.

Most of those present had worshiped Kweshrima in one way or another. No one knew why the goddess had destroyed the Aathal. Some —like Mylora—refused to speak of, or even acknowledge Kweshrima's role in the Aathal's destruction—and the world's subsequent decline.

"And your other research, Commander Mylora?" Svemakuu asked, warmly. "Concerning escaping Efruumani through a means other than the stars?"

Mylora gave him a thankful smile. "We've been able to confirm that the oruu do—or did—exist in another plane of existence most of the time, only passing through to ours when they choose. That, combined with certain legends of the gods' origins, leads me to believe it is possible for mortals to cross over to such a plane of existence—this realm of the spirits. Whether we will find a home there, or find a way through to a new home remains to be discovered. We should only need a small percentage of our georaurals to conduct those tests, however, so the rest are at your disposal."

"We should use our combined resources to hurt the Imaia," said Vila. "We can launch an attack on a position far from our bases—they will comb that area for a time while we regroup. Maybe their railways—

something that will make them pull back into their city for a time and let us be."

Raima sighed, shaking her head. "We all share your motivations, Vila, but we have to keep the Imaia active along those railways. Even with water piping and Icevein's farms, we need their supplies. Your engineers and Nightstone's scientists are resourceful, but we have no foundries or factories capable of producing cleaning supplies, medicines, modern weapons, or any of the other supplies the Imaia keep stocked. Disrupting those supply lines will hurt us as much as it hurts them."

"Then we will strike somewhere else," Last Shadow's commander insisted. "We need to make them bleed after what they did to Bonde and the others, even if he had grown too extreme in his methods."

"No, Vila," Raima said. "We must focus on survival, not vengeance."

She paused, looking around the table. "I believe Tepjo and Kogen had the right idea. Somewhat, at least. We should lie low and let the Imaia forget about us. We'll use the spies Kogen and I placed inside Mjatafa Mwonga to plan quiet, targeted raids that have little impact on the Imaia, but great reward for us. Ideally, we would make them less intense each time, so the Imaia think we are losing manpower or support."

"And how do we get off the planet after that?" Narvyk asked. "Finding a way onto Myrskaan Station is our best chance, and it won't be easy to get all our people there if we do. Not with the tech and ships we have now."

It wasn't good enough. Estingai wanted more than anything to escape this world—to fly through the stars, free to look for a new home. But leaving others to die with Efruumani would drain all sweetness from that victory. A glance at Svemakuu told her he felt the same way. His mouth was a thin line, eyes down.

"We could steal more of their vehicles," Mylora suggested. "If we got our hands on some of their troop transports, my scientists and Vila's engineers should be able to use their technology to make something that can get us to Myrskaan Station. Some of those new mini rail guns would also help. There's a reason the Imaia carefully controlled the use of firearms."

"It's not big enough."

Everyone looked to Svemakuu. Estingai's husband still wore a contemplative expression.

"Would you mind elaborating on that, Iceborn?" Narvyk asked.

"A troop transport isn't big enough," Svemakuu said. "Getting only some of us off Efruumani is not an option."

He met the eyes of each commander with a hard expression. "If our end goal is only getting a handful of our people off Efruumani, we will have to choose who lives and who dies. That could break every one of our factions, never mind any unity between us. It also makes us no better than the Imaia. Worse, actually. They're leaving us behind because they see us as monsters. If we surrendered, they'd likely kill or imprison us, but they wouldn't leave us behind."

"You have a solution in mind, Svemakuu?" Raima asked.

"I do," said Svemakuu. "First, we are no longer six factions. We can't think of ourselves that way if we are truly united, which is the only way this will work. No more Icevein or Frozen Phantom or Last Shadow, save maybe to refer to the different primary bases."

"Then what do we call ourselves?" Mylora asked.

"The Remnant." Svemakuu let the word hang in the air for a moment. "We are all that remains of those who fight the Imaia. Kweshrima may have doomed Efruumani, but the Imaia began stripping the planet of resources long before then."

"I can agree to that," said Kogen after a moment of silence. "I assume you think it would be best to redistribute our people through our bases?"

Svemakuu nodded. "Some won't like moving, but it won't be any worse than the upheaval we've already experienced."

"And once we do that?" Vila asked.

There was a hint of skepticism in the woman's tone.

"Then we get the Imaia to attack us with one of their capital ships."

All eyes around the table grew wide. Svemakuu had incredible ideas. They just didn't always come out of his mouth the right way.

"Right." A grin slid onto his face. "While I agree we should eventually try to lie low, we first need to give them a reason to send one of their capital ships out of Mjatafa Mwonga. Whether it's dealing with us, or some other reason our spies can feed to the Imaia's high command."

"And what then?" Vila asked. "We steal it?"

Svemakuu shook his head, grinning wider. "We blow it out of the sky."

That caused even more confusion. He'd probably done that on purpose.

"I believe what my husband means," said Estingai, "is that if we try to steal one of the Imaia's larger ships, they will know that we have it and will be motivated to reclaim it. If we instead destroy it—ideally without too much damage—they will believe we did so for supplies and weapons, rather than for the craft itself. They might not consider salvaging the wreckage worth the effort."

"Exactly!" Svemakuu said. "And we won't need to commandeer the Imaia's space station. Was that not clear?"

This time Estingai sighed.

"Tepjo, do you have any caverns large enough to rebuild a capital ship?" Raima asked.

He thought for a moment, then shook his head.

"We have one that might work," said Vila. "We've used it as a gathering area, a hospital and farming space, since it has no connections to the outside. If we could have some Shapers to widen it and make it accessible, it might work. With some georaural reinforcements from Nightstone, of course. Once we open it up enough to fit a cruiser in, however, we won't be able to hide it in there again."

"What if critical components are damaged when we take it out?" Mylora asked. "We won't be able to replicate reactors or power cells of that size. And the ones on the ships we've already stolen won't be big enough."

"Our spies can help with that," Raima said. "It will be dangerous, but if we need to replace any parts we can't fabricate ourselves—"

Estingai stiffened, tuning out Raima. For a moment, she'd thought she'd sensed...

Estingai rolled her shoulders and moved her head from side to side to cover a glance around the room, as she brightened her blacknodes.

Nothing. She couldn't sense Svemakuu, but she should have felt anything coming from outside the immediate area of his shroud.

Still nothing.

She could have been mistaken. Or it could mean that whoever she'd sensed had dimmed their biogems and was still there, invisible to Estingai's senses.

She flared her blacknodes in a burst of power, only for a few seconds. But that should have allowed her senses to reach out even farther, possibly all the way to the surface or down one of the long tunnels.

But again, nothing.

Estingai considered brightening her opalnodes, allowing her to flare and burn out her blacknodes in one massive burst—something only full Auroraborn like she and Svemakuu could do. Opalnodes were ultimately useless on their own.

She decided against it, instead brightening her clearnodes to enhance her other senses. It took her a moment to adjust as all her senses increased twelvefold.

"If we wait until just before a supply shipment goes out on rail to one of their Darkside bases, or their people at the end of the railway, and create a roadblock..." Svemakuu sounded as though he was speaking directly into her ear. "...something that they can't easily clear in a day or two, we could have our spies encourage the decision to send out supplies on one of their older capital ships, with a minimal crew..."

Estingai tuned the conversation out again, focusing on other sounds. There weren't many, save for the occasional creaking and clinking of fabric and armor. The stark chamber's cool temperature and dim lighting made it easier for her to adjust. Her vision sharpened into greater contrast and she became more aware of the slight chill against her face, the weight of her clothing and armor. Her mouth was parched and tasted of the dried meat ration she'd eaten before the meeting. She tuned out the slight body odor from those around her—including herself—and the spike of arousal that always came with brightening one's clearnodes.

Closing her eyes would have allowed Estingai the greatest focus on sound, but she didn't want to alarm anyone without cause.

Even if I did sense someone, these tunnels twist and turn and intersect for miles, and Svemakuu's shroud will keep us concealed.

The soft clink of an armored footstep near the back of the room.

The lights went out.

Estingai whirled around, priming all twelve pairs of biogems. She donned her mask, seeing only through her enhanced senses and the dim light of reflected gemcrests . Despite her Samjati blue skin, she didn't possess the golden eyes and natural night vision of those with stronger Samjati blood like Svemakuu.

What she saw turned her veins to ice.

A tall, imposing figure outlined by points of Auroralight shining in all twelve colors strode from the darkness. It wore armor of polished iron that Estingai knew well, infused biogems reflecting on the metal.

Estingai's hands flexed toward the weapons at her waist, but she drew neither. Swords did little good against a lightforged. She didn't have enough rounds to shoot the creature until it could no longer heal, and the rail gun on her back would take too long to charge.

But Estingai could create her own weapons. Better ones.

The rasp of titansteel and click of firearms told Estingai that the others had drawn their weapons. They didn't have better options—only she and Svemakuu had rednodes.

Something was off about the lightforged's armor. It wore the usual full helmet with a detailed faceplate, mocking the Samjati tradition. Tall, wicked antlers sprouted from its forehead, the helm crafted to accommodate them, like Svemakuu's. The iron armor had no effect on the lightforged, but burned anyone else, Natari or Samjati. That was all normal, but this lightforged seemed more impressive than those Estingai had fought.

Is it more ornate? Did the Imaia send an officer after us?

As far as she knew, lightforged only had one commander among them...

No.

Estingai froze just as crystals of frost and motes of flame shimmered around the lightforged's outstretched hand. In a moment, they formed into a massive blade of silver and gold, as long as the lightforged was tall. The blade extended from an arched cross guard, thickening near the end where a small crescent of metal had been removed, golden cracks webbing out over the silvery metal, so that the weapon ended in a wicked hook.

"*Kifrytari!*" Someone breathed from behind.

Estingai steeled herself even as her heart pounded and her legs threatened to collapse.

Kifrytari -- the Imaia's Deathknight, commander of their twisted, all-but immortal lightforged. The creature that had murdered and broken many Estingai held dear. Most lightforged carried iron weaponry, but that cursed blade was synonymous with the Deathknight.

Estingai brightened her greynodes, increasing her speed and reflexes, and her rednodes.

Two golden shields formed in Estingai's hands, each over a meter and a half wide. Hardlight didn't cut as well as a metal sword, but the blunt edges would work better for Estingai's purposes.

Svemakuu had formed his own darklight shields, the deep violet substance fadeing into wisps at the edge.

The Deathknight stopped a few paces away and leveled its massive blade at the two of them. With a flick of the wrist, it switched its grip and slammed the blade almost a quarter of its length into the stone floor, then fell into a ready stance.

Estingai leapt forward with a roar, knowing Svemakuu would follow. Her cry echoed off the walls, bolstered by the voices of the aides.

"Protect the commanders!" Svemakuu barked.

Estingai rushed the Deathknight, raising her shields as she flared her violetnodes, directing twin bursts of blue-violet lightning toward the Deathknight.

The creature raised its own hardlight shield, blocking Estingai's attack even as it sent a burst of violet fire toward Svemakuu, forcing him to shelter behind his shield. At the first sign of pressure from her foe's shield, Estingai twisted away, avoiding being thrown back by the wall of hardlight. She thrust for the creature's armpit, where the armor was weak, but the Deathknight blocked the edge of her shield with its armored wrist and spun, missing Estingai with its kick, but connecting with Svemakuu's side, knocking him back.

Don't worry about him. His greynodes protect him from that.

Iceborn like Svemakuu used their greynodes to enhance strength. It also made him more durable, able to take that blow without shattering his ribs.

Estingai looked to her husband. He met her eyes through his elk-like mask and nodded.

They would attack as one.

Estingai flared her greynodes and violetnodes, leaping toward the Deathknight as energy roared through her. She aimed high, again throwing lightning.

Svemakuu aimed low. Just as the Deathknight conjured another hardlight shield, Estingai's vision flashed white-blue. She bared her teeth as the Deathknight blocked that too.

Estingai dismissed her hardlight blade and instead used her rednodes and violetnodes to send darts of hardlight wreathed in violet flames at the Deathknight. Svemakuu threw needles of violet ice. The Deathknight countered both with another shield—this one of darklight, deflecting the projectiles back at them.

Estingai had expected that.

Flaring her greennodes, she ripped chunks of volcanic rock from the floor and hurled them at the Deathknight—one low, one straight at the darklight shield.

The lightforged conjured another hardlight shield to protect its feet, but stumbled as the second rock hit its darklight shield hard enough to bend it, and hit its mark. The shield absorbed enough of the blow, but both hardlight and darklight had a drawback: the more force brought against a construct, the more Auroralight one had to feed into it to maintain the structure.

That was the only way to defeat a lightforged skilled in Auroramancy —wear down its Auroralight. They used Auroralight to heal, and that was finite. Estingai just hoped she and Svemakuu could hold out that long.

They danced with the Deathknight in fire, ice, lightning, stone, darkness and light, pushing Estingai to the limits of her abilities.

Starless nights, can we win this?

She was beginning to doubt.

Estingai had one ability she hadn't used yet, one she only used when absolutely necessary. It consumed Auroralight at the fastest rate. Svemakuu hadn't used it either, and nor had the Deathknight. Estingai's blacknodes granted her the ability not only to detect someone using

Auroramancy, but which biogems they brightened. It took training to recognize the individual signatures, like rhythms and melodies, but she'd done it. The Deathknight had yet to brighten its ambernodes.

Just as Estingai primed her own ambernodes, the Deathknight forced them back with twin walls of hardlight.

Estingai braced herself, keeping upright as her boots slid over the smooth floor. The cave already hampered the more acrobatic fighting style she and her husband were trained in, and their opponent's capabilities eliminated their usual close-quarters advantage.

Flaring her rednodes, Estingai created her own hardlight barrier and pushed back until the Deathknight released its own.

Estingai glared up at the Deathknight.

Burn it.

"Dim clearnodes!" she barked, hoping the Deathknight would take a moment to do so. Estingai flared her greynodes and ambernodes, allowing her to draw and cock her revolver with supernatural speed, and unload on the Deathknight. She brightened her rednodes as she pulled the trigger, creating small hardlight shields around her ears.

All six rounds of her first moon clip unloaded on the Deathknight, two center mass, two to the head, and one to each kneecap, aiming for the gemstones when she could. Her ambernodes allowed her to anticipate where the Deathknight's shields would appear.

The speed she pulled the trigger would have jammed most firearms, but she carried one made for Auroramancers.

Greynodes still flared, chewing away at her Auroralight, Estingai released the spent clip, loaded a new one and repeated the pattern. She did the same with her third clip, conserving the last two rounds. Holstering the firearm, she dismissed the shields around her ears. They only rang slightly.

She'd dented and scratched the Deathknight's armor in a few places and cracked one gemstone, but the number of rounds at the creature's feet told her most had hit its shields. Svemakuu had emptied his clips too – there were more spent rounds than she'd fired.

Estingai tensed, ready to go again, when the commanders' aides rushed past, weapons raised, gemcrests shining with Auroralight.

That thing will slaughter them.

Estingai took half a step forward when something caught her arm. She whirled to find Svemakuu beside her. He'd erected a darklight shield between them and the Deathknight.

"Get the commanders out of here," he said. "I'll wear it down and follow you out."

"Neither of us have taken down a normal one alone," she answered. "You expect me to leave you here with that?" The Deathknight easily killed the first two aides with spikes of violet ice through their necks. Estingai's stomach knotted in fear. "I'm not sure we can take that *together*."

Svemakuu wobbled his head, the corners of his eyes crinkling. "All the more reason for you to leave."

She shook her head firmly. "Not without you."

"Please don't fight me on this." His voice strained. "I'll occupy it long enough, then lose it in the tunnels. I can stay down here longer than it can."

He had a point. Running out of Auroralight made one lightless, but the next aurora fixed that. Lightforged died without it, from what they'd gathered. At the very least, they could be killed once their Auroralight ran out. If Svemakuu could trick it into following him deeper into the tunnels...

"Fine," she relented, "but you *run* when the time comes."

He nodded. "I promise. Now go."

Estingai gazed at him through their helmets for one last moment, wishing she could kiss him.

With a strangled grunt, she ripped her arm from his grip, stalking back toward where the commanders, still around the table, stood tense and spellbound.

"Out!" Estingai gestured to the nearby tunnel. "Don't stop until you get to your extraction points."

As they moved to the exit, Estingai stole one last look at her husband, just to see the last aide crushed against a wall. Svemakuu looked back at her, his darklight shield still intact.

The creature strode toward him, stepping over corpses like so much rubble, one hand crackling with energy as a blade of violet ice formed in the other.

"Svemakuu!"

Her husband whipped around, shield dissipating into violet-black wisps as he formed a blade of darklight large enough to match the Deathknight's own. He moved with speed nearly matching a Natari with flared greynodes.

His blade connected with a sickening crunch. The Deathknight staggered back a step, reaching for its face.

Estingai blinked, eyes wide. Svemakuu's strike had ripped off its faceplate.

When the Deathknight revealed its face, the chamber seemed to grow cold. Estingai's knees threatened to buckle.

"No," she breathed, horrified, mind rejecting what she saw.

No. Darkness, please, no.

The skin was a pale white-grey instead of dark blue, the markings glittering gold instead of black, matching the glowing eyes. But Estingai knew that face.

"Kojatere," she whispered.

Svemakuu went rigid, darklight blade fading to smoke.

No. It can't be.

The creature wearing the face of Kojatere, former Champion of the Union and leader of the Knights Reborn, stared at him, then turned to Estingai.

Estingai hadn't seen the woman die herself—she and Svemakuu had been far across the battlefield—but people they trusted had told them that her mother-in-law was dead. Slain by the God King himself.

"Estingai," Svemakuu cried, "run!"

But she froze as the Deathknight looked past her and clenched its hands into a fist. Green light glowed at the creature's brow and breastplate. The cave rumbled, cracks echoing through the chamber.

Estingai realized the Deathknight's plan with a sharp chill. She turned to the commanders, raised a warning hand. But the cry of "Move!" died on her lips as the tunnel collapsed in a cloud of dust and rubble.

Goddess...

They were gone.

Every commander, buried.

No time to dig. No time to mourn. Svemakuu needed her.

Come on, Estingai!

She turned to see the Deathknight raise its massive blade. Her husband stood alone before it.

She had to get there. To help him.

Another resonant crack stopped her cold. Estingai looked up to see her own dark shape reflected in the slab of obsidian dropping toward her.

Estingai woke in darkness.

The first breath she sucked in came out in a coughing fit that stabbed at her side. Something there was broken. Dust itched beneath her mask and the air was stuffy, thick with the smell of sweat and blood.

Her mind... wasn't working right.

And she hurt. Everywhere.

She couldn't move. Her aching muscles pushed, but something was stopping her.

Light. She needed light.

And air.

Estingai reached for her jacket zipper. She could manage that, at least. Loosening it, she tugged at her padding and shirt. But the light that should have been there didn't come.

It took her clouded mind a moment to process what that meant.

I'm lightless.

Estingai closed her eyes, fighting down the panic, trying to remember what had happened. It was hard. People could function while lightless, but the absence of Auroralight depressed them in every way. It dulled emotions, thoughts, sensations, even pain. The last of those worried Estingai the most.

She'd been fighting, about to run, when she saw...

How? Kweshrima and the others wouldn't have lied. They would have made sure—

Even her lightless mind couldn't dull the horror of that memory.

Don't focus on that. Not now.

The ceiling had caved in. She'd flared her greennodes and rednodes at the last moment, pushing back at the rock and throwing a hardlight shell around her. That saved her from being crushed, but used most of her remaining Auroralight. After that, even flaring her opalnodes hadn't been enough to move the rubble. The strain and sudden lack of Auroralight must have made her pass out.

I'm trapped.

Trapped and lightless.

1

Return

"Though the Ministry of Science has been so far unable to run any tests on the Champion's blade, Ilkwalerva, a survey of reports referencing the blade has gathered the following information: The blade is able to cut through any substance, organic or inorganic, and grants its owner even greater Auroramantic abilities than afforded the Redeemed. There is also its supposed ability to create more Redeemed."

Exodus countdown: 23 days, 25 hours, 7 minutes

Skadaatha Modibodjara, Vizier of the Third Imaia of Atonga, stepped through a tear in the fabric of reality into apartment 636 of Mjatafa Mwonga's House of Innovation. Her home.

She fell to her knees on the living room carpet the moment the portal to a realm of molten red and icy violet closed behind her. The pouch in her hand fell to the floor as she caught herself. Traveling through that fiery realm often required most of the Auroralight she could hold within her four crests of biogems, and she'd spent longer than usual on that plane this time.

Taking a deep breath, Skadaatha drew in a small amount of Auroralight from the biogems set into her armor to stave off lightlessness. Then she glanced toward the kitchen just in time to see her husband, Vysla, turn from where he stood washing cookware.

He smiled at her at first, as he always did. Then his eyes widened. He dropped the pan he'd been holding and rushed toward her.

"Skadaatha!" he gasped, looping one of her arms around his shoulders and picking up the fallen pouch. Once he bore most of her weight, he helped her to her feet and toward the balcony.

Skadaatha tensed at first but dismissed the urge to push him away. Instead, she forced herself to smile, focusing on his touch, muted as it was through her titansteel armor and the padding underneath. It wasn't easy. That she'd had that impulse in the first place infuriated her.

I'm supposed to be past that.

A month away from Vysla, however, with only herself to rely upon, may have brought back old reflexes and instincts.

It didn't help that she felt so weak. Skadaatha had drawn in enough Auroralight to prevent becoming lightless, but that was no substitute for when her gemcrests shone like the auroras themselves, investment flowing through her body.

Vysla opened the balcony door and guided her toward the railing. By the second step, Skadaatha straightened, removing her helmet and hanging it from her belt. She adjusted her long white braid as it fell over her shoulder, and closed her eyes, breathing in deep as investment filled her to bursting. It wasn't Auroralight, the invested light that filled all of Mjatafa Mwonga and gave it life. Today was Kojoa, the day after Auroraday. The energy source that filled her with life was even more potent.

Opening her eyes, Skadaatha found a genuine smile on her lips as she gripped the balcony railing and looked out over the city.

They weren't incredibly high up on the sixth floor of the building, but few buildings near the city's center rose much higher. Still, the height allowed them a vantage few saw on a daily basis. One Skadaatha hadn't realized she'd missed so much. She brightened her clearnodes to take it in properly.

Their balcony faced north, looking toward the center of the city. It allowed for a view of the Central and Military Districts, the residential complexes and Inner Sea beyond, and the high walls of the Vale at Mjatafa Mwonga's center from which light spilled forth like an overflowing cup. She ignored the iconography and other propaganda, instead focusing on the city's beauty.

Lush white, black, maroon, and dark teal foliage covered the city, appearing on every street and building in addition to the cultivated parks and gardens, with blossoms and fruits providing the occasional bloom of color. Skadaatha's enhanced vision allowed her to make out the individual petals and leaves on some buildings close by, and detect the subtle differences between their different shades and hues. With her clearnodes brightened, she could hear the people below on the street, milling about, nearly picking out bits of conversation. Efruumani's sun warmed her skin, and as she breathed in deep, she caught hints of the flowers and herbs potted on lower balconies.

"I still find myself shocked at times that we managed this," she said, looking out over the city that would save them from Efruumani's death. Skadaatha turned to her husband as he rested his arms on the railing beside her. "I think I almost forgot how impressive it is. And how beautiful."

He raised a dark eyebrow. "Didn't you spend the last month in the Ice Wastes?"

The simple, familiar expression somehow washed away Skadaatha's lingering frustration and disappointment at the day's events. Not all of it, or as much as it usually would have, but even the small amount was enough to bring a smile to her lips as she rested a gauntleted hand over his. She took in his short black hair, slim, yet fit build, the deep red-orange of his skin and narrow, vertical black stripes on his face that marked his Taryngai heritage, and his kind, inquisitive golden-brown eyes with their crinkles at the corners. Vysla wore his long, voluminous yet breathable robes that marked him as a man of science. The cutout over his collarbone displayed his crest of violet biogems, and patterns of gold and red down the front and back distinguished his field of engineering, as did the pattern on his squat cylindrical kuufi that he'd left on the kitchen table, as usual. The sleeves of his robe were bunched up around his upper arms, and his hands still dripped with water and suds.

Auroras, I've missed this man.

"Not exclusively," she said. "The Wastes are scarred and empty, but even then, the shining windswept plains spreading for miles..." She trailed off for a moment, conjuring Darkside's dark, cool palette in her mind. The strange, faint blue-orange glow of the ice gave the land an eerie atmosphere even in that hemisphere's perpetual shroud of darkness, its wounds giving it the appearance of shattered, treacherous craglands.

She met Vysla's gaze. "Their beauty is unrivaled."

Vysla's smile made her heart swell, heat rushing through her body.

"What's inside?" he asked, handing her the pouch, which she tied to her belt.

"You left the water running."

Vysla's eyes bulged, and he dashed back into their apartment. The water stopped, and a few moments later he was back at her side, gazing out at the city.

"You're late," he noted.

Skadaatha let her eyes wander over Vysla again, drinking him in. It seemed strange to her that she'd only known Vysla for sixty-two of this world's cycles around its sun—one hundred and twenty-four years by the Atonga calendar—less than a tenth of the time she'd been on this world.

"Late?"

He grinned at her. "You left me with the dishes."

Skadaatha snorted, shaking her head before looking out at the city again.

She hesitated for a moment, then put her hand over his. "I missed you."

The emotion in her voice surprised Skadaatha.

She *had* missed Vysla. Spending a month away from him had been an idiotic idea, especially with how it had ended.

Skadaatha pulled her husband closer as he wrapped his arms around her, but it wasn't enough. Her armor got in the way.

"Did things take longer at the mountain, or at the final station?"

Skadaatha tried to keep the frown from her face, yet she could not.

"The mountain," she said, pulling back from his embrace and gripping the railing, eyes down, staring at nothing, "I failed. It wasn't there."

Vysla remained silent as Skadaatha took a few deep breaths, trying to force down her disappointment at that failure. The Vale caught her eye, however, and that disappointment turned to anger.

Skadaatha clenched her teeth.

"Dear—the railing."

Skadaatha glanced down at the railing, then released it and dimmed the pairs of greynodes that enhanced her strength. She didn't know when she'd brightened them. She'd squeezed the metal rail hard enough to form it to the curves of her clenched fists.

Skadaatha dimmed her clearnodes as well, then turned toward the apartment and stalked through the white-walled main living area to the bedroom, trying to calm herself with deep, measured breaths. She stopped halfway when she glanced toward the kitchen and noticed what sat on the table. Other than Vysla's kuufi, datapad, and a stack of papers.

Vysla's footsteps followed her in, the glass door to the balcony closing a moment later. She turned to him, some of her tension fading. "You made me *kaabelgaaz*."

He smiled, raising a hand to her cheek. "I didn't think you'd be able to find any on Darkside, so I wanted to have some ready for you when you got back."

Skadaatha's mouth watered as she looked back toward the plate of small, crescent-shaped cookies. She started taking off her gauntlets.

He even dusted them with sugar for me.

Which meant he'd dipped them in citrus blossom water as well.

Skadaatha brightened her clearnodes just enough to breathe in their wonderful scent from where she stood. She knew that if she got too close right now, she'd have a hard time keeping herself from stuffing every last one into her mouth.

With effort, she took only two, popping them into her mouth and licking her fingers clean, as she continued to the bedroom. She'd begun to sweat from Lightside's heat. Even with the building's climate control, the temperature would take some getting used to after six weeks in temperatures consistently well below freezing.

Skadaatha bit her lip as she set her helmet on its stand.

She didn't want to talk about her time away—that would only make her more temperamental.

I want to be with my husband again.

Her time on Darkside without him had been necessary, but not enjoyable.

She knew, however, that if she did not talk to him and work through her emotions, she would explode sooner or later. At him or someone else.

"I took a bit longer than planned at the station as well" she said, setting down the gauntlets and busying herself with the straps of her armor as Vysla entered the room, "I used too much Auroralight searching for the Throne to travel back here through Manakera."

Vysla's fingers joined her own a moment later.

"I see."

He was quiet. When he did speak, his tone was neutral. "Were you still able to obtain the materials we need?"

Skadaatha's jaw tightened for a moment, but she unclenched and nodded. She unlatched the now-dim brace of biogems she'd worn at her waist and set it on a small table next to her armor stand. Then she fished out the pouch and tossed it onto their bed. Neither of them made for it at first, however, instead continuing to remove her armor. It was a sort of ritual for them whenever she returned home wearing it.

First, her pauldrons came off. Then her arm harnesses, followed by her cuirass, greaves, and cuisse, and finally her heavy sabaton, leaving her in her padded uniform. Skadaatha shed the sweaty garments and her underclothes as well, allowing herself a smile at the way Vysla's eyes ran over her body. When she stood naked before him, clothing set aside for laundry, Skadaatha gazed at her husband for a moment, and could see a desire in his eyes that mirrored her own. Her body reacted immediately, and another warmth only Vysla could bring out spread through her like wildfire. For a moment, Skadaatha wanted to throw aside everything that had happened before her return home and lose herself in her husband's arms.

She was unable to put aside her stresses completely, however. Despite her desire for Vysla and her desire to bury her stress, her turmoil remained.

Why am I like this?

Skadaatha gave her husband a tight smile as she strode toward the washroom of their apartment. The large tub caught her eye, and the impulse of seducing her husband into joining her for a long soak blossomed before being dampened by her other emotions. Sight of their shower did the same, yet Skadaatha suppressed that impulse as well.

She knew what she was doing. Rather than fight her frustration, Skadaatha had let it become a feedback loop. She hated how weak she was in that respect. At the same time, she knew that seducing her husband would merely give her the illusion of reconnecting with him while the emotions and problems she'd tried to take care of with some time apart festered.

Taking two small cloths from a drawer, Skadaatha wet both and lathered some soap into one before walking over to the shower with them. She didn't turn on the water, but instead scrubbed herself with the soapy cloth. A hot shower would have been nice, with or without Vysla, but she needed to speak with her husband, and the rushing water would be too loud. This way, however, she wouldn't leave spatterings of water all over the bathroom floor.

"What have you been working on?" she called.

After a moment of silence, Vysla walked into the washroom. At first, he said nothing, eyes drinking her in. Skadaatha smiled at that, squeezing her thighs together at the arousal his gaze created within her.

Then Vysla seemed to remember her question. He blinked, then furrowed his brow. "Hmm?"

"On the table in the living room."

His eyes widened for a moment before he nodded to himself, "Ah, yes. I've been looking at the city's cooling and energy supply systems that connect to the engines and palladium reactors. They're quite exposed at the moment, if well-disguised, but I believe there should be a way to fix that. If we concentrate all five reactors instead of having them spread out, I believe we can save resources, limiting the amount of necessary repairs and replacement parts while still keeping them accessible for maintenance."

"Isn't that something you should leave for Makahaba and her people?"

Skadaatha usually found her husband's tangents—the way he would get so passionate about something that his mind would become consumed by a single task—endearing, as well as how flustered he became when forced to change subjects. Recently, however, Skadaatha found she had less and less patience for the quirk, as it brought her only irritation.

She hated that.

Patience. Patience always wins out in the end. It will for Ezthyl, and for me.

"We're all part of the same Imaia, dear."

Skadaatha sighed. "You're too good at using my own words against me."

Vysla's lips quirked in a quick grin, and Skadaatha decided to turn for his benefit as she moved to scrubbing her lower half of any sweat and grime.

"Is that an invitation?"

Skadaatha almost laughed, knowing her husband could see *exactly* what his words did to her from that angle.

Would it really be so bad to throw off those robes and pull him in here with me?

Skadaatha held in a sigh. If she'd sat down and talked things through with him instead of running off for a month, maybe not. She was already procrastinating enough as it was, however.

"Set my *kalasa* and the beaded underdress out on the bed?" she asked with a smile once she'd finished rinsing and wringing out the soapy cloth. She hung it from a hook inside the shower and began the same process with the other one to clean off the soap. The grin she caught on her husband's face as he went to retrieve the diaphanous garments warmed her.

By the time Vysla returned to the washroom, Skadaatha had finished with the damp cloth and was drying herself with a fluffy white towel. She tried to ignore the double-axe and sun sewn into the fabric. It was appropriate for one of her station to have such paraphernalia in her home, yet Skadaatha would have preferred décor of a more personal nature.

As she hung the towel up and walked with Vysla back into their bedroom, grabbing a few more of the *kaabelgaaz* on the way, Skadaatha was acutely aware of the crest that hung on the wall over her armor stand. Though the other rooms of their home each bore a few Imaia wall-hangings or something of the sort, the crest had been the only item she allowed in their bedroom. It was the one place she could escape the burdens of the Imaia for a time when needed.

Skadaatha allowed herself a small smile at the garments Vysla had laid out on their bed: A beaded net-like sheath-dress that covered little, her diaphanous kalasa wrap, and a bead-fringed mantle. She ate the small cookies and licked the sugar from her fingers, then slipped on the beaded dress. It cinched beneath her breasts, then clung to her all the way down to her calves, where it ended in beaded tassels.

With Vysla's help—she didn't *need* it, but appreciated it as well as his touch through the thin fabric—Skadaatha arranged the wrap so that the top draped over her breasts, shoulders and arms, leaving a diamond shape open over her upper abdomen, then wrapped around from behind to meet at her waist, where it layered over her lower half. The hem of the skirt stopped just above the tassels of the beaded dress. She secured it at the waist with a simple belt of red cloth, then slipped the beaded mantle on over her shoulders. Skadaatha made sure to dress without looking at their mirror, as she always did when wearing something that did not completely hide her scars.

Once she was dressed, Skadaatha smiled at Vysla in thanks for his help, and a shiver ran down her spine at the desire in her husband's eyes. Her eyes darted to his lips, and another impulse rose within her—it had been over a month since she'd seen him. The pouch on the bed caught her gaze. Skadaatha sighed.

This needs to come first.

She wanted to scream.

I can't even make myself just talk and open up to my own husband, the best man I've ever known.

As with the mountain and the Throne, however, Skadaatha did not let her failures stop her. She moved onto the next tactic, which in this case, was her and her husband's shared interest in science.

In particular, a project of theirs which utilized resources that Skadaatha had committed something akin to treason in acquiring, as they were not being used for any official project.

Is it really treason if my word is law?

That, unfortunately, depended on the other two in the Imaia with the same power. And the one above all three of them.

Skadaatha picked up the pouch and handed it to her husband. "How long before it is ready for testing?"

Vysla blinked, taking the fist-sized pouch and pulling at the drawstrings. "Yes, right."

Skadaatha followed her husband as he headed out of their bedroom and down the short hall toward the office they shared. She grabbed a few more *kaabelgaaz,* then missed a step at the grief that pierced her heart like needles of ice as she passed their... their spare room. It happened every time.

Every damned time.

Skadaatha flinched, tensing at the gentle fingers that closed around her wrist, and had to force herself to unclench when she looked up and saw the compassion on her husband's face.

"Sorry," she said, embarrassed at her reaction.

"You don't need to be. Not for that."

Skadaatha gave him a tight smile as he tugged her into their office. It was a modest, six-walled room just large enough for two people to share comfortably. Two desks and chairs stood against adjacent walls, a long, Imaia banner hung just beside the door, and three large maps of Efru-umani hung on the remaining walls. One was of Darkside, one of Lightside, and one, a stylistic starmap of the Myrskaan system—named after the gas giant that dominated Darkside's sky and worked with the sun to tidally lock the moon they lived on within the star's habitable zone. They had learned in recent years that their world's position was an improbable stellar occurrence, and only the power of the God King held it in check now.

Their desks stood over computers with large, hexagonal screens rising up out of the back of each—luxuries afforded them due to their positions. Skadaatha and her husband planned to see that they became necessities available to every home and building in Mjatafa Mwonga.

Once inside, with the door closed behind them, Vysla emptied the small pouch onto his desk, then set the fabric aside.

Rough nuggets of three of the four most valuable metals on Efru-umani gleamed under the room's artificial light. A few were the size of a finger-joint, others as small as the nail on Skadaatha's little finger. Vysla separated them into groups by color, taking great care as he did so. The black metal with silvery-white flecks was currently known as darksteel. Caught in the right light, it had a strange, pale blue-violet gleam. The air around it misted, and Skadaatha knew from experience that it was near-freezing to the touch. The other two metals, both silver in color, though one had a reddish cast to it while the other's was violet, were named zidanio and aikanuum respectively.

The official purpose of the mining at Saanad station was to gather iron, titanium, aluminum, and palladium for Exodus, and before that, Skadaatha's mag-rail project: the Fingers of the Imaia. The unofficial purpose, known only to a select few in the Imaia's upper echelons, was to gather these three metals for testing, along with a red-gold metal known as lightiron. Skadaatha's position had allowed her to grant Vysla leadership over the project, but she'd made sure to secure some material off the record so she and Vysla could conduct a few of their own tests in private. Though none of the metals had been officially classified yet, Skadaatha knew that Ynuukwidas was aware of the origins of lightiron and darksteel, as she had been from the moment she first held some. The other two, however, mystified even her.

She and Vysla had looked into the metals for their own purposes before Exodus or the discovery of Mount Saanad, researching stories of people who often experienced minimal effects without knowing what caused them. These had given rise to legends all across Efruumani of people blessed with prodigious strength, supposed foretelling abilities, or supernaturally quick reflexes. Given that, and what she and Vysla had learned since getting their hands on some of the metal, they could be the key to restoring her power, as after her failure tonight, the power of a Throne seemed mere fantasy.

That soured Skadaatha's mood again, and she found herself glancing back toward the spare room. The combination of the two brought up thoughts of her and Vysla's first encounter with the metals and the blade that hung above the wide doorway connecting their kitchen with the house's main living room.

She stiffened despite herself, a perfect image of the weapon in her mind.

The weapon, *Ilosuuo*, Protector of my Joy, was fashioned after the old Akrafena style of the Batekuue people, the Imaia's progenitors. The pattern of its broad, heavy blade glittered black, silver and gold, with cutouts of the sun and double bladed axe at the thickest part, just beneath the small hooked point. In a normal weapon of war, such an adornment would have weakened the blade. Ilosuuo was more than an ordinary weapon, however. The black of its blade came from a titanium-darksteel alloy, while the gold came from an alloy of titanium and light-iron. With those two compounds pattern-welded together with what small traces of aikanuum and zidanio they had been able to find and isolate, the resulting blade had yet to break or dull.

The hilt, however, was the weapon's real treasure, integrated with various georaurals, studded with small biogems, and banded with dark-steel and lightiron. The weapon had been worth more than some nations while nations other than the Imaia had remained. The heirloom tax she and Vysla paid to keep the memory of their son was heavy.

But worth it. I will see that you get justice, Aiolo. One day.

If Vysla's work with the materials she'd acquired turned out as promising as he hoped, that day would come soon.

"This is perfect, Skadaatha."

Skadaatha looked back to her husband, catching a glimpse of herself in the dark, reflective screen of Vysla's computer as she did so. She didn't stop her frown or the hand that rose to her face. Upon arriving on Efru-umani, Skadaatha had given herself markings similar to that of the Natari in an effort to seem somewhat less alien while still standing out. Though her marks were white, matching her hair. Once, she had thought herself beautiful. She could still be called that, if only from the left side of her face. The discolored scars on her cheek and jaw she had received upon her unexpected journey to this world had long-since served their purpose, and the one on her back she'd received before then was worse. Now they served only to remind her of her failure, separation, and pain.

Vysla never cared about that, though. He was curious, but never looked upon me with disgust.

He liked her hair, too. Skadaatha would have preferred to keep her hair short or shaved, but Vysla liked the long braid she had worn to keep up appearances when they first met. He wouldn't object if she cut it all off, but she'd come to enjoy the way he would run his fingers through it when unbound.

And the way he pulls on it sometimes.

Skadaatha's pulse raced at the thought, but she contained the emotions. Now wasn't the time for that.

As much as I wish it were.

"These are raw? Straight from the earth?"

Skadaatha nodded. "Those were the instructions I gave my contact."

Vysla grinned, picking up one of the larger pieces of the silvery-violet aikanuum, about as big as the first joint on Skadaatha's thumb. Neither of them had ever handled such a large amount of this metal in an unrefined form. Skadaatha watched as her husband studied it.

He took a notebook off his desk and handed it to her. "Back up against the wall and toss this at me. Don't wait for me to be ready."

Skadaatha raised an eyebrow. "With the screen right behind you?"

Vysla possessed many wonderful attributes. Quick reflexes and hand-eye coordination were not among them, and those monitors were expensive.

Her husband's cheeks darkened as he scrubbed a hand through his black hair. "Fair enough. I'll stand over there."

He rose from his seat, walking over to stand against the wall.

Skadaatha tossed the book at him the moment he turned back to her. She aimed to the side of his head, just to be—

Skadaatha's eyes widened as Vysla snatched the small leather-bound notebook from the air. He'd moved faster than she could ever remember seeing.

Grinning, he held up the six-sided notebook in one hand and the small chunk of aikanuum in the other.

"It quickened your reflexes?" she asked. "Or improved your coordination?"

"The first. I just snatched it out of the air the moment I realized it was in reach. Pick up the zidanio."

Skadaatha turned and picked up the silvery-red metal. The moment her fingers touched it she felt stronger, more energetic, but she'd known about that effect. Zidanio was more common on Lightside than Darkside

—save at Saanad, though even there, the veins they'd found were few and far between compared to the mundane metals.

"Now, brighten your violetnodes," Vysla said, golden-brown eyes shining with excitement. "Just enough to make a tiny flame appear above your finger."

Skadaatha did as her husband instructed, raising her index finger, and started when the violet flame that blossomed above her fingertip was almost three times as large as she'd intended. It burned out immediately as she dimmed her violetnodes and turned to her grinning husband with a curious expression.

"You knew that would happen."

He shrugged, walking back to her. "I thought it would. Though, I hadn't been able to test my hypothesis until we had a sufficient amount of the material. I'll need to see exactly how much it increases the output of Auroralight used when compared to flaring a pair of biogems or using an ability in conjunction with one's opalnodes."

He held out a hand, and Skadaatha dropped the zidanio nugget into his palm, blinking at the sudden lack of energy.

"That makes me much more hopeful about our objective," Skadaatha said. "How long until you have something we can test?"

"With these, I should be finished in half a week."

Skadaatha nodded. For some reason, the thought dampened her mood.

Three days.

They would leave the planet in twenty-four, yet still three seemed too many.

"Yes," Vysla continued, a spark entering his voice as he held one of the silvery-red nuggets up to inspect it. "With these, fueling the blade will become a non-issue. If I can just figure out the right structure for the georaural..."

Vysla's excitement was almost enough to bring a fond smile to Skadaatha's face.

Almost.

For the moment, she was too irritated. She glanced out the window in an attempt to distract herself, but the ever-present propaganda outside just soured her mood even further.

Here in the heart of Mjatafa Mwonga, every building bore a double-axe and sun banner hanging from a wall or flagpole, or over the entry-way. Many bore reliefs of Imaia heroes and iconography on their facades, and Skadaatha knew that every park and square had at least one statue. The very streets of the city themselves broadcast their loyalty to the Imaia loud and clear.

Do any of them find it as redundant and limiting in décor as I do?

Her informants told her that most of the people's support of the Imaia was genuine. And why wouldn't it be? The Imaia gave people food, shelter, and clothing. It gave them education, medical care when they needed it, and a community and cause to be a part of.

All it requires is the knowledge that if you step out of line, you won't be given the chance to do so again.

There were better, more fair ways to rule. Those where the fear that one's rights could be violated at any time without warning or recourse didn't linger in the back of every citizen's mind. Where the people had a choice in who governed them and how their taxes were used.

Skadaatha might have taught the people of Efruumani how to make those types of societies work, had that been her goal here, but that was far from her concern. The Imaia needed their obedience. It was up to them to find happiness serving it.

The course of the Imaia is no longer entirely in my hands, anyway.

"Why aren't you surprised?" she snapped, whirling back to glare at her husband.

Vysla blinked, looking up from his study of the rare metals. He frowned but did not answer.

"You could at least show some disappointment that I returned empty-handed," she huffed. "Instead, you seemed almost relieved."

Vysla sighed, folding his hands.

"How do you think I should feel, Skadaatha?"

His voice was soft as he met her gaze, golden-brown eyes unflinch-ing. He was one of the few people that could do that. It was almost enough to quell her anger a bit.

"Should I feel excited that my wife is so desperate to find a power that will raise her to godhood again? Should I be pleased that you are so willing to steal time and resources and break the laws of the society you have worked so hard to build and maintain?"

"Little things," Skadaatha shot back. "They—"

"Pile up enough pebbles over time and you make a mountain, even if you weren't misappropriating my time as well," Vysla's voice rose a bit, arms tensing. "You should know that better than anyone else. "

Skadaatha wanted to bare her teeth but held back.

You don't think properly when you let your emotions control you. You make stupid mistakes. You should be above that. You are *above that.*

Vysla rose from his seat. "You are an incredible woman, Skadaatha. Your drive is one of the things I love about you. But think about how it makes me feel that you are trying to find something that will effectively end your time as a woman—if a very long-lived one—that I can relate to and truly call my wife? It's already hard enough for me to measure up as it is. I could accept that as long as I had the certainty that you would be *mine* to measure up to. Now, I'm not so sure. Am I disappointed that your lead didn't pan out? Of course I am, but I think I'm allowed to be relieved that it means you will be my wife for a while longer."

"How can you say that?" Skadaatha forced through gritted teeth. "How can you believe I would—?"

"Because you told me so," Vysla snapped. "You confided in me the difficulties your descent brought about and regaled me with the joys you found in the difference."

His jaw tightened.

"You made it quite clear that one of the new wonderful things that made your present status bearable was your ability to love me the way you did—the way I hope you still do. If losing your power allowed you to feel such a thing for the first time, the only logical conclusion is that things will change should you ascend once more."

When Skadaatha said nothing, simply holding his gaze, unable to dispute his statement, Vysla sighed, flexing his hands before running one through his hair. "Even if that didn't change, we barely spend any time together. If we do, it's to talk about ways for you to get an edge, like now, and you're always irritable and not yourself."

"*I'm* irritable? You're the one yelling," she barked.

"I'm Natari. According to you, I'm genetically inclined to do so. You, however, are not."

Vysla's eyes flashed with those words. He looked about to say something else, but closed his mouth, nostrils flaring as he breathed in deep. He raised a hand toward her, then let it fall back to his side.

"You're not yourself these days," he breathed, suddenly seeming far more tired than when Skadaatha had returned. He met her gaze. "Forgive me for yelling at you. I'm sorry. We do need to talk about this, though."

"I know," she forced out. "You know I'm terrible at...at being vulnerable. Being direct about that, at least. That's why I wanted to talk with you about this." She gestured at the nuggets of metal. "Seducing you seemed like it would provide only a temporary fix, but I thought this might help us reconnect."

Vysla blinked, mouth opening and closing a few times, "No. No, I suppose you're right."

He sighed, running his fingers through his hair. "Why do you need the Throne and its power so desperately?"

Skadaatha frowned. "You know why."

"No, I know why you *want* the power," Vysla said, an edge to his voice, "not why you're so obsessed with it that failure can send you into such a terrible mood. Or why you wanted to avoid talking about it so much that you left for a month to hunt something that could have irrevocably changed you when you found it."

Skadaatha's anger bubbled up like magma within her, but she said nothing. She had no answer for Vysla. None that seemed good enough, at least. That was the source of her emotion. She knew why she wanted the Throne. She had a list of things she could accomplish with its power, yet none of them warranted her desperation.

"You don't need the Throne, Skadaatha," Vysla said, his voice soft once more. "You couldn't beat him with brute force and vast knowledge then and won't now. Your strengths lie in your patience and cunning, which is what we're doing. You once told me you were of the mountains, that you *were* the mountains. Mountains wait and outlast."

I am the mountains. The mountains endure.

But how long could she truly endure without that power to sustain her?

"Why are you so desperate for the Throne?"

The mountains are strong.

Skadaatha found that if she looked deep enough, she had an answer. One she did not wish to accept the truth of. The weakness of.

I need it because it left a rent in my soul. You patched it up, my sweet, wonderful husband, and with Aiolo's aid you began a more permanent fix. But his death bored through that patch like cannon fire. His killer's escape from justice is another blow every time I see her—every time I hear her name. I need the Throne to have any chance of killing her.

And I need to survive long enough to see the Imaia's purpose fulfilled. I will not leave that to Ynuukwidas.

Skadaatha glanced at her husband. If Vysla had shut down and ignored her the way she did now, Skadaatha would have stormed out in a cold rage or glared daggers at him at the very least. Yet he sat there, patient, compassionate.

She loved him for it, yet at the moment she couldn't take it.

"I need to go," Skadaatha said, turning out the door and into the hall before Vysla could stop her. "I—"

Vysla's hand closed upon Skadaatha's wrist, cutting her off before she made it halfway down the hall. She didn't flinch or pull away. She just stopped.

I can't tell him.

His hand rose to her upper arm, and with a gentle tug, he turned her back around to face him.

"Skadaatha," he said, those kind eyes holding her captive. "My love. Please."

But I need to.

"I can't help if I don't know why you feel this way."

Skadaatha bit her lip.

I need to. I can.

"Seducing me might only make things better for a brief time," Vysla said, brushing aside a stray lock of hair and tucking it behind her ear, "but it might be what we need at the moment."

Skadaatha's body grew hot as Vysla rested a hand at the small of her back and pressed her to him.

"It might even work a bit better if I seduce you instead."

Skadaatha laughed, a sound that hadn't passed her lips in over a month.

It made her feel...

Good. It feels good to laugh again. To be in his arms. I can do this.

Vysla leaned in. "I did make you *kaabelgaaz*."

Skadaatha closed her eyes.

A knock at the door sounded even as Skadaatha's lips parted.

Like that, the spell was broken. Her eyes were no longer captive. Vysla's sigh as she looked toward their door was like an icy spike to her heart.

"Vizier Skadaatha," a muffled voice came from the doorway, "The God King requests your presence at the Vale of Boaathal."

Skadaatha held in a curse.

Of course, he knows I returned.

Though she did not hold even a fraction of the amount of power she once had, she was still invested enough for a being like Ynuukwidas to sense her presence at this proximity if he bothered to search.

Skadaatha turned back to Vysla, but before she could say anything, he turned back toward the office.

"I'll head to the lab," he said, tone neutral. "With what you brought, it shouldn't take more than two or three days to have a working prototype. Now that most of us are simply on standby, we're allowed to pursue personal research until the launch, provided we use none of the reserve materials. It limits what I can do, but...you've said I often work best in those circumstances."

Skadaatha stood motionless, unable to think of the right words to say, as her husband strode back into their office. All she could do was follow him with her gaze, chest tight.

Before he strode through the doorway, he looked back to her with a tight smile. "I'll see you tonight, my love."

It took a few moments for Skadaatha to move. She wanted to roar, to punch a hole through their wall, slam her fist down on the table so hard it collapsed. Instead she steadied herself against the wall, freezing her anger and all the other useless emotions that swirled within her at the moment.

How does he do it? Even when he fears he will lose me if I achieve my goal, he still works to aid me in its completion.

Worse, he was likely right. Skadaatha's knowledge was vast, yet still only a single drop in the ocean of existence. Power changed individuals in more ways than mortals often spoke of; the more power, the more drastic the change. She did not know if she would still be able to love as she did now once she ascended. She hadn't before.

But I need that power.

She needed it for something larger than Vysla and herself, or even the Imaia.

Still, it did not have to come to that. She could find a compromise. If she found the Throne of Darkness, weakened as it was, the power might not change her immediately or as drastically as before. If it did... ownership of a Throne afforded one certain abilities.

She looked back to the office.

I have to make things right.

The knock came again. "Vizier Skadaatha?"

But the God King waits for no one. Not anymore.

Reigning herself in with a few deep breaths, Skadaatha strode to the door.

She pressed one button to unlock it, then a second to open it.

The door slid open to reveal a pair of priests. Both were male and Natari, bare-chested save for the mantles of white, gold, and black that covered their shoulders and upper clavicles, and matched the ankle-length skirts that fell from ornate bands of fabric encircling their middle. One bore a crest of opal biogems and wore a net of beads on his head, a Buunta practice. The other had attached violet tassels to the hem of his mantle and skirt, remnant of the Hythe religion. His biogems were grey.

Skadaatha met their eyes with an icy glare as she stepped out the door, "Take me to the Vale."

2

Questions

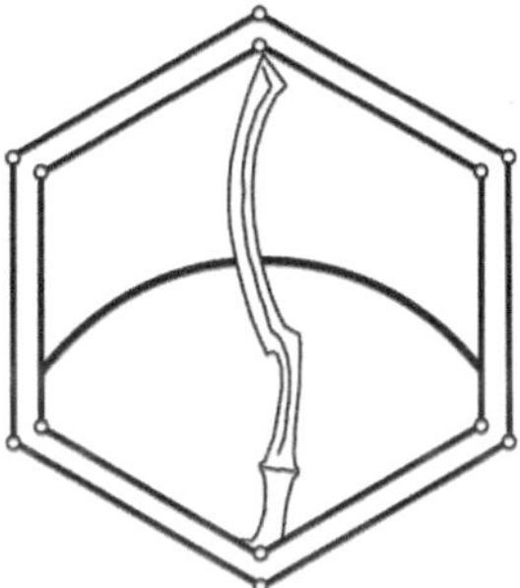

"Vizier Skadaatha believes that while the blade is certainly involved in the process of creating new Redeemed, it is not wholly responsible for such an incredible feat. As to the blade's origins, she believes that it is at least partially a physical manifestation of Lord Ynuukwidas' power, similar to the gold markings many Redeemed bear upon their bodies. Her other thoughts about the blade's origins are quite... unsettling, and should not be recorded into anything that might become a matter of scientific record at this time."

Exodus countdown: 23 days, 23 hours, 23 minutes

Othaashle Mestari, Champion of the Imaia of Atonga, jerked awake with a gasp as her sense of reality fuzzed before coalescing into the cockpit of her 4-Tail.

She looked wide-eyed at the control panel and relays of her fighter, then put a hand to the harness at her chest, heart pounding as she sucked in deep, almost ragged breaths. The autopilot was still engaged, keeping her at cruising altitude, and she hadn't overshot her destination.

Emotions and sensations lingered: a slight hangover, exhaustion from running and greenpushing from a city to a suburb, longing and melancholy at a handsome man with a disarming grin waving back at her as his transport drove off.

The vision—Othaashle knew by now that they were not dreams—had been even more gripping than the previous five. In this one, as in the rest, she'd seen through the eyes of a young woman named Kojatere; a lonely, troubled girl whose older brother seemed her only friend. She'd been little more than a child in the previous few, and in this one she still hadn't even reached her tenth cycle.

Why am I seeing through the eyes of such an unruly, delinquent young woman?

The girl had almost missed seeing her brother off before he left to return to his posting as a soldier. Kojatere apparently had even tried to lie about her age and become a soldier herself, both because of her drive to fight and the pain of being apart from her brother. Othaashle could respect the first, but found the second just...sad.

She hoped the girl eventually became a soldier—that would fix her lack of discipline, among other things.

The visions had caused Othaashle problems she had never thought she would have to deal with, but knowing *why* she was having these strange visions would have made them at least slightly more bearable.

Whatever the Aathal did to me is what started these visions.

She was sure of it. And if the World Tree had done this to her, there must be a good reason for it.

Shaking herself back to the present, Othaashle looked out of her cockpit just in time to see the last natural island before her destination pass by. A squat fortress with the shining tower of an Imaia relay station topped its highest hill.

Though it had likely once possessed another name, most referred to it simply as Outpost One. In addition to the fortress and relay station, it had also housed most of the Imaia's navy before Mjatafa Mwonga's docks and shipyards had been completed. The island had also once possessed a thick jungle that covered it completely, leaving it largely unsettled for most of Efruumani's history. Now it was just a barren slab of blue-black rock that jutted out of the red-orange waters where the Polar and Atonga Seas met. All of its resources, and local flora and fauna, had either been transplanted to one of the conservation parks, or had been harvested to fuel Mjatafa Mwonga's construction.

Outpost One zipped by before Othaashle could blink, leaving her for a short time with nothing but sea and sky as her 4-Tail soared through the air. The pale red sun and its light dominated the sky, which bled into the red-orange sea—something distinctly Lightside. Othaashle had heard once that this connection of sea and sky had inspired the first engineers and shipwrights that thought of taking to the sky, a notion romanticized in many contemporary works on the rise of the Imaia and its continual technological progress.

The thought made Othaashle look down at her lap. She frowned, then reached down under her feet to pick up the book she'd been reading before her vision. Othaashle had picked up *Journey to the City of Light* before leaving on her trip to check on the Darkside conservationists and find out what Skadaatha had been up to. She usually didn't care much for fiction—especially romance; the Redeemed didn't care about that sort of thing—but the story was one of the few that included Redeemed in more than just a passing manner without being *about* them, and therefore carefully written not to offend. Othaashle had only read about half the work so far, but she hoped that she could glean something of the average person's honest opinion of her and her people from it by the time she finished.

When Othaashle looked back up, the light of what seemed for a moment a miniature sun appeared on that line, dividing sea and sky.

Mjatafa Mwonga, or as many had begun to refer to it, the City of Light, shone like a beacon on the horizon, growing in size with every passing second. There, the God King Ynuukwidas, Lord of Justice, embodiment of the Scarlet Light, resided, along with Boaathal, Efruumani's last remaining World Tree. Othaashle had left Darkside on Auroraday, and so had missed the brilliant ribbons of color that danced over the city with the regular solar flares, but Boaathal's light gave the city its own unique beauty.

"Incoming 4-Tail fighter, please identify," her fighter's radio crackled as she neared the city walls. Two Trident-class fighters headed toward her in an arc that would let them fall in on either side of her from behind. The trans-atmospheric craft were not only some of the Imaia's fastest aircraft, capable of speeds of up to 1,300 kilometers per hour in-atmosphere, but also the most deadly. In addition to twin rotary cannons set onto the wings, a large gauss cannon ran down the middle of each craft beneath the cockpit, giving the vehicle its trident-shape.

"Control, this is Othaashle, call sign Mestari, returning from Darkside," she said, pressing the button that transmitted her audio.

"Standby."

Othaashle dropped the left wing of the fighter a bit to give herself a better view of the city as she waited for Control's response. Her earlier impatience had faded—the visions had not come this close together so far—and she let the air traffic personnel do their job.

Hundreds of meters below, the thick outer walls of the city and the mechanisms they hid passed behind her, giving way to the Mwonga Sea, the wide ring of water that encircled much of the city proper, and contained the original reefs that had protected Boaathal and its atoll from discovery for thousands of years. Railways hung suspended almost a hundred meters over the waters in twelve vectors, connecting the main bastions of the wall with the center of Mjatafa Mwonga.

"You are cleared for entry, Supreme Commander," Control called. "Welcome home, Mestari. Escort, fall in with Commander Othaashle."

"Thank you, Control."

Othaashle passed next over the massive constructs of the conservation band. The three main sections were housed by materials that would filter the ever-present light of Boaathal and the sun to mimic the conditions of each part of Efruumani, as well as contain the airborne species that resided there, with each of the three divided accordingly into different ecosystems as needed. Both planning and building those habitats had been projects of incredible scope, but Othaashle and much of the Imaia believed it would be worth it. Beyond that, and integrated with the habitats, lay the Fresh Water Sea. The red-orange band echoed the Mwonga Sea, though this one branched off in all directions inward and outward. It not only supplied Mjatafa Mwonga with fresh water, but allowed it to feel like a true city, rather than a monolith of different metals, stone and wood, as the initial design had been.

Instead, the Fresh Water Sea allowed the city to live.

Within that red-orange ring lay the heart of the Mjatafa Mwonga.

Divided into six districts, the city proper seemed at odds with its name. The so-called City of Light was covered in patches of white, black, dark teal and bursts of color. Grasses of every kind, gardens, and even small patches of forest covered every available surface in the city. Their presence gave it a more natural presence, and would mean less energy spent on recycling air after Exodus.

The Agricultural District made up the outer ring, with the Military and Manufacturing Districts coming next, and then finally the Central District, and the city's heart. Othaashle's escort broke off, returning to their patrols of Mjatafa Mwonga's airspace as she accelerated her descent, turning in an arc toward her target.

The Isle of the Redeemed—a true island in this artificial landscape—sat just outside the jewel of the city: the Vale of Boaathal, ringed by Lord Ynuukwidas's palatial temple. The brilliant light of the World Tree permeated everything in the city, filling Othaashle's biogems to the brim and recharging the georaurals integrated into her 4-Tail's design. She passed over Imaia High Command and the House of the Innovation, and finally settled onto her landing pad atop the Spear—a high, slender tower that housed all military functions on the Isle of the Redeemed. It sprouted up from the Isle and the Village of Light, rising high above any buildings between it and Boaathal's light—the only building in the entire city privileged enough to look down upon the Vale itself. It, like many other buildings and structures near the city's center, was hexagonal. The architecture grew a bit more varied and pragmatic toward the Manufacturing and Military Districts and the residential areas that bridged the different sections of the city, but Othaashle had often thought that the city looked like a honeycomb from up high.

Once over the landing pad atop the Spear, Othaashle began the landing process. She lowered the energy levels from the aircraft's palladium reactor, then engaged the georaurals fixed at five points to the bottom of her vehicle. She tethered the ship to the polished volcanic rock set into the landing pad and gently pushed down against them. Newer pilots always had a rough time with georaural-assisted landings, but to Othaashle, it had become almost instinctual.

Once her 4-Tail rested securely on its landing pad atop the flight deck, Othaashle took a moment to steady herself. Her view of the City of Light in all its shining glory had calmed her and allowed her to forget her anxiety, to forget even the visions themselves for a time.

Now, however, as Othaashle watched her entourage approach—no doubt notified by Air Traffic Control—the full weight of her responsibilities returned, as did the uncertainty of whether or not she could bear them as she once had.

Othaashle needed to project strength, but she still felt a little dazed. Sitting back, she let herself glance toward the sky. Lightside's usual pale red-orange sky did not touch Mjatafa Mwonga. Here, the light of Boaathal—and once a week, the auroras—bathed everything in a bright, white light that gave the city its name.

After a few more deep breaths as she waited for the reactor to power down entirely, Othaashle switched off the shield that protected her and the rest of the ship from the reactor's radiation, then collected the ship's remaining Auroralight in the georaurals near the rear of the craft for easy energy-replacement.

Othaashle shook her head a moment later. She had no need to replace the biogems in the georaurals while in Mjatafa Mwonga.

Light, it's good to be back.

With one last deep breath, she unlocked the cockpit's hatch and brightened her pair of Samjati greynodes before leaping from the aircraft. She landed on bent knees before three Redeemed and one Natari woman waiting for her, as expected. Othaashle breathed in the fresh air and closed her eyes for a moment, basking in Boaathal's light and letting it refresh her, washing away some of her worries, before looking to those waiting for her. They stood at a safe distance from the craft, up against the lush, overflowing planters that bordered the roof of the hexagonal tower and continued down off the sides of the structure. Even on a landing platform, life flourished in Mjatafa Mwonga.

Yndlova met Othaashle's gaze with a crisp salute a split-second before the others, as usual, though all were the picture of military professionalism.

Adjunct Yndlova Ingonja, Othaashle's second-in command, wore a fine military uniform of black, red, and white with thread-of-gold embroidery that would have marked her station even without the various medals and insignias on her breast or the adjunct's markings on her cuffs and epaulets. Yndlova's buttons, firearm and side-sword all shone like mirrors, her trousers were straight and pleated, the black line of the Destruction Campaign—where the young woman had caught Othaashle's attention—standing out stark against the sky-red fabric, her boots were polished to perfection, and her cap sat at just the right angle atop her head. Othaashle couldn't find a line or dark hair out of place as she looked the woman up and down, returning the salute.

"We're glad to have you back in Mjatafa Mwonga, Supreme Commander."

"Thank you, Yndlova. Hopefully, I won't be leaving it again any time soon."

Yndlova nodded, her hard, golden-brown eyes taking on an even harder cast than usual. Everything was set in motion now. Even a single delay could have massive consequences for Exodus.

Othaashle took a moment to meet the masked gazes of the Redeemed, returning a salute to each one. The reforged soldiers were her charges, as she was the first of their kind. Most looked at each other as brothers and sisters, but they all looked to her as a sort of mother. At times, she held that responsibility as more sacred than those that came with her position as the Imaia's Champion and supreme commander of its armed forces

"Adjunct Itese," she said to the one closest to her and Yndlova, her second adjunct, and second among the Redeemed. Itese's position afforded her the honor of being the only other Redeemed to wear armor more ornate than the rest of their kind, though not as ornate as Othaashle's own, of course. The woman herself was tall and lanky, especially for a Samjati, yet wore her hair in a Natari style of several tight, thin braids woven into one thick one that hung down her back. The mask of her helmet was styled after a lion, with pronounced brows and cheekbones, and a white mane covering the back that her braid often blended into.

"Welcome back, Champion."

Othaashle turned to the other two Redeemed. One, Akete, was an Unbound Redeemed: one whose soul had been recovered and reforged even when the body had not. Redeemed like Othaashle and Itese bore pale grey-white skin, platinum and gold hair, and golden markings and patterns about their remade bodies, and wore masks to cover their faces. Unbound wore bodies seemingly constructed of light itself that, with great practice, could become malleable after a fashion. Akete's current form stood a head taller than most Redeemed with flared shoulders and a delicate, heart-shaped face.

The other, Taizak, bore Samjati antlers like Othaashle and Itese, though his were more slender than Othaashle's own. She knew them by the patterns on the masks that obscured who they had once been. "Redeemed Akete, Redeemed Taizak."

"Ynuukwidas's light shine on you, Champion," they both said, inclining their heads.

"Were there any concerns you noted on your journey?" Taizak asked. His mask was styled after one of the elk that had once roamed Darkside, matching his thick, fanlike antlers. He was one of the more senior Redeemed that Othaashle and Itese often trusted with high-level matters, but he seemed determined to help out even on the more mundane jobs like vehicle inspection and refueling.

Not with my ship.

Othaashle shook her head, unbuckling the brace of biogems she'd worn for extra Auroralight while on Darkside and handing it to Akete, "Just look her over as you refuel, and take this back to the gem reserve when you're through."

The two Redeemed engineers nodded, then strode past her toward the ship and began their work.

Othaashle looked to her two adjuncts, then nodded toward the lift at the edge of the deck and set a quick pace toward it. As the three of them boarded the lift, Othaashle could see the question in Yndlova's eyes, but said nothing. Such things were not for the ears of other Redeemed. Not even Itese.

I can't have her worrying, too.

Othaashle did not welcome the silence, however. It spurred her mind to think on what she had seen on her journey home.

The girl's name, Kojatere, meant nothing to her. The brother's name, however, unsettled her. Her memories from shortly after her Redemption in Ynuukwidas's light had grown hazy since the incident, but she remembered the name Suulehep in connection to one of her missions shortly after the destruction of Darkside's former World Tree, Yrmuunthal.

Stop. Focusing on these visions will do nothing now but raise more questions you cannot answer.

She needed to look through the archives for information. Despite the technology that allowed datapads and her 4-Tail's autopilot, Othaashle still needed to use a terminal within Mjatafa Mwonga to access the Imaia's vast archives of information.

"Have there been any incidents while I was away?" she asked once the lift doors closed, looking between her two companions. "Specifically any involving Samjati?"

Both shook their heads.

"I can look through the Ministry of Justice records," Yndlova said, "But there's been nothing notable enough to come to my attention, Commander."

Othaashle frowned. Reports not getting the proper attention or not being filed in the first place could be part of the problem. Things like that were not supposed to happen in the Imaia, but people were people, and the last fifty or so cycles had left figurative and literal scars on all of Efruumani.

"Did you find out why Vizier Skadaatha spent a month traveling around Darkside?"

Othaashle's frown deepened. Both at her adjuncts' seeming lack of concern over the previous issue and her answer to the question.

"Nothing that deviated from her official purpose of checking in on the mining stations, cultural sites and Project Heirloom," Othaashle said, "Though I wasn't able to get as close as I would have liked. She covered her trail well."

As Vizier, Skadaatha oversaw the Imaia's Ministries of Culture and Science, but Othaashle always kept in mind that the woman had once commanded the Imaia's armies, spies and assassins when there had been a need for the latter. Skadaatha likely knew almost everything about Othaashle, while somehow shrouding herself in mystery from everyone save the God King himself. That troubled Othaashle. She trusted Lord Ynuukwidas, but could not properly protect the Imaia and its people from unknown elements.

"The trip was not a complete waste, however," she continued, realizing how long she'd been silent. "Darkside is harsh, but beautiful, even with the scars left by Yrmuunthal's destruction. The last team I visited had managed to cultivate a svenyblossom garden near their base, and had even managed to rescue a large group of mommothem and amajuuros for the conservation band. The people we sent there seemed truly invested in their work, and sad that they would soon need to leave it for good."

The lift grew silent after that, only broken by the chime that signaled their arrival at ground level.

"How is the Ambernet project coming along?" Othaashle asked Itese as the lift let them out on the ground floor of the tower. She'd wanted to stop on floor thirty-six, where her apartments were, but she knew it would be more prudent to start on her research first and gather some materials to take back to her rooms.

The Village of Light's library took up the entirety of a squat, six-story building adjacent to the Spear, but the archives were more securely guarded in an underground facility beneath the island that connected all the buildings with each other as well as High Command and an access tunnel to the military district. No one expected an attack on Mjatafa Mwonga until well after Exodus, but preparation for such times was at the soul of the Imaia.

"We're making progress," Itese said, "But High Command and Vizier Skadaatha's Ministries are being very...meticulous in what archives they allow us to link to our own."

Yndlova snorted. "Paranoid is more like it."

While Yndlova assisted Othaashle in a strictly military capacity, Itese served as more of a liaison to other branches of the Imaia, though both assisted in administration. The Redeemed were a largely military organization, but with no one to fight—well, almost no one—they were allowed pursuits like that of any other citizen of the Imaia. Under Othaashle's leadership, they now had a presence in each of the Imaia's six ministries that allowed them to contribute to the Imaia's endeavors, and give the Redeemed access to the skills and resources to pursue projects of their own. Itese oversaw most of those and kept Othaashle apprised of them.

"They have a reason to be," Othaashle pointed out. "As do we, considering our taboos."

Itese nodded. "Which is why I've only given the other ministries a gentle push."

"The wireless connection to Myrskaan Station continues to improve, though?" Othaashle asked.

The Ambernet project had started as an alternative to spending valuable resources to transport data-servers between Efruumani and Myrskaan Station, but over the last three years, the project had grown to add more and more of the archives and terminals to the collection.

"The connection still goes out due to the flares every Auroraday, but we've gotten to where it starts up automatically, and the average transfer speed has increased by five percent even over the weeks you were gone. We've also had some possible breakthroughs in our research of mundane communications technology."

Othaashle nodded as they exited the Spear and stepped out into the Isle's main plaza, "Good. Let's keep at it. Exodus is in only four weeks, and we'll need to make long-range communication with the station as fast as possible."

Lush snow-white foliage covered the plaza before them, with patches of blossoms providing wonderful splashes of color to bring even more life to the scene. Redeemed milled about, walking from one building to another, alone or in groups, heading over the bridge to the city, sitting on some of the park benches and reading or simply enjoying the plaza around them.

Itese sighed. "We're working on it, Commander."

"I don't want excuses, Itese," Othaashle said, cutting the woman off.

At a glare from Yndlova, she softened her tone. "You and your team are some of the Imaia's best. You'll find a way."

As Itese nodded, Othaashle specifically did not look toward Yndlova again. She could feel the woman's sustained glare regardless.

Othaashle didn't want to snap at Itese, but she needed an excuse to send her off so she could speak with Yndlova in private. The Redeemed protected the Imaia, but Othaashle protected them. She'd rarely need to do so until now.

"For now," she said, stopping and turning to Itese, "I want you to check on security and safety measures regarding the refugees and the Samjati."

Itese nodded. "Of course, Commander. Is there any particular reason, just so I know what to check for?"

Othaashle frowned. "I spoke to a lot of the people we'd sent to Darkside while I was trying to investigate Skadaatha. They grew... tense at the sight of me. I got the impression that most of those who volunteered for projects there did so because they didn't feel welcome in Mjatafa Mwonga. They shouldn't feel that way simply because they once stood against us. Once they realized they had been misled, they owned their mistakes and sought sanctuary under the Imaia. We need to make sure Mjatafa Mwonga is the sanctuary we promised. For all of them."

That was still a sore subject for many of those Othaashle had spoken with. When the subject had come up, she'd seen something broken behind their eyes—those that had actually come to grips with the fact that the goddess they'd worshiped had done such a terrible thing.

"I want an evaluation of trends among them regarding their integration into Imaia society: what jobs they typically hold, if there are enough cooled and covered areas of the city for them to feel welcome, things like that. I want to find the problems and work to fix them as quickly as we can. Ideally we'll be able to make some tangible progress by the time most return from their assignments on Darkside. Work with Makahaba's and Skadaatha's people on it to make sure that appropriate cultural and legal regulations are both in place and properly enforced. Skadaatha might take that the wrong way when she hears about it, but that's just something we'll have to deal with when it happens."

"Lord Ynuukwidas's light shine on you, Mestari. It is good to have you back."

Itese saluted her and nodded to Yndlova, then trotted off toward the bridge that led to the city's center, shining mane and braid swishing with the movement.

When Othaashle looked to Yndlova, she wasn't surprised to find a frown on the Natari woman's dark red face. Before Othaashle could speak, Yndlova made a curt gesture toward the side of the plaza.

Othaashle let out a sigh, then nodded, a bit of shame blossoming under that gaze.

"How many?" Yndlova asked once there was no one within earshot.

Othaashle blinked for a moment at the directness of the question, but then, that was Yndlova.

I've been among Samjati too long.

They tended to talk around an issue more than Natari did.

Much of the reason Othaashle kept Yndlova around was because the adjunct would speak to her frankly. She'd been the one to pull Othaashle out of her self-imposed isolation after the first two visions had come unexpectedly.

"Three. One on the trip back. The first was in private, but the second... I'm glad most Samjati have no idea that Redeemed shouldn't be able to just faint like that. Thankfully, whatever I said during that vision apparently came out mumbled, and they just thought it was something that happens to Redeemed if we don't get enough Auroralight."

The Samjati reservation against directness had been invaluable as well. Redeemed could not lie, and Othaashle was no exception to that. She didn't know what she would have done if one of them had asked her a direct question regarding that... episode.

She looked to Yndlova. "Was it that obvious?"

The woman shrugged. "You're not normally so pensive, sir. You don't normally snap at anyone, much less Itese. And I'm usually the one you send to deal with Skadaatha, since she seems to actually like me for some strange reason."

Othaashle sighed. Itese would definitely ask about that later.

"You need to pull it together."

Othaashle frowned but nodded. She kept the matter of her visions secret from the other Redeemed—even Itese—to protect them and the people of the Imaia. Seeing their commander, their Champion, experience such weakness would be bad for morale. If they started wondering if the same might happen to them... that would be much worse.

Though Othaashle still needed to research the events she had witnessed so far, she had a sickening suspicion as to their nature. If she was right, it would conflict with far too many of the taboos surrounding her kind.

"Thank you," Othaashle said, trying to express with her voice what her masked face could not.

Yndlova returned the implied smile. She knew Othaashle better than anyone.

"Do you want to talk about them?"

Othaashle shook her head. "I want to look into them, though. I can't have another vision in public, but I can't confine myself to quarters again, either."

How can the people expect me to protect them if they see me, one of the Redeemed, simply falling unconscious? They would doubt all of us.

Taking a deep breath, Othaashle straightened her spine and looked to Yndlova.

"I need pre-Destruction records of a city known as Kaldakia. Ones that will list families that lived there and soldiers that the Union recruited from there. I also want everything we have on the Aathal. Both of them. Legends, data, everything."

"I'll procure both of those for you, sir."

Othaashle raised an eyebrow, then cocked her head. Part of what she taught new Redeemed—when there had been new Redeemed, at least— was a set of expressions and body-language that accounted for their masks, but their bodies still defaulted to the mannerisms of their former selves. Even for her.

"I assume there is a reason I won't be going with you?"

"One of the Redeemed—Mjaktie, I think; the one with his mask styled after a scarred bear—came to me with a message from one of those standing vigil at the God King's temple today."

Othaashle smiled under her mask. Most outsiders saw the Redeemed as something akin to faceless automatons—if respected ones —addressing them simply as 'Lightforged,' yet Yndlova had made sure to learn the name and mask of each one. She even knew most of the Unbound, who changed their faces often to suit their mood.

But she is not truly an outsider, is she?

"He reported that Vizier Skadaatha had returned from her tour of the Darkside stations, and that Lord Ynuukwidas had summoned her. Unscheduled."

Othaashle frowned at that.

"How long ago?"

"The summons went out maybe an hour ago. I don't know when she arrived."

Othaashle blinked when she realized she had been biting her lip, and felt the heat rise in her cheeks. This was not the first time she'd been grateful for her mask's shrouding of her emotions. She wanted to return to the safety of her quarters. She could do her research from there, and if another vision struck her, no one would be around to see. But she couldn't let a chance pass to spy on Skadaatha. And Lord Ynuukwidas could provide an easy solution to her problem.

If not, I will need to figure out a way to predict when these will come, at the very least.

"Thank you, Yndlova."

"Do you wish for an escort to the Vale?"

Othaashle shook her head. It was bad enough that she had to rely on Itese and Yndlova as much as she did to assist with her duties. That made her a liability. Normally, an unscheduled meeting between Skadaatha and Lord Ynuukwidas would have merely intrigued her. Now, it worried her.

I am Champion because of what I have accomplished and the power I wield to protect the people of the Imaia. The visions threaten my ability to wield that power as needed.

She had no illusions about how easily Lord Ynuukwidas could take that power from her and give it to another.

"Sir."

Othaashle looked up at the address, surprised to find Yndlova still there. She cocked her head.

"I know it would be a bad idea to do so directly," Yndlova said, "but no one knows more about the Aathal than the God King, and he saw it attack you. Show an interest in the Aathal when you speak with him."

Othaashle nodded. "Thank you, Yndlova. And please, relay my apology to Itese for snapping at her and sending her off that way. I will apologize to her myself, later."

Othaashle's adjunct saluted, then turned toward the archives.

"Yndlova?"

The adjunct stopped and turned around, expectant. "Yes, Commander?"

"How did your and Itese's research project go while I was gone? Were you able to make any progress?"

Yndlova blinked. "Sir?"

Othaashle cocked her head. "Didn't you ask for some time to spend in the military archives for a historical research project?"

Yndlova blushed for some reason, making Othaashle once again thankful that her mask shielded most displays of emotion from others.

"Oh," Yndlova said, seeming flustered. "Yes, I did. I was able to find time to work on it, but it's a look into more recent history, so lots of dead ends. That was a personal project, though. Itese is not involved."

"My mistake," Othaashle said. "Itese was working on some project as well regarding different battles in recent history. I figured you two were working together."

Yndlova shook her head. "No, I didn't know about that."

Othaashle nodded. "Well, I'm glad you were able to find some time to work on it, even if you didn't make the progress you'd hoped. Let me know if I can provide any assistance, and extend that to Itese and her project, as well."

Yndlova smiled. "I will, sir."

"You are dismissed."

Othaashle looked after Yndlova for a moment as the woman walked toward the Isle's archives, then set off for the Vale of Boaathal. She was so preoccupied with what she had seen, and what Skadaatha and Lord Ynuukwidas could be discussing, that she barely noticed the people or the beautiful architecture of the district as she strode through it. She barely remembered to greet the Redeemed at their posts outside the Vale.

Only the sensation of the power within the Vale managed to pull Othaashle from her thoughts. It made her hesitate, remembering what had happened the last time she'd entered this place. She also realized she'd brightened her Natari greynodes at some point to speed herself along. She shook her head. Auroramancy required intent to direct its power, but that didn't mean it had to be conscious intent. That was doubly true for Redeemed.

Steeling herself, Othaashle slipped into the Vale and brightened her clearnodes to enhance her hearing and other senses, then made for the spot she'd discovered long ago that had proved best to listen in on Skadaatha's meetings with the Imaia's God King.

3

Lord of the Imaia

"Georaural technology allows for simple storage of extra power, though an artificial crest would be far more practical for such things. If I am to construct a weapon that can hope to match Ilkwalerva in both power and convenience, much more complex and precise design is required. Even then, I would be stretching georaural technology to its limits, if not for the discovery of zidanio."

Exodus countdown: 23 days, 23 hours, 5 minutes

The walk to the Temple of Light from Skadaatha's apartment in the House of Innovation took about half an hour down Crimson Causeway, one of the central district's main boulevards. The House of Innovation, like High Command, the Isle of the Redeemed, and other structures where those who ran the Imaia lived and worked, all stood in close proximity to the Vale and its surrounding temple as a symbol of status. Between those buildings and the temple lay the People's Circle. The people of the Imaia were its heart, so they should have places to gather close to their god and the heart of the city that sustained them. The Circle was essentially a large park and community center, with extensive gardens, amphitheaters for plays and concerts, gymnasiums, plazas where food purveyors could set up carts and stands, and anything else the people needed to find some enjoyment. Railways leading to the outer districts ran down the center of every major avenue, letting off at different points around the Circle, allowing it to be constantly filled with people of all ages, professions, and backgrounds.

Skadaatha's costume drew a plethora of different reactions as she strode down the Causeway with her escort. Admiration, curiosity, lust, shock, and even a bit of disgust from a few more conservative pedestrians were all directed her way. Skadaatha ignored them all, instead finding pleasure in others she glimpsed wearing the *kalasa*. Most wore it in different styles—wrapped tight around the body and looped around the upper arms like voluminous sleeves, wrapped just below the breasts and over the shoulders, bearing the crest of biogems at the chest, or even just worn as a loose cover over other clothing. All Skadaatha saw were of a thicker cloth than her own, though some not by much.

As they ventured closer to the Temple's fortifications, disguised as sections of wall bearing elaborate reliefs, Skadaatha noticed many different fashions of both Samjati and Natari on the passing people, even a few where one wore an approximation of a fashion from the opposite culture.

Skadaatha's position as head of the Ministry of Culture afforded her the fashions—modern or traditional—of whichever culture or society she wished. The Atonga style—the ancient empire that the Imaia had given life to once more, and one of the few cultures she had not been able to experience herself—was Skadaatha's favorite, especially in Mjatafa Mwonga's heat. The beaded dress she wore under her kalasa wrap had initially been one of high status for Atonga women, but it covered almost nothing. Skadaatha had made great progress in eliminating the taboo of nudity within the Imaia. She considered it a foolish one, especially considering that the common people of Atonga and many other cultures had gone about with little-to-no clothing for centuries. Even now, all Natari cultures left some part of the chest bare when they could, due to their biogems. Ameta Makahaba, and her role in the Imaia's history had helped with that.

Despite how Skadaatha regarded her as a person, the Whore Mother of Atonga was one of the few mortal-born Skadaatha had encountered that seemed to truly use her power for the good of those beneath her, and rarely balked at working with others. Skadaatha had used the influence of their two positions to set a number of fashion trends and eliminate an equal number of taboos.

In such a diverse body as the Imaia, however, compromise was necessary. Given their freezing home climate, most Samjati saw the absence of clothing as something scandalous or reserved for when in private. Mixing with Natari cultures over the years had changed that, yet the idea was still ingrained in most of their cultures, and Skadaatha did not want to alienate such a large portion of the Imaia's population. Most of whom, likely already felt so.

So, she wore the diaphanous kalasa wrap over her beaded dress. The garment on its own provided scarcely more cover than the beaded dress, yet wrapped in the right way over that same clothing, it claimed just enough modesty to be appropriate.

Other compromises had to be made, of course, as Natari had no antlers to adorn, and Samjati could not wear Natari hats. Natari would try as much as they could to keep some part of their chests and torsos bare, while the Samjati had to keep their bodies and faces almost completely covered in Lightside's constant strong sunlight. Their blue complexions could bear the light of the Twilight Band in most places, but here, the closest point to the sun on Efruumani, the ultraviolet radiation acted like poison against their bare skin and could easily blind their sensitive eyes. Skadaatha had long-since assigned a team at the university to work toward remedies for that, if only due to the heat of the city alone. For now, many Samjati chose to stay inside or—if they could afford them—wear thermal georaurals about to compensate for the heat.

As Skadaatha passed through an opening in the Vale's disguised defensive ring, the power that resided within sang to her, filling her with energy as Boaathal's light, reflected out of the Vale by great mirrors, saturated her gemcrests to the brim with power.

Once, only a solitary atoll at the center of a shallow sea had stood where she walked. Now, a grand temple surrounded the Vale.

Lightforged of both types stood at their posts along with spirit sentries that dotted the Temple's grand architecture and gardens and added to the light that flooded the area. Though light created shadow, very little of the latter could be found here.

The Type-One Lightforged, or the Redeemed, as they preferred to be known, stood vigil at the outer posts, differentiated only by their ever-present masks.

The Type-Two Lightforged, or Unbound Redeemed, stood in their hardlight bodies, echoes of the God King's own chosen form. They were incredibly effective in battle, but despite the relatively familiar features and body-types, even Skadaatha found them discomforting to look at.

It irked Skadaatha that Ynuukwidas had discovered such a technique when she could not. The ability to snatch a soul just before it disappeared through the Gates of Death and restore it to the physical realm would be invaluable against the Enemy. Even worse, the God King had effectively forbidden Skadaatha from researching it directly. He'd said nothing to her, but after creating the first few Redeemed, the God King had declared it taboo to speak to the warriors of their past. That they had no memory of their past lives—one of the costs of the second chance at life they were given—only made things more difficult.

Six of each type flanked each side of the Temple's main gate with its hexagonal towers and massive doors, the double-axe and sun emblazoned on the metal gate.

Within, spirits and priests milled about. Though their outfits all bore certain similarities to mark their stations—the mantles and skirts or trousers of white, gold and black—no priest she could see matched another exactly. There were almost too many denominations of the Atonga Kanisa to keep track of, but all were present and allowed within Mjatafa Mwonga so long as they adhered to two rules: practices must not violate any laws or infringe upon the rights of others, and Ynuukwidas must be acknowledged as god. The latter was hard not to do for the common people once they looked upon the Temple, especially when all Efruumani's remaining oruu were gathered here. The spirits that served the God King rarely took forms that resembled anything close to Efruumani's sapient species, but that was expected of them.

Each one Skadaatha saw was an ornament of propaganda. Yet they were also dangerous.

Ynuukwidas has never been known for his subtlety.

The Temple's architecture was a strange mix, blending what Skadaatha assumed was the ancient style of Ynuukwidas's homeland with modern materials, infrastructure and improvements, and the number six.

Hexagonal towers and parapets rose from the tops of squatter buildings or at junctions in the walls. Every window had six sides to its outline. Buildings that might have been round without the influence either had six, twelve, or at points even eighteen sides. Even the surrounding wall formed a dodecagon.

Aia, was I ever that obsessive?

She hoped not. Skadaatha had held her power longer than Ynuukwidas, but she'd been born to it, where he had not.

As she passed deeper into the Vale, more propaganda assaulted her. Some of it was subtle—actual art—worked into ornate reliefs or sculpture, though that was due to the discretion of the artists rather than Ynuukwidas's own tastes. Those displayed the six ancient Orojo kingdoms involved in Ynuukwidas' ascension, as well as statues of his supposed pantheon. Still, Skadaatha found it a little much. It made her... jealous.

The emotion surprised Skadaatha—it was not one she had often felt.

Do I not have a right to feel this way?

None of the art referenced her, despite the fact that the Imaia was her creation. Her masterpiece. Most of it did not even reference the Imaia's true origins on this world, but instead Ynuukwidas's origins, as many histories had been altered to make the Imaia seem something he'd had a hand in from the start.

No. No, I do not. I made my decision.

While the Imaia had been Skadaatha's idea, she knew that it would not have worked if she had set it up to be a body she ruled over. She'd had to make the people of Efruumani believe it their own idea. That way they would care for it and take responsibility for its survival and improvement. She had made herself simply a harbinger and a source of knowledge for Atonga's advancement. Even with Ynuukwidas at their head, the people of Atonga saw it as their own, as many had legends linking both herself and Ynuukwidas to their own cultures and ancient religions.

That, Skadaatha had played a part in.

With her mind on the propaganda, Skadaatha did not realize that she had entered the Vale until its sense of peace washed over her. Her mind and body felt relaxed yet energized at once. Her four gemcrests—two at her brow and two at her clavicle—shone bright.

Under her feet, hard paving stones gave way to spongey black soil and dark teal grass with shocks of burgundy. The more sterile scents of metal and stone gave way to the fresh, clean aromas of flora and life. Trees surrounded this part of the Vale, their white, black and dark teal leaves pearlescent in the light. To someone ignorant of this place's power, it might have been a palace garden.

Most palace gardens, however, did not center around a massive Aathal.

At the Vale's center, roots thicker than most Samjati rose from the ground. They twisted together, merging into a trunk thick enough that ancient peoples likely would have tried to carve a small dwelling out of it.

If the tree had let them get close enough.

The trunk rose high into the air, taller than any of the spires that dotted the surrounding temple. Its canopy spread out to cover the entirety of the Vale to the point that a mundane tree would have cast the entire area in shadow, starving the grass and other plants of light.

Despite its thick trunk and massive roots, Boaathal somehow managed to bear a resemblance to every species of tree that grew on Lightside. That alone made it awesome to look at. Among its leaves and branches, however, lay the true wonder: its biogems.

The biogems in themselves were nothing special—every life form on Efruumani, flora or fauna, possessed them. Yet while those absorbed Auroralight for consumption, Boaathal's biogems *produced* such light, shining brighter than any individual's, almost too bright to look directly at. They seemed to sparkle with every color imaginable. Their light—Boaathal's light—not only allowed the nearby plants to grow, but fed them with unparalleled energy, making the surrounding flora more magnificent and vibrant than possible anywhere else on the planet. Boaathal provided everyone and everything in the surrounding area with a constant source of Auroralight. Even had auroras not danced almost constantly in the sky above it, everything in this area was bathed in light, eliminating the possibility of anyone becoming lightless, and providing unparalleled potential for technological growth. Skadaatha and her husband had designed Mjatafa Mwonga with Boaathal's light in mind, just large enough for everything within its borders to be in reach of the light and its power.

Skadaatha and Vysla had often wondered what they could do if they managed to harvest one of the Aathal's biogems as they harvested those of other flora and fauna, what studying them would reveal. Some believed they held the secret to Auroramancy's origins, but that was far less mysterious than most liked to believe. Power manifested on certain worlds. On others, it did not. It was the manner in which that power manifested, and the role that the Aathal played in that process, in which interested Skadaatha.

She stopped a short distance from the Aathal's roots, hands rising toward her scars.

Despite feeling drawn toward the tree, Skadaatha knew from painful experience to tread carefully around Aathal. They had wills of their own and did not suffer fools or the mal-intended.

Someday, I will learn their secret, and not just for the Imaia's advancement.

An Aathal's power had been used to send her to this world. Skadaatha shivered and had to force her hands away from her scars. Yet as soon as the chill came, Boaathal's presence washed it away. The warmth of peace spread through her. The warmth of contentment. Of well-being.

"Skadaatha, you are late."

The deep, rich voice that resounded in her mind and pressed into her like a physical force surprised Skadaatha. Yet with the calm of the Aathal spreading throughout her body, Skadaatha had no need to restrain herself from whirling toward the voice's source.

The God King himself had entered the Vale. His presence washed over her like a wave of heat and energy. He stood tall and imperious, his posture perfect as he crossed the Vale toward her. Ynuukwidas's form was scarlet fire and molten gold in an amalgamation of the different Natari phenotypes. A large mane grew from his head, tumbling over his shoulders and down his back and chest. Spots and stripes of pure white adorned his face and other exposed areas of skin, the patterns shifting every few minutes. This form was not composed of flesh, but something more alive, more powerful. It was not the living, quasi-hardlight of the Type-Two Lightforged, but something more raw. The God King was power incarnate. Skadaatha herself had once been able to take a similar form.

The God King radiated power, yet if Skadaatha brightened her Natari blacknodes and concentrated, she knew she would be able to distinguish between the God King's power and that contained in the slim, golden crown set with twelve biogems that rested upon his brow.

That crown was the true Throne of Light. The throne in the main hall of Ynuukwidas's temple gave off a similar power signature, but Skadaatha had long-since realized that it was a decoy made for show.

The thought brought a rush of frustration, making her tense.

Ynuukwidas can manipulate the form of the Throne he took. Could Kweshrima have discovered how to do so as well?

If so—what did that mean for her search?

Remembering herself, Skadaatha dropped to one knee and inclined her head to the God King, "Lord Ynuukwidas, what did you wish of me?"

It grated her to play such games with him, but they were necessary.

For now.

"Rise, Vizier. Tell me of your tour of the outposts on Darkside."

Skadaatha stood and met the God King's eyes. The amusement on his ever-changing features rankled Skadaatha even through Boaathal's calm. She was never sure how much he knew of the world outside Mjatafa Mwonga, save that his vision ended at the twilight band. He had yet to reveal to her his method of hearing mortal prayers, and at the present, she suspected he never would.

"Everything is progressing as expected, Your Majesty."

This was not one of the scheduled meetings in which she and the other ministry heads reported to him, but Ynuukwidas seemed to enjoy speaking to her unofficially as well. She knew why and took advantage of it.

"None of the stations reported any raids or outright attacks. All transports are headed back on the railways, and should be here in two weeks, with eleven days to unload possessions and supplies and integrate themselves into Mjatafa Mwonga."

"What quantities of the rare metals were our workers able to recover?"

"I don't have exact figures yet, Majesty, but the transports were heavily laden with each of the metals. There is more left at the sources, of course, but we have gathered all we can and there should be enough to sustain us until we find a new world with elements of similar properties."

Skadaatha had no idea how long that would take. She knew there were other inhabited worlds like Efruumani, yet she knew only of six systems that would undoubtedly have such elements present, and she knew the location of none of them. Not even her own.

"What of your search for the Throne? Fruitless, I should guess, as you still bow to me, and I do not sense its power."

The question shook Skadaatha from her thoughts. She met Ynuukwidas's gaze and had to melt the ice in her voice before she spoke.

"You are correct, Your Majesty. I found the mountain and the pool of power there, but my search of the cognitive plane was in vain. I believe that Kweshrima—if she still lives—or whoever took control of the Throne after her still has enough power to hide it, whether in the physical or cognitive plane. I can neither sense it nor find it where it should be."

Skadaatha clamped her mouth shut, jarring her teeth, at the frustration that had slipped into her last few words.

I've searched all of Darkside, physical and cognitive planes, and have nothing to show for it, and little time to think of or execute another plan.

Skadaatha took a few breaths to calm herself, then gazed up at Ynuukwidas, studying him. The God King's eyes were distant in thought. Though his features shifted in a subtle manner, so that over the course of every forty-hour day his features represented that of every ethnic group of Natari, his eyes never did.

Skadaatha found that frustrating. She had often wondered what the God King looked like before. As a mortal or even as a god new to his powers. She was certain he was of the Oro-Buusa ethnic group, but she had never been able to pin that down or tell others of her findings. That would undermine the careful balance they had set for the mythology surrounding the God King.

"It is probably for the best that you failed in your search."

Skadaatha blinked, eyes focusing on the God King's own. Even through the Aathal's peace, anger bubbled up within her, yet Ynuuk-widas's expression cooled it somewhat. His features held no trace of mockery or amusement, only contemplation.

"While power is always needed," the God King elaborated, turning to pace around Boaathal; even he gave the Aathal a wide berth, "you are much more useful to the Imaia in your current form."

He stopped, looking back at her. "Do you find reason to disagree?"

Skadaatha held back a frown. "I see your point. In my current state, I can break and bend the rules that restrict your use of power and would restrict me should I find such power of my own. Still... I know my time is limited without that power, and so I remain undecided on which outcome would be more beneficial to the Imaia."

Anger flared again as a grin tugged at Ynuukwidas's mouth, but Skadaatha forced it down.

"Yes... yes, you would remain undecided," he said before turning back to his pacing, "Do not worry, Skadaatha, your current form will remain long enough."

Skadaatha felt an impulse to touch her scars again as Ynuukwidas rounded the tree's perimeter, thinking.

Does he see the same potential in Boaathal as I? Does he wish he had a way to study it?

Though Ynuukwidas was a god, even he was subject to the power and judgement of the Aathal. Skadaatha had warned him of that, relaying her own tale of misfortune to enforce the point, back when they had been on nearly equal footing.

As Ynuukwidas disappeared behind the tree, Skadaatha found her gaze and thoughts drawn to the Aathal again.

There should be some way to study or use it, otherwise they wouldn't be here, would they? Or are all the elements of an Aathal purely just for show?

Some parts of Skadaatha's memory from before she had come to Efruumani felt like wisps when she reached for them, puffing away to mist or slipping through her fingers, leaving nothing more than faint impressions. She knew that there must be a safe way to interact with the

Aathal. She just hadn't found it yet. And she had yet to discover how Kweshrima destroyed Yrmuunthal, Boaathal's twin.

At times, that knowledge seemed to be better left in the dark like the goddess herself, but it frustrated Skadaatha that the goddess of Darkness and Mystery had discovered something she could not.

At least we are able to use Boaathal to power the city and our escape from this dying world.

She just hoped they would be able to take the Aathal with them when they left the planet, as she knew its connection to Efruumani was not merely physical. They had fail-safes in place if her fears turned out to be correct, but things would be a lot easier if the Aathal did not resist their departure from its home.

As Ynuukwidas came back into view, Skadaatha noticed something she had not before.

It was subtle, but the God King's shoulders seemed bowed, burdened by the same stress and worries she carried, yet at the magnitude of beings far beyond her current state.

"Has the strain grown worse?"

Skadaatha did not hide the concern in her voice. It was not concern for Ynuukwidas himself, but for the Imaia and the promise it held with him at their head.

Ynuukwidas stopped, looking for a moment as if he was surprised to still find her here. That alone gave Skadaatha her answer, yet the God King nodded slowly.

With her question answered, Skadaatha could pick out the strain in the God King's voice as he spoke.

"I must reduce the radius of the auroras again before we leave. Perhaps in a week or two. I need to be ready if anything goes wrong during our departure."

Skadaatha nodded gravely. "Is there nothing else you can do to reduce the strain?"

The God King shook his head. "Even after I gained knowledge of the celestial bodies, I do not believe I truly realized how... precarious our position is until Yrmuunthal's destruction threatened to disrupt the careful balance. If I lessen the strength I lend to Myrskaan's hold on us, we risk falling out of its Lagrange point and into the sun. Even simply moving into a closer orbit would scour Efruumani of life, melting and evaporating Darkside's icecap. We are so close to the edge of our sun's habitable zone that even the slightest variation in our path could cause catastrophe in the four weeks before we launch."

Skadaatha sighed. The question had been a stupid one. She'd been the one to make many of the calculations about Efruumani's solar system. Of course, she hadn't realized the factor that the Aathal played in stabilizing the system's irregularities.

"It isn't just that, though, is it?" Skadaatha asked.

Ynuukwidas studied her for a moment, then nodded, almost to himself.

"It's the auroras and Boaathal's light. I have to resist feeding off them. That was never a problem before, but with so much of my energy devoted to merely keeping the planet stable... I sometimes wonder how those on Myrskaan Station survive without the light of the auroras. Even with the substitute I provided."

The thought made Skadaatha shiver and frown. Though she believed those who manned and lived on the station orbiting Myrskaan to be fools for agreeing to such an experiment, she could not question their bravery. What troubled her most about the station, however, was how Ynuukwidas had managed *something* built into the station to ensure the georaurals kept working and no one went lightless. He had shared the secret with no one—not even Makahaba—and forbidden research into its workings.

"Anything to report on your ministries?"

Skadaatha shook her head. "I haven't been fully debriefed yet, but nothing of note, save that the Ministry of Science has completed all tasks needed for departure and they stand ready to deal with any problems that may occur. Most are simply checking over calculations or inspecting the various systems."

"And your husband? He is well?"

Skadaatha chose her words carefully. Ynuukwidas had an uncanny ability to detect lies. She had yet to figure out if that was something of the man or the power he had taken for himself.

"He looks to innovate, as always. When I returned home, he was working on a way to better connect all of the city's infrastructure and make it more accessible for maintenance while making it less vulnerable to shutting down completely should any malfunctions occur."

"And the Ministry of Culture?"

Pride swelled within Skadaatha as she spoke, though she made sure to keep it from her face and tone. Ynuukwidas already had too much to use against her if he wished.

"The composer Dymbajat should be close to finishing his latest work, and all stations reported a generous amount of heirloom materials recovered or turned in. I do not know that they will yield a substantial amount of the metals that give them their power, but at the very least, most should be effective weapons when we come into contact with the Enemy."

Skadaatha did not know as much as she would have liked about the Enemy. That had been Odentho's area of expertise. Yet despite all the work she had put into the Imaia's creation, all she had suffered through to get to this point, she hoped she never had the need to learn any more about it. It was a foolish hope. She knew it was out there. It had been defeated for a time, but that had taken more power than even Ynuuk-widas could imagine.

It will be back. We just need to be ready for it.

"We need to refine and distribute as many weapons as possible that utilize georaurals and the rare metals," the God King said, as though reading her thoughts. "Our people know war, but their experience is of fighting soldiers and warriors like themselves. Ones that can suffer wounds of the heart and soul as easily as wounds of the flesh. We must be ready."

Skadaatha's jaw clenched, but she smoothed it. Though his tone was that of the learned informing the ignorant, Skadaatha knew he did not mean it in that way. She had been the one to inform *him* of such things.

I started the entire program.

At times, it seemed Ynuukwidas forgot the role she served for the Imaia. That worried her. Holding such power, even for a short period of time, changed one irrevocably. Ynuukwidas was not the same person he had been before taking the power of the Throne of Light for himself. He was not even the same person he had been shortly after his ascension.

Is 'person' even an adequate description of him anymore?

Regardless, though power changed a person, it should have *enhanced* his capacity, not caused him to overlook things. She hoped it was just the strain of holding Efruumani together. Once they departed, Atonga's god and most powerful weapon would be as he should again.

"Did you find any information that could aid Othaashle's conservation efforts?" The God King asked suddenly. "I am certain the last of the draakon died out decades ago, if not centuries, but if we can find even one that survived, it would be a priceless treasure."

Skadaatha barely kept herself from snarling at the mention of that name.

"I have enough to focus on with my own two ministries, Your Majesty," she grated, "I don't have the time or resources to help the Supreme Commander in her misguided search for skeletons of the past."

Ynuukwidas turned to her, and the amusement—no, condescension—on his molten features made anger boil within Skadaatha.

You are the mountains, steady and immovable. You are the ice that tops the world—cold, careful, above petty squabbles. Control yourself.

"You must bury your anger toward Othaashle, Skadaatha," Ynuukwidas said, smile fading as his tone darkened. "*Othaashle* has been reborn in my cleansing light. *Othaashle* has given you no reason for such hatred. Or am I incorrect?"

Skadaatha swallowed her anger. Anger at herself for showing such a strong reaction, at Ynuukwidas for bringing up her name, and at the cursed woman herself.

"You are correct, of course, Your Majesty. Othaashle has done nothing to earn my hatred."

Though the woman takes great enjoyment in putting herself above me every chance she gets.

Ynuukwidas nodded. "Good. You are dismissed, Skadaatha."

Skadaatha sighed, but bowed, then turned to leave. Unofficial meetings like this were always abrupt, as they began and ended at Ynuukwidas's whim. It had not always been that way. Once, she'd—

"Skadaatha."

Skadaatha stopped, turning back toward the God King at the sound of her name. "Yes, Majesty?"

Ynuukwidas hesitated for a moment, expression pensive.

"Did you... sense anything in the past day? A strange resonance? I cannot be sure, but it felt like it was somewhere near the center of Darkside."

Skadaatha almost shook her head. But her curiosity won out.

"I did. It was only a flash, barely a second long, but it felt as though it came from near Yrmuunthal's Grave."

"Do you believe it was something to worry about? The Enemy?"

Skadaatha held back a frown.

So, he doesn't know either.

"It was unfamiliar to me. I did not have time to pursue it, but... I doubt it has anything to do with the Enemy."

Ynuukwidas remained silent for a moment.

"And what of the legend of the seed of Boaathal? Do you think that has any connection?"

Skadaatha blinked, then shook her head. "That supposed sanctuary either died out or never existed to begin with, Majesty. You would have been able to find them unless they fled to Darkside. Even so, the signature I felt was brief, but distinct enough for me to believe it has little connection to the Aathal."

Ynuukwidas nodded, then turned away from her, looking toward Boaathal in silence. Skadaatha stood there for a while before she figured the God King had dismissed her presence. Then she left.

Time was at a premium.

ONCE CERTAIN SKADAATHA had left the Vale and the temple beyond, Othaashle stepped out from cover. She strode toward her distracted god, careful to keep her distance from Boaathal. The calming effect of the World Tree was welcome, dampening her anxieties for a time, but the last time Othaashle had come too close, the Aathal had struck her, and she'd succumbed to the first of the visions that now assaulted her without warning. The young Samjati children she'd seen then were the same two from her most recent vision, though grown. The brother's name, Suulehep, itched at something in her memory—something beyond the block—but the girl's name, Kojatere, meant nothing to her.

But they seemed so real. Especially that one where they visited Yrmuunthal.

"How much did you overhear, Mestari?"

Othaashle blinked, the deep, commanding voice pulling her from her thoughts. She turned toward the God King and knelt before what seemed a statue of scarlet light and molten gold.

"Enough to know that Skadaatha has once again failed in her search for power, Lord Ynuukwidas," Othaashle answered, satisfied and relieved at the words she spoke, especially given her current situation.

"Rise, my child. Do you believe someone else reached the Throne of Secrets before her, claiming its power?"

Othaashle shook her head, standing now. "We would know. Only the Remnant could have claimed it before her, and they are desperate enough that they would have wasted no time in using that new power against us."

"You believe it was moved, then?"

Othaashle nodded. "Leaving the Throne near its original location is something even Kweshrima was not foolish or reckless enough for."

And... Othaashle blinked as the realization washed over her. *Leaving it anywhere related to Darkside or the goddess is too obvious.*

As though he could read her thoughts, Ynuukwidas sent Othaashle a knowing smile.

"You believe you know its location."

"Not an exact location," Othaashle said, wondering how she could find that. "But more than Skadaatha has."

Ynuukwidas grinned at that. He often seemed amused by the rivalry between her and Skadaatha, though Othaashle didn't see it as such.

"Be on guard if you seek the Throne and its power, Champion. I would welcome a companion to ease my burden and know what it is to hold such power, but that power has... consequences."

Othaashle nodded slowly at the God King's tone, considering, then hesitated.

This could work.

"My Lord, when you reforge us—the Redeemed—who we were is erased save for the bodies we wear, correct? No memories return?"

The God King seemed troubled by her question. His words came slowly.

"Memories of who you once were are gone, never to return. It is the price you must pay for a second chance to serve the Imaia. Remnants of your former self remain in intellect, skills, personality, and other small ways, but otherwise, you and your people are seared clean of your former lives when you are Redeemed. Why do you ask, Mestari?"

Both reassured and troubled by her god's response, Othaashle voiced the first excuse she could think of.

"The Throne, my Lord. It is of Kweshrima's power. I know by my body that at the very least, I was once of her lands, if not in her service. I worry that if I find the Throne and take its power, it could undo some of your own."

Ynuukwidas let out a rumbling laugh, his earlier wariness gone.

"You need not worry about that, my Champion. The power that Redeemed your soul is beyond that of Kweshrima and her Throne."

"That is reassuring, my Lord."

"Your conservationists have wrapped up their work on Darkside," he stated, changing the subject. Othaashle knew what he sought.

"Yes, Lord Ynuukwidas. Though they could find only the remains of draakon."

The god nodded, expression solemn. "I expected as much."

They entered into a short silence, and for a moment, Othaashle contemplated telling her god of the visions she'd had.

If anyone could heal them or know what I am seeing, it would be him, but...

Boaathal caught Othaashle's gaze.

Even he does not know everything about the Aathal.

"Will we be able to create more Redeemed before Exodus?" she asked instead, turning back to the god. "Keeping Auroraborn dissidents within Mjatafa Mwonga, even as lightless under heavy guard... I don't like it."

"No. Merely holding this world together requires too much of me. Once we are safely out of the system, out of the path of the solar flares, we will forge a new generation of Redeemed to lead the fight against the Enemy."

The strain in her god's voice chilled Othaashle.

He needs strength from his champion, not a liability.

That sentiment, combined with the contempt he'd shown for Skadaatha's earlier weakness, made Othaashle's decision for her. She could *not* let Ynuukwidas know of her weakness. Not until Exodus was complete, at least.

If I don't find my own solution first. The Throne...

If Othaashle could find that, not only would she have the power to stop these visions, but she would gain a significant source of power for the Imaia.

"If I may be dismissed, Lord Ynuukwidas, I wish to look into the location of the Throne of Secrets myself."

"You are dismissed, my Champion." Ynuukwidas turned his gaze to Boaathal. "I wish you fortune and caution in your search."

Othaashle bowed, then strode away from the Aathal and out of the Vale.

Once she was a few paces away from its border—something about the Aathal and its power interfered with mundane technology at times—she raised her comm, opening a line to Yndlova.

"Yes, Mestari?"

"I'm headed back to the Isle. I need all reports on Remnant activity since Yrmuunthal's destruction ready for me when I return."

"Of course, Mestari."

Othaashle shut off the comm as she strode out into the streets of the District of Light. She specifically did not look back toward the Vale and the light of Boaathal that illuminated the sky above it.

Even Ynuukwidas does not know everything about the Aathal.

The Throne of Secrets might not give her a way to stop these visions, but it was the best she could hope for.

As she neared halfway between the compound and the Vale, another thought occurred to Othaashle.

She grinned beneath her mask.

If I take the Throne of Secrets and its power, Skadaatha will be furious.

That was often a reward in of itself.

4

Lights Out

"In this first design, zidanio plays a critical part, found both in the georaural framework, and integrated into the weapon itself, particularly the grip. I have constructed six interlinked georaural frameworks, integrating three into the guard, and three into the pommel. Not all Auroramantic functions will be critical to this weapon's use, and keeping economy of space in mind, I have been very precise in my selection of which functions to include."

Exodus countdown: 22 days, 30 hours, 23 minutes

The reverberations of *slaipenhair* and skilled fingers tugging and plucking on tightly wound metal strings filled the rehearsal room, the walls of the space crafted to make the fading sound seem a perfect chorus for the instruments and musicians who coaxed the wonderful music from them.

The musicians sat in a small arc, eyes either fixed on the sheet music before them or staring far off in concentration, notes memorized, focus consumed in bringing nuance to the performance.

Skadaatha smiled, reveling in the sonorous waves that flowed through the air around her. Music was one of the few things that could make her smile as easily as Vysla. Well-performed music, at least.

In theory, Skadaatha should have been a composer, and a masterful one at that. Her talents with music lay elsewhere, however. She had yet to find a way to translate them in a manner that would allow her to create such incredible, living art, and she had forgotten much of what once had been instinctual and intuitive to her.

What I would have given for the foresight to write down such melodies.

She wasn't even sure that Ynuukwidas was aware of the mechanics of his actions at this point. She planned to keep it that way as long as possible.

Taking a deep breath, Skadaatha attempted to calm herself and simply enjoy the music rather than be frustrated by the forgotten melodies it reminded her of.

Melodies of power.

Dismissing the thoughts, though not without effort, Skadaatha returned her attention to the music, clearnodes on a low burn to help her better appreciate the slight changes in timbre and dynamics, and orangenodes bright to help fix the performance in her memory.

For a while, it enthralled her.

The only thing that kept this experience from being perfect at the moment was that she could not enjoy this wonderful, intimate experience alone with the musicians. Dymbajat, the composer, sat a few feet away from her. She had nothing against the man—he was actually one of the few people whose company she enjoyed—she simply preferred to experience music alone with the performers. A quiet, older man, he always seemed sad, on the verge of tears, though Skadaatha supposed that was to be expected given the loss of his wife, Zuula, a talented singer in her own right, and obviously her husband's muse.

The loss was not recent, but then neither was Skadaatha's own. She had rarely heard more than two words out of Dymbajat at a time, save for greetings, farewells, and musical direction to those who brought his works to life. Skadaatha remembered the longest string of words she had ever heard from the man's mouth that had not fallen into those categories: "An artist's reply to despair and violence is to make music more intensely, more beautifully, more devotedly than ever before."

Where he had once composed joyous, triumphant works still performed by the Imaia's military bands during parades and ceremonies, his music had taken a darker, more melancholy turn since his wife's death.

Yet, it was even more beautiful.

The current piece had not been commissioned by the Imaia as many of Dymbajat's earlier pieces had, with clear directives and a scheduled debut at some parade or celebration in one of Mjatafa Mwonga's many plazas. Skadaatha had quickly seen how such orders had stifled Dymbajat after his wife's death, and had taken over the man's patronage, both personally and through her Ministry via the University of Culture, which she headed, as she did all of Mjatafa Mwonga's learning institutions save the military academy. This was one of the few areas where Skadaatha would have abused her bureaucratic power and responsibilities if needed. Inventing an excuse had been quite simple, however.

She hadn't been able to continue Dymbajat's access to large bands and orchestras for his compositions as much as he had previously enjoyed, yet through an initiative to further perfect and explore the capabilities of musical instruments—especially the ones from more isolated cultures the Imaia had absorbed—she had found the funding to allow Dymbajat as much time as he wished to create music, and the performers to bring that music to life. The composer had said nothing to Skadaatha beyond a few words of thanks, yet she suspected he enjoyed the direction she had given him in exploring smaller ensembles and working with tunes of cultural significance.

This was one such piece, taking the melodies of older folk tunes and weaving them together for an intimate ensemble. The quintet was quite standardized with its roster of two *gojere* fiddles, the larger *goja* and *goja kira*, and kora harp, yet the common instruments brought an unexpected complexity to the simple tunes, and the composition itself pushed each instrument to its limits.

As the piece came to an end, signaled by the increasingly intense harmony and a need for resolution, Skadaatha closed her eyes, surrendering to the music. She breathed in deep at the frisson that washed over her as the last chord faded into the air.

"Very well done," she said, looking first to the musicians, then to the composer. "You are a true jewel of the Imaia, Dymbajat."

The man seemed to wince at that, but nodded. "Thank you, Vizier Skadaatha. I am interested to hear your take-away, as always."

Though Skadaatha made sure to attend many private performances and rehearsals of musicians and ensembles throughout the city, this particular session served as a chance for her to review and approve the piece before Dymbajat could release the music for live performances and eventual recording. Despite using old folk melodies as his building blocks, Dymbajat had woven textures and harmonies a bit more sophisticated than those the general masses appreciated. Such music was not strictly in line with the normal art funding, but Skadaatha suspected this was something Ynuukwidas allowed as a mercy to her, even though the ministers below her often agreed with such tastes.

With Dymbajat, Skadaatha had yet to encounter a piece she would deny funding. This piece in particular had been beautiful, the performance just as much, yet Dymbajat's writing had pushed those instruments to their limits.

"Toward the end," she said, rising to walk over to the musicians, "in the fiddles, I believe. There was a section where the timbre grew quite shrill and thin. Was that on purpose?"

Dymbajat looked at his folder that contained the parts of each instrument recorded on paper. Though the system no longer amazed her —she had been the one to spread and standardize it through Efruumani's various cultures—seeing individuals like Dymbajat and the musicians exercise their fluency in it sent a thrill through her.

"Yes," the composer said, running a finger down one page of the music. Asking about his music was the only way Skadaatha had found so far to prompt him to engage in conversation. "It fits the proper emotion, I believe. Though I have been experimenting with natural and artificial harmonics in that section as well. The techniques would work better with a larger section for each note rather than a single instrument, but if anyone can coax the right sound out of their instruments, it is this group."

I'll have to get him a larger ensemble to work with.

The composer hefted and scanned through a large sheave of papers he'd been holding to his chest.

"This is the updated anthem arrangement that integrates 'the March

of the Redeemed' you requested for the performance following Exodus'
success," He said, handing her the papers, "I believe it should be to your
liking. It is more... passionate than the originals."

Skadaatha nodded, allowing a faint smile to touch her lips as she
took the sheet music. "Thank you, Dymbajat. I will look them over as
soon as I can."

He bowed, then walked over to the musicians.

Skadaatha left the composer to work with his musicians and
wandered out toward the music hall's main entrance, suppressing the
small bubble of anger that rose at Dymbajat's mention of the
Lightforged.

As she walked through the halls, passing many rooms that hosted
different ensembles rehearsing within, Skadaatha caught the lyrics of
the Imaia's Anthem being sung by a particularly large choir that had left
the door open a crack.

She paused for a moment to listen.

> "There, out in the darkness,
> A threat waits, lurking
> Enemy of life
> Enemy of peace
> Ynuukwidas witness,
> We never shall yield
> Till freedom reigns
> Until freedom reigns
>
> We go to fight the true fight
> We who refuse to be slaves
> Millions look on the axe with hope,
> Millions of hearts beat as one
> And if one falls as Matsanga fell
> The flame, the Axe
>
> We shall spread through the stars
> Braving all dangers
> Fighting the darkness with order and light

We shall be the sentinels
Forged in battle
Keeping watch for the night
Keeping watch for the Night

We know our place in Aioa
We hold to justice and truth
And We weep for the fallen both friend and foe
But we cannot turn aside
And those who fall as Kweshrima fell,
Will fall in Flame

And so it must be
Arise the Imaia
Raise your golden banners high
The fallen march with us in spirit
And in the Light

Lord bring us our enemy
So that we may all know your justice and peace
So that our deaths are not in vain
We will never rest
Until your light shines unhindered
This we swear by your Light"

Despite her annoyance at the credit the lyrics gave to Ynuukwidas, who would have been ignorant of the Enemy if not for her, Skadaatha couldn't help but smile as she continued down the hall. Crafting them had actually been fun. Even if they'd somehow turned out sub-par or too heavy with propaganda, Dymbajat would have found a way to make them ring in the hearts of the people.

Skadaatha's path took her out of the building into the university's main plaza, where students, researchers and professors mingled and crossed paths among the various buildings, bursts of dark foliage, and occasional monuments, all moving a bit quicker than usual.

Many in the Imaia bureaucracy thought these centers within the university to be a waste of time and energy best spent elsewhere, but Skadaatha had fought hard to keep them alive. Regardless of how far she had fallen from her former state, Skadaatha still wielded considerable power in the Imaia, backed up by that of those who followed her, and those who appreciated the fruits of her patronage of the arts.

A few students hurried past Skadaatha toward the stairs that led to one of this campus's hanging rail stations. Skadaatha had commissioned the project, which connected all campuses of the Imaia's university, as a test for the technology used in the Fingers of the Imaia.

The entire city was preparing for a temporary shutdown to switch from running off the power of the auroras and Boaathal's light to the power grid connected to the city's palladium reactors that would act as the main power source for Exodus.

Thoughts of Dymbajat—specifically the grief that permeated his music—and the power-switch led Skadaatha toward the engineering building that housed Vysla's lab and office. When she realized where she was going, Skadaatha paused, almost turning away, but instead continued on into the building. She hadn't found a good time to speak to her husband since their argument after her return to the city.

With effort, Skadaatha remembered to be personable. She asked the first student she encountered, a young Natari woman, if she knew where Vysla was. The woman wore a colorful, ankle-length dress that left a large triangular portion of her torso uncovered. She pointed Skadaatha toward one of the communal work areas near the building's center.

As Skadaatha walked in that direction, passing by the different offices and workspaces, many with their doors cracked or wide-open, she glanced through, searching for her husband.

She found Vysla overseeing the work of a few students.

Skadaatha did not disturb them, instead watching her husband work.

He, like her, was not one who needed to constantly be around people, talking and interacting with them, but he didn't have to try nearly as hard to be good with people as she did.

I do not deserve that man.

"Vizier Skadaatha?"

Skadaatha blinked at the address. Warm ripples spread through her as Vysla walked toward her wearing his usual crooked smile. The appreciative glance at her dress didn't hurt, either.

She'd chosen a nondescript outfit today—a simple violet dress in the fitted cut of the Nimikadeka with a neckline low enough to leave the two gemcrests at her clavicle uncovered.

She did not embrace him—that was something meant for the two of them alone—but took his hand and returned the smile.

"I thought I would join you during the shutdown. And I hoped we could talk."

Vysla nodded before waving to the students he'd left behind and gesturing back out the door.

For a while, they walked in silence toward the lift that would take them to Vysla's office. It soon grew too much for Skadaatha, however.

"Are there any particular projects I should take notice of?" she asked as they neared the lift. No one was around to hear, but she and Vysla had long since grown used to speaking in code unless in their own home. Their project was not exactly treasonous in itself—ideally it would benefit the Imaia nearly as much as the palladium reactors—yet if the wrong people found out, word would no doubt reach Ynuukwidas and the project would be handled by someone else at the very least.

"Three," Vysla said, as the lift opened before them. "Maybe four." He grinned at her, "I'll tell you which ones I'm thinking of after we're through."

Skadaatha snorted, yet couldn't keep the corners of her mouth from quirking up in a smile. They often played games like this to keep each other sharp on the other's area of expertise. She, quizzing him on the folk tunes worked into more formal compositions, or what instrument originated from which culture, and he on the nuances of various laws of reality or of factors of current research as they related to her interests for the Imaia's future and their own within it.

The ride up to the sixth floor took only a few minutes, but the walk through the lab seemed to take hours. Each person they passed or that Vysla stopped to speak to seemed to be able to sense Skadaatha's emotions and paled if she so much as glanced at them.

Skadaatha sighed, closing her eyes as she drew her fingers from her temples to the middle of her forehead.

I should be able to weather this. I should let all this flow past me as the mountain endures, despite the storms and gales that seek to make it crumble.

As with most things in her new life, that was far easier said than done. Skadaatha did make an effort, however, to focus on each workstation she and Vysla passed, and the details of what he asked about when he stopped to speak to someone.

"So, what are your guesses?" Vysla asked with a sly grin once they entered his personal lab—a perk he'd earned as one of the Imaia's top minds. Thick one-way glass comprised the exterior walls, tinted so that the sun's rays would not harm any Samjati who entered the room, while still allowing for a clear view of the campus and the city beyond.

Skadaatha thought for a moment, walking over to the window to look out at Mjatafa Mwonga.

"The augmentation and energy transference were obvious," she said, glancing back at her husband and allowing herself a smile at Vysla's nod. "The third would be... one of the reduction efforts? The palladium reactor?"

Vysla barked a laugh, shaking his head. "No. No, no. We're looking for a way to reduce the size of the reactors enough to comfortably fit them on something smaller than a capital ship, but the designs for something a single person could carry might not even be possible."

"Then which ones?"

Vysla walked over to his data terminal and opened a few files with blueprints. Skadaatha scanned them, then raised an eyebrow at her husband. "Hardlight for the blade?"

He nodded. "Most of our focus on hardlight has been directed at its force field-like properties, understandably, yet there are records of Auroramancers who used hardlight as tools, some of which functioned as an inclined plane."

Skadaatha stepped closer, reading over the notes. She resisted frowning at one of the listed possible applications: Weapons for Redeemed or their support troops.

"Whose project is this?"

"Suuri Kwangeta."

"Clever girl," Skadaatha breathed. "She isn't Auroraborn, is she?"

Vysla smiled. "She is not."

That made sense. Skadaatha could form hardlight to a sharp edge if needed, but the amount of concentration necessary to maintain such an edge was too great to focus on much else at the same time. She, as it seemed most Auroraborn with the ability, shaped hardlight in other ways that required less focus.

Georaural technology allowed for much more precise control than a mortal mind, however, and a scientist without the prejudices of an Auroraborn would see a much greater range of possibilities.

Skadaatha tried not to frown at that. She had a greater capacity than most, yet she still had not thought of this.

"I assume the hilt will have a high percentage of the aikanuum?" she asked, refocusing.

"And the zidanio," Vysla said. "I'm hoping that with the augmentation working correctly, the lesser amounts can work more efficiently."

Skadaatha nodded. "And the others?"

"Power storage and hardlight heating?"

Skadaatha frowned at that.

"Hardlight he—"

The lights went off. The hum of various machinery and systems went silent.

That was sudden.

She'd expected a warning or announcement of some sort.

Light from outdoors still shone in through the windows, but as Skadaatha looked out at the city—Vysla walked up to join her—she found herself in awe of how much light the buildings of the city themselves emitted. Within a minute, the city took on a dull cast as all lights went out, despite Boaathal's light and the ever-present light of the sun overhead. Only the distant floating guard-towers—relics of the age of Samjati naval dominance—remained lit and powered up.

"How long until the reactors take over?" Skadaatha asked. The Imaia had eliminated nearly all groups that could pose a threat to them, especially here surrounded by miles of ocean. Still... this seemed like the perfect time for something to go wrong.

"About five minutes."

Skadaatha glanced at her husband, taking his hand.

"I never apologized," she said.

"For what?"

From anyone else, Skadaatha would have taken that as a challenge, but she knew Vysla meant the opposite. Despite his incredible memory, he was a proponent of the 'forgive and forget' practice.

She squeezed his hand.

He squeezed it back, filling her with that wonderful warmth.

I can tell him.

That would mean admitting how broken she was.

He doesn't care about that.

That made it easier, but harder all at once.

I'm supposed to be the strong one. The one he *can rely on. Not the other way around.*

"Vysla, I—"

A loud, distant *boom* cut Skadaatha's words short. Flashes followed by billowing smoke appeared on the city skyline. Skadaatha tensed, priming her biogems. Moments later, an alarm blared.

Mjatafa Mwonga was under attack.

Skadaatha turned to Vysla. "Any chance you have a working prototype?"

Vysla's eyes widened even further than they already had at the alarm. "Never mind."

She twitched toward the doorway, then remembered how she'd left Vysla last time. Skadaatha grabbed Vysla and pulled him to her in a quick but fiery kiss that left him dazed and her with a racing heart. Despite the blaring alarms and the adrenaline making its way through her body, Skadaatha smiled at that as she pulled back.

"Stay safe, husband. I love you."

Skadaatha flared her Natari greynodes for speed and primed her ambernodes for foresight, then bolted out the door toward the nearest exit.

5

Mestari

"As this weapon will be exclusively handled by Vizier Skadaatha, I decided to include a single amethyst setting to allow for the production of lightning, the regulation of temperature and the production of fire or freezing temperatures for an Auroramancer that can call on both polarizations of each biogem."

Exodus countdown: 22 days, 29 hours, 42 minutes

Skadaatha's greynodes burned bright as she raced through streets crowded with frightened people. Other far-off explosions echoed through the city. A single glance upon exiting Vysla's lab had indicated the nearest point of attack: one of the airborne, icy guard-towers that hovered high above the freshwater sea had been hit and started to fall from the sky. Skadaatha ignored her comms for now—soldiers and Lightforged would handle any other threats, but she was one of the few who could bring the tower down safely. No one would be crushed if a tower fell into the Fresh Water Sea, but nearby people and infrastructure would suffer if the tower fell too fast.

If it drifts enough to fall on part of the city...

Skadaatha shook the thought from her head as she came to an intersection. The only light around her was that of the sun and the Aathal. The entire city's power grid would be offline for at least two more minutes. The attack could be over by then. She brightened her clearn-odes—though not to the point where the sensory input would over-whelm her—and set her ambernodes and Natari blacknodes to a low burn. The former would enhance her sense of premonition, while the latter would allow her to detect any nearby uses of Auroramancy.

They knew. They planned an attack for the first time in years that the city has been so vulnerable. And so close to Exodus.

That meant a spy deep within their midst. Announcements had gone out this morning, but only the higher-ups of the ministries had been informed beforehand to plan accordingly for their domains.

Skadaatha almost launched herself into the sky so she could take the most direct route, but her clearnodes, ambernodes, and adrenaline-heightened senses alerted her to the low thrum of a fighter through the blaring alarm just in time to throw herself to the side as the whir of rotary guns sounded. She rolled into a crouch, looking up as an Imaia Horseshoe fighter soared past.

The Remnant? Or just dissidents?

Shallow ruts sizzled in the street where the fighter's turrets had torn through the pavement down to the metal foundation beneath. The pilot's aim had been off from where Skadaatha had stood.

Rising to her feet, Skadaatha brightened her clearnodes and primed her violetnodes, vision locked on the fighter as it sped toward the falling, wobbling guard-tower.

Then she noticed the huddled, frightened people pressing them-selves against the building wall beside her. Two men, one Samjati and one Natari, held an adolescent Samjati girl to them. All three trembled, gazing at her with wide-eyed terror.

"Stay down and against the wall," Skadaatha said, straightening; "Sur-prise is our enemy's only advantage, and they've just given that up."

The Natari man raised a shaking hand, pointing past Skadaatha, "M-my son!"

Skadaatha followed the man's gesture. Most people on the street had cleared out after the fighter's pass, huddling low against walls like these or ducking inside the buildings.

Except a young Natari boy, frozen in terror.

Skadaatha should have sensed him, but there were too many people around, and the boy's attention was not on her. She didn't need to follow the boy's gaze to know that his eyes were fixed on the enemy fighter, swooping down for another pass.

Skadaatha bolted toward the boy, drawing on her strength to give her a burst of speed toward him. She tackled him, rolling and shielding him with her body just as she heard the hiss of the fighter's weapons.

As she came to a stop, Skadaatha looked down at the boy. He trembled and tears flowed freely down his orange cheeks, but he did not sob.

A painful sensation of familiarity hit Skadaatha as she looked down at him.

No time for that.

"You'll be okay," she told him.

Rising to a crouch, Skadaatha hefted the young boy in her arms, ready to deliver him to his family while the enemy fighter circled.

Another fighter came into view before she made it halfway across the street.

Skadaatha brightened her Natari rednodes and threw up a golden hardlight barrier between herself and the new fighter, bracing for the impact of its weaponry.

The concussion never came, and Skadaatha heard a gasp from the direction of the boy's parents.

She looked back toward the fighter just in time to see a figure that shone almost as bright as the sun itself shoot into the air. Blue-white light flashed, leaving the afterimage of a thin bar connecting the fighter and the glowing figure. Hardlight of gold and darklight of black-violet surrounded the aircraft. A moment later, it slammed to the center of the empty street twenty meters back.

A roiling, white-hot anger burst to life within Skadaatha as she watched the shining figure rise into the sky. The impulse to flare her opalnodes and Natari violetnodes simultaneously and knock that figure out of the air with a bolt of lightning rose up within Skadaatha. She didn't immediately suppress it. There weren't too many witnesses to take care of, and she could blame it on the attack. Othaashle wasn't a god. And it would have been her fault for exposing herself like that, anyway. She always needed to show off. One good hit...

Skadaatha waited too long, however, and watched with jaw clenched as Othaashle bound away toward the city's military district. Cheers followed.

Skadaatha let out a low growl.

No. You're supposed to be better than that. These are your people. Othaashle is not worth their lives.

With great effort, Skadaatha forced herself to swallow that anger as she straightened and jogged back over to the boy's family, now standing and looking after Othaashle as they cheered. She couldn't blame them for their excitement or praise. Few ordinary citizens had ever witnessed any of the Redeemed in battle, and now these had been saved by Othaashle herself. A hero slain by the enemy, then reforged in Ynuukwidas's light to fight once more.

The worst part was, they would likely still praise her if they knew the truth as Skadaatha did.

"All of you, get inside!" Skadaatha said, pushing the boy back to his family, who huddled around him immediately. "Take shelter until the alarms cease. Ynuukwidas's light protect you!"

With that, Skadaatha glanced back toward the falling icy guard-tower and snarled as she took off running.

This is cutting it far too close.

OTHAASHLE GLANCED BACK over her shoulder as she bounded away from the downed fighter. The city guard would secure it and help get those around it to safety. After watching long enough to confirm that Skadaatha was headed toward Tower Five, Othaashle turned her attention back toward her destination.

"Yndlova, report," she called over her comm, using her Natari greennodes to tether herself to a fighter that zipped through the air toward Tower Two and the Military District. Another Horseshoe fighter.

"Multiple explosions, Mestari," Othaashle's second reported, "And the power is still down. They hit the repair yards in Military, three factories in Manufacturing, a few of the turrets around Bastion Eight, Airfields Two and Eleven, and hangars all around Military and Central, including those in the Towers. The explosions seem to have ceased for now, but we're getting everyone away from defensive structures and military buildings."

Damn.

This was bad. An attack like this with so many widespread explosions going off at once during a shutdown of the entire city took serious manpower, planning, and infiltration.

Looks like I'll be hunting some spies after this.

"Any chance the factories hit produce weapons?"

"Looking into that but haven't been able to confirm it. Towers Five, Three and Two were hit, though none of them report the same type of damage. The remaining towers are scrambling fighters now and we received one report that an insurgent was apprehended fleeing one of the attack sites near the outer wall."

Something pricked at Othaashle's mind, and she halted her pursuit of the traitorous fighter. Though she continued tracking it with her gaze.

"What about the Warehouse District between Manufacturing and Agriculture?"

Silence over the comm. Then: "Nothing reported, Mestari."

Mouth drawing to a line, Othaashle brightened her Fireborn greennodes and pushed herself off one of the obsidian plates set into Mjatafa Mwonga's streets, straight up into the air, high enough that her tether began to strain. Anywhere else on Efruumani, sustaining a push this high would have used up all Othaashle's Auroralight. This close to Boaathal's light, however, her Auroralight replenished even as she used it.

"How many rogue fighters, Yndlova?"

"Nineteen reported so far, Mestari."

"Including the one I just took care of?"

Othaashle heard her adjunct's snort through the comm. "Eighteen, then."

Gazing down at Mjatafa Mwonga, clearnodes burning bright, Othaashle searched for the pattern. Something wasn't right. The fighter she'd downed near Skadaatha hadn't fired on any of the nearby buildings despite the obvious clusters of people near them. None had tried to finish off the wounded towers or targeted any civilian structures either.

What is their game?

"Have Jynos send me a fighter, Yndlova. I need a ride. A Trident, preferably."

Othaashle could move fast with her greennodes, but not as fast as any of the Imaia's fighters.

"On it. Standby, Mestari."

As Othaashle waited, she opened up a second channel.

"Adjunct Itese, report."

Two seconds of silence.

"Mestari, I've deployed the Redeemed to secure the city. Our best warriors and pilots are working with Wing Commander Jynos and Adjunct Yndlova to take to the air and secure the points of attack. I've deployed everyone else to work with the city guard to lock down the city and keep citizens out of harm's way."

Othaashle grinned "You barely even need me to give you orders anymore, Adjunct. Good job. Keep me apprised of any updates."

"Yes, sir, Mestari."

"Mestari," Yndlova's voice came over the comm, "I've got a Trident headed your way, callsign: Redtail."

"Good work, Yndlova," Othaashle said, scanning for the approaching fighter.

Found it.

"Keep working with Jynos and Itese, and let me know of any updates. Give Redtail the code to open up a channel with me."

Othaashle dimmed her greennodes just as the Trident zipped toward her, dropping into a crouch on its wing between the main body and its left rotary gun. She brightened her greennodes again to tether herself to the strips of obsidian set into the wing and pressed down hard, ensuring she wouldn't fall off too easily.

"Mestari—er, Supreme Commander—it's an honor," the pilot's voice came over Othaashle's comm. "What can I do for you?"

"Mestari is fine, Redtail," Othaashle said to the young woman. "Name and rank?"

"Tuuski Bekalma," the woman answered, "Airman First Class."

"How good of a shot are you, First Class Tuuski?"

"One of the best, Mestari."

Othaashle laughed. "Let's hunt some rogue fighters, then. You take them down, I'll make sure they don't damage our beautiful city when they fall."

"Can we find a few trainees to drop them on, Mestari? Their heads should be hard enough."

Othaashle grinned. "I like you, Redtail. On my mark—dive!"

"COMMANDER EKAIJE," Skadaatha barked, jogging into the command center on Tower Five's third level. Men and women in uniform stood at their posts in the large room, some facing a projected, three-dimensional display of the tower as it descended toward the sea and city below, others facing a wall of visual relays. "Status report, now!"

The Natari woman in the commander's uniform, biogems glowing violet, a small, oval-cut sapphire hanging down below her cap onto her forehead, started, as did most in the room. She recovered before Skadaatha had to repeat herself.

"Hangar doors are still blocked, and repulsors one and three are damaged, Vizier," she said, snapping a crisp salute as Skadaatha came to an abrupt stop beside her. "The guard-tower is falling at two meters per-second for now."

Skadaatha gritted her teeth. These towers had been used to test various thrusters and stabilizers that they'd used on spacecraft and trans-atmospheric fighters, but they hadn't been renovated since then—not enough time or resources. Most of the tech was georaural, not mundane, and harder to work around in a crisis. With two of its four repulsors damaged, Skadaatha was surprised the tower hadn't already hit the water below and caused a tidal wave to wash over the nearby district. That would cause casualties they couldn't afford right now. Of the citizenry and the city's infrastructure.

"How long until we hit the water?"

"Three minutes," the woman said. "We're doing what we can to keep stable and minimize damage to the city, but it still won't be good."

Skadaatha clenched her teeth.

Cutting it close is an understatement.

A display of the tower's continued descent caught Skadaatha's gaze and snapped her thoughts back to the present. She held up her comm and switched the channel feed, ensuring that the commander saw what she was doing.

"Broadcast on channel five," Skadaatha ordered, heading back out of the room, "and assemble teams of all greenskaters and redblockers you have. I have a plan to get this tower to the water safely. Gather those teams and open the channel. Wait for my command... and brace yourselves."

Skadaatha ran down the hall toward the nearest balcony. She brightened her Samjati greennodes, creating a tether between herself and the fortress's icy walls, then hurtled over the railing and out into the air.

OTHAASHLE WHOOPED from where she crouched on her fighter's wing as Redtail hit the engine of another Horseshoe fighter with her Trident's gauss cannon. This was the fourth fighter they'd brought down together, and Othaashle caught it with hardlight and darklight in a now-practiced motion. She guided the craft down with gentle nudges and bounced it toward a section of a wider street that the city guard had cleared of any citizens. She grinned when she saw a few Redeemed run out onto the street to secure the craft now that it was safely on the ground.

"Nice one," Othaashle said. "Mind if I take a shot at the next one?"

Redtail laughed over the comm. "As you wish, Mestari. What do you need me to do?"

"Just find another fighter and get me close enough. I'll take it from there."

"Yes, sir!"

As Redtail searched for another fighter, Othaashle tried to make sense of this attack. Rather than shoot up buildings and installations, the rogue fighters were dogfighting. They hadn't tried to attack any more of the guard-towers or even the Vale. Not that the latter would have been a particularly wise or successful endeavor.

There's got to be something I'm missing.

"Mestari, target acquired."

For now, however, Othaashle was content to dogfight.

Zeroing in on the fighter Redtail had spotted—a 4-Tail like her own craft, but much less formidable—Othaashle primed her Natari violetnodes.

T̲WELVE̲.

Skadaatha plummeted through the air, using lashings to keep herself little more than a meter from the tower's narrowing base as she descended. She slowed upon reaching that bottom point, adjusting her tethers to keep her steadily floating a meter from the icy tip. She formed a small hardlight disc with a cone-shaped bottom beneath her to keep her hair and clothing from whipping about as she descended toward the small sea below but made no effort to hold the disc up.

Eleven... Ten...

"Now!" Skadaatha barked to Ekaije. "Cut all thrusters and keep this channel open."

A moment of silence, then, "Cutting now!"

Nine.

The roar of rushing air drowned out all other sound as the ice-made tower dropped toward the ground with no resistance, pushing Skadaatha along with it. She looked down through her disc at the fast-approaching water. The guard-tower's commander had calculated exactly how long she should wait. She had to time this perfectly, or her barrier might shatter, and the station's impact would send a massive wave toward the surrounding area.

Eight... Seven... Six...

Skadaatha continued to count down in her head to when the tower would drop to twice its height from the water's surface.

Five... Four... Three...

"Brace!"

Skadaatha roared as she flared her rednodes, violetnodes, blacknodes, greennodes, and opalnodes all at once in a massive blast of power.

With her Samjati violetnodes, Skadaatha shot a blast of cold through her feet, freezing the water beneath her for a radius of twenty meters in an instant. That done, she used her Samjati greennodes to tether that chunk of violet ice to the plummeting icy fortress above and pushed the two apart with as much strength as she could bring to bear, flaring her Samjati greynodes to keep the resulting forces from crushing her body. The two bodies of ice jolted, and Skadaatha shattered the ice beneath her with her greennodes, sending it flying in all directions and creating a depression in the water that she then used her Natari rednodes to fill with a barrier of hardlight the size of the entire base of the guard-tower. She sandwiched that between two layers of darklight that softened the impact of the tower against the hardlight and that of the hardlight against the water below. Skadaatha then tethered herself to the fortress with her Samjati greennodes and pushed away with all her might at the last moment, torpedoing herself deep and away into the water at the last moment. The water felt like a sheet of glass as she crashed through it, but the enhanced strength and durability she gained from her Samjati greynodes protected her body. Even with all she'd done, Skadaatha felt her barrier of hardlight and darklight jolt the tower rather than cushion it, but no alarms blared over her comm.

Not for the first time, Skadaatha wished tethers would work while in water so she could propel herself to the side and come up for air. Instead, she flared her greynodes and moved her body like a whip, kicking her way up to the edge of the tower's shallow base.

Skadaatha's Auroralight all-but ran out just as she reached the surface. She dimmed her gemcrest the instant before going lightless— water distorted Boaathal's light the same way it did normal light, unfortunately. When her head broke through to the sweet, life-giving air, Skadaatha reflexively gulped in breaths—the reflex of a mortal.

She floated onto her back for a moment, allowing herself to catch her breath as the less-potent reflected light of Boaathal replenished her gemcrests. Once a comfortable amount filled her, Skadaatha brightened her violetnodes and froze the water beneath herself before brightening her Samjati greennodes and tethering herself and the ice on her boots to the ice beneath. She pushed so she floated above the water, then spoke into her comm, "Status."

"Some damage from the impact, but nothing too serious so far," the Ekaije reported. "Weapons are operational if any more fighters try to target us. There is some damage to a few of our fighters, but nothing major. Thank you, Vizier."

"Good," Skadaatha barked. "Get those hangar doors open so the fighters can protect us if the attackers pull any more surprises."

Skadaatha let herself breathe for a moment, mind racing as she looked between the tower and the rest of the city.

Firing at random citizens on the street but not the buildings they shelter in or a massive falling target that can't defend itself?

If this was the Remnant, this attack made no sense. The rebel group was small with few resources—Skadaatha was surprised they even had two ships left—but they were smart. Every strike she'd seen since the group's formation had been calculated for maximum damage to the Imaia. Except this one.

Skadaatha opened her comm to the Urban Corps. and High Command channels.

"This is Vizier Skadaatha, I need a report on what's happening."

"Mestari!" Yndlova's voice came over the comm as Othaashle carefully lowered her and Redtail's eighth downed fighter—there had to only be three or four left now.

"Yes, Yndlova, report!"

Redtail pointed them in the direction of another fighter running from two other Trident fighters.

Othaashle slapped the wing twice and gave Redtail a fist-pump as they hurtled through the air toward the group.

"A report came in of four fighters and two shuttle-transports carrying some sort of wreck over Bastion Eight."

That's what it was.

"Should we pursue, Mestari?"

Othaashle thought for a moment.

"Negative, Yndlova. I have an idea. Have the outposts keep an eye out, but do *not* pursue."

"Yes, sir."

Othaashle focused on the rogue Horseshoe fighter again as Redtail fell in with the two Trident-class fighters already in pursuit. She brightened her clearnodes to make out their insignias.

"Tri-six, Tri-thirty," she said, switching her comm to the direct channels to those two pilots along with Redtail. "Hold—"

Othaashle's vision flashed. For a moment, something flashed before her eyes. She sat in a room filled with hardened men and women in combat uniforms. Mjatafa Mwonga and the three fighters returned.

"Tri-six, Tri-thirty, Redtail," she repeated, releasing her Natari greennode tether to Tuuski's fighter and vaulting off toward Isle of the Redeemed. "I've got to go investigate an urgent report."

Othaashle tethered the obsidian in her boots to that in the nearest building. "Chase the rogue out of the city but do *not* shoot it down."

As if in response to Othaashle's orders, Skadaatha's voice came through the open fighter channel.

"All fighters, one of the traitors is fleeing the city. Shoot it down over the Salt Sea."

She'd said it on the channel even the rogue pilot could hear.

Othaashle's vision flashed again. This time she stood with two officers before a plethora of maps and reports, and a Samjati man in all black.

Dammit, Skadaatha now is not the time to be stupid.

"Belay that," Othaashle barked over the main channel, tethering herself to another building. So much for her plan. She switched to the private channel. "Damage it once it is out of the city, but do not shoot it down."

Her vision flashed back to normal, showing her the area she had aimed for, and she switched over to a direct channel to the Imaia's wing commander.

"Jynos, this is Mestari Othaashle. Disseminate these orders to each of our pilots individually: damage the enemy fighter, but do not pursue beyond the city walls. Inform the Vizier of my orders, then kick her off this channel."

"Understood, Mestari."

Her vision flashed, and she was in a dark, damaged, but finely built structure, fighting. Odors of blood, black powder, ozone, and gore assaulted her senses. Pain lanced through her like a lightning bolt.

"Yndlova," Othaashle hissed, through a direct channel to her adjunct, reversing her lashings to slow herself as she neared the secluded grove of trees. She stumbled as she landed, vision returning to normal but pain persisting. "I need you at our meeting spot in the park."

More pain. Injured soldiers all around her. Some were dying. Others were already dead.

Othaashle stumbled forward. She could still feel the spongey grass beneath her, the roots and trunks of the trees as she pulled herself between them. Then her sense of touch began to switch, and a white light appeared behind her eyes as it had each time.

"Quickly."

6

Imaia High Command

"Similarly, I decided not to include an aquamarine setting, as manipulation of fire and ice has proven terribly cumbersome when performed with georaural technology in comparison with practiced Auroramantic abilities. I believe the presence of zidanio will increase the innate alertness provided by aquanodes far beyond what a georaural could accomplish."

Exodus countdown: 22 days, 27 hours, 56 minutes

"Vizier Skadaatha, I would feel much more comfortable if we waited for Commander Othaashle to arrive before we begin."

Skadaatha kept her expression neutral at Admiral Kanysile Takina's defiance. Even in her middle years, the woman seemed too pretty and delicate to have served despite her numerous commendations that adorned her uniform, complemented by the emerald gemcrest on her collarbone. As the Imaia currently had little use for any sort of traditional navy beyond shipping at the moment, her arm of the military had taken to working with the Winged Legion and providing more manpower and resources to the intelligence agencies.

Skadaatha, Takina, and the other heads of the Imaia's armed forces stood around the central display terminal of High Command's overbridge meeting room, a small, hexagonal chamber situated just across the hall from the much larger main War Room of the overbridge where officers and technicians currently milled about.

"I agree with the admiral," General Hanbarka Sioro said, the orange gemcrest shining along with his medals as he stood straight-backed, broad chest puffed out. Many officers in the Imaia's military shared his same Auroramantic ability to see into the past and the enhanced memory that almost always accompanied a sunstone crest. Sioro's drive to examine every battlefield he could, and his incredible ability to analyze those battles and gain insight into the tactics and strategy, was what had sent him hurtling through the ranks. The man's keen sense for logistics hadn't hurt either.

"As do I," echoed Wing Commander Chapi Jynos. The slender man's golden eyes seemed to constantly dart between each person around the terminal. Unlike the admiral and general, Jynos was not an Auroramancer, though the Auroralight in his ruby gemcrest gave him quicker reflexes than most.

Skadaatha remained silent as she met the eyes of each of the Imaia's high officers, ignoring the aides and adjuncts that waited at their heels. Each wore a crisp uniform with patterns and colors denoting their specific branches of the Ministry of War, as well as a large patch of medals and commendations on their right breast, conveying to all that they had earned their lofty positions.

"Unfortunately," Skadaatha said in a level tone, "We don't have time to wait for the supreme commander. I need damage reports, forces prepared for a counterstrike, and a strategic assessment of the attack. These insurgents caught us off guard during a moment of weakness, using our own aircraft against us, and could discern no clear purpose from their actions."

She couldn't let anything get in the way of Exodus.

We're too close.

"While I agree that time is of the essence," Takina said, "Commander Othaashle's leadership—"

"I have led armies and peoples since before Atonga's first queen sat on her throne, Admiral," Skadaatha said, her voice ice as she cut the woman off. "That should be enough to assuage your concerns. Now, I saw on the way back that our priests and medics are ministering and aiding the injured. I would hope that our military engineers are out as well, surveying the damaged areas of the city for repairs."

The high officers exchanged uncomfortable looks. A few of their aides had gone pale. Skadaatha knew she'd put them in an unenviable position between her and Othaashle. She didn't care.

After giving them another minute under her icy gaze, Skadaatha called up a real-time map of Mjatafa Mwonga on the terminal before them.

"All guard-towers are safely down on the water," she began, "I have reports from Towers Two, Five, and Six, that most of the damage was—"

The hiss of doors sliding open at the other end of the room cut Skadaatha off, and her mouth drew to a thin, hard line as Othaashle strode into the room, titansteel armor gleaming, antlers and cape giving her an intimidating silhouette. Her adjuncts, Yndlova and Itese, flanked her and took up positions behind her similar to the other aides once they reached the central terminal, though both far outranked every other aide present. Yndlova, as always, was the picture of military professionalism— even her multitude of braids somehow seemed all in their place—while the tall, lanky Samjati Redeemed for some reason saw the need not only for a stylized mask, but added flamboyance like that ridiculous mane.

Still, the officer snapped a crisp salute the moment they noticed the trio.

"Supreme Commander Othaashle," Skadaatha said, trying to smooth her expression and tone despite the anger that rose within her. "You're late."

"I am," the woman said simply, masked face unreadable. "I stopped on the way to get what reports I could and reassure our people that they are safe, and Exodus has not been threatened in any way."

She paused, looking around the table. Though Skadaatha couldn't see the woman's eyes through her Lightforged mask, she knew Othaashle's eyes were on her as the she continued.

"I expect that I will not be told I've lied to our people."

"That is what I was attempting to review when you arrived, Commander," Skadaatha refused to address the woman by honorific. "The others insisted on waiting for you, however."

Othaashle looked around the room, then sighed. "While I appreciate your adherence to protocol, Commanders, Vizier Skadaatha has long-since proven to be an asset to the Imaia in military matters."

Skadaatha ground her teeth. She'd been expecting Othaashle to take the side of her underlings. Why did the woman's acquiescence make Skadaatha want to hit something?

Othaashle paid her no more mind and turned to Jynos. "Wing Commander, I recommend giving one of your pilots—callsign: Redtail—some sort of a promotion or medal. I was very impressed by her during the attack. I'll submit a formal request later."

Then she turned to General Sioro. "Reports on the damages, General?"

"They are incomplete, Commander, as reports are still coming in. Preliminary findings indicate only superficial damage so far to anything non-military, though Bastion Eight and Tower Five received significant damage, the latter of which, the vizier can testify to. Our inspectors are working with Vizier Skadaatha's people to ensure nothing is missed and all damage is properly assessed."

"The one thing we have not been able to figure out so far," Takina cut in, "is how such a widespread attack was planned and coordinated without our knowledge. The level of manpower and intelligence needed for this would be too large to go unnoticed."

"I can shed some light on that," Othaashle said, turning to Adjunct Itese, who handed her a ruined, small mechanical device that looked like a receiver of some sort. The commander held it up for all to see. "I believe devices like this significantly reduced the manpower needed to carry out an attack on this scale. We could be looking at as few as nine-teen infiltrators who simply took their time in planning this attack. Vizier, I believe you'll be able to enlighten the others on this device I found."

Skadaatha frowned, watching as Othaashle passed the device to Sioro, who studied it. A troubled expression crossed his features before he passed it along. When it came to Skadaatha, her eyes widened after a moment. She looked around the display. "This is a receiver for a remote detonator. We theorized that they'd used devices like this before, but constructed of georaurals. It is relatively new technology for us, just past the testing stage..."

How had rebels hiding in caves managed to surpass her *in advancement?*

"They will have needed to infiltrate our ministries' joint military-science division," Othaashle turned to Jynos again.

"Wing Commander, were any reports made of strange-looking craft firing upon us? Have we compared reports of craft seen and shot down with those missing from our hangars?"

"No reports of non-Imaia craft so far, Commander," Jynos responded. "We are missing nineteen operational trans-atmospheric fighters in total, and nineteen were shot down, including the one you ordered not to be pursued."

"I'm still waiting on an explanation for that," Skadaatha said.

The supreme commander's masked face turned toward Skadaatha. "We will give you a report of our findings, Vizier. I would prefer, however, that you focus on any damages the attack may have made to our infrastructure. I noticed at least one residential building damaged by the attack on my way here. I would appreciate it if you would lend the Whore Mother's workers some aid in repairing it."

Skadaatha narrowed her eyes at Othaashle. The woman was being far too agreeable.

"Of course, Commander."

Othaashle turned back to Jynos, "Wing Commander, do you have any reports from the outer shipyards or our outposts beyond the city? Yndlova reported a group of rogue fighters transporting some sort of wreckage over Bastion Eight while it was still inactive."

Jynos shook his head. "I will have some for you in a moment, Commander."

The two aides behind the man immediately grew much more interested in their datapads.

"While we wait for that," Othaashle said, "we need to address the possibility of spies in our midst. We had at least eight that we knew of and watched up until this attack. I don't doubt there are more lying low in the wake of today's events. Tell your spymasters that I want this done quietly. If possible, I want any possible agents we find watched rather than rounded up. Most importantly, however, I want to know if this is the Remnant. What is left of them, at least."

Skadaatha flexed her fingers behind her back as Othaashle turned to her. "Vizier, I would appreciate it if you could lend your experience in this area to the Imaia's spymasters."

Skadaatha nodded slowly, unsure if this was some sort of jab at her former position.

"Pardon me, Commander," Jynos said, taking the datapad handed to him as he and the others nodded, "it looks as though four fighters and a transport—all under repair—were taken from Shipyard Seven during the attack. We also have reports of attacks on two capital ships that were being re-outfitted for trans-atmospheric flight."

Skadaatha peered at the supreme commander, frustrated with her inability to see through the woman's mask.

"Your thoughts, Commander?" she ventured.

The woman remained silent a few moments longer before speaking. "I have recently reviewed our reports of Remnant activities since Yrmuunthal's destruction and their effective collapse. About five and a half years ago, one of their attacks damaged an early Akane-class capital ship on a supply run back from Darkside. The terrain was unsuitable for salvage, and we had moved on to the Draakon-class by then, so we bombarded the area and that was it."

Skadaatha nodded along with the other officers. She remembered the incident.

"Even before today, we knew that we had not eliminated every last cell of the Remnant," Othaashle continued. "I worried they had been too quiet and were working toward something big rather than simply giving up hope and dissolving in truth.

"Today's attack... the timing, the superficial damage, the stolen ships in disrepair—combined with the downed capital ship—this all makes me believe that the Remnant salvaged that ship and just stole the parts they believed necessary to make it work."

Skadaatha raised an eyebrow at that, considering.

"Pardon, Commander," General Sioro said. "But for what purpose?"

"They want to escape," Skadaatha said.

Othaashle's masked head swiveled toward Skadaatha. For a moment, the two stared at one another. The mask prevented Skadaatha from meeting the other woman's eyes, but Skadaatha could feel her gaze.

She'd already figured it out, and she doesn't like that I came to that conclusion. Why?

Othaashle turned back to the others.

"I believe their spies informed them that Exodus will likely render Efruumani uninhabitable in a short amount of time," Othaashle continued. "They hope that they can make it off-system with what they've salvaged and pieced together, as Vizier Skadaatha guessed."

"I agree with General Sioro, Commander," Admiral Takina said. "To what end? Do they seek to take Myrskaan Station? How do they plan to make it past the Draakon ships stationed in low-orbit?"

"Even if they did make it past our cruisers," Jynos put in, "they would need coordinates and the necessary navigational systems to travel through Aathalspace to hope to reach another system, much less one that is habitable."

"*We* may know that, Commander," Skadaatha said, "but the Remnant —if this *is* in fact the Remnant—is likely making decisions out of desperation. Maybe they hope to travel in our wake or blend in with our other cruisers. Regardless, this narrows down the areas in which to search for their spies. I will—"

"Assist the spymaster with locating any insurgents in our midst," Othaashle said. "Once they are found, we will take things from there. As I said, your focus on repairing any damages to Mjatafa Mwonga's infrastructure is far more important. I will also grant any resources you need to improve fortifications or security at key points if you believe it necessary."

Skadaatha forcibly relaxed herself, remaining silent as she nodded her assent.

"Good," Othaashle said. "I will handle pursuit of the ship we shot down personally, and find out if this is the Remnant, and what their plans are. If necessary, I will eliminate those I find. Any spies within our ranks will be unable to warn them in time. Meanwhile, we need to hunt the remaining spies. Round up those who try to flee and hold them for interrogation until I get back. I want no premature deaths or anyone getting lost in the camps. Report your findings to Adjunct Yndlova."

The commander paused, then turned to Skadaatha, "Vizier, I will need you to coordinate with High Judge Omuura. Have your cultural ministers coordinate with the city guard and her judges to ensure that Samjati areas are watched and that any offenses against Samjati citizens are handled quickly and harshly. Tell Omuura to make an example, if needed. Any questions?"

Silence. Then:

"When will you depart, Commander?" Admiral Takina asked.

"Immediately."

7

Nothing to Fear

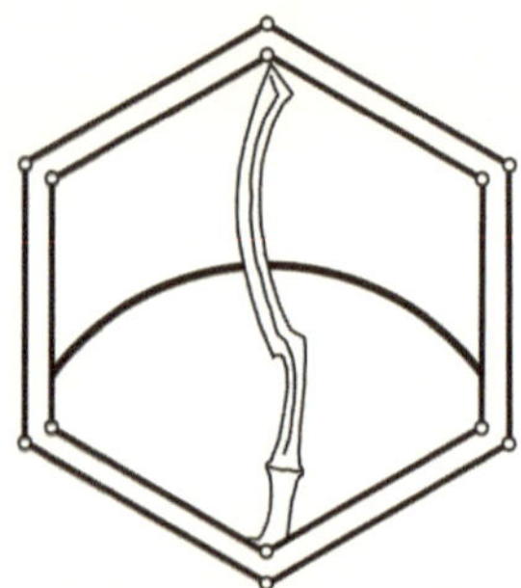

"The ability to push and pull on water and volcanic rock seems unsuited to a weapon of this sort, but I have included two emerald settings for healing. Though the effect is negligible and unsuited for use in battle under normal circumstances, I believe zidanio will amplify the effect to the point where it may be of use. I pray, however, that Skadaatha will never need to test this effect save under controlled circumstances."

Exodus countdown: 22 days, 26 hours, 27 minutes

"Do we have a list of the exact parts and ships lifted by the Remnant?" Othaashle asked Yndlova as they and Itese strode through the Isle of the Redeemed's main plaza toward the light reserve. "Or what damage was done to the capital ships to mask the theft?"

As Yndlova answered her question, Othaashle tried to dwell on the mission ahead. Thoughts from before tugged at her attention, however.

How did Skadaatha know?

Then there was her...vision. Several of the Union's most pivotal strikes at the Imaia—at what would become the Imaia—had been executed by Symuuna Team. Most had been before Othaashle's rebirth, but the Ministry's records detailed the brutal efficiency with which that team operated, even compared to the other strike teams that had made up Operation Phantom.

Most of the visions she'd seen before had to do with this Kojatere. They showed her childhood and adolescence, with vague impressions of the woman's adult life. Othaashle could think of no reason why she experienced these visions. Save for the one she didn't want to think about, at least.

Until now. Until Symuuna.

As far as Othaashle remembered from her research, Symuuna Team had never truly been disbanded. The Imaia's information on the team was limited, provided mostly by a former member who had defected after Yrmuunthal's destruction.

Mnene, right? One of Skadaatha's people.

Othaashle would have to look into him when she got back.

A renewed sense of purpose rose within Othaashle, quickening her step.

This must be it. The Aathal is trying to warn me of a spy in our midst. A former member of Symuuna.

So far, her visions pointed toward this Kojatere as that spy, but if that was the case, her research had yielded far less information than the visions. The name wasn't too uncommon on Darkside, and her search had pulled up a champion ice-dancer, several soldiers, a politician, and a notable Auroramancer slain during the war. Almost all had fought the Imaia. She hadn't been able to connect any of them to this Kojatere of Symuuna Team so far, though, and if Symuuna's reputation held up, any further attempts to do so would be fruitless.

"And do we have any reports on the trajectory of the downed craft?" she asked, coming back into the conversation.

Two Horseshoe's, a Trident ship, a 4-Tail, and a trans-atmospheric transport shuttle.

The list of potential parts stolen was too varied for Othaashle to think of a use for each one, yet enough of them contributed to the various propulsion systems to support her theory.

Even if I'm wrong about this, I still have a lead on the Throne.

Unless she was wrong about that, as well. Othaashle did not see much room for doubt in either, however. Both made too much sense.

"They set off at two degrees," Itese provided. "They will come danger-ously close to our outpost if they maintain that trajectory."

So, they're heading toward Old Atonga.

Othaashle almost laughed at the irony that would present if she found the Throne of Darkness in the birthplace of the Natari.

"Pardon, Commander," Yndlova said as they entered the large, fortress-like building, striding through the lobby toward the storage racks. "Are you sure about going alone? I do not doubt that you could handle whatever salvage crew they send, but if you do stumble onto an entire operation, surely some support would be welcomed."

Othaashle's mouth thinned as she opened the inner door. Her second's words, coded for Itese's sake, were a cold reminder of the danger her visions presented.

If I could figure out a way to control when they come—

No. Even if that was a possibility, it was far beyond her current abili-ties. Only the Throne would grant her such power to change that.

"I am certain," Othaashle said, taking one belt fixed with biogems of all twelve colors, one with moonstone biogems, and another with emerald biogems. The first was standard for any Redeemed leaving Mjatafa Mwonga, the second was for strength and speed when traversing Atonga, and the third was to help her speed across the ocean and that lay between Mjatafa Mwonga and the ancient continent. "Stealth and speed are key. If only I am gone, no one will notice, and even if they do, I can reach the rebels before any warning. If more leave, that is less certain."

"Yes, Commander," Yndlova said, cheeks a bit darker red than usual. "Forgive me. The attack and its timing in relation to Exodus have me nervous."

Othaashle turned to the other woman and nodded. "You have nothing to fear, Yndlova."

She looked between her two adjuncts and laid a hand on each of their shoulders. "I need both of you to keep an eye on Skadaatha. I may have been too harsh during the council meeting, and the woman has claws. She may try to move into the investigation or even move against me during my absence. Give way if you feel you must, but keep an eye on her."

Both nodded. "Yes, Commander."

Othaashle smiled, though she knew neither could see it.

"Itese, find and clear the nearest entry to the underground. I've wasted enough time as it is."

As her adjunct trotted off, Othaashle took a deep breath, steeling her resolve.

I need to be right. I—

"Commander."

Othaashle turned to Yndlova. "Yes, Adjunct?"

The woman thrust a closed, gloved fist toward her. Curious, Othaashle placed her open palm beneath it. A small device similar to the receiver they'd found earlier dropped into her hand. The only noticeable feature was a small red button.

"Hide this somewhere it won't be found if you're searched," Yndlova said. "Press the button once when you find the Remnant to send us the coordinates. After that, only send a second or third beacon if you need support or transport back to the city."

Othaashle frowned, but sighed, pocketing the beacon.

"You *were* a bit harsh on Skadaatha during the meeting," Yndlova said. "She was out of line, but you know she doesn't like you. I want to set a tail to follow you out of the city and once you return."

Othaashle shook her head. "That won't be necessary, Yndlova. As much as Skadaatha dislikes me, I am the Imaia's Champion. She knows she could not easily replace me, and that stifles any impulses she may have about taking me out. Her moving against me politically, however, is what you and Itese need to look out for while I'm gone. Use your judgement on keeping her away from the prisoners."

Yndlova frowned at that. Her full lips made her appear as though she was pouting.

"What?"

"Itese's starting to get suspicious, and I don't like lying to her," Yndlova's lowered voice carried an edge. "The excuse I gave her when I went to find you was utter slag and she knew it. You need to let Itese in on what's been happening to you, Commander. We're your adjuncts. We—"

"No."

Othaashle paused, reigning herself in. "Yndlova, she is Redeemed. If I am experiencing these visions, the rest of my kind might experience them as well once they've been Redeemed for as long as I have. The visions incapacitate me. I can't have the other Redeemed panicking or losing confidence in me. I won't have Itese second-guessing herself or her commands."

"Then tell me, at least," Yndlova hissed. "I don't even know what these visions are about! Just that they wrest control of your body away from you and that the first few shook you to the point that I had to practically drag you out of your quarters." Othaashle's adjunct let out a deep breath. "I can't help you if I don't know what's happening to you."

Othaashle gritted her teeth, wanting to lash out.

No. Not at her.

Yndlova trusted her. Enough to follow her orders when she might be compromised, even if it meant letting her go on a dangerous mission alone with nothing more than a beacon to call for help.

"You're right," Othaashle sighed. "As usual. I'll give you a full account of the visions when I return. For now, though, I want you to look into the Symuuna strike team."

Yndlova blinked, golden eyes wide. "Of the Union's Operation Phantom?"

Othaashle nodded. "In my latest vision, I saw through the eyes of a woman who had just been chosen for that team. None of them made sense before, but after this one, I think these visions may be trying to warn me of a spy from that strike team in our midst. My incapacitation when I receive this knowledge must be the price for it."

Yndlova looked troubled. "That... right before Exodus?"

"My thoughts, exactly. Hopefully, the Remnant will give me some answers about that as well."

Yndlova sighed. "I hope you're right."

"Me too."

I am right.

She had to be. If she was, the Remnant, the visions, and Skadaatha would all cease to trouble her. If she was wrong...

I won't be.

8

Ambush

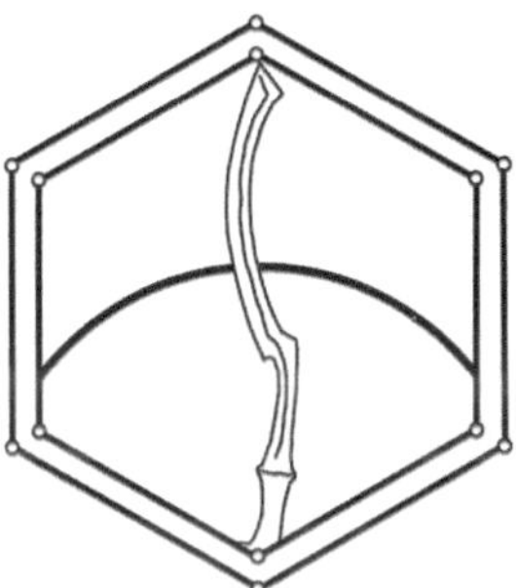

"As I know of nothing that can reliably reproduce Ilkwalerva's ability to cut through any substance, I have included six settings of moonstone divided equally between two of the frameworks. They should increase the durability of both the blade and the hilt, and a bit of extra strength and speed could provide a useful edge on top of the reserves already available to Skadaatha."

Exodus countdown: 22 days, 2 hours, 8 minutes

Othaashle released a heavy sigh, dimming her Fireborn blacknodes and greynodes and brightening her Iceborn blacknodes as she came to a halt under the cover of a nearby rocky outcrop. One of many in this barren, scoured land.

Mjatafa Mwonga's beauty makes it all too easy to forget what lies beyond its walls.

The city's construction had required heavy terraforming due to its size and location, but even after moving mountains of rock and earth from the nearby coasts to extend the perimeter far beyond the Shallow Sea's natural reef border, Mjatafa Mwonga still lay at the center of the Polar Sea, beyond the horizon from even the southernmost coasts. The nearest islands had long since been converted to outposts or reduced to flat slabs of land harvested for their raw materials. A few had been lost beneath the sea after Yrmuunthal's destruction. Even from the old Imaia islands, the nearest coastlines were beyond the horizon.

Due to the city's position, Imaia fighters had been designed to float even if heavily damaged, something the Remnant had taken advantage of.

Despite the time Othaashle had lingered, making preparations, the Auroralight reserve she'd worn—now almost entirely depleted—had allowed her to race across the sea, hovering at the front of a thin trail of ice. It had taken hours to cross the sea and hours of searching this now barren continent once she made landfall, but with her blacknodes brightened, Othaashle had finally sensed use of Auroramancy. All Redeemed bore two gemcrests: that which they'd been born with, and that which Lord Ynuukwidas blessed them with upon Redemption. The latter was always a full Fireborn gemcrest, bearing all twelve pairs of biogems. This allowed Othaashle to use every Auroramantic power available. At first, it had taken some getting used to, but now she could use both pairs of blacknodes at once to shield herself while listening for Auroramantic signals.

Peering carefully around the rock that sheltered her from sight, Othaashle grinned as she noticed the damaged Trident and a team of six. Three of them bore cables from a larger transport, attaching it to the downed fighter. All save the pilot, who wore an Imaia pilot's jumpsuit and rough, mismatched armor that only managed a semblance of a uniform. They tucked loose pants into calf-high boots with tread-like soles, below loose shirts and coats topped off by mask-like helmets and head-wraps. All were shades of grey, blue, and green that helped them blend into their surroundings in these bleak coastal lands they had made their battlefield.

The larger transport that hovered nearby made Othaashle more confident in her theory regarding the stolen parts. It was of Imaia design —the same shuttle model that had been stolen during the attack. It had the standard rear and ventral thrusters, georaurals giving off a bright green light rimmed the bottom of the craft.

They augmented it with repulsor georaurals for the uneven terrain.

It was quite ingenious. Atonga's terrain was rocky highland and desert, and a modified craft such as this would be able to hover high enough to negate any terrain interference, while remaining low enough to not stand out.

But how did they get it here?

This area wasn't too far from the coast, but still...

Othaashle brightened her Fireborn blacknodes and focused on the extra sense they granted her, honing in on the *thrum* it allowed her to perceive, then picking out individual frequencies.

Grinning, Othaashle brightened her clearnodes, enhancing her eyesight, then looked between the six insurgents. All had the antlers and full-coverage clothing of Samjati.

Two of those helped attach the cables while the third lounged against the nose of the damaged fighter.

Tree, Sleepy, and Arms.

A single look told Othaashle the posture was a front. The two men and one woman were the type that could appear disinterested or distracted one moment and have a knife in your back the next. They watched their surroundings carefully.

Othaashle took out her beacon and sent a signal back to Yndlova. She would need a transport soon.

The other three finished attaching the cables on their side, and Othaashle turned her attention on them. Their weapons and bits of armor told Othaashle they were soldiers, though she suspected that was a secondary function, as they did not share the same air as their companions. One examined the damage to the fighter while another— the pilot—sat on the ground and leaned back against the craft, shoulders slumped, head tilted back.

Mech and Pilot.

The last—Medic—examined Pilot. Though shades covered his eyes, something about the man—it had to be a man from the build—tugged at Othaashle even from this distance. Something she could not place.

Othaashle watched Medic as he examined Pilot, eventually helping the other man to his feet and steadying him. Then Medic turned to the ship and the other soldiers and waved.

They would die for their attack on the Imaia.

Now.

Othaashle flared her Iceborn greynodes, launching herself in an arc toward the center of the rocky clearing. She brightened both pairs of violetnodes, then her Fireborn rednodes. Blades of ice, tongues of flame, then thin arcs of hardlight shot forth as she whipped her arm toward the transport. Two of the thick cables connecting the damaged fighter to the transport snapped.

Not enough.

As she reached the top of her arc, Othaashle stretched one hand out to the side. Mist and motes of fire flashed before her splayed fingers.

Sleepy and Tree saw her, weapons readied before Othaashle hit the ground, but once she was among them, it was too late. The fire and mist around her hand had coalesced into a sword as long as Othaashle was tall: Ilkwalerva. Its blade shimmered like ice even as it glowed with an inner heat.

Ilkwalerva met blades of titansteel and hardlight wreathed in violet flames, and Othaashle's enemies flinched back in shock.

They recognized Ilkwalerva. It had slain many of their number, though Othaashle doubted they knew it had also turned many of their fellow terrorists against them.

Othaashle's blade also sheared through those of her enemies.

A report sounded from behind Othaashle before she could press the two warriors. She brightened both pairs of rednodes, throwing up a barrier of interwoven hardlight and darklight to stop the lethal projectiles. The barriers cracked and gave, but they did not break. The projectiles bounced back the way they'd come, though no longer with lethal force, and Othaashle whirled, dismissing the barriers while simultaneously flaring her Iceborn violetnodes.

Blue-white light flashed. Atonga's hot, humid air crystalized into violet ice as a beam of flash-frozen air connected with the shooter. Mech fell to her knees, clutching at the ice at her chest as tiny shards dropped to the rocky ground between her and Othaashle.

Othaashle spun back around just in time to catch Sleepy's hardlight blade—she'd reshaped it—on Ilkwalerva's flame-like back.

Othaashle smirked.

Then she began to dance.

Othaashle could have obliterated all six of the warriors with ease, and they knew it, but she needed to leave one of them alive to take her back to their rat's nest. If possible, she wanted the shuttle to leave and come back with reinforcements.

Though Othaashle wielded her massive sword, she did not fight as a swordsman. Rather than meet her attackers blow for blow, keeping her distance until the last moment, Othaashle rushed in close, using Ilkwalerva almost like a spear at times. Sleepy seemed prepared for this. She extended her hardlight weapon to mimic a staff or spear as she met Othaashle's attacks.

Impressive.

Forcing hardlight to hold an edge sharp enough to cut took an impressive amount of concentration and will. The woman must have drilled herself over and over again to be able to do so while changing her weapon's shape.

The men were not prepared. Three lightning-quick jabs to the torso and skull felled Arms. Tree fell to his knees as his head dropped from his shoulders with a dull thud.

Pilot drew his sidearm and let loose an enraged roar in time with another burst of reports. Two of them this time. Again, Othaashle shielded her back with a darklight and hardlight mixture as she engaged Sleepy. The Remnant woman was good, better than either of the men had been, but she fell all the same. Othaashle managed to make Sleepy focus on her attacks so intently, that her eyes went wide with shock as Othaashle conjured a hardened, razor-thin blade of violet ice and split her neck with it just before plunging Ilkwalerva through her middle. She fell, and Othaashle spun upon the shooters. This time, she shoved her shield forward to smash the two remaining insurgents against the rock wall. Othaashle rammed Ilkwalerva through Pilot's chest before the man could recover. When she turned to follow through with Medic, however, the man was gone.

Where is he? I just need to—

Othaashle caught the knife in midair and moved her barrier to catch the missiles that followed. Medic gave her no room to breathe, however. He came at her with a flaming hardlight blade in one hand, and a pistol in the other. She couldn't see his eyes, but she saw the man's rage in his posture. His weapon had given away his strength: he was an Auroraborn.

Othaashle barely blocked the second burst of projectiles and formed a hardlight shield over her forearm to block the man's blade. He had come too close, too quick. Why had she hesitated?

Why do I know this fighting style? So relentless.

The thought rose unbidden, and Othaashle's mind started to spin. She slammed it down, sharpening her focus to a razor's edge as she set her stance, slapping the man's pistol aside and shoving him back a pace. She slashed Ilkwalerva through the air where the man's chest should have been. Rather than stumble backward, however, the man had twisted and rolled. Had Othaashle been anyone else, been even a slower version of herself, the man's next two bursts of missiles would have hit her as she followed through on the swing. Rednodes running low, Othaashle threw up only a darklight barrier this time. The missiles bounced off.

Othaashle set her jaw.

This boy doesn't need arms to lead me to the Remnant.

They would make him a better Redeemed, however.

Othaashle exchanged a few blows with the man, then gave him the opening. The man took it, firing three bursts from his pistol. Othaashle threw up a hardlight shield but strengthened it with darklight and sent it racing toward her foe before it had formed completely. The man dodged, but only partially. The shield clipped him as it sped past, sending him sprawling on his belly, weapons dropping from his hands.

"Impressive," Othaashle commented as she approached, Ilkwalerva leveled. "You will do well as a—"

Othaashle's words cut off, tongue frozen, entire body gone rigid as Medic scrambled to his feet.

His helmet had fallen off, revealing a face only partially shrouded by his hood.

Biogems of all twelve colors ornamented strong, yet delicate brows. Sweat plastered his silver hair to his blue forehead. Golden eyes sat atop high cheekbones, and a slender, proud nose protruded from above full lips. His face was slender, but his chin strong.

He winced in pain at the light, yet those defiant eyes let only a hint of the man's fear show as they flickered between her and Ilkwalerva.

Othaashle didn't understand it. She'd never seen this man before, yet...

I know you.

Othaashle's head spun. Images of officers giving orders, soldiers fighting, and soldiers dead and dying flashed before her eyes. She was vaguely aware of hitting the ground. Emotions coursing through her, bringing flashes of the visions Boaathal had shown her.

Blackness took her.

9

Lightless

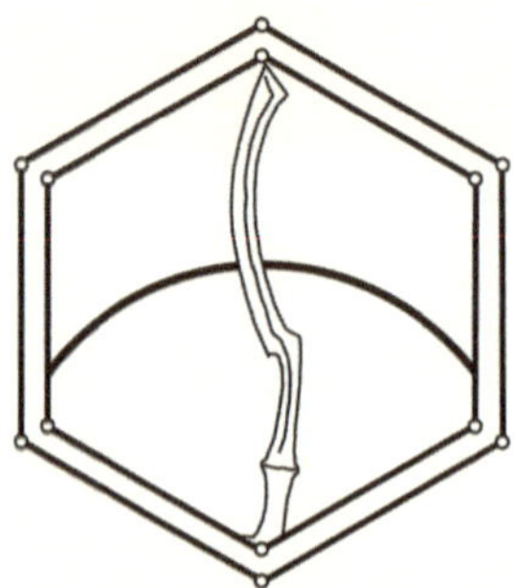

"Diamond's ability to increase the senses is useful, but does not affect the weapon in any manner that warrants its inclusion. I have included opal settings with each structure as a last resort, though I must admit, I am somewhat frightened of what a zidanio-enhanced power flare could produce in the hands of someone like Skadaatha."

Exodus countdown: 21 days, 34 hours, 29 minutes

"Why are you being so stubborn about this?"

A thick morass surrounded Othaashle's thoughts as she returned to the present.

"Because you never learn, Koruuksi."

Those voices... A young man, frustrated, exasperated. And a stern, annoyed woman. Older. Who were they?

"And you're okay with this?"

Why did it leave off there? Why didn't I see what happened?

Why did she care?

"It was *my* idea, idiot."

A young woman this time, angry.

All three voices were muffled by something, though not by much.

The voices were an annoyance. Unimportant.

Why didn't matter at the moment. Right? *Right.*

She *did* care.

Don't I?

Yes. Out of more than just curiosity.

Othaashle groaned. Even as she tried to form complete thoughts in her mind, they slipped away.

What was that supposed to show me? That Kojatere is not the spy? That it's this Phantom? Or is this showing me that Kojatere is a warrior worthy of my respect. Worthy of Redeeming, perhaps, if I encounter her?

Why was it so hard to think?

"You know Estingai—"

"—'s position is honorary, so she is not my commander, nor is she yours. My position is honorary, as well, which is why *I* should be punished, not Uuchantuu. I asked her to cover for me."

Othaashle tried to focus on something other than the vision, but her thoughts were constricted. They moved. So. Slowly.

"And I *agreed*, Koruuksi. I decided to take responsibility for you— something you should think about if you ever manage to pull your head out of your ass."

The voices? No, they seemed too unimportant.

It was so vivid.

The vision hadn't simply played out before her eyes. Othaashle had experienced the woman's emotions. Her anger, her frustration, her turmoil. Those emotions lingered.

Stop it! Your thoughts are... clouded. Get your bearings and see if tracking the Remnant is even still possible!

"I agree with Uuchantuu, Koruuksi, if... not in the same terms. You have to learn that you can't just run off and attach yourself to whatever team you feel like at the last moment."

Silence.

Finally.

With effort, Othaashle relaxed her mind.

Then—

"Did I defy orders?"

"No, but—"

"Did I defy your orders, Commander?"

Othaashle pushed, reaching out beyond the morass, regaining awareness of her body.

The older man sighed. "No, no you did not."

Pain.

It helped pierce through her muddled thoughts, clearing her head, but *light*, that pain.

Not the dull throb of concussion or cramps of muscles that had remained motionless for too long. Not even the pain of wounds. Othaashle had never known pain like this. Yet...

"So, this was something you came up with on your own, Uuchantuu? Making her punish you for no reason?"

"Haven't you been listening? My reason is that even when you're not deliberately disobeying orders, you still find some way to make a mess of things."

Setting her jaw, Othaashle forced everything from her mind—frustration, pain, thoughts of the vision—feeding them into an emptiness that devoured all thought and emotion. It took time and will—more than it should have; *light, the pain!*—but she managed it.

The young man spoke again, an edge to his voice. "They would have died even if I hadn't come along, Uuchantuu. You... If I hadn't, we wouldn't have her. I don't know what I did, but I brought her back."

He sighed. "It is, her, isn't it?"

Something about that pricked Othaashle's mind through the remaining fog.

"Yes. It's been so long since I last... but, yes, I believe it is."

She opened her eyes.

"We should tell Estingai and the others then, shouldn't we? And prepare to move her?"

My helm.

It was gone. No mask hid her face from the world. A part of her went cold at the violation of something her people held to with such fervor, yet.

"Yes. Just watch her. Send for me if she wakes. Uuchantuu."

Focus.

She heard footsteps. Booted? Definitely on a hard surface. They were disappearing. Yet they echoed.

I'm... underground?

Or in a cave, perhaps. That made sense.

A rough sound, like someone punching a cloth sack echoed faintly. A grunt followed.

"Ow! What the—"

Another similar noise followed, though the grunt that followed was more surprised than pained.

"Uuchantuu, what—?"

Focus.

The walls—what Othaashle could see of them—and ceiling were smooth, rounded in a way no chisel could manage and polished to the point that they gleamed, reflecting the room's electric lights.

"You need to stop, Koruuksi. Every time you run off like that, I ..."

Lava tubes? No, no, that's not right. The ceiling wouldn't be flat, would it?

"It's a coin toss on whether or not we come back alive every time one of us leaves, Uuchantuu."

Why were her thoughts still so muddled? Even her body felt like lead. And that pain. That searing pain! It burned worse than any fire, yet Othaashle smelled nothing.

"You're not just 'one of us' and you know it. You're more important."

Othaashle brightened her clear—

Her eyes went wide.

Nothing. Nothing happened.

No.

"To you?"

Othaashle tried to turn her head. She hissed with pain even as her efforts were rendered futile.

She tried grey.

"Yes, idiot. To me, to Estingai... you can't push away everyone, Koruuksi. Even if you did, you'd still be important to every single person that's left."

Nothing.

"I never asked for that."

The voices started to fade into the background, as though Othaashle's ears rang after a rifle's report.

She tried red to push at her bonds.

Nothing.

"None of us asked for any of this. Doesn't mean we don't have to deal with it. At least Estingai—"

"I'm not my sister. You should know that better than anyone."

Othaashle checked her gemcrest. They were empty. Each one.

I'm lightless.

The young woman sighed. "Can you at least be more careful? Or take someone with you next time?"

Lightless.

The realization hit her like an icy dagger.

I'm... dying.

Lightlessness merely acted like a heavy depression for most. For her kind—souls pulled back from the brink of death by Lord Ynuukwidas's blessing, bodies reforged by investment, lives maintained by investment —it was a death sentence.

"I had to go, Uuchantuu. Edendo was in bad shape. In any other situation, I would have been the only reason he made it out alive. In this one... well, I'm the reason we have her."

A vague sense of respect came through the numbness that had begun to settle in Othaashle as her mind processed the young man's words. She still had yet to see any of the speakers.

Lightless.

She was dying.

"Yeah, and now you get to be part of the interrogation while I have to escort the first round of parts back to Remnant One."

I'm dying.

"You know I'd rather be in your place."

Yndlova... she was right. I should have brought someone with me. Visions and morale be damned. Uncertainty isn't worth death. I should have—

No. No! She was Othaashle, Mestari of the Imaia. She had destroyed armies and nations, shattered the Union and the Remnant that fought on even in defeat. She had broken Matsanga himself. She—

But what can I do?

"I'm sorry. I was so scared and angry I didn't even think—are you alright?"

The beacon!

But she couldn't move her hands.

"No. But I'll deal with it. I have to, don't I?"

Silence. It seemed to affect Othaashle's thoughts.

"When do you have to leave?"

"I'm probably holding them up as it is."

"Go on then. I need some time to think anyway."

"No running off until I get back?"

"So I *can* run off once you come for round—Hey!"

"Idiot."

"Be safe, Uuchantuu."

"Take some of your own advice, Koruuksi."

The quick, echoing footsteps brought Othaashle's mind back to the present situation.

I need to do something.

Othaashle tried moving again. Her entire body this time, not just her head.

Again, that searing pain. Again, her efforts proved futile. She was laid out on her back. The bonds held her like—

Her thoughts couldn't make the connection. Iron would do this to mortals, but it didn't affect Redeemed in the same way. That was why they made their armor from it.

A growl of disgust and frustration rose in Othaashle's throat.

I can't die like this. I can't.

Something scraped against the rock, the noise grating. Something Othaashle couldn't see. It made her almost nauseous. She froze, closing her eyes, forcing down the nausea.

Out of fear? Aren't I better than that?

But she'd never been lightless before.

"So, you're awake."

Othaashle hesitated, then relaxed her eyes.

A young Samjati man with piercing golden eyes, short-cropped silver hair, and a proud nose stood over her. He wore a thick headband just above his eyes, covering his gemcrest, and pursed a set of full lips.

Him.

It was Medic. The only surviving member of the recovery team she'd ambushed. She hadn't realized before how handsome he was.

Was that young woman his lover, then?

Though Othaashle's mind still worked slowly, the vision was somehow still crisp.

She realized that the young man bore a striking resemblance to Kojatere's commander, Aiteperit.

He also looks a bit like Suulehep, doesn't he?

A strange warmth filled Othaashle at the thought. Then it chilled her almost as much as the realization that she was lightless had.

Is this young man Aiteperit's son? Grandson? Maybe Suulehep's?

She wished she could remember how long ago Symuuna Team had operated. This young man couldn't be more than sixteen cycles, if that.

Stop! Focus on the mission. Not this young man.

Seeing his face had triggered the vision though, as far as she could tell. Othaashle couldn't remember if there had been triggers before that.

Is it because of his resemblance to the men in my vision? Boaathal, what are you trying to tell me?

Othaashle met the man's gaze. She couldn't read his expression, though he had what seemed a perpetual hardness to his eyes. This man had seen his share of horrors.

Medics see more than most. The worst of war's horrors, at least, though they commit less.

"I'm right, aren't I? It really is you. Or, it was, at least."

Othaashle narrowed her eyes at that. How could he not know who he was? And what did that last part mean? He'd seen Ilkwa—

Othaashle's eyes bulged.

Ilkwalerva! Damn my lightless mind.

The young man raised a silver eyebrow, and Othaashle was reminded that nothing hid her face or her expressions as she was used to.

"Do you recognize me?"

Othaashle ignored the man's words. How had it taken her this long to remember Ilkwalerva? The blade was a part of her.

And it requires no Auroralight for me to summon it.

Othaashle reached out to Ilkwalerva, willing it to appear. It would drop into her grip no matter what.

And I can flex my fingers, at least. That's the mistake that will end them.

Othaashle felt her connection to Ilkwalerva. The blade was there, but manifesting it was like trying to pull her uniform through a hole no larger than her fist.

Still... the chance was there.

Othaashle pulled.

"No, of course you don't."

Something about the young man's tone prickled a memory.

"It is her, isn't it?" he'd said. Then, "It really is you."

Those words lead to something else. Something the young woman had said?

Othaashle closed her eyes, trying to recall the conversation she'd only barely registered, sifting through the words and the way each was said for something important.

"I didn't want to believe... but no, I can't ignore it, now."

The young man sighed. She could hear him pacing, though his footsteps were soft. When he spoke again, there was a bite to his words.

"Just the mention of your name strikes fear in so many, yet take away your Auroralight, bind you in aluminum and silver, and you're just as helpless as any other prisoner."

The reminder of her lightless state—that she was slowly dying—sent a spike of fear through Othaashle. More, she didn't know exactly how much time she had until she absolutely *needed* investment to survive.

Yet, Ilkwalerva...The blade would be her salvation, but not now. Not yet.

Aluminum. That's why they're not worried about my weapon. Fools. And... silver? Is that what burns?

The idea seemed familiar...

Othaashle opened her eyes, fixing her gaze on the young man. He didn't flinch, and she gained a bit of respect for her enemy.

"I will destroy you," she said, stating a fact.

Othaashle wanted to summon Ilkwalerva but couldn't. Not yet.

Parts, that was it. The young woman—Uuchantuu—she said she had to escort the first round of parts to their main base. That's where the Throne must be.

And if she was escorting the first batch of parts, that meant they were more here. More for Othaashle to examine.

Or I could sneak onto one of their shipments, slip into their base unseen.

That idea was definitely wishful thinking, especially with how little information she had on this whole operation.

"Then why didn't you?"

Othaashle barely caught herself before she let her expression give anything away. She had no answer for that.

"I couldn't make sense of it either," the young man—Koruuksi, she believed—said. "Not until I removed your helmet, at least. Then..."

"Who do you think I am, insurgent?" she asked, studying the young man. That, she thought he might actually have an answer for. Such questions were taboo for Redeemed, but then, the greater taboo was to let one's face be seen.

Koruuksi hesitated for a moment, shook his head, barking a bitter laugh. "You all internalize that propaganda, don't you? Your people started all of this, Kifrytari."

"My god didn't bring about the world's end."

"Didn't he? Isn't that what you plan to do with your city?"

Othaashle blinked. She'd caught the young man's hesitation, but barely, as brief as it had been. And then there was his comment.

This Koruuksi has spoken with the Remnant spies.

"You're better informed than I thought you'd be," she said. "I could see how it might seem that way to those who refuse to accept Ynuuk-widas's protection. Efruumani is dying—it would be dead already if he did not work tirelessly to hold it together. Mjatafa Mwonga will leave behind an empty world to save its people and give them a chance at a new home. Your goddess is the reason Darkside has been reduced to a desolate wasteland with no auroras to bring it life."

Koruuksi's mouth drew to a thin line, but he did not respond in anger. From what she had heard earlier, that meant he was using great restraint to hold himself back.

I need to bait him somehow. I need information about their plans and Kweshrima.

"That's why you attacked us, isn't it?" she ventured, "You fanatics must continue your insane goddess's work. You would endanger the salvation of millions."

"We attacked none of your people, Kifrytari," Koruuksi spat back, "We only—"

"Koruuksi!"

The young man cut off at the gruff voice—the same one from earlier.

He kept out of Othaashle's vision, and must have beckoned Koruuksi to do the same, as the young man walked out of sight a moment later.

Othaashle could barely hear them.

"You're talking to her? I told you to come get me when she woke."

There was frustration in the man's tone, but beneath that... fear.

That I can work with.

"With all due respect, Commander, I didn't think it was a good idea to leave her here alone once she woke."

The older man sighed. "No, I guess I can't blame you for that. You shouldn't have spoken to her, though."

Silence. Then a sigh.

"Apologies, Commander. She baited me."

"That's why we have trained interrogators, son. Come on, Aiandi and Uuluutho will guard the door. I want to be done with this as soon as possible."

The scraping came again, though this time it ended with the unmistakable sound of a heavy door closing, followed by the click of a deadbolt.

The lights went out and muffled footsteps echoed in the corridor beyond.

When they faded, Othaashle was left in silence and darkness.

The part of her mind dominated by lightlessness threatened to succumb to that darkness, but she pushed back.

I may be robbed of light, but I still have Ilkwalerva.

Othaashle remembered something and concentrated, bringing her awareness down to her right thigh. It was difficult, especially as numb as lightlessness made her—to everything save pain, at least—but she felt the almost imperceptible pressure in her trousers against her inner thigh where she'd hidden the tiny beacon.

She could free herself this instant and call the Imaia down upon these insurgents, but it would be much easier to get these fools to tell her what she wanted to know if they believed they had power over her.

I just need to make sure I get it out of them before the lightlessness takes me.

Othaashle closed her eyes—not that it made a difference in this darkness—and planned.

10

Decisions

"Topaz settings were an obvious inclusion a matter of tradition to bless the weapon and its owner with good luck during battle. After some deliberation, I also have decided to include a single sunstone setting as part of one of the frameworks. While its facilitation with viewing past events is unneeded, I am curious to see if the memory enhancement will extend to muscle-memory when combined with zidanio's effects."

Exodus countdown: 20 days, 21 hours, 40 minutes

Frustration seemed the lot Skadaatha had somehow chosen in the past week. Frustration at her search for the Throne turning up empty, frustration at Vysla's progress on the weapon, frustration at her lack of authority in the investigation, and lastly, frustration at the man before her and his silence.

Torni Hyhainen was a stern, broad-shouldered man with dark blue skin and thick, shovel-like antlers. He wore the *dakafti*—a fashion most Samjati men in the city had adopted that blended the colorful patterns of the Takani *dashik* with the long-sleeved and ankle-length cut of the Jusanariti'i *kafta*. His mask and broad-brimmed hat sat at one end of the unadorned aluminum-iron table between him and Skadaatha. Altogether unremarkable.

Save for the man's biogem eye and the surrounding scars.

He was also one of the suspected spies.

They sat in a sterile room beneath the Lightforged compound on the Isle of the Redeemed. Aluminum sheets covered doors and walls of thick, solid iron to nullify any attempt by Auroraborn at breaking out, mirroring the cuffs.

If they were iron, the man wouldn't have kept silent for so long.

That wasn't allowed, however. The man still had his rights. Othaashle had ensured that. The woman's orders had almost barred Skadaatha from learning the man's identity much less getting into this room with him.

The knowledge that even that would have been denied her if Othaashle was still in the city rankled her. It made her look for an excuse to cause pain to the man before her.

That would be even more fruitless, however. Torture was the tool of the sadistic. Done correctly, it could create a leashed wretch for a time, but almost always it proved unreliable for extracting information.

Skadaatha checked her timepiece and held back a frown.

She'd sat in silence with this man for an hour. He hadn't even tried to stare her down. He hadn't avoided her gaze, but he'd never given her anything more or less than a placid, almost bored expression, chin high, shoulders back, like he believed he was in control.

I've wasted enough time with this man. Let Othaashle waste her energy trying to pry anything from him without violating his rights. I'll deal with him once he's thrown in Makala.

Without a word, Skadaatha rose from the table and strode out the door.

She made it halfway down the hall before hurried, approaching footsteps echoed off the walls.

"Vizier Skadaatha, a moment?"

Skadaatha turned and studied Yndlova as the woman came up beside her. She held her cap at her side, and myriad tight braids fell down her back and over her shoulders, each capped off by an amber bead, matching the gemcrest her pristine uniform hid. Despite the woman's affiliations, Skadaatha respected the adjunct. The woman always acted professional and in the interest of the Imaia. She'd seen an opportunity for advancement and taken it, and as far as Skadaatha could tell, was hyper-competent in performing her duties. It didn't hurt that the lack of a Lightforged mask made her easier to read.

It's not her fault she doesn't know what I do about her commander.

Skadaatha took a deep breath. "What is it you need, Adjunct?"

Yndlova studied Skadaatha for a moment, full lips pressed together. Her hard golden eyes narrowed as though surprised at the response.

A moment later, she nodded and gestured to one of the other rooms. "If you wouldn't mind, Vizier. This is a sensitive matter."

Intrigued, Skadaatha followed the other woman into the room and closed the door behind her, flipping on the light. She put the room's stark table between herself and Yndlova.

She looked at the adjunct, waiting for the other woman to initiate, but Yndlova's attention seemed elsewhere.

"Adjunct?"

The woman blinked but did not blush. Instead, she sighed. "Forgive me, Vizier. As I said, this matter is sensitive. If I tell you, you will be the third person to learn of it, and I would have you swear to secrecy."

Skadaatha nodded slowly and brightened her yellownodes ever so slightly for luck. She could guess who the other person was. "Go on."

Yndlova hesitated, but after a moment, the woman drew herself up, squaring her shoulders.

"The supreme commander has been afflicted by... something," she said. "Episodes that leave her temporarily incapacitated."

Skadaatha blinked, genuinely surprised, then crossed her arms.

"Why are you sharing this with me? You know of the... tension between your superior and I."

"Because both of you serve the Imaia and are vital to its success," Yndlova said, a slight edge to her voice, "and I'm worried. If an episode strikes her while she's fighting the Remnant... I know she wouldn't die, but she would be incapacitated, allowing them to restrain her. If they can keep her lightless for eight days..."

"Then the Imaia loses its champion," Skadaatha finished. The admission was... unsettling at the least.

"And whatever knowledge she managed to glean from the Remnant," Yndlova added, tugging at one of her cuffs.

Despite her feelings that Othaashle shouldn't be the one to hold the position, Skadaatha could not deny the importance of the Imaia's champion. Ynuukwidas was too removed, too grand for people to truly wrap their heads around or relate to. Othaashle managed to just sidestep that line. The common people regarded her akin to a hero of legend, much as they had Matsanga before his betrayal. And she commanded the absolute loyalty of the Lightforged without demanding it, so far as Skadaatha could tell.

A blow to morale like that for both the Lightforged and the common people this close to Exodus would be catastrophic.

Even without the panic it could inspire in the Imaia's citizens, if the Remnant managed to accomplish such a feat, it might encourage them to try something even more drastic against the Imaia.

Skadaatha frowned, "You want me to go after her."

Yndlova bit her lip, then seemed to catch herself, and nodded. "To shadow her, at least. She took no form of communication with her save for a beacon she was to activate once to mark her location, twice if she needed support or extraction. Before the episodes, that wasn't uncommon, but once they started, she would check in with me regularly, especially if she was out of the city."

Skadaatha's eyes widened for a moment and she brightened her yellownodes further. Even she wasn't entirely sure of the exact mechanics of yellownodes, but it couldn't hurt.

"Do you know what caused them? These episodes?"

Yndlova shook her head. "I believe it has something to do with the strain on Lord Ynuukwidas."

Skadaatha hid her surprise at the statement.

Othaashle trusts her more than I expected.

Skadaatha only trusted Vysla that much.

Are they...? No... Yndlova doesn't sound like a woman concerned for her lover.

Unless she had severely underestimated the woman's ability to reign in and disguise her emotions. She tended to do that with Natari, even after all these years with them.

Something the adjunct had said earlier stood out to Skadaatha. "You said I would be the third person to learn of this. Did the Mestari not ask the God King for help?"

Yndlova arched an eyebrow in a suffering loo., "Is that a serious question, Vizier?"

Skadaatha almost laughed at that.

Almost.

"Where was she headed?"

Yndlova peered down at her datapad and pulled something up before turning the screen toward Skadaatha. "I received the first signal marking the location she found them at over three hours ago. Nothing since then."

Skadaatha peered at the display.

So... they're hiding in Old Atonga. Very clever.

Skadaatha looked back to Yndlova. "Is there any more information you can give me?"

The adjunct's lips drew to a thin line. She spoke slowly, as though mulling over each word before allowing it past her lips.

"Before she left, Mestari Othaashle mentioned something about Symuuna Team and Operation Phantom. She believed these episodes were trying to warn her that one of their number still lived and had infiltrated the Imaia's ranks."

Skadaatha started to shake her head.

Impossible. Torni is the last of them. Mnene would have—

Skadaatha's eyes widened as she realized the implication of Yndlova's words.

"That would be of great concern, if correct," Skadaatha said, covering her reaction, "I'll leave within the hour."

"Vizier."

Skadaatha paused halfway out the door.

"I hope my trust in you is not misplaced."

Skadaatha blinked at the edge to Yndlova's voice, then looked back toward the woman twitching the corner of her mouth in a smile. "I will do what is best for the Imaia."

"You look troubled."

Skadaatha looked up from the straps of her armor, a warmth already spreading through her from her husband's voice. That warmth grew further, spreading rare contentment through her as she met his eyes.

She let herself smile. "Only because you know how to read me."

Vysla's eyes twinkled before he moved to help her with the straps. She didn't need the help, especially with this newer style of armor, but appreciated the gesture just as much as she appreciated the way his fingers occasionally brushed against her.

"Are you going to share what's bothering you? Or keep it to yourself."

Skadaatha frowned, then relaxed. The tightness in her chest that had developed on her walk home had yet to disappear.

I owe him more than that.

"I've been given an opportunity."

"For you, or the Imaia?"

"For the Imaia... and *us*."

Vysla's hands paused. "Oh."

Skadaatha sighed, leaning back against her husband.

So strange that I can take such comfort in the mere touch of a mortal man.

Even after all these years, it amazed her.

But Vysla is not just any man.

Skadaatha straightened, then turned to meet her husband's gaze. "I might be able to end her, Vysla."

"But?"

Skadaatha clenched her teeth and had to take a deep breath before she continued.

"But would that be what is best for the Imaia?"

"I have a feeling that you're the only one who can answer that question."

Skadaatha sighed. "That's the problem."

"You have to go after her at the very least."

She looked down. "I do."

"Skadaatha."

Skadaatha looked up, meeting her husband's eyes and taking comfort in the love and warmth that radiated from them.

"You need to start taking more of the Imaia's workings and doctrine to heart, my dear, if you want it to succeed. You still think of Othaashle as who she *was*. Before Lord Ynuukwidas remade her. This could be the opportunity you need to put that behind you. Go after her, allow yourself to see what becomes of this mission with the Remnant. She will prove herself to you one way or another."

Skadaatha couldn't help the smile that curled her lips. "Even after so long, you still manage to amaze me."

Vysla raised an eyebrow. "Me?"

She nodded. "You, Natari and Samjati in general... I was born with Aioa, yet you who live such short lives are capable of providing wisdom to those who have seen and known far more than you ever will."

Vysla shrugged. "Sometimes a different perspective is all that is needed. I imagine us mortals have a wildly different outlook to those not subject to the passing of time."

Still smiling, Skadaatha met her husband's lips. He responded immediately, wrapping his arms around her. Skadaatha couldn't resist brightening her clearnodes and leaning into the enhanced sensations.

This—the warmth, the peace that spread through her when she touched her husband this way, the way her entire body seemed to stir to life—this was an experience Skadaatha had never known before losing her power, and one she treasured all the more for it.

Even the way it left them both breathless when their lips parted.

Especially the way Vysla's cheeks grow so dark red whenever we kiss.

Her husband cleared his throat, scrubbing a hand through his hair. "When do you have to leave?"

Skadaatha frowned. "As soon as possible."

Vysla sighed. "I expected as much." His lips quirked in a smile. "You owe me when you get back."

Skadaatha grinned, then raised an eyebrow when Vysla squeezed her hand. "Wait here."

Skadaatha looked after her husband as he rushed into his office. Once he was out of sight, she dimmed her clearnodes and busied herself with checking the straps on her armor and strapping on her vambraces. She had only her helmet left when Vysla returned, holding forth a slim metal rod with a few buttons, and rings of small biogems infused with Auroralight encircling either end.

"Take this," Vysla said, handing it to her.

Skadaatha took the rod and looked it over. One end housed a flat, polished red biogem with metal rims to shield it, while the other looked almost like a pommel. She felt its innate power immediately, spreading from her hand into her body. Her mind became more alert, her body more solid. Skadaatha's eyes widened as she looked up at her husband. "Is this...?"

He nodded. "It's a prototype. I don't know if you can depend on it, and I hope you won't need it. I don't know if it can measure up to Ilkwalerva, but if it comes to violence, this might come in handy."

Skadaatha looked at the weapon and noticed a small clip on the end. She secured it to her belt, then embraced her husband.

"I'll see you soon, my love," she whispered in his ear.

"I'll hold you to that," he said, completing their usual exchange whenever she headed toward potential danger.

For a moment, Skadaatha hesitated. She didn't want to leave her husband's arms, didn't want the warmth only he could bring out in her to fade, as she knew it would once she started toward her objective. Even with her clearnodes dimmed, she wanted to sweep her husband into her arms and toss him onto their bed. That fire still burned in her.

The fate of the Imaia, however, was a charge laid upon her shoulders since before Vysla had been born.

Reluctantly, Skadaatha stepped out of her husband's embrace, heart swelling at the way he resisted letting her go just for a moment. She raised a gauntleted hand to his face and stroked his cheek with her thumb. "Thank you, my love."

Skadaatha took her helmet and put it on as she strode out the door.

She would kill Othaashle or bury the woman she'd once been.

11

Vizier and Champion

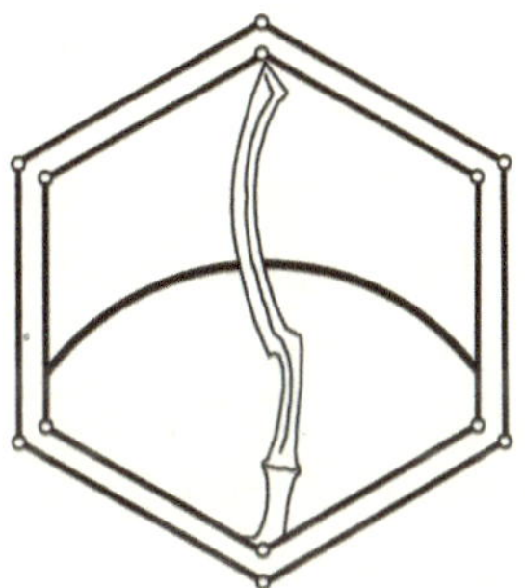

"Ruby settings took up half of each twelve-setting framework. With Miss Kwangeta's breakthrough in hardlight technology and zidanio's unique properties, I believe that this weapon will not only produce a hardlight blade that can maintain a cutting edge, but that the edge will resist any attempts at deformation and cut through whatever surface it encounters. I used only one setting to assist with quickened reflexes."

Exodus countdown: 19 days, 34 hours, 32 minutes

Othaashle grinned as the 'professional' interrogators left the room, taking a break to regroup. Koruuksi took up a post next to the closed door, leaning against the wall. The surface Othaashle was strapped to had been angled so that her interrogators didn't have to crane their necks to watch her expressions. It also gave her a better view of the room and those in it. Koruuksi watched her but did not meet her eyes.

The boy—young man, she supposed—continued to intrigue her. Whatever semblance of military organization the Remnant still held to, Koruuksi managed to defy it. Whether it was something to do with this 'Estingai,' his sister, or some status as an irregular, Othaashle did not know.

None of the Remnant displayed their biogems, hiding them with masks, shirts, helmets, and thick headbands, so Othaashle had no indication anyone's abilities other than Koruuksi, especially lightless as she was. Was it his standing as an Auroraborn that allowed him such pull within this organization? Whatever it was, he had somehow wormed his way into the majority of her interrogation sessions. Strangely, though, he had remained silent for most of it.

Over the past two days of 'interrogation'—that was how long she thought it had been at least; lightlessness dulled her time-sense—Othaashle had done her best to only speak the truth to her interrogators. She loved the way it made them squirm. Security demanded a certain number of secrets, but even the Imaia's few secrets were useless to the Remnant. The disparity in power was just too great. The extended time in silver restraints had also numbed her to the pain somewhat. Or maybe that was her lightlessness. It was hard to tell.

What frustrated Othaashle, however, was that she had yet to figure out why this young man's face had made her freeze. It didn't help that her lightless thoughts seemed to drift listlessly unless she used all her focus.

What do I find so intriguing about him? And why does he seem more intrigued by me than frightened?

There was some fear there, of course. Her reputation and the name the Remnant had given her demanded that much, at least. For some reason, however, this young man betrayed far less fear when he looked upon her than his commander or her interrogators.

Despite his near constant presence, Othaashle had been unable to speak to him with the others in the room, lest she give away her intentions.

Until now.

Othaashle took a deep breath, gathering her thoughts.

"Why do you resist?"

Koruuksi's eyes flickered to hers only for a moment, but Othaashle knew she had him by the way his jaw bunched.

"Do you truly serve the Enemy now that your goddess is dead?" she prodded, brow furrowed.

His mouth twitched at that.

But at which part?

"Every Remnant life you lose and every Imaia life you take only serves to weaken resistance against the Enemy," she continued. "Or do you not believe in the Enemy, writing it off as Imaia propaganda?"

"We never denied the Enemy's existence."

Finally.

Koruuksi's voice carried an edge. "We just didn't want to be conquered."

"You rejected peace, as well."

Koruuksi snorted. "Matsanga told us all about the 'peace' the Imaia offered. For a people that preach justice, you seem quite detached from the ideal itself, assassinating those among your own ranks who did not fall in line, fueling insurrections across the world."

Othaashle grinned. "In that, the Imaia is little different from the old Samjati nations. We were just more efficient at achieving the desired results. And our insurrections favored the people rather than the oppressors."

"It was the Imaia that manipulated those older nations into doing so. And every death that resulted from their actions served the Enemy. Or does that only matter when it doesn't serve your interests?"

Clever boy.

"The unity that resulted from our conquest far outweighed those deaths. It allowed the Imaia to take to the stars and is what will allow us to leave this dying world that your goddess doomed along with her people."

"So, you believe the end justifies the means?"

"Kweshrima certainly did."

That silenced him.

"What is your objective, anyway? Patch together an old cruiser in the hopes of leaving this world? Even if you manage that, you'll need coordinates and faster-than-light travel to have any hope of finding a new world to settle. Not to mention the fact that you'll all be lightless."

Koruuksi's expression dropped, and Othaashle knew she'd been right. Still...

They can't truly be as short-sighted as I suggested to the council, can they?

There was the possibility that even with whatever authority this young man had that kept him outside of the chain of command, he did not know all the details.

Of course, there is something that would allow them what they need to survive. Or someone.

But how to pry that out of the young man? He'd reacted only with silence and retorts when she mentioned Kweshrima, giving away nothing save perhaps his inability to defend the goddess.

A deal might work. Best to approach that with care, though.

"Why not come to Mjatafa Mwonga?" she ventured, a part of her mind knew the conversation was losing direction. Now that she had gotten herself speaking, however, it was hard to stop. "The Imaia took in every refugee that fled from the broken remnants of the Union. We do not cast aside potential warriors or resources."

Koruuksi snorted. "You really think I'm dumb enough to believe that the Imaia would accept into its ranks those it labels insurgents and terrorists?"

"Are those labels unearned?"

"You prove my point, Kifrytari."

"We would vet you all, of course. Those of your women and children, and those who followed your orders simply because they were born into this life and felt like they had no choice. might be allowed to live simple lives as citizens or join our soldiers to fight against the true Enemy."

"And those of us who hold you responsible for our present situation?"

Othaashle grinned. "Those of you with such misguided outlooks would no doubt fall under my command. Lord Ynuukwidas and I have ways of treating your ignorance and ensuring loyalty to the Imaia."

The young man's face hardened.

"So that's how you did it."

Othaashle barely caught the words, dulled as her hearing was by her lightless state. She opened her mouth to press further—

The question died on her tongue as Koruuksi straightened, then tensed. Something flashed in his golden eyes.

Othaashle tensed by reflex in response, then hissed as the silver bit into her skin. For a moment, she peered at Koruuksi. Then it hit her.

"Someone is using Auroramancy."

Koruuksi didn't respond, instead inching toward the door. Othaashle knew she was right, however. Most Auroramancers with blacknodes kept them at a light brightness almost constantly. Especially soldiers. And Koruuksi was Auroraborn.

"More than you expect to feel..." Othaashle continued, trailing off as she realized what that meant.

"Get down," she hissed at Koruuksi, flexing the fingers of her right hand. "Play dead."

Ilkwalerva, come to me.

The young man's gaze snapped to hers. He blinked in surprise. "What?"

Othaashle could feel the frost and motes of fire at her fingertips. Ilkwalerva wanted to come to her, but something blocked it. The aluminum shouldn't have worked like that, but then again, she'd never tested her weapon in this manner before.

Othaashle gritted her teeth. *Come on.*

Her heart started to race as doubt entered her mind.

"Just do it," she hissed again, mouth dry, squeezing her eyes shut.

Almost there...

Power flooded through Othaashle with the force of a bursting dam as Ilkwalerva dropped into her palm. Out of the corner of her vision Othaashle noticed Koruuksi's wide-eyed disbelief as she deftly used the blade to slice through her silver and aluminum bonds as though they were made of cloth.

Gasping in relief, Othaashle stumbled free of her searing bonds and rolled her shoulders as she drew upon Ilkwalerva's innate power. Koruuksi's gaze flickered to the biogems at her brow, eyes widening further as the power filled Othaashle. She pulled on the investment within Ilkwalerva and brightened the greynodes on her brow, and both sets of clearnodes and blacknodes, filing herself with strength, the clarity of heightened senses, and gaining the ability to sense use of Auroramancy while hiding her own.

Othaashle didn't even need to pick through the different frequencies. The amount of Auroramancy she sensed in use could only mean one thing: a fight.

She glared at Koruuksi. "Why are you still on your feet?"

Koruuksi's expression hardened. He opened his mouth, then closed it and crouched to the floor huddling against the wall.

I hope this plays out and the boy doesn't stab me in the back.

Othaashle shook and flexed stiff muscles, then moved behind the silver and aluminum table, angling herself so that it was directly between her and the door.

Only one person would disobey my orders.

With her enhanced senses, Othaashle heard the screams and shouting far before the footsteps approached the door. She moved Ilkwalerva behind the table, out of view of the door.

The thick door of iron, aluminum and silver slammed open with such force that it nearly hit Koruuksi's huddled form. To the boy's credit, he didn't even flinch.

In the doorway stood Skadaatha, fully armored, biogems glowing behind the hardened glass of her helmet, designed to allow them exposure to auroras even while she wore armor. A corpse lay slumped against the doorway just behind her, smoking. The scent of burning flesh made her nose wrinkle.

"What have you done?" Othaashle hissed, not giving Skadaatha the chance to speak. "I gave orders for no one to follow. You might have just ruined everything."

Skadaatha cracked her neck but said nothing.

The realization that she couldn't read the other woman's face—that it was hidden beneath her helmet—made Othaashle realize her own face was exposed, and she wore no armor.

There was something to Skadaatha's posture. She was too stiff.

She's always had a problem with me. Not Yndlova, not the Redeemed, but me... And now she can see my face...

Othaashle glanced down toward Koruuksi and caught Skadaatha following her gaze. The woman tensed, then looked back toward Othaashle, posture suddenly predatory. Her biogems glowed brighter as she raised her hands. One toward Othaashle. The other toward Koruuksi.

No.

Something snapped inside Othaashle. She couldn't explain it. She didn't try.

Flaring her greynodes and opalnodes, Othaashle kicked at the back of the metal slab she'd spent three days strapped to.

The explosion of strength in the kick snapped the table free of its supports with the scream of tearing metal. It flew toward Skadaatha and slammed into her, throwing her back through the doorway.

Othaashle started forward to follow up on her attack, but movement to her side halted her. Koruuksi groaned, slowly pushing himself up onto his elbows.

"Stay down," Othaashle hissed, angling Ilkwalerva to guard her center line as she advanced on Skadaatha.

I have to get her away from him.

She still didn't know why, but she knew she could *not* let anything happen to the young man.

Outside the room stretched a long, wide hallway lit by strips of blue-white lights two-thirds of the way up rounded walls of smooth, polished stone. Smooth enough to make Othaashle unsure of her footing. She'd noticed her lack of footwear while bound, left only in her padded uniform, but hadn't registered it until now as she dropped into a fighting stance, preparing to strike at Skadaatha. Her clearnodes made her acutely aware of the smooth, cool stone beneath her bare feet.

Othaashle's foe heaved the metal slab off of her, armor nicked and dented in a few places, but otherwise whole, and Othaashle dodged, careful not to let the metal touch her.

"You came here to kill me, is that it?" Othaashle asked, continuing toward the other woman. She leveled Ilkwalerva and primed her gemcrest, but did not attack yet. "I never thought of you as the treasonous type, but maybe you just thought you'd take the change to settle a grudge and blame it on the Remnant. Maybe seize the power of your old position in the wake of my downfall?"

"The Imaia will be better off without an arrogant bitch like you at its head," Skadaatha growled, thrusting her hand out to the side.

Othaashle frowned at that, then raised an eyebrow as she noticed the slim metal rod in Skadaatha's hand.

What is—?

Skadaatha pressed a button protruding from the metal. The rod hissed, the sound amplified by the stone walls around them, and

Othaashle's eyes widened as a length of both hardlight *and* darklight extended from the metal rod.

No... a blade.

Othaashle didn't see how that was possible. She'd managed to weave hardlight and darklight together as shields but getting either substance to hold a dangerous edge was too difficult to be worth the effort, even for her.

A moment after the blade extended fully—about a meter from the hilt—it crackled with electricity. The blue-white bolts of energy threw wild shadows about the hall.

How is she powering that?

It took Othaashle only seconds to grasp the mechanics of the weapon, but none of the gemstones were large enough to—

Othaashle barely knocked aside Skadaatha's thrust aside in time to avoid experiencing the effectiveness of her foe's novel weapon. The woman had moved with Auroralight-enhanced speed and would have struck home had Othaashle not already brightened her grey and clearnodes.

Not amber, though. Not yet.

Those used up Auroralight too quickly.

As the two blades met, sparks flashed, and for a moment, she worried, bracing herself for the shock.

Instead of running down Ilkwalerva's length to Othaashle's hand, however, the biogems set into the blade flashed bright, absorbing the power.

Othaashle looked from the blade to Skadaatha, and grinned.

She attacked.

Skadaatha parried and counter-attacked with the same enhanced speed, strength, and dexterity that Othaashle could call upon. Othaashle was far more skilled with a sword, however. If the other woman was truly as ancient as she claimed, none of that had been spent practicing with the weapon.

As if Skadaatha had heard her thoughts, the woman conjured hardlight, throwing it at Othaashle.

The close quarters of fighting in a halfway—even one as wide as this one—should have made wielding a blade of Ilkwalerva's size difficult without the need to dodge expertly thrown hardlight missiles. For Ilkwalerva, however, stone was no hindrance.

Othaashle wove through the attacks, using her blade's superior reach to knock aside the hardlight and push Skadaatha further back down the tunnel. None of the missiles would hold an edge, but without armor, they would hurt at the least. At worst, they might crack a rib or put out one of her eyes. She could have used her rednodes to form shields and block the attack, but she would need more Auroralight for that. The power she drew from Ilkwalerva burned quickly just to sustain her. One of the few disadvantages of being one of the Redeemed. Instead, she used only enough to match Skadaatha, using her physicality to her advantage.

At one point, a uniformed man came into view behind Skadaatha. Without missing a beat, Othaashle's foe whirled out of the way of an incoming thrust and sent two missiles of hardlight flying down the hall toward the Remnant man.

They hit simultaneously. One hit his throat, crushing his windpipe, the other the middle of the man's forehead. He dropped like a stone.

Othaashle's eyes widened at the precision of her foe's attack.

Skadaatha turned back to Othaashle.

Then *she* attacked.

Suddenly, it was all Othaashle could do to keep that crackling hardlight blade from her. Skadaatha began to push her back, but Othaashle managed to reverse their positions so that the woman maneuvered her away from Koruuksi and that dead-end of a room. She stumbled back past the corpse of Skadaatha's victim, as well as a few others, taking hits from the hardlight.

As the tunnel opened up around her, Othaashle barely raised her weapon in time to block a bolt of lightning that shot from Skadaatha's fingers.

A blinding white-blue light flashed, leaving an afterimage the color of darklight. Othaashle dropped to one knee, her right shoulder numb. Her hand spasmed, and she almost dropped Ilkwalerva.

No!

Growling, Othaashle tightened her grip on the blade's hilt and drew power from it even as she threw herself on her back, out of the way of a second iceflash.

Looks like I'm out of options.

Othaashle rolled to the side and sprang upright, throwing a hardlight shield up before her. Taking advantage of the brief moment of safety, Othaashle spun around to take in her surroundings.

The tunnel opened up much more than she had expected into a large cavern with some source of natural light that she couldn't directly see. The walls bore carved and painted reliefs, ridges, and alcoves, though strips of electric lighting, racks, curtains, and other more modern accoutrements covered many. A few vehicles and what she assumed were some of the stolen capital ship parts filled the large chamber, as well as several concentrations of equipment that gave the place the look of a temporary base of operations. Lifeless and barely moving bodies lay scattered throughout the room

Othaashle committed it to memory and whirled back around, setting her stance.

She dismissed the hardlight between her and Skadaatha.

Then Othaashle brightened her ambernodes.

An incredible clarity settled over her. Othaashle focused on a single goal: victory.

Skadaatha struck with Auroramancy and blade as one, but Othaashle moved even as her foe did. Her body simply knew what to do. She slipped between the crackling hardlight blade and hardlight missiles Skadaatha threw at her and reached for Skadaatha's helm.

I can't kill her. She knows too much that the Imaia needs.

She could disable the woman and take her new weapon, however.

Just as Othaashle's fingers curled under the rim of her foe's helmet, Skadaatha tilted her head down sharply.

The movement wasn't enough to crush or sever Othaashle's fingers, but it hurt. More importantly, it threw her off-balance.

"I heard you've begun to lose your mind, Mestari," Skadaatha growled, spitting the last word.

Othaashle's brightened ambernodes and Fireborn greynodes let her anticipate Skadaatha's counterattack and gave her the speed to avoid it, but Othaashle no longer held the upper hand. Skadaatha had brightened those pairs as well.

"That you remember Symuuna Team," Skadaatha continued, "Do you remember anything else?"

Othaashle gritted her teeth as they traded off blow after blow of Auroramancy and swordplay, uncaring when their attacks went wild and damaged or outright destroyed the nearby equipment and vehicles. Circuits sparked and smoked around them, some catching fire and filling the air with an acrid scent.

"You remember the boy, don't you? I recognized him, too."

Othaashle drew power at a steady rate, but she could feel Ilkwalerva's well diminishing. The blade would recharge over time—at least she thought it would; she'd never been able to test its limits before—but once it ran out, lightlessness would follow. With Skadaatha's ambernodes brightened, Othaashle's foe would be able to predict her movements and end her within seconds. And she was willing to bet Skadaatha had more Auroralight to draw upon than she.

"Don't worry. Once I'm done with you, I'll deal with him."

I will not *let her end me. I have to—*

Othaashle's vision flashed. A dark, cliffside manor—no, a fortress— loomed above her. Her ears rang with from nearby explosions and reports.

Her vision flashed again. Skadaatha thrust the crackling blade toward her, but Othaashle had already moved out of its path.

No! Not now!

She was pressed up against a rocky outcrop, bullets flying inches over her head. A dead man lay beside her, one of her comrades. The foul, metallic mixture of his blood and emptied bowels filled her nostrils.

She fought Skadaatha. The woman attacked with blade and hardlight this time. Othaashle moved to dodge, then threw a darklight bubble up around her at the last moment. Skadaatha pulled her strike at the last minute so her arm didn't snap back at her with the rebound. The hardlight missiles still bounced off, but Skadaatha moved out of their paths effortlessly.

That's it.

Even as Othaashle's vision flashed again, bringing her back to that rocky hillside, she focused on Skadaatha's weapon, attacking that rather than the woman as she flared her grey.

She stood over a Natari man in armor and combat fatigues. One like her own. He would never use his arm again.

Skadaatha stumbled as Othaashle scored a hit on the crackling blade, almost knocking it from her foe's hand. Othaashle pressed that advantage. Maintaining hardlight or darklight took a fair amount of Auroralight even when one did nothing with it. Maintaining an edge took more. Forcing the substances to keep their shape as they were struck took far more energy—one of the reasons hardlight armor was mainly ceremonial.

Othaashle attacked relentlessly. Flaring her rednodes like this would have rendered them dim within a minute in any other circumstances. Drawing power from Ilkwalerva allowed her to direct the energy to whichever node she wished, however, rather than simply using the light each node had absorbed during the aurora.

Othaashle's vision flashed again and again, pulling in her other senses. Her attacks became more desperate, frantic. Her heart raced, muscles tensing.

Not now. Not now! I won't let her—

Othaashle stumbled back as Skadaatha's crackling blade shattered, the darklight rebounding her strike even as it faltered.

For a long moment, both froze. Skadaatha's helmeted head moved, looking between Othaashle and the smoking, broken weapon. At a swell of power from her foe, Othaashle tensed, readying another attack.

A rent opened up in the air beside Skadaatha, and the woman leapt through it. It vanished before Othaashle could follow her.

Othaashle's vision flashed again, and she dimmed all her nodes. Ilkwalerva burst into motes of flame and frost as she released it. The sudden lack of energy and strength sent her to her knees.

I hate that she can do that. Cheap lightless trick.

Othaashle let the vision take her.

12

One Night

"Lastly, I included one amber setting and one onyx setting for an added edge with premonitions and investment interference respectively. Amber's ability for foresight is best kept to an Auroramancer, as are onyx's abilities to detect and shroud Auroramantic signatures, though if the chance arises, an onyx sensor may be an acceptable inclusion, and aikanuum could react with amber in a very advantageous manner if my suspicions are correct."

Exodus Countdown: 19 days, 32 hours, 17 minutes

Skadaatha had lost track of how long she'd sat with her arms tight around her knees, eyes closed, back pressed up against the wall, when the hiss of the sliding door and brief influx of ambiance from the hall outside signaled Vysla's return.

Another way that I'm less than I was since coming to this world.

She tracked her husband's movements with her ears as he made his way into the house—he kicked off his shoes, set down his briefcase on the table just inside and made his way to the kitchen.

His footsteps stopped.

Skadaatha didn't know if he saw her in one of the room's mirrors or polished surfaces or if he'd simply glanced over toward the main room.

"Skadaatha?"

That warmth that only Vysla could bring out blossomed within her at the sound of his voice and hurried footsteps, yet rather than cheering her up, it made her want to weep.

Skadaatha held back her tears as her husband knelt beside her, laying a hand on her shoulder. She could barely feel the touch through her armor. She wished she'd taken it off.

"Skadaatha, what happened?"

Skadaatha gritted her teeth, barely holding back her tears as she forced the words out.

"I failed."

Skadaatha sagged back against the wall, arms falling to the floor. With those words, the reality—the sheer selfish stupidity—of what she had done finally set in.

She's the champion of this Imaia, of my creation. I was supposed to watch her back, to help her toward our success, and instead I've put myself and Vysla in danger.

Once, she might have been immune from such consequences. But Ynuukwidas led the Imaia now, and he was a god of justice. Skadaatha did not worry for her life, but there were worse fates than death.

If Othaashle gets word to him of my betrayal, it won't matter that she struck first.

She knew Vysla wouldn't be satisfied with that answer, but he didn't prod her.

I don't deserve him. He's too good for me.

He rose from where he'd knelt before her and walked off toward the kitchen. Running water reached her ears, then a few clinks of metal and porcelain, then cupboards opening and closing, before Vysla returned to kneel before her, placing a hand on her armored knee. Again, she cursed herself for not taking it off.

At times like this, Skadaatha had to wonder if she was just being hard on herself, or if thoughts like that rang truer than she cared to admit.

"I couldn't... I couldn't stop myself," she said eventually, voice wavering.

With effort, Skadaatha met her husband's gaze, forcing down her shame as she spoke. It took effort to keep her voice from catching.

"I tried to kill her, Vysla. She had already freed herself and knocked out the guard when I arrived... I think I recognized him. They'd taken her helmet off. When I saw her face..."

Skadaatha trailed off as anger rose up at the memory of that woman's face, even transformed as it was.

"I didn't even try for subtlety in finding her," she continued. "I cut through every Remnant man and woman in my way. When I found her..."

Skadaatha took a deep breath. "I tried to kill her. I still want to. Yet I failed. I thought I had her at a disadvantage, and yet I still fled. I don't know what's more troubling. That she bested me, or that I couldn't stop myself from attacking her."

She was the mountain. She was implacable, immovable, as was her will.

Yet even mountains burst if the fire within becomes too much.

Her chest tightened. A small, minuscule part of Skadaatha, a part of her she had thought long-since done away with, resented the very need for such comfort. A goddess should not be so vulnerable as to need such reassurance, especially not from a mortal.

But you are not the goddess of the mountains any longer and have not been for some time.

She looked up at Vysla. The kindness in his golden-brown eyes, the only eyes that truly knew her, brought a weak smile to her face.

I may have lost my power, but I have something far better now.

Still... the pain and shame of defeat lingered.

"If I don't even have my control..." Skadaatha rasped, taking a breath to calm herself, "I feel so small and useless. I hate that. I hate it because what I have with you is far more precious than any power I once held. I hate it because I wouldn't have you if I still had my power, yet a part of me still wants it regardless."

"And you hate that you want it so that you can kill Othaashle for taking our son from us," Vysla said, his voice so soft, soothing, "because as much as you want to kill her, you know the part of her that killed Aioilo is gone, and that her past life should be forgotten. She is the Imaia's champion—our sword and shield against whatever we may encounter until Ynuukwidas recovers."

Skadaatha sighed. This time she clutched Vysla's hands instead of his legs. She hated how right he was, yet loved how well he knew her.

"You are right, as usual. You were right before, as well. I need to be more like myself again. More cool-headed and in control. I apologize for being short with you earlier."

"Which 'earlier' are you sorry for, exactly?"

Skadaatha leveled a half-hearted glare at her husband but could not help the deepening smile on her lips. "All of it. I've been a poor wife lately."

"You carry the weight of worlds and the future of an entire people on your shoulders."

"That doesn't excuse my behavior."

Vysla's eyes twinkled. "We mortals don't have the mysteries of divinity to hide our flaws."

Skadaatha rolled her eyes. "Thank you."

Then she remembered something. She sighed. Before she could speak, however, a faint whistling sounded from the kitchen. Vysla held up a finger, shooting her a warm smile, then rose and walked over toward the kitchen.

Rather than look after him, Skadaatha lowered one hand to her side, fingers resting on the damaged prototype.

Vysla walked back a few minutes later with two mugs and carefully sat down before her, handing her one.

Skadaatha took the mug and breathed in deep.

"Icepepper?"

He nodded. "It steeps quickly."

Skadaatha smiled. "I love you."

Vysla returned her smile. "Now will you tell me what you were sighing about before I got up?"

Skadaatha frowned. "I need to apologize for something else."

Vysla raised an eyebrow, and Skadaatha lowered a hand to her side. She brought up the broken hilt of the weapon he'd made for her, proffering it to him.

"She overloaded it by attacking the blade. It seemed deliberate on her part."

Vysla took the weapon, studying it. "Yes, I thought that might be an issue."

"I haven't been able to think of a way to compensate. Anyone familiar enough with georaural mechanics will recognize how it functions and be able to exploit the flaw."

"If they can last long enough to figure that out," Vysla pointed out, "and if they have a weapon that can match it. Currently, only Othaashle and those with ruby biogems have anything that this won't cut through. Still, I'll see what I can do."

He paused and Skadaatha found herself grinning as her husband seemed to stare at something far off.

"If I use the hardlight and darklight to merely shape the magnetic field rather than weaving them together to make the blade," he murmured to himself, "I could use mundane energy and recycle..."

He stopped, shaking himself, then set the broken weapon on the floor and smiled at her. "I can worry about that later, however. " He took her hands in his own. "Are you alright?"

Skadaatha wanted to tell him she was, but shook her head. "When I decided to flee, it was the first time I can remember truly fearing for my life since I became mortal. It doesn't excuse my actions, but that is part of what's been bothering me, I think. Before Ynuukwidas took my power, my own death wasn't a concern, and the deaths of those around me were as natural as the passage of time. Even once I became mortal, I don't think I truly thought or worried about death until... until Aiolo. After him, it became all too real. For him, and for us. "

Vysla sighed. "Unfortunately, I don't think that's something I can fix."

Skadaatha ran her hand over his thumb. "I know you'd try if you thought of a way, though."

He gave her another tight smile. Then his expression sobered.

"What do you plan to do about Othaashle?"

Skadaatha sighed, forcing down the anger that rose at the woman's name.

I should have reigned myself in long ago.

But it had been easier to hate. To fear.

"I need to act before she can return to the city. I don't know if she'll go to Ynuukwidas with this or use it to blackmail me, but I won't give her the chance to do either."

She paused, taking a deep breath. "I can't defeat her alone, so this time I'll overwhelm her."

Vysla let out a long breath but nodded. He knew this had to be done.

"Can you wait one night before you go after her?"

Skadaatha blinked at her husband, confused. Then she saw the glint in his eyes, and an entirely different heat that only he could bring out spread through her. The hair at the nape of her neck rose as a shiver ran through her.

Skadaatha rose to her feet, hands still in his, tongue darting out to wet her lips.

She kissed him. He responded immediately, deepening the kiss, hands moving to her face. Sparks danced around his fingertips as they touched her skin. Skadaatha let herself become lost in her husband and the emotions only he could inspire in her.

When she finally pulled back, both were breathless. She traced one of the black stripes on his face with the pad of her thumb, biting her lip.

"I'll take that as a yes?" Vysla asked, eyes glazed over.

With a grin, Skadaatha bent low and got a surprised yelp out of her husband as she threw him over her shoulder and started toward the bedroom, brightening her clearnodes.

His laughter filled the room as she tossed him onto the bed.

13

A Bargain

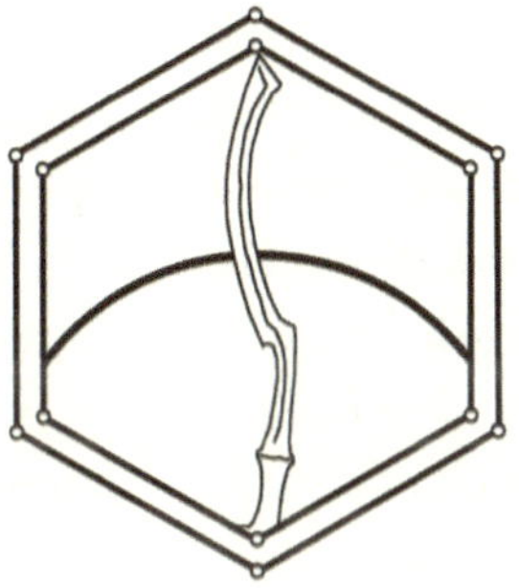

"An abundance of sapphire settings were also necessary, as Skadaatha insisted on testing the weapon's ability to function as a power siphon. I believe the inclusion of three sapphires per framework in my design will allow it to both siphon power from another's gemcrests and transfer the stored power to her own when needed. I declined to include any sapphire settings calibrated to affect aging."

Exodus countdown: 19 days, 29 hours, 53 minutes

After a long trek through Atonga's barren landscape, flashes of the bloodshed from her vision and the carnage Skadaatha had left in her wake haunting her, Othaashle found Koruuksi. Her heart swelled upon recognizing him, confusing her even further. He slumped against a rock, boots off and coat undone, sidearm still in its holster and helmet at his side. He had chosen a spot shaded by the rocky outcrop. By the stumps growing out of cracks in the shadowed rock, he'd also found some nutritious shadow-plants to eat. His eyes were closed, silver hair matted, head tilted back, but Othaashle didn't believe he was sleeping. She'd brightened her blacknodes as she crossed the last ridge before spotting the boy, hiding herself from his Auroramantic senses. Without her armor, it was easier for her to keep silent as she approached, even in this rocky, uneven terrain.

Before making herself known, Othaashle circled the location in case of a trap. She ended up creeping over the foundations of ancient Atonga buildings, but other than that, found nothing. A few tracks, droppings and plants, but no animals. Not even lizards or insects that had once seemed ever present on Lightside.

That doesn't seem right. How did those at the base feed themselves?

This area was well within the foraging range of those caverns. She knew that the Imaia had done extensive trapping on Lightside to transplant as many animals as they could to Mjatafa Mwonga's conservatories, but surely there were some left here, weren't they?

Or did our activity upset their habitats too much?

The ruins were as much of a surprise as the lack of animals. Mjatafa Mwonga's construction had required extensive terraforming, resulting in the harvest of mountains of stone, soil and sand for that alone, not to mention the stockpiled raw materials for Exodus.

Did we do as much damage to Lightside as Kweshrima did to Darkside?

No.

The Imaia had only taken such measures after Kweshrima's destruction sent Efruumani into its death throes. They took what they needed to ensure a new life for their people.

Once satisfied that Koruuksi had no trap laid for her, Othaashle summoned Ilkwalerva and let her footsteps be heard as she approached him.

Rather than dart away or jump to his feet, the young man opened a single golden eye and looked her up and down as she towered over him.

"Changed your mind, then?" he asked. "Come to finish me off like everyone else in Wolfden? Or did you spare me because you remembered who you are?"

Othaashle blinked, not just at his nonchalance.

"You know me?"

Koruuksi raised an eyebrow, then sighed. "I do."

Maybe I can work with that. I could leverage what I've seen in the visions to gain the Remnant's confidence.

With that, she could do far more than eliminate an enemy or gain the Throne's power.

But I need more from him.

Othaashle waited for him to elaborate, but he did not. She almost prodded him for more, considered threatening him, even, but her earlier surprise that had overcome the taboo had faded.

It's bad enough I have nothing to cover my face with.

"I didn't kill your people," she said, unsure why, "they were already dead by the time I engaged Skadaatha."

The young man gazed at her in silence, full lips twisted in a frown.

Why do I care what he thinks?

"Why did you come after us?"

Othaashle frowned at the question, "You attacked—"

"No. Why did *you* come after us? Don't you have more important things to do like run the Imaia?"

"Your spies are quite well-informed. It's a shame they'll all be in chains by the time I return to Mjatafa Mwonga.

Koruuksi shrugged. "Our spies knew they would get burned following that attack. They won't give you anything. And you didn't answer my question. Isn't the Imaia supposed to 'embody the light of truth' or some pompous shit like that?"

"Silence isn't dishonest. I came after you personally to avoid alerting any of your spies."

Koruuksi studied her for a moment.

Why does that expression seem so familiar?

"Are all of you Lightforged such bad liars?"

Othaashle found she had no answer to that. The words weren't untrue, but...

The young man took a deep breath, then closed his eye. "I don't suppose you'd agree to just let us go? There's bad blood between us, but most of us just want to leave Efruumani before we die along with it."

Othaashle almost barked a laugh at his use of 'bad blood.'

"Unless the parts left in that base were unnecessary for the repairs you need to make on the cruiser you salvaged, that is no longer an option."

Koruuksi's shoulders slumped, jaw bunching. A moment later, he stiffened, face a deep purple. Blazing golden eyes fixed upon her own. "Do it, then. Kill me and be done with it."

Othaashle held that gaze, so hard for one so young. She leveled

Ilkwalerva at him, the tip a mere finger's breadth from his chin. "With this, it wouldn't be 'done'."

He tensed, eyes widening. Normally, Othaashle would have grinned at the fear one showed when she threatened to chain their soul to Ilkwalerva. For whatever reason, she felt only disgust at herself when it appeared in Koruuksi's eyes.

"I still have use of you, however," she said, shoving the emotion away as she pulled her blade back just a bit. "If you get me what I want, I'll provide you and the rest of your insurgent group with a Draakon-class cruiser. They're built to house 46,785 crew and passengers—though I'd be surprised if you have even half that number across all your remaining cells— and are stocked with supplies for two full years, and carry a complement of tanks, transports and fighters. Most importantly, it will have a star map showing the coordinates of theorized habitable planets, and Aathalspace drives."

She didn't mention how those drives were still somewhat experimental. Exodus would rely mostly on Ynuukwidas for that.

Koruuksi's eyes bulged.

"Interested?" she asked, raising an eyebrow.

The boy seemed to regain control of himself and narrowed his eyes at her, jaw set.

"And what exactly do you think I can provide you that's worth such a valuable resource?" he asked, guarded. "Every Auroramancer we have left? So you can twist them into Lightforged?"

Othaashle did not respond immediately.

Do I tell him?

She'd already wasted enough time.

"The Throne."

His eyes widened, and Othaashle knew she'd picked the right one to spare.

"Kweshrima no longer deserves it," she continued. "She lost the right when she doomed this world and everyone on it. And I believe you know where it is."

Koruuksi rose to his feet and crossed his arms over his chest. He was tall enough that she had to tilt her head up a bit to meet his gaze.

"If I did," he said, carefully, "how do I know you'd keep your end of the bargain? What do you want with it?"

"Her power, of course. The Imaia needs every resource it can get its hands on to fight the Enemy. I should be rounding up every last person in your Remnant to forward the Imaia's goals, but the power of that Throne is worth far more."

She grinned. "Think of it this way: if you retain the Throne's power, you could still be a threat. For all I know, Kweshrima has spent these years in hiding looking for some other way for you to get off world. The Imaia can't have that. If I take that power, the Imaia has no need to pursue a few thousand refugees fleeing to a likely-deserted planet where you'll spend the next few generations merely adjusting to life if you don't die first. With this trade, both of us win."

Koruuksi stared at her for a long while, expression unreadable. Then he closed his eyes and took a deep breath.

"Deal."

Othaashle smiled.

14

The Remnant

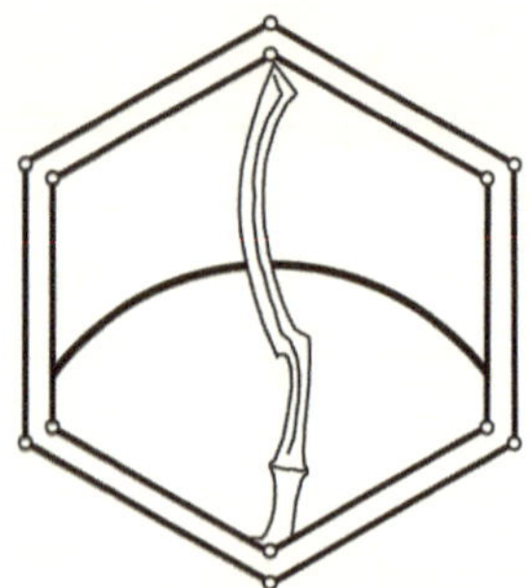

"For now it will need to be handled with bare hands, or at least bare palms, though I have several theories about surpassing that barrier in later tests. Though the zidanio increases the power of one's Auroramancy, that same power does not translate the georaural technology. Aikanuum, however, has proven quite useful in recent tests as an alternative."

Exodus countdown: 19 days, 18 hours, 44 minutes

Othaashle frowned when the shadowed cavernous entrance to the Remnant's base finally came in sight. As large as it was, she only picked spotted it because Koruuksi pointed it out and told her to brighten her clearnodes.

She couldn't sense any use of Auroramancy from that direction, even when she flared her Natari blacknodes. It should have been a faint pulse even at this distance despite any blackshadows they had working to cloud their presence. Even with her enhanced sight, she saw no soldiers or scouts that would have caught her and Koruuksi's approach.

The lack of any Auroramantic signatures strengthened Othaashle's conviction that the Remnant had the Throne.

And it's finally within my grasp.

"Will we be attacked if we approach the entrance?"

Koruuksi, hood pulled up over his helmet, shook his head. "I'll take care of that. I'd still keep your rednodes ready, though."

Othaashle nodded and gestured for him to go first. She almost summoned Ilkwalerva as they started forward but thought better of it. The features of one of the Redeemed would intimidate Koruuksi's comrades enough as it was.

Or shock them, apparently.

Over their long trek the past day, Koruuksi had said nothing more about how he knew her, and Othaashle had not asked. She'd experienced another vision—they eschewed regular intervals so far, but were growing more frequent—when they had stopped so Koruuksi could rest. To Othaashle's relief, the boy had been asleep when it happened.

When she'd asked about the greave he wore, and how he'd acquired them, he'd remained silent. Othaashle was certain which one of the Redeemed they had belonged to, however.

Between what she'd seen this time and the taboo all Redeemed held to, she'd found herself both unwilling and unable to prod the young man about whatever connection he had with who she had once been.

Hyhainen was there again, but other than that—

No.

Othaashle shut down that line of thinking. The questions it led to... well, she didn't want to think of the most likely answers.

No one popped out of the barren, grey-blue landscape of rocks and crags as Othaashle followed Koruuksi, but she did not drop her guard. The shadow of a tall, jagged outcrop loomed before them, at the base of one smaller mountains that bordered the Uumfuulai basin, casting a long shadow.

How fitting that one must leave the sun's touch to enter their base.

As they neared the entrance, however, Othaashle noticed signs of stonework and rubble, even the remains of some tools.

"Was this a mine?"

Koruuksi nodded. "One of the old Atonga goldmines that the Imaia or Iron Empire expanded into an iron mine. They did a nice job of cleaning out all the iron within and around the mine for us."

Othaashle snorted. The Remnant was a group of insurgents, but they were resourceful. That thought made her frown.

Resourceful enough to become a threat if I give them a capital ship?

It didn't matter. She needed the Throne to combat the visions.

I told Koruuksi I'd give them a ship and let them get away. I didn't say the Imaia wouldn't follow once we've established our own new home and wipe them out.

Once they drew close enough to the entrance, Koruuksi stopped just as four men and women in the dark, rough jackets the Remnant favored stepped out, leveling rifles. Othaashle couldn't recognize the make from this distance. All wore helmets to protect their skin and eyes. Surprisingly, only one had antlers.

"Identify yourself," one of the men said.

"Hynaia?" Koruuksi asked, "It's me, Koruuksi. I—"

One of the women—the one with antlers—gasped, "Is that...?"

She took a step closer, posture showing curiosity and... disbelief? A moment later, she stiffened, rifle pointed directly between Othaashle's eyes. She recognized it now: a Synarra 632 rail rifle. Good weapon. Precise, and it didn't have a long power-up time like the heavier weapons.

It wouldn't kill her, but the hole it could leave would take a bit longer to heal than Othaashle preferred. At this range, the round would travel fast enough that Othaashle would need to already have her ambernodes brightened to dodge or throw up a shield in time. She brightened them just in case.

"Koruuksi," the woman said, masked face turning toward Othaashle, "what are you doing here with one of those? Is it just the two of you, or is this a trap? You—"

"It's just me and her," Koruuksi said, cutting the woman off. "I've made a deal to get us out of here. We give her what she wants, and we get a capital ship to get us off world."

All four lowered their weapons for a moment before they remembered themselves.

"Get Estingai if you need to," Koruuksi said again before the guards could speak.

Othaashle raised an eyebrow, impressed at the way he took command.

"You'll probably need to have Uuchantuu come along, too," he continued, then paused, voice tense when he spoke. "She's here, right? The convoy made it here with no problems?"

Othaashle peered at Koruuksi, still unable to determine the nature of his affections for the young woman.

"She's fine," the first man—Hynaia—said. He paused, then turned to the others. "I'll get the commander. Watch her."

"What the hell, Koruuksi?" the woman with the antlers asked once Hynaia was out of earshot. Her rifle's muzzle remained pointed at Othaashle's brow, unfaltering as she spoke. "We were so close."

"Everything back at the Wolfden that we stole is destroyed or too damaged to be of any use, Zofja. This is our only chance, now. And it's a better one than we had before."

None of the guards replied, though their postures grew more hostile.

"Can I at least come out of the sun while we wait?" Koruuksi asked, patting the side of his helmet. "It's hot in this thing."

Zofja nodded and the guards moved aside, letting Koruuksi through. The young man leaned against the cavern wall behind them and removed his helmet, smoothing the sweaty silver hair from his forehead before wiping his coat-sleeve across his brow.

Othaashle made no move forward. She had the impression that the guards would all fire their weapons if she so much as shifted her weight. Instead she studied the Remnant soldiers.

Their dark uniforms bore no markings or medals of any kind. They looked unbearably hot to Othaashle, but a force of mostly Samjati on Lightside would need uniforms that covered them completely. Everything they wore and carried was dark, camouflage for the shadows of their caves as well as the surrounding environment.

As she waited, Othaashle started to feel restless. Though the visions had not come at anything even close to approaching regular intervals, each one seemed to come sooner than the last.

If one takes me before I get to the Throne...

That would be as bad as if Skadaatha had left her lightless and wounded beyond her ability to heal in that other base.

Othaashle tried to force the creeping worry from her mind, but as the minutes passed, it grew more difficult to do so.

When she finally heard the padding of booted feet approaching,

Othaashle nearly jumped. She let out a breath she hadn't realized she'd been holding.

The guard, Hynaia came into view first, followed by two young women in dark, armored jackets, both carrying helmets at the hip—the taller one's was strange, more ornamented. One was shorter and pretty, almost petite, with full lips, a larger nose—though one that fit her face—and tilted, light golden-brown eyes that would have made Othaashle think the woman of Kysuuri heritage if not for the deep red skin. The hair added to that: dark waves threaded with white and silver strands.

Uuchantuu?

The name didn't fit save for the eyes and hair.

The other woman had no antlers and her skin was a light blue-violet with black stripes. She was more handsome than pretty, at least compared to the shorter one, but that might have been due to the stern expression and tight, angular jaw. Two scars that appeared to have been from the same wound—one through the middle of her right eyebrow, the other at the top right point of her upper lip, giving her cupid's bow a lopsided look—added to the effect along with her golden eyes and styled blue-black hair that was shaved on the right and long on the left, swooping down to fall over her face.

Othaashle's eyes went wide when she took another look at the strange harness the Samjati woman wore over her jacket. A glint at the Natari woman's arms caught her attention as well, and Othaashle glanced to Koruuksi again, then back to the Samjati woman, looking her up and down.

Is this her?

All three wore pieces of the armor given to the Redeemed, though they'd done something to dull the armor's reflective surfaces.

The Samjati woman had done something else to modify her breast-plate. At the center of the chest, she'd attached the mask of one of the Redeemed.

I was right.

She bore no insignia, but from the way the others guarded her, this woman was one of their commanders.

This is Estingai. The last of the Knights Reborn.

Othaashle met the woman's gaze—

"You!" Estingai hissed, eyes widening as she lunged at Othaashle, dropping her helmet.

It seemed Koruuksi and Uuchantuu had expected this, as each grabbed an arm and held her back even as she struggled.

Estingai barely paid them any mind. Her wild eyes focused on Othaashle. "You monster. You took everything from me!"

Othaashle raised an eyebrow. "And you took one of my Redeemed from me. Though in Epekora's case, I believe you'd done me a favor."

That seemed to enrage the woman further. Koruuksi's greynodes brightened in response, and Uuchantuu's expression grew strained.

"Get a hold of yourself, Estingai," Koruuksi managed through gritted teeth, "I'm the irresponsible one, remember?"

Are they siblings then? They don't look alike. Or is he her second?

That would explain the young man's seeming lack of adherence to the rough command structure these insurgents maintained. Though it spoke poorly of a commander who would let a subordinate speak to her like that simply because they were family.

Unless he's her adjunct. If the Remnant even keeps to formal military structure.

Estingai rounded on Koruuksi, growling as she ripped her arm free of Uuchantuu's grip, "How could you bring her here? You should have let her kill you first."

"I'll try to remember that next time," Koruuksi said, glaring at the woman. "I need you to let me bring her inside."

"What possible reason could you have that makes you think I would let that happen?"

The fact that I could cut through all of you in an instant if I wished?

As the two argued, Othaashle noticed a strange pressure coming over her. A dampening like that of lightlessness. She tensed.

What is this...? A trap?

She reached out to Ilkwalerva reflexively, but before a single heartbeat had passed, Othaashle's vision flashed, a battlefield appearing before her.

No. No!

Othaashle fought through the vision, willing Ilkwalerva to her.

She was back before the cave.

Troops in uniforms and armor of dark blue clashed against those of the Imaia.

Five.

The cave again. Koruuksi and Estingai had stopped arguing. Wide eyes focused on her. Motes of fire and frost swirled around her fingertips.

Six.

Ilkwalerva coalesced from fire and ice, dropping into her hand.

It shattered into flame and frost as the vision took her.

15

Compromised

"Test of the blade against darklight and other hardlight surfaces proved successful. Each impact placed the device under great strain, however, and required great strength from handler even with zidanio's enhancements, especially during prolonged periods of contact."

Exodus countdown: 19 days, 8 hours, 25 minutes

The soft, rhythmic lapping of the polar sea against Mjatafa Mwonga's outer wall—what would be the outer hull after Exodus —helped Skadaatha center herself as she waited, gazing out at the horizon.

Skadaatha had arrived before the others to allow for some time to think. She was resolved to end Othaashle if necessary but didn't feel entirely certain about it. A night spent with Vysla had cleared her head of the heightened, lingering emotions of near-death experience, leaving her with questions she had yet to find a good answer to.

Do I want to kill her only because it is necessary? Or am I letting my desire for vengeance influence my reasoning?

A part of her wished she'd simply been able to stay in bed with her husband.

Othaashle was supremely valuable to the Imaia. Skadaatha could not dispute that. Yet neither could she trust the woman to act as if their fight —one Skadaatha had initiated—had not happened.

Skadaatha knew she wouldn't if their places were reversed. She would either accuse the woman of treason immediately or wait until it benefited her most.

More than that, Skadaatha would need to lie to those who would help her eliminate the threat Othaashle presented. She'd already lied to Yndlova about how she'd been unable to find Othaashle and wanted to regroup with some of her best people, just in case. That should satisfy the woman for a while.

Skadaatha sensed the first of her former lieutenants approaching long before he came within earshot. Skadaatha had kept her blacknodes at a low brightness since her return to the city, even while she slept. Boaathal's light allowed her the constant source of power to do so.

"You said this was urgent," Kwaasa Kotoka said in his rich tenor as he stepped up beside her. "Does it concern Exodus?"

She'd chosen one of the smaller, less-used harbors along Mjatafa Mwonga's outer wall as their meeting place. It was well-maintained, but that was about it. She'd had Kwaasa procure the craft they would use to cross the sea. He was good at things like that.

"It might," Skadaatha said without turning to face the man. "Let's wait for the others."

She could feel a few more not far off.

Within thirty minutes by the timepiece Vysla had crafted for her, Skadaatha stood with her back to the calm, red-orange waters of the Polar Sea, facing a semicircle of her seven most trusted lieutenants: Kwaasa Kotoka, Aarnal Meri, Abdal Kirim, Ljamyla 'Lady Death' Palyken, Synova Kobolan, Symen 'Vulture Eye' Nomokon, and Mnene Folonja. Each wore a brace of shining reserve biogems, and had come fully armed, as had she.

They were not truly her lieutenants any longer, though square jawed Aarnal Meri worked in the Ministry of Culture where he oversaw the relocation and resettlement of refugees that had fled their homes after the Destruction. The refugees—mostly Samjati—trusted him with their welfare, as his blue-violet skin and shovel-like antlers proclaimed his shared heritage, despite the fact that he'd fought against the Union.

When Skadaatha had recruited him for his incredible ability to keep fighting and leading men even after taking multiple wounds—even for a greyarm—she'd asked him why he chose to fight for the Imaia. His answer had been a simple statement:

"When the fight came to Alatai, our participation became inevitable, and only a fool could have believed otherwise. Every Alataina had just one decision to make: whose side to take in that bloody fight--the Imaia or the Union. The Imaia was a single, united body, while the Union was held together with thread at the time. My choice wasn't that hard."

Synova Kobolan, a solid woman of mixed blood with red skin, tall antlers, and black spots decorating her skin, worked in the Ministry of Science helping to develop new armor both with her experience operating the vehicles, and her knack for finding ways to rip them to shreds.

Skadaatha had helped set them up in positions there both to best utilize their skills and to keep a pulse on areas of the Imaia she might not normally deal with.

She'd done the same for the rest of her former comrades in the time between Othaashle's appointment as supreme commander of the Imaia's forces and the effective destruction of the Union. Save for Symen. He had continued his service in the Imaia's armed forces training marksmen, though so far none could compete with his incredible natural skill.

She'd brought along each for a specific purpose. Aarnal and Kwaasa for their offensive Auroramancy, Abdal and Mnene for stealth, Synova to take care of any vehicle Othaashle might return on, and Ljamyla and Symen to pin her down or take her out from a distance if needed.

Skadaatha hoped to encounter Othaashle in the rocky Atonga cragland, ideally near some well-placed caves.

You're distracting yourself. Just tell them.

"Commander Othaashle may have been turned or compromised by the Remnant," she said, meeting the eyes of each of her comrades in turn. "I called you here because we need to rescue her if possible..." she paused, "or kill her if necessary."

Their reactions were varied. She had expected as much. All knew of her rivalry with Othaashle, though only Mnene shared Skadaatha's knowledge of the champion's former identity. He'd been one of Kojatere Mestari's comrades before coming to the light.

Ljamyla and Symen remained stoic, but with a hint of expectancy. Their loyalty had been to Skadaatha long before Othaashle had come into the picture. Aarnal merely raised a skeptic eyebrow. Kwaasa nodded, rolling his broad shoulders. Abdal fingered one of the many explosives he carried about his person. Mnene remained impassive.

"Forgive me, Comma—er, Skadaatha," Synova said scrubbing a hand through her thick, dark hair, "I don't mean to question you, but I simply cannot believe it. Othaashle is our champion. Why would she betray us? And how would the Remnant best her in the first place?"

"I share Synova's concerns," Aarnal said slowly, "though I will do as you command, Vizier."

Skadaatha looked to Mnene and arched an eyebrow. He studied her for a moment before his eyes widened. Only for a moment, however. Once he regained control over himself, he nodded.

"This is... taboo to reveal to anyone else," Skadaatha said, looking to the rest of her comrades, "but Mnene can confirm it. Before Lord Ynuukwidas Redeemed Othaashle, she was Kojatere Mestari."

Several jaws tightened, eyes narrowing. A few looked to Mnene, who gave a grim nod in confirmation.

"I know many of the Redeemed are powerful Auroramancers Othaashle killed," Aarnal said, "but Kojatere herself?"

"This is why you have the feelings you do toward her?" Ljamyla asked Skadaatha.

"Part of it," she answered. They all knew what had happened to her son.

"Does this mean all Redeemed are suspect?" Abdal asked, hand going to one of his many knives this time.

Skadaatha shook her head. "I don't believe so. Othaashle has apparently been having visions that leave her incapacitated. I found her after one of these in a Remnant base, and she attacked me. There might be some other explanation, but she fought as though she wanted my head. I would like to merely bring her back to the Imaia if she has been merely captured, but if she has turned..."

Skadaatha trailed off and paused for effect. "If there is any chance that the woman who presides over our armed forces, our peacekeepers, and our courts is truly working against us, we have no choice but to eliminate her."

"And if Commander Othaashle merely attacked you because of a grievance against you, Vizier?" Symen asked.

"That's why I want you all with me," she lied. "This could be a failure on whatever barrier to past lives that Lord Ynuukwidas creates in the Lightforged, either due to some attempt by the Remnant to reclaim their fallen champion, or simply due to time. That is part of what we need to learn, so that we can be ready if this is something that might affect the rest of the Lightforged."

"That seems like something for Lord Ynuukwidas," Kwaasa said, "not us."

Skadaatha frowned, then sighed. "The strain of holding Efruumani together is too great for him to be bothered with something like this. He has already begun drawing the range of the auroras back from the Twilight Band."

Most of them stiffened. None pushed Kwaasa's suggestion.

"Are you with me?" Skadaatha asked, meeting each of their gazes in turn.

Each nodded.

"You know we are, Vizier," Abdal said.

Skadaatha nodded to Kwaasa. "Bring the craft around."

The man jogged off. A few minutes later, Skadaatha heard the hum of an engine on the water below.

Straightening, she turned in that direction and leapt off the edge, brightening her greennodes, and tethered herself to the water below the boat, pushing herself up just enough to slow her impact on the small craft's deck. The boat was orange to match the water, simple and shallow, with just enough room for weapons, supplies, and some room to stretch out if needed, just big enough for their number. Moments later, Skadaatha's comrades leapt down beside her. She caught most of them, as only Mnene was a full Iceborn. Once they were all secure in the craft, Skadaatha moved to the helm. Once there, she hesitated for one last moment, steeling her resolve.

She pushed forward on the throttle and the craft lurched forward.

Toward Othaashle.

16

To the Throne

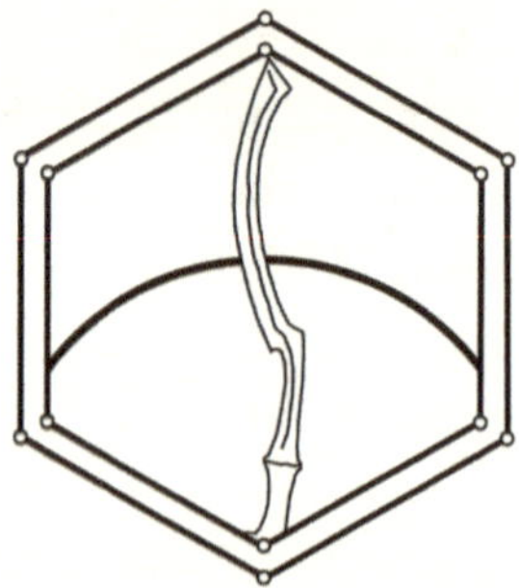

"After Vizier Skadaatha's feedback gained from an extraordinary field test, I have polarized half of the ruby settings. The framework is one of several designs that I produced with help from Miss Kwangeta, though for the moment, they are purely theoretical. The Vizier's notion of combining darklight and hardlight to allow the blade to flex as one made of steel is seems so obvious that the only reason I can find for not originally attempting it is that I have no clue if it is even possible."

Exodus countdown: 19 days, 6 hours, 36 minutes

The frustration of defeat lingered as Othaashle came back to herself.

These visions grow more vivid each time.

They took purchase in her mind, more like memories than dreams. The implications of that raised uncomfortable questions.

Blinking, Othaashle took in her surroundings, forcing those thoughts away.

She was in a cavern once more, away from the sun's light, yet she was not in a cell. That did not seem to be the room's primary function, at least. There was enough room for two guards she did not recognize to flank her, while Koruuksi, Uuchantuu, Estingai, and a woman that looked only a few years older than Estingai, with deep blue skin, black stripes, and no antlers spoke in hushed tones. A sapphire gemcrest shone at this woman's brow.

Othaashle turned her attention back toward herself. She wasn't lightless, but bindings of silver and aluminum enclosed her wrists and ankles, linking them to each other and forcing her into a kneeling position. Someone had also affixed an aluminum mask over the lower half of her face. She moved her jaw, testing, and found that it didn't prevent her from speaking, but would prevent her from producing fire and ice with her breath.

Clever.

But not entirely secure.

If she were merely a violethand, she wouldn't have been able to direct the fire or ice she created, but as a fullborn, her aquanodes would allow her to direct the energy however she pleased.

Othaashle didn't try that just yet, though. She still sensed the dampening pressure around her that she'd noticed just before her vision. It made her unsure how her abilities would function.

She also wanted to hear the argument between her minders.

The older woman bore an insignia on the breast of her armored jacket—a superior or fellow commander, maybe?

"What about this?" Estingai demanded, shoving something toward Koruuksi. "Did you know she had this on her?"

Othaashle narrowed her eyes, focusing on the small object.

The beacon.

So, they'd actually bothered to search her this time. It wouldn't make much of a difference.

Koruuksi raised a silver eyebrow at the commander, looking back and forth between her and the device she held. "You say that like I'm supposed to know what that is."

Estingai bared her teeth at him, the scar at her lip twisting her expression into a fierce snarl.

"It looks like a remote detonator," Uuchantuu said, looking to Estingai. "Isn't that a bit useless without explosives?"

"It's a transmitter," Estingai said. "Likely how the Imaia found Wolfden."

Koruuksi frowned. "That doesn't make sense. She fought whoever it was that came and destroyed everything. I think she might have even saved me."

Estingai growled. "If she did, it was part of a plan to bring you here so she could call a strike and wipe all of us out."

"And how would she have activated it while bound to a slab of metal?" Koruuksi demanded.

Estingai's jaw bunched, golden eyes flared, but it seemed she had no response to that.

"This is our best chance, Estingai," Koruuksi hissed, "we've been over everything that could go wrong. It all ends the same way. Most of our plans end in death one way or another, and you have yet to provide one good reason why we shouldn't."

"You weren't there." Pain and fury made the woman's voice raw as she spoke, "You didn't see—"

"I said a good reason," Koruuksi's voice was firm. "You know you wouldn't accept something like that from me."

"He has a point, Estingai," the older woman said, "I don't like it, but this seems like our only option."

Othaashle watched the woman's posture as frustration, anger and disbelief mixed.

"You want me to betray her?"

"What has she done for us?" Koruuksi asked, "Kept us hidden so that we can eventually waste away against the Imaia or with the dying world she doomed us to?"

Yes.

That was her confirmation. The Remnant knew where Kweshrima was, and that dampening pressure had to be her. She was close. Likely in this complex.

Skadaatha never found the Throne scouring Darkside because Kweshrima had already hidden it right under our noses.

And now, Othaashle would seize it.

She almost summoned Ilkwalerva and drew enough Auroralight to flare her Samjati greynodes and rip free from her bonds.

Instead, she brightened her Natari blacknodes and concentrated.

It took a few minutes, and she had to tune out the rest of the argument, but she heard it: a faint melody—similar, yet contrasting that of Ynuukwidas.

"She's awake."

Othaashle blinked and noticed Uuchantuu staring at her. The rest turned their eyes on her as well.

"The boy is right," she said, directing a grin at Estingai—she seemed the most likely choice. The aluminum mask hid most of her expression and muffled her voice somewhat, but she was able to make it work. "Give me what I want, and you will be able to leave this world and search for a new one in comfort. It's a far better deal than your goddess has been able to offer you."

She nodded toward the beacon. "I would be careful with that if I were you. I didn't activate it when I found this base, but if you do, it will tell my subordinates I need support."

Teeth bared, Estingai dropped the small device before her and crushed it under the heel of her boot. She smoothed her hair out of her face—an ineffectual gesture—then marched toward Othaashle, rednodes lighting up as she shoved Koruuksi against the wall with a hardlight bar when he tried to hold her back.

"I don't make deals with monsters like you," she growled.

Just a bit closer.

One.

Othaashle shifted in her bonds, readying herself.

Two.

"Just monsters like your goddess? Tell me, how does the death of an entire world measure up against soldiers and insurgents killed in combat?"

Three.

The woman's eyes flashed with rage. "Combat?"

Four.

She leaned in closer, grabbing at Othaashle's collar. "You murdered them, assassin. You murdered my—"

Othaashle flared her greynodes and opalnodes. That pressure inhibited her, but she pushed through it, burning through all the Auroralight in her opalnodes and Samjati greynodes in one brilliant flare. She roared as the incredible strength rushed through her and with, twin snaps, shattered the restraints on her wrists and jaw.

Five.

She brought her hands around to her front, grabbing Estingai with one, and pushing herself to her feet with the other.

Six.

Othaashle stretched out her free hand and kicked her legs apart, breaking the chains there, just as Ilkwalerva materialized. She brought the edge to Estingai's neck.

"Weapons down," she commanded, looking to the two stunned guards flanking her.

They looked to Koruuksi and the older man.

Othaashle brought the tip a bit closer to Estingai's throat and shot hard looks at both the Samjati. "Now."

Estingai struggled against Othaashle's grip, but with Ilkwalerva, she was able to pull more investment into her body, replenishing her Samjati greynodes to let her overpower the younger woman.

Koruuksi nodded and the guards put down their weapons.

"How could you?" Estingai rasped.

Othaashle ignored her and looked to the guards. "Good, now get over to the other side of the room."

"Just kill me, monster," Estingai growled.

"Maybe," Othaashle said, "if you continue to irritate me. For now, though, you're going to take me to the Throne."

Estingai barked a bitter laugh. "You're insane."

"From what I've seen so far, I'm far more stable than you," Othaashle said. "Though I have a feeling you'll find some way to lay the blame for that at my feet."

"I won't take you to it," Estingai grated, "just kill me."

"Estingai," Koruuksi said, voice tense.

"That's the thing," Othaashle said, wiggling Ilkwalerva's point before the woman's face. "With this, I won't merely kill you. If I have to feed your soul to Ilkwalerva and I don't get what I want, I'll ensure you are Redeemed in time to be tasked specifically with eliminating the Remnant."

"You're bluffing," Estingai said, though she couldn't hide the fear in her voice. "We know you've stopped making new Lightforged."

Othaashle shrugged. "I'm sure I could convince Lord Ynuukwidas to make a special dispensation in this case. You are the last of the Knights Reborn, after all."

"Estingai," Koruuksi said again, "just give her what she wants."

"No!" the woman grunted.

"If I have to take your soul and those of your fellow insurgents here do give me what I want," Othaashle continued, letting her irritation show in her voice, "I'll still honor my end of the deal, but I'll make sure that you are the Redeemed tasked with hunting them down for the Imaia to eliminate once we've found our new home."

"I won't take you to it."

"Don't be stupid, Estingai," Koruuksi said. "You say she took everything from you? What about me? What about Uuchantuu? Do you want her to take everything from us, too?"

"Either we both win," Othaashle continued, "or I win, and you and your Remnant lose. I can't see why this is such a hard choice for you. Unless you really just want to die."

The woman stiffened under Othaashle's grip.

Damn. I wanted unstable, not suicidal.

Koruuksi stepped forward. "Estingai, please."

The young man met Othaashle's gaze. "We give you what you want, and you let us escape, right?"

Othaashle nodded. The Imaia could use whatever base they established on their new world as a colony. Pre-existing infrastructure would be well-worth the price of a capital ship and a brief campaign.

Though I might keep you.

The young man had titansteel in his spine.

She could take the Throne, give them the cruiser, then take the boy and threaten reprisal if they didn't just fly off with her generous gift.

Though, I'll likely have to take Estingai as well. That might unhinge her enough to throw away her life doing something stupid and reckless.

"I'll take you to it."

Othaashle raised an eyebrow at the young man.

"Koruuksi, no!" Estingai began but cut off when Othaashle laid Ilkwalerva's flat against her jaw.

"Stop, Estingai," Koruuksi hissed. "Or are you going to make her kill you and abandon me and Uuchantuu?"

That seemed to get through to the woman. Enough to make her go still, at least.

"The others will stay in here," Othaashle said, nodding toward the guards, Uuchantuu and the commander. "And I'll be bringing Estingai with me to ensure she doesn't decide to do anything stupid."

Koruuksi nodded, gesturing for the others to move against the wall of the small room, leaving a clear path toward the door for Othaashle and Estingai.

"You first. Tell me which way I need to go," Othaashle said.

"Left," Koruuksi said, walking toward the doorway.

"You exit to the right. I don't want any surprises."

Koruuksi did as she said, and Othaashle shoved Estingai forward, then walked her with one hand gripping her shoulder and Ilkwalerva at the woman's back. Keeping her greynodes and blacknodes bright and adding her yellownodes for a bit of luck, Othaashle followed the young man out into the hall.

17

The Throne of Darkness

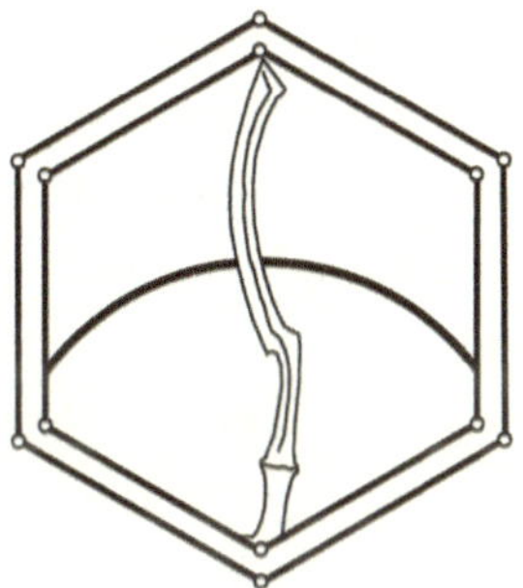

"Given how the blade overloaded, I have lengthened the hilt hollowed it out to an extent, including more moonstone and sapphire settings wherever there is space available in order to both keep the blade and weapon together, and allow for greater storage of power."

Exodus countdown: 19 days, 6 hours, 27 minutes

As Koruuksi led Othaashle and her captive through the system of caves and tunnels, some natural, some carved, all dimly lit by thin strips of lights, Othaashle grew increasingly more certain that they were approaching the Throne.

At first, the dampening pressure had waxed and waned as they moved through different corridors and chambers, but after a certain point, it had begun to grow stronger. The air grew colder, the darkness more tangible with every passing step. With her blacknodes brightened, the melody Othaashle had sensed earlier repeated over and over, growing louder and more insistent as she grew closer. Othaashle shoved down the discomfort it brought. She was finally close.

Though they had long since left the complex's larger areas behind, their passing has caused quite a stir. Civilians had shied away, and soldiers had gripped their weapons tight, some raising them, but all had enough sense not to be reckless. They knew of Ilkwalerva and the

Redeemed, even if most had never seen either. What other weapon could it be?

They knew the kind of slaughter Othaashle could leave in her wake if she wished. They wanted none of it. It didn't hurt, of course, that Koruuksi and Estingai shook their heads when soldiers met their eyes.

When Othaashle caught the flashes of disbelief and horror some faces expressed upon seeing her, it unsettled her. If she had not been so close to the Throne, so close to an end to these visions, it might have troubled her. She shoved the thoughts aside.

None of that matters anymore.

Finally, they reached a chamber the depth of which Othaashle could feel. With Atonga's volcanic activity, Othaashle would have expected warmth this far beneath the surface, yet the cold bit deeper than that of Darkside's Wastes. The darkness was a black fog around them. The melody would have deafened her had she perceived it with her ears.

As they continued further into the fog with slow, careful steps, something started to coalesce. Pale blue and deep violet shimmered, giving off a light that illuminated nothing.

Othaashle's heart began to pound with anticipation until finally the vague shimmer solidified into a great, austere Throne of ice and darkness given form atop a tiered dais. It looked carved of great blocks of obsidian, yet Othaashle knew it was nothing so mundane.

Drawing in enough power to fill her gemcrests completely, Othaashle shoved Estingai to the side and leveled Ilkwalerva. She approached the throne, a satisfied grin spreading across her face. Stretching out one hand, she rested her fingers onto the slab-like seat. They tingled with the power of the Throne.

Flaring her Iceborn bluenodes, Othaashle raised Ilkwalerva, then rammed it into the Throne.

Cracks spread throughout the Throne as Othaashle drained its power with her bluenodes, letting the ocean of energy flood through her. The room lost its chill. The palpable darkness began to fade.

Then it stopped.

Othaashle frowned. She was filled to bursting with power, invested beyond anything she had ever experienced. She felt as though she could sprint for hours without stopping, leap canyons in a single bound, lift monuments with no effort at all.

Her breath caught. The world around her, even in this dark chamber, felt more real, more alive than it ever had before. Details were sharper, contrasts heightened. Her surroundings slowed. She found she was aware of every passing second. Othaashle knew the exact time of day, how long it had taken her to arrive here from the chamber she'd woken in. Everyone on Efruumani had a timesense, but it was nothing like this.

The melodies of every soul in this complex called to her senses.

Yet...

There's still something missing.

The Throne shattered.

Othaashle stumbled back in surprise, leaving Ilkwalerva driven into the icy stone that remained.

Natari blacknodes bright, Othaashle felt the presence behind her just in time to whirl around and roar as a hand darker than night grabbed her forehead. Her mind barely registered the trap Kweshrima had laid for her, the trap she had run headfirst into, before the goddess's overwhelming power drove her to her knees.

The pressure, the thick miasma of darkness, the icy cold, all returned tenfold, crashing over her.

Let me in, child, and I will give you what you wish.

The voice chilled Othaashle to her core as she gasped desperate, ragged breaths.

No.

Somehow, she managed to push back the pressure on her mind.

No, I will not *let you in.*

Mustering all the mental fortitude available, Othaashle flared her blacknodes and tried to analyze the different power signatures in and around her even as she desperately fended off Kweshrima's assaults on her mind.

There has to be a weakness somewhere. Something I can exploit.

The power radiating from the goddess was deafening, overwhelming everything, even with Othaashle's own increased power that boiled till she thought she might burst. Her arms and legs quivered with the effort of holding her up despite her kneeling position.

All her effort went into holding back the intense pressure that bore down on her, into keeping her body from succumbing to the freezing cold. Only the tiniest sliver could be spared to try and discover some weakness to exploit in the goddess's defenses.

Come back to me, my child.

The goddess masked her twisted heart with a tender voice as she spoke.

Ynuukwidas has stolen who you are. I can restore you.

The shock of that statement almost won Kweshrima the battle, but Othaashle caught herself just as she began to slip.

Is she behind the visions? Was the incident with Boaathal just a coincidence? Or something she managed to exploit?

But if she had the power to do that, why hadn't she simply crushed Othaashle?

Othaashle's eyes bulged.

Because she can't.

Everything turned on its head for Othaashle.

She had succeeded in siphoning power from the Throne, but not all of it. Kweshrima still held onto what power she could with a connection to the Throne that had been strengthened over hundreds of years. Yet it seemed it was all the goddess could do to fend off Othaashle.

I can beat her.

Teeth clenched in a rictus grin, Othaashle pushed back at the goddess's attack, searching for a weakness with renewed purpose. All her skill in Auroramancy amounted to nothing in this fight, but she was more than an Auroramancer, more than one of the Redeemed.

I am Mestari, the Deathknight, and today—

She found it—the nexus where Kweshrima's power connected with the Throne's.

Today, I claim the life of a goddess.

Othaashle flared her gemcrests, throwing every scrap of power she could gather at that nexus even as that dark, icy pressure began to suffocate her.

Her arms gave out. She barely noticed. All her will—her entire being—was focused on eliminating that node of connection between the goddess and her Throne.

You want to know the truth, don't you, my child? The truth Ynuukwidas stole from you? I can give you that.

No.

Othaashle did not want to know who she had been. That woman was dead. She wanted an end to her wondering. And an end to the visions.

I can give you that, too.

The node burst. A screech filled Othaashle's mind. Physical pain like a massive blade rending her from shoulder to hip flooded through her as the goddess reeled from the agony of being severed from her Throne.

Othaashle reached for the power of the Throne, that dark, icy miasma. If she could anchor herself to that, she could take even the goddess's own power.

It lay just beyond her grasp. She strained, barely able to keep Kweshrima's overwhelming power from obliterating her.

Then she grasped it and flared both sets of bluenodes, linking herself to the Throne.

The power came upon her suddenly. The power of the Throne.

And that of Kweshrima.

They consumed Othaashle.

The Darkness of a sky without Myrskaan's pale light, the cold of the Wastes, swirled together and pressed down upon her. It burrowed into her body, forcing its way into her gemcrest, her ears, the pores and openings in her skin, even her eyes. She opened her mouth to scream, and it rushed in, choking her.

When it filled her completely, she began to burn.

Not the burning of fire, but the cool burn of chewing too much mint or a dish with too much icepepper. The way Samjati biogems burned when they brightened. This sensation, however, didn't come just from Othaashle's gemcrests, but from her entire body. Her skin and muscles flared. Even her bones seemed alight with an icy blaze.

Othaashle gasped, realizing that the power no longer choked her, and looked down at her hands.

She glowed with those same violet and pale-blue lights that illuminated nothing. The power within her had grown from a vast lake to an endless ocean. It threatened to burst from her, like the strength she drew from her Samjati greynodes magnified beyond her imagination. Or it would have been, had the power not begun to expand her mind, allowing her to comprehend what she had become.

Even as Othaashle reveled at the possibilities of her new power, something snatched it, then started to burn it away.

"No!" Othaashle cried.

But it was too late.

They came separately, at first. Thoughts that were not her own, sights and sensations, memories of movement. Sounds, aromas, taste, knowledge. And finally, emotions and passions.

Othaashle roared as they hammered into her mind like spikes. It was like the visions, only fragmented. Her mind felt pulled in a thousand different directions at once, shredded even as it tried to hold on to some semblance of control.

Othaashle felt something being stripped away from her as though her very skin was being flayed.

They merged.

The world exploded.

18

The Price of Power

"After days of testing, Miss Kwangeta and I have finally managed a blade of layered hardlight and darklight that allows for a razor edge as well as strength and flexibility. I cannot sufficiently test the durability and power storage, unfortunately, but these modifications should do for now."

C. 35 years, 3 months, 3 days before the Destruction of Yrmuunthal

I *can't miss him.*

For a moment, as Kojatere raced over streets on one of the neighborhood's skating paths, greennodes bright, Kojatere wondered if leaving to go to Aiella's last night been worth it. An escape from her parents was welcome any time even without the added bonus of clearnode-enhanced sex on a rooftop on Auroraday, but...

Will I still feel that way if I miss saying goodbye to Suule?

A lateoruu popped up and stuck its tongue out at her, while another made more ticking noises.

Kojatere swatted at them and brightened her greennodes further, pushing off the icy path and speeding toward home.

Broad streets zipped by below, with people on bikes and a few of the new, more affordable electric motorcarriages. A part of her wished it wasn't near the end of the snowy season, and she could skate across an entire street instead of on a thin line, but then she wouldn't have been able to enjoy Aiella's company again this morning. Instead, she would have been up early, working to clear the snow off the streets and walkways before Atjakuu rose into the sky.

Kojatere glanced back to the path before her just in time to flare her greennodes, pushing up into the air and into a tight flip as she cleared the antlers of the messenger stopped off on the path before her.

"Sorry about that, Kinga!" Kojatere called back. She thought that was her, at least.

"These are for Union Messengers only!" the woman—maybe Kinga—called, words barely audible to Kojatere as she raced onward.

Kojatere soon passed into her neighborhood, and felt a sense of comfort as she took in the familiar houses. The lack of snow made the streets of long, tall apartment buildings—each crafted to look like several individual houses pressed up against one another—look more stark, and less welcoming than usual. Without that, the sense of stagnancy stood out more. One of her many reasons for fleeing to the city on occasions like last night. Here, she didn't fit in with the quiet, simple lifestyle that her parents and so many others enjoyed. She didn't exactly fit in within Rovani either, but no one did. The city was so full of progress and people that no one stood out there, because no one and everyone belonged at once.

When Kojatere's home came in sight, she smiled as a few luckoruu burst into the air around her. Suule and her parents stood in the yard, the slightly askew street number hanging over the door a few paces behind them. Kojatere winced when she saw that her window was still open from when she'd snuck out last night.

I knew the latch didn't close all the way.

Her parents had definitely noticed that.

As she slowed and caught Suule's eye, her brother smiled. Kojatere thought of the time, and smiled back as a few timeoruu popped up, showing her she'd made it home with five minutes to spare.

Then Kojatere's parents noticed her. Neither the disappointed expressions they wore, or the impatienceoruu that popped up around them—folded arms each tapping a finger to mark the time—surprised her.

At least Suule's happy to see me.

Her mothers both wore the simple, finely-cut morning robes they wore most mornings while sipping their hot tea, relaxing in the morning, or doing any chores they needed to attend to before going off to work with the rest of the neighborhood.

Kirsi, her Samjati mother, in her pale green robe that complemented her skin, somehow always managed to be fashionable. Matching silk slippers covered her feet since there wasn't enough snow on the ground to soak them. Aminata, her Natari mother, wore a robe with pale grey snowfox fur lining the collar. She had adjusted to Darkside's cold better than most Natari women who came here, but she was still Natari—born of a land of warm, eternal sunshine rather than Darkside's cold winds and starlit skies. She wore boots.

Kojatere held in a sigh as she stopped just a few feet from the three of them and looked at her adoptive mothers, Aminata's arm around Kirsi's waist. They always looked so happy for each other, and had done so much for her and Suule.

Sometimes, lately, they're just a little...much.

After giving them a quick, tight-lipped smile, Kojatere looked to her twin brother and grinned.

Suule wore his Darkside Union uniform. Standard issue: A white, button-up shirt and thick, plain white trousers tucked into calf-high boots under a long, white, knee-length double-breasted coat with blue trim. He held his hooded mask and cap at his hip, forgoing it for now. He was also Kirsi's son, so Kojatere caught the shine of thin silver patterns filling in the trim on his coat. The silk, silver-white scarf around his neck was also new, and the new strap Kojatere had bought her brother for the guitar at his back already bore his personal touches as well. She smiled at that, then looked her brother up and down, lingering on the trim and the scarf, "That gonna pass an inspection?"

Suule rolled her eyes, "That your way of saying it looks nice?"

She smirked.

"I'm glad you made it back before he left, Kojatere," Kirsi said, "Where were you?"

"And why is there snow on your shoes?" Aminata asked, then sighed, "You didn't use one of the messenger paths again, did you?"

Instead of denying it, Kojatere gave her mothers as sweet a smile as she could manage, "I did. Don't worry, though, I made sure to say hi to Kinga. I think it was her."

As both her mothers sighed, Kojatere glanced back as Suule, still grinning.

"Just because you're a celebrity doesn't mean you get special privileges, Kojatere," Aminata said.

Kojatere rolled her eyes, "Doesn't it, though? Kinga and Adorjan and the others haven't done anything yet."

Both frowned at her, and Kirsi stepped out of Aminata's embrace toward her, "Kojatere, this—"

She paused, and Kojatere winced as her mother wrinkled her nose, "Why do you smell like violet—"

"Aiti, Bamama," Suule said, stepping over and putting an arm around Kojatere's shoulder, "Why don't you go over and chat with Eha and Amaruuk? Hamado will be here soon, so I only have a few more minutes with Tere. You can both have the entire rest of the day to interrogate her."

Their mothers shared a look, then sighed and nodded. Both hugged Suulehep tight before walking over to where their neighbors sat by the fire.

Once they'd sat down , Kojatere looked to Suule, and shot him a thankful smile before throwing her arms around him, taking care not to rattle his guitar in its case. As he returned the embrace, wrapping his arms around her, a warmth radiated through Kojatere, melting the tension in her shoulders.

I still have some time with him.

"I'm gonna miss you," she said into his collar, "A lot."

Suule laughed, "You'd probably miss me a bit less if you hadn't ran out last night."

She sighed, pulled back, "I know. I just needed a break after all the Auroraday activities."

He raised an eyebrow, "Then why—"

Kojatere shrugged, "You know how they love all that. They wanted to spend the day with you again like before you left, and I didn't want to take that or you away from them."

"And last night?"

"I just couldn't take it anymore after dinner. I figured you would have enjoyed the time with them."

Suule snorted, "I did. Until they went to bed way earlier than either of us usually do. You smell like you had a good time, though. Violet-sage, some minty liqueur, and..."

Her frowned, wrinkling his nose, "Do I want to know?"

"I went into the city to meet up with a girl. Ajeda."

He made a face, sticking out his tongue, and she punched him lightly in the chest, "Hey. *You* don't get to give me shit about sleeping around."

Suule grinned, then raised an eyebrow, "Wait. Ajeda—why do I recognize that name? What does she look like?"

Kojatere frowned, "Nice lips, long, black hair, high cheekbones, lean, but not too lean, why?"

Suule's eyes danced as he raised a hand to his mouth, and Kojatere sighed—that usually meant he was trying not to laugh.

"What?"

"You just have a type."

She punched him in the arm.

He just grinned, running a hand through his blue-black hair that shone with a few silver strands.

"Well, I definitely wouldn't have been able to provide *that* kind of entertainment," he said, digging his other hand into a coat pocket, "*but...*"

Kojatere blinked, then grinned as Suule pulled out a small hexagonal tin used to contain the pungent violet sage inside. He held it out, and she palmed it, slipping it into her own pocket before their parents could see.

Then she frowned, "Well, now I feel like shit."

Studying her twin, Kojatere remembered the odd look on his face earlier, "Did you need to blow off some steam last night, too?"

Suule shrugged, then nodded to their parents, "Can you try to go a bit easier on them? They are a bit much sometimes, but they miss me just as much as you do. Probably more."

Kojatere snorted, "Not possible."

Then she took a deep breath, sobering, "It's just...I don't want you to go. You're my only friend."

Suule frowned, "What about Ajeda, or your teammates?"

Kojatere shrugged, "You know how cutthroat it is."

He snorted, nodding, "That's why I got out."

"And because I was better."

"Then we would have been partners."

"Will you just admit I was better than you?"

He grinned, "Only when it stops frustrating you that I won't."

She stuck her tongue out at him, then folder her arms, "I just feel...I don't know, stifled?"

Suule threw her a flat look, "Tere, you're the captain of the national team. You've been to the Union Games once with me and we won. Now you're also touring with the Church's Historical Dancers to keep you in shape for competition and the next Union Games. When you're not here, you're traveling all over Darkside. How are you stifled by that?"

Kojatere shrugged, "It's not just that. Doing all that shows everyone that I'm the best, but...I want to be out helping people like you are, not just performing for crowds and competing for some sort of meaningless national pride."

Suule pursed his full lips for a moment. She always thought they looked a bit big under his short nose and didn't fit his strong, angular jaw, but men and women threw themselves at him just as much as they did at her, so apparently they liked that.

"That national pride may mean nothing to you, Tere," he said, cutting right through her words, "But it means a lot to a lot of people. Including the men and women I train with. Even if it didn't—remember that you may be the best at ice dancing, but there's always someone better than you at something else. Like being the captain of the team."

"What's that supposed to mean?"

Suule sighed, frowning, "I recommended you for captain because I thought it would help you grow. You're the best. Instead of seeing your teammates as beneath you, use that skill to help teach the others you compete with. That's how you can help people without any training or signing away years of your life to serve in foreign lands. Instead of resenting how much time our mothers have to focus on you now, embrace it. Help them deal with one of their children leaving home. Help them deal with how often you travel and how much they want to see you every time you perform."

"I guess I can try that," she sighed, "But I'm still going to join the

Union Forces after. I'll be the best soldier there is, and do the same there."

Suule grunted, "Good."

Kojatere nodded, then glanced back at their parents before grinning at Suule, "So, you going to tell me about the new weapons now that our moms aren't listening in?"

Suule rolled his eyes, but grinned, "I got to try one of the railgun cannons we replicated from the Imaia's technology."

"What?" Kojatere knew she was grinning like an idiot, "What was it like?"

"Heavy. With a hell of a recoil. I had to brighten my greynodes to use it properly."

"Were they specifically designing that one for use by Auroramancer's only?"

They talked for a few minutes about the weaponry and technology Suulehep's position allowed him to try out. About the pirates the Union often fought, and the island paradises she knew Suulehep would get stationed at because life was always far more fair to him than it was to anyone else.

Eventually, though, he turned the conversation back on her.

"I don't think you'll want to leave as badly if you actually try to make an effort here, Tere."

She sighed, "It's not that I want to leave. I always miss home when I'm traveling, and I like coming home, but I don't like the gossip or the prying and negative attention I get from just living my life. Or the pressure."

Suule snorted, "You think those things don't exist in the Union Forces?"

"Not this way," Kojatere protested, "Like you said, I'd be just one of thousands of soldiers. Plus, you'll be there. Now that you're gone, I always have to be the hero or the accomplished one."

He shrugged, "Make friends with someone annoyingly exceptional."

"You know I'm bad at that."

Suule looked like he was about to say something, but Kojatere picked up padded footsteps, then grinned as Suule smiled past her. Kojatere turned around just in time to meet Muusti—their neighbor Anara's large, fluffy, white dog—in a big bear hug before setting his paws back down onto the street and smiling down at him as she scratched his head.

"Muusti would disagree," Suule commented.

"Muusti loves everyone, though," Kojatere said, trying not to slip into her dog-voice as she crouched down to pet the soft fur between Muusti's ears, "He doesn't want me to change or behave or be like everyone else."

She glanced up at her brother, "I hope you're not trying to do the same."

He arched an eyebrow, "I'm not."

Then he looked over toward their parents, "Honestly, I don't think they are, either. You shouldn't not change just because you're stubborn though."

Kojatere let out a small growl, then bit her lip to keep from laughing as Muusti echoed it.

"I'm not saying become a different person entirely," Suule said, "Just try a little harder in some areas. Maybe choose like...six rules to actually follow."

Kojatere rolled her eyes, "I'll do that when the world ends because someone didn't follow the rules."

Suule snorted, "Even then, you'll find some way to get around them."

Kojatere smiled at that, then rose to her feet, keeping one hand on Muusti.

"If you don't tell me before you go, I'll embarrass you in front of Hamado."

Suule studied her for a moment, expression unreadable, and Kojatere blinked as Suule took a deep, tired breath.

"Are you really sure you want to join the Forces?" he asked.

"What do you mean?"

"Things aren't as great and simple in the Union Forces as everyone seems to think, Tere," he said bringing his mask in front of him. He stared down at it, playing at the edge with his fingers, "We do help people, but...I'm not even entirely out of training yet, and I've seen things I didn't sign up for. I knew it wouldn't be easy. I just—"

Kojatere took her brother's hand as he cut off with a sigh.

He smiled at her, then his gaze grew firm, "Serving means following orders, Tere. Even orders that you may disagree with that come from officers who haven't earned your respect or just plain don't deserve it. That's something you'll need to prepare for."

Suule took a deep breath as his words sunk in, and the smile was back, "Don't waste your time whining about Aiti and Bamama or about how no one gives you a challenge anymore. Teach or help others here, and try putting more effort into making friends. And don't try to get out of your contract and enlist again—you're the one that stayed on."

Kojatere sighed, "I know. I won't. I was...in a bad place when I tried that. I just wanted to be back with you again."

Suule gave her a tight smile, "I'm sorry I wasn't there."

He glanced toward the street then, and a few more timeoruu blipped in and out as he looked back to her.

Kojatere started to look in that direction, when Suule drew her into a tight hug, "Remember what I said, okay? And try to think of at least *some* options besides enlisting."

Kojatere threw her arms around her brother, squeezing him as her chest and throat grew tight.

"I'm going to miss you a lot," she whispered.

"Me, too."

They held onto each other for a while before Kojatere picked up the soft hum of an electric engine, and released Suule to glance over at its source.

A Natari man wearing a uniform nearly identical to Suule's stood up in the driver's seat of his motorcarriage and waved from the street. The white coat was striking against the man's maskless, red face. After studying him for a moment, Kojatere smirked at Suule.

He waved back, then frowned down at her, "What?"

"Hamado?"

"Yeah."

"Just a friend?"

Suule rolled his eyes, but Kojatere caught the grin tugging at his lips.

"I'll miss you."

"You just said that."

"I know. I need you to feel bad about leaving."

Suule shook his head and gave her another hug before petting Muusti, then walking over to their mothers. Muusti followed, leaving

Kojatere alone, leaning against the lamp post. When Suule finally walked over to Hamado and climbed into the motorcarriage, he embraced his friend, then smiled at Kojatere again and waved before putting on his mask.

Kojatere took a few steps forward and looked after them as they drove off down the street. For a moment, she considered racing after them until they reached the town limit, but she heard footsteps approaching from behind her a few seconds before two sets of arms wrapped around her.

Taking a deep breath, Kojatere took a hand in each of hers. Today, she would try to face her mothers without snapping at them or running up to her room. She could do it, but she had to make herself want to. *I'll make you proud, Suule. I'll do better. Just stay alive long enough for me to join up and serve alongside you.*

The world swirled black, violet and blue.

Exodus countdown: 19 days, 6 hours, 8 minutes

Othaashle gasped as she came back to reality. She'd lost count of how many visions had come back to her now, replaying moments in time from Kojatere's youth that she'd lived through since the incident with Boaathal. Now, however, she knew them not as mere visions, but—

Light flashed white, red and gold.

C. 32 years, 2 months, 19 days before the Destruction of Yrmuunthal

Kojatere leaned over the railing of the small, dark motorboat, breathing in the salt air as she basked in the heat of Lightside's ever present sun. Despite the wind created by their craft's movement, a warm damp breeze rose up every now and then off the rippling orange waters, making her light-cover seem even heavier and more constricting. She must have twitched or squirmed, because she heard Asuuri laugh from behind her.

Turning around Kojatere glared at her Natari friend, even though her mask hid the expression.

"Stop enjoying yourself."

Asuuri smirked at her. The gorgeous Natari woman had kicked off her boots and taken off her shirt, which sat at her hips, the sleeves tied like a belt. She wore a thin, sleeveless white undershirt, but between the hot, sticky air, and the spray from the water, it clung to her, leaving very little to the imagination and displaying her moonstone gemcrest. Kojatere certainly didn't mind the view.

"Jealous?" The other woman asked, as though reading her thoughts.

Kojatere rolled her eyes and tried to concentrate on the view rather than her friend. A few oceanoruu sped alongside the boat, taking the forms of tiny fish and dolphins as they hopped in and out of the water.

The island itself wasn't exactly what Kojatere had imagined when she thought of Lightside. Rather than pristine beaches backed by thick, lush forests, gnarled, overgrown shrubs reached out over the rocky coastlines. Their leaves were still dark green, teal, pink, purple, and red, but all more subdued than she'd imagined.

At a contented sigh from Asuuri as the woman stepped up to the boats railing, Kojatere glared at her again, "You're giving our driver quite the show."

Asuuri glanced back toward the rear of the boat, and Kojatere followed her gaze. A Samjati man wearing an unadorned black mask that seemed to blend in with his dark light-cover sat right next to the motor, hand on the rudder, keeping them on their course. So far, he hadn't spoken, despite the few questions they'd thrown his way.

When Kojatere looked back to her friend, she found Asuuri grinning, "I don't mind. If we're going this far out from the port, he probably doesn't see too many attractive women that often."

Kojatere rolled her eyes, then turned back to their driver, "Are there any beaches where we're going? Ones a bit less rocky?"

The man didn't even glance her way.

Asshole.

For a moment, Kojatere thought about pestering him, but Asuuri turned her back toward the railing, angling her to the front of the boat.

"Don't bother with him," Asuuri said wrapping her arms around

Kojatere's waist as she looked over her shoulder. She pointed up ahead, "Look! I think we're almost there."

The boat began to slow as they neared a rocky mouth formed by two arms of jagged stone. Once they were close enough, Kojatere grinned as she took in the cove. A wide, sandy beach stretched from one rock wall to the other. Military tents on concrete bases sat back from the water, and Kojatere thought she saw an opening and a dirt road way near the back. Off to her right, a concrete jetty stuck out past the shore into the water. Two figures—both in fatigues—stood at it's edge, looking toward them.

Kojatere grinned, squeezing Asuuri's hands, "I think I'm gonna like this place."

"Me, too."

As they drew closer, Kojatere brightened her clearnodes just enough to let her make out the faces of the two figures on the jetty.

She groaned.

How did he even get here?

"What is it?" Asuuri asked.

Kojatere sighed, "Better put your shirt back on. That's Aiteperit."

Aiteperit, her brother's friend, had met them at a bar in town, prepped them, then led them to the boat with their mysterious driver before saying he had something to do in town.

Asuuri let go of her waist, and as Kojatere heard her friend getting dressed, she brightened her clearnodes even further—as much as she could without the noise from the motor and the waves hurting her ears.

That was definitely Aiteperit. She'd known he would a part of this operation, but hadn't realized he would be a part of the welcoming committee.

And why is Mnene with him instead of Suule?

She thought that was Mnene, at least. His mask had the same markings.

Kojatere caught the movement of their lips, but even if she'd been closer, the waves and the boat's motor would have drowned out their words.

As the boat slowed, and the wind created by their passing disappeared, so did the windoruu. Heatoruu replaced them. Little bulbous figures that danced on Kojatere's arms where she felt the sun's heat most. When she flicked or swatted at them, they grew little faces that looked aghast she would do such a thing.

Looking back toward the jetty, Kojatere dimmed her clearnodes and studied the two men waiting for them.

Aiteperit looked basically the same: high cheekbones, full lips, red-orange skin just a bit lighter than Asuuri's. He was of a medium, if fit, build, with short black hair, a pointed nose, dark Natari eyes, impeccable posture, and black spot-markings that helped obscure the occasional blemish on his skin. What looked like a patienceoruu stood on his shoulder—a little violet figure with folded arms and a posture just as stiff as Aiteperit's.

Mnene wore a light-cover version of military fatigues, just like Kojatere. His mask was simple, bearing a light feather pattern. Like all Samjati soldiers, rather than forgoing a name or stylizing the letters, he had his name spelled out in both scripts. Atongan characters on one side, snowscript on the other.

When they pulled up alongside the jetty, their driver tossed one rope to Aiteperit, and Kojatere tossed the one at the front to Mnene. Once they were secured, both men extended their hands toward Kojatere and her friend. Kojatere took Mnene's arm, and Asuuri, Aiteperit's.

"Good to see you again, Mnene," Kojatere said, wobbling her head as she clasped the man's arm, "I didn't realize you were a part of this unit."

The stocky Samjati man wobbled his head back, "Good to have you here, Kojatere. I was part of the initial team. When I heard we had new blood coming, I hoped it would be you."

Kojatere caught the hint of nerves in the man's voice that meant he still had a crush on her, and frowned under her mask. Mnene was nice, handsome and well-built under those clothes, but not her type.

And if I'm not sleeping with Asuuri while we're here, I'm definitely not sleeping with him.

Kojatere wobbled her head and turned to Aiteperit. She grinned as she spotted something on his fatigues.

"Aiteperit," she said, "Looks like you're slipping."

He frowned at her, and she pointed to the sleeve of his uniform, "Missed a spot, grease monkey."

Aiteperit sighed, "Good to have you here, Kojatere."

Kojatere grinned, then looked back toward the opening of the cove.

"Are we going to need to come in like that every time?" she asked, "That was a long, annoying trip."

"Yes," Aiteperit said, "Due to the nature of this outfit, unless we drive into any of the smaller towns or villages by the backroads, we will need to take precautions when entering and exiting this base."

Kojatere rolled her eyes, then scanned the tents behind the beach, frowning. She looked back to Aiteperit, "Where's Suulehep? Why isn't he out here?"

Aiteperit rolled his eyes and looked toward the boat, "Can you just stop already?"

Kojatere frowned, about to follow Aiteperit's gaze, when two large arm wrapped around her pinning her arms at her sides.

"Miss me, 'Tere?"

Kojatere's eyes went wide at the sound of her brother's voice, and she pushed out of his grip, whirling around.

She punched him in the chest, "Asshole! I almost threw you into the water!"

Suulehep wobbled his head, laughing, "Do you know how hard it was to be silent the whole way over?"

Kojatere growled, but hugged her brother, "Idiot."

She pulled back, "What's with the mask?"

Aiteperit sighed from behind her, "He wanted to surprise you."

Kojatere raised a fist, ready to punch her brother again, but he waggled a finger at her, then gestured to his chest, pulling back part of the fabric and revealing a sergeant's arrows.

"Be nice," he chided, "I outrank you now. If you beat me up or mouth off, I can beat your ass or assign you to latrine duty and no one will say anything."

Kojatere sniffed, then grinned, folding her arms over her chest, "So you admit I can beat you up."

Suule barked a laugh and pulled her into another hug, "I missed you, 'Tere."

"Me too, Suule."

He wobbled his head when he released her, nodding toward Aiteperit, "He outranks you, too."

Kojatere blinked, then turned toward Aiteperit.

Shit.

She didn't know how she'd missed it before. Sewn just above Aiteperit's left breast pocket was the single silver bar of a lieutenant. Kojatere herself was still a corporal, as was Asuuri.

Kojatere took a deep breath and saluted Aiteperit, "Forgive me for my lack of respect, sir."

Aiteperit grinned, surprising Kojatere.

"Forgiven" he said, "Though if you're not careful, you might get put on leak duty."

"Understood, sir."

Aiteperit glanced at Suulehep, then back to her, "Relax, Kojatere."

Kojatere lowered her hand.

"Sirs," Asuuri said, stepping up behind Kojatere, "Forgive me, but given the importance of our outfit, I thought we'd have more than, well..."

"It doesn't look like anything special," Aiteperit said as Kojatere looked around, "Because it isn't supposed to. Our guards and patrols are hidden as well. We have everything we need hidden underground and inside the rock walls of the cove. Beck in those caves, we have a few larger vessels that hold equipment."

Kojatere frowned, scanning the cove and its beach again, then blinked.

"The concrete."

"Exactly," Suule said, "To anyone passing by, this just looks like an offshoot of the naval base at the port, because the Union is not officially or openly affiliated with Mahela."

"That would threaten the island's trade routes," Asuuri said.

Aiteperit nodded, "And with those, the livelihoods of its people."

Kojatere nodded to herself, then glanced at Asuuri and realized her friend was glaring at her.

Right.

Kojatere's cheeks grew hot under her mask.

"Everyone," she said, pushing Asuuri forward, "I'm sure you know from our files, but this is Asuuri. Asuuri, this is my brother, Suulehep, Mnene, an old friend, and Aiteperit, our..."

"Commander of your unit," Aiteperit finished, extending a hand to Asuuri. He looked between her and Kojatere as Asuuri shook his hand, "I selected you two because I believed you would be a good fit for our outfit here. You are both skilled auroramancers, have shown exemplary tactical and leadership skills in getting your previous units out of tough situations, and seem to have a flare for...creativity in fulfilling your orders. I hope I'm correct in my assessment."

He paused, glancing back toward the base, then looked to both Kojatere and Asuuri once more. He saluted, then gave them each a tight smile, "I have to report into Operation Command and finalize things now that you've arrived, but Sergeant Suulehep is my second. He will show you around. Mnene, with me."

Mnene wobbled his head at Kojatere and Asuuri, then started after Aiteperit as the Natari officer turned back toward the base. Aiteperit paused after a few steps and looked back.

"Oh, and welcome to Operation Phantom."

The world swirled black, violet and blue.

Exodus countdown: 19 days, 6 hours, 8 minutes

Memories.

Kojatere—Othaashle? Othaashle—lay on her back now.

These were memories, not just visions. Boaathal hadn't been trying to show her a spy within the Imaia. Instead, somehow it had begun a process that restored her memories. Yet even as it had done that, the Aathal had damaged other memories. Those of her earliest days as Othaashle. The way they—

Light, again.

C. 30 years, 3 months, 20 days before the Destruction of Yrmuunthal

Clear orange water surrounded Kojatere. Even after being on Lightside for so long, it still fascinated her that she could actually see without brightening her clearnodes or attaching a light to her goggles.

And the water was warm. That was the best part.

She'd always loved swimming, even in Darkside's freezing, black oceans, but here she felt like she could really explore.

This cove and the reef that lay beyond, hidden beneath the waves were excellent spots for her, too.

As her lungs started to burn, Kojatere kicked to the surface and sucked in a deep breath of humid, salty air.

On instinct, Kojatere glanced back toward the base.

The others laid on the beach or floated in the surf where their feet could still touch the rocks and pale grey sand beneath, but swimming farther out was what relaxed Kojatere. Being here pushed her to always be doing something, so she found peace in making the most of her down time.

Drawing in another deep breath, she dunked her head back beneath the water and used a greynode enhanced kick to propel her down toward the reef. The flippers helped, especially with her antlers. They'd probably been great for shoveling through snow back before her ancestors had created wood and metal shovels, and now they were great for fashion and the occasional close-quarters fight where Kojatere's opponent didn't expect her to use them; they were ill-suited for swimming.

At least there's no kelp around here.

That had been a mess she never hoped to repeat.

As Kojatere came closer to the reef, she smiled at all the coral and the little schools of shining, slivery-orange fish that swam by. There were others that had bright colors and stripes and patterns, and Kojatere even glimpsed a marlin and a few orange-fin tuna swimming through the waters, their bright orange coloring shimmered under the light that shone down from the surface.

Those were supposed to be deep water fish, but something about these reefs and the currents around the islands made them draw close every now and then, which made for wonderful meals when they got the chance to catch them and prepare them right out of the water.

The thought made Kojatere's mouth water.

She swam around a while longer, using her greynodes to help propel her through the water, her greennodes to create small currents to help speed her even further or guide fish close, and her clearnodes to help her spot little fish and crustaceans that camouflaged themselves among the coral and anemones.

Though Samjati and Natari were the only life-forms on Natari with full gemcrests and the ability to use auroramancy—except for the legendary Draakon, of course—all plants and animals had biogems that helped them adapt to life Efrumani's different, often extreme biomes.

Most species only had one or two types, and many of those were the easiest to harvest for georaurals.

Normally, she would be worried about depleting her auroralight reserves on the chance that they needed to immediately deploy for an urgent mission, but everyone in their unit carried an extra gembrace, even here. Kojatere's was strapped around her waist over her wetsuit that doubled as a full lightcover.

After exploring the reef for a bit, Kojatere came up for another breath, then let herself sink back down about a meter. She closed her eyes for a moment and let herself just hang suspended in the water. She opened her eyes when she felt a bit of movement around her in the water, and grinned when she saw a few fish coming toward her to swim around her antlers.

When she could no longer hold her breath, Kojatere kicked herself to the surface again. This time, she didn't duck down immediately. Her lungs were getting a little tired of that.

Instead she treaded water and looked toward the shore, brightening her clearnodes.

Asuuri and Mnene lounged near the edge of the water with Suule, who had his guitar out. She couldn't tell if he was playing a song or just absentmindedly fingerpicking, but Asuuri kept smiling over at him and twisting so her body was in full view. Kojatere hadn't had the heart to break it to her that Suule preferred men.

For a while, Kojatere had thought her brother had a thing with

Mnene, but the man's recent attempts at flirting with her had put that to bed. She hadn't done anything more than flirt back, however. Mnene was attractive, but so was Asuuri. Kojatere and her friend had enjoyed each other's company as regulars, but they'd agreed that it would be bad continuing with that in such a small, tight-knit group like this. Sticking to that wasn't always easy, though.

While those three lounged, Luujyndama, Hambruus, and Akna swam in the surf, riding waves and splashing each other. The other four on their team, Rykard, Samuuka, Ngonda, and Yende, were running around on the sand throwing a ball back and forth.

Gulls and pelicans sat on the cove walls or flew overhead, occasionally diving into the water after some of the smaller fish. Kojatere frowned at the birds, tempted to try and skewer one with an ice lance.

She and the others had cleaned enough bird shit off the tents and buildings for several lifetimes.

A metallic glint caught Kojatere's eye, drawing her attention to the garage at the back of the cove. She brightened her clearnodes further.

Aiteperit leaned over one of the motorbikes they kept for going into town and the occasional scout around the island. He had his coat off, tied around his waist, leaving him in a white, sleeveless shirt that clung to his torso with sweat. With her clearnodes, she could even see the few grease-stains on the shirt.

For a moment, Kojatere let herself admire her commander. He wasn't as stuck up as she'd initially thought, and the man knew how to lead a team, even if he didn't go on every mission with them. He was still a bit stiffer than she would have liked, though. She tried to admire his arms and his ass, especially since he bent at the hip instead of the back, but it ruined it for Kojatere knowing that he did that to make sure he didn't compress his spine or risk ruining his perfect posture.

It did reassure her, though, that even stoic, implacable Aiteperit needed to decompress after a mission.

This last one hadn't even been bad. They'd had a few injuries, but nothing to serious, and no losses. Still...that didn't make what they did any easier. Taking out fanatics and insurrectionists who hurt innocent people needed to be done, but the clandestine nature of their team meant they rarely received any praise for it. All they saw was violence, and just how cruel people could be when religion or greed was involved. Sometimes she was so desperate for an escape...

She and Asuuri had almost broken their rule after a few particularly bad missions.

Kojatere shook herself and looked back to Aiteperit. She sucked in a deep breath and plunged back beneath the water just as he looked toward her.

She turned as she sank, and when Kojatere stopped herself, using her arms and legs to hang in the water once more, she found herself gazing out at the open water.

Her chest grew tight at the tendrils of dread that crept over her as she looked at that impenetrable orange wall. *That* reminded her a bit too much of darkside.

People had always thought she was crazy for swimming in those waters, especially when there were no auroras to light the skies. Swimming in a river or walking in the surf was one thing, but most people went no farther than that.

Kojatere always had, though that didn't mean she wasn't scared of that vast, impenetrable expanse. The fear of that unknown was balanced by the thrill of venturing so close, and the awe and wonder that made her skin tingle at such a sight. Kojatere had never been this deep in Darkside waters, though. She'd never hung a few meters below the water and looked out into a wall of water that seemed to hide nothing, when it hid so much. Doing that now, she could see why most people ventured no farther than they could walk into Darkside's black waters.

A low hum reached her ears, snapping Kojatere out of the trance-like state just in time for her to look up and to the left as a boat sped overhead, cutting through the water and toward the cave.

Kojatere flared her greynodes and shot up to the surface. Just before the boat disappeared into the cave, she caught sight of a stylized, twelve-pronged snowflake of Kweshrima's Knights on the side.

How did I not notice that sooner?

She looked to the shore and saw Suule and the others on their feet. Those in the water stood waist-deep, looking after the boat, and the other four had stopped playing ball.

Brightening her clearnodes, Kojatere saw Aiteperit standing rigid next to the motorbike he'd been working on. She took that as her cue to head in, and flared her greennodes and greynodes.

When reached the shore, she headed for Suule and brightened her violetnodes before tossing him, Mnene and Asuuri each a ball of salty, violet ice to cool off with.

"That boat had the symbol of the Knights on it, right?" Kojatere asked her brother, holding a forth ball of violet ice to the back of her neck. The water was warm and refreshing, but now that she was out of it, the heat and humidity were already starting to sink in.

"I've seen that symbol before," Suule said, pressing the ice to his forehead, "I think that's Phantom."

Kojatere blinked, cocking her head as she detached the goggles from her mask. Suule had eventually admitted they had no evidence one way or another that this Phantom was *the* Phantom, though he'd told her that Aiteperit believed he *was* that Phantom, and that the legends about him were under-inflated, if anything.

"I didn't realize our outfit had anything to do with the Church."

Suule shrugged, "I don't think it does. Not really, at least. It could just be one of Phantom's people. Aite and I ran into them a few times even before we were recruited to Symuuna."

"I'm guessing we have orders, then?" Asuuri asked. She and Mnene already had their towels over their shoulders.

Suule didn't answer. Instead, he cocked his head and turned back toward the tents.

Kojatere looked past him to find Aiteperit trotting up to them, jacket still undone, though he'd stripped off the undershirt.

Kojatere took a deep breath when she realized she was staring at her commander's well-muscled torso. The Natari stripes and deep red of his skin only served to emphasize his physique. Not for the first time, Kojatere found herself grateful for her mask.

"Mnene, Asuuri, make sure everyone is dressed and ready to deploy if necessary."

The two soldiers saluted, then started waving to the others as they headed for the tents.

Aiteperit looked to Kojatere and her brother. A patienceoruu—she wasn't sure if it was the same one that was almost always with him, or if he just managed to attract whichever one was near—floated over his shoulder in a double-ring pattern.

"I think that's Phantom," he said, nodding toward the cave, "I want you two with me."

"Any idea what to expect, Captain?" Kojatere asked.

To her surprise, Aiteperit frowned, looking down with a hand to his chin. He usually made a point of looking people in the eye—even Samjati.

"I'm not sure," he said, "I usually get orders through the base, and they're usually quite general. Part of the reason I took this post was that I would be able to work relatively autonomously within some general guidelines."

He took a deep breath and straightened, looking both of them in the eye.

"Let's get cleaned off and dressed in fatigues. And quickly. Phantom is not a patient man."

Exodus countdown: 19 days, 6 hours, 8 minutes

Slipped from her mind even now as she grasped at them was due to something more than just the passing of time. Why had it—

Light flashed.

C. 30 years, 3 months, 20 days before the Destruction of Yrmuunthal

"This isn't right."

Kojatere glanced at her brother to find him staring at the projection, features intense. She could practically the gears turning in his head.

"Something you want to share, Lieutenant?" Phantom asked.

"This seems like a trap, sir."

Phantom folded his arms over his chest, "Go on."

Suule nodded.

"Our outfit's existence has been kept secret so far, but our actions have not gone unnoticed. The Union or a mercenary company will fail, and then within a week, their mistake is corrected. A peacekeeping mission or relief effort will be threatened. As soon as anyone hears about that, the threat is eliminated. I'm usually the one that goes into town, sir, or the one who scouts out an area and gets information from the locals when needed. People whisper about us and the other teams Captain Aiteperit has under his command. Usually, it's connected with the Phantom of legend, but I've even heard talk when we've returned home on leave."

"Your point, Lieutenant?"

"The Imaia won't attribute to Kweshrima or her Phantom, sir," Kojatere said, "They're too smart and too experienced for that. And so are the peoples that have resisted their efforts at colonization. Then there's the girl. Her family may have the resources that House Juusaran is demanding, but I think they are being over-inflated for our benefit. Saltpeter isn't exactly rare—most mines that were destroyed in the Cabal's time have been found and rebuilt. The horses and eagles are rare enough, but House Olvia would have more power and influence than they display if they were really worth the life of their heir. This is about drawing us out and either exposing or eliminating us. That's what I would do."

"And what exactly is your plan of action, Lieutenant?" Phantom asked, "Of course this is a trap. If we let it slide, then the Imaia grows more confident, feeds the corruption within the Union, and robs us of valuable resources. After that, they won't even bother with a trap, because you will still be a problem for them to eliminate, and they'll have more intel and resources. That is why I brought this to you, and not any of the other Phantom teams."

"It doesn't matter if we're the best," Kojatere snarled, jabbing a finger at the projection of the Juusaran estate, "Look at that terrain. There's no good approach. Members of your best team *will* die doing this. Don't you—"

"Silence."

Kojatere snapped her jaw shut and looked to Aiteperit. He didn't acknowledge her, and Kojatere had to hold in a sigh. He'd earned her respect, but she still had problems reading him.

She looked back to Phantom to see his masked head swivel as he studied each of the three of them.

"This is your job, soldiers. This is what your team was created to do. We strike out at those who deal with the Imaia and pursue petty attempts to enrich themselves at the cost of a greater good—especially when that happens within the Samjati. Darkside needs to be free. You *think* you know what the Imaia is capable of, but I've seen it firsthand. If they set a trap for us, we need to spring it and come out on top. Is that understood?"

They all nodded, though Kojatere's jaw was tight, "Yes, sir."

"Good."

He pointed to the table with one hand and reached into the folds of his lightcover with another.

"This image is a few months old. When I had it scouted for this mission after hearing of the girl, my people were able to retrieve these. I expect this mission to be carried out with your usual ferocity and effectiveness."

"I would actually like to discuss a few more details about this mission, sir," Aiteperit said.

Phantom cocked his head, but nodded.

"Lieutenant Suulehep," Aiteperit said, "You are dismissed. Lieutenant Kojatere, wait outside for me."

Kojatere clenched her teeth as she and Suule exited the room. She knew she shouldn't have called Phantom an asshole, but that wasn't exactly inaccurate.

Once they were out of the room, Suule shot her a sympathetic smile and squeezed her shoulder before walking past her toward the stairs.

Kojatere drew in a deep breath and leaned back against the wall.

Aiteperit and Phantom didn't take long to finish whatever they were talking about. The vents and the door's soundproofing interfered with her enhanced hearing, unfortunately.

When they came out of the room, Phantom didn't even seem to acknowledge her as he walked past. Kojatere didn't acknowledge the man either. She waited until she heard the other doors hiss and click behind him before glaring at Aiteperit.

To her surprise, he didn't look like he was going to reprimand her. His shoulders looked a bit more bowed than usual as he studied her.

"You know we have to do it."

Kojatere frowned, looking down, "Doesn't mean I have to like it."

He nodded, "Phantom may be cold, but he's right. If we don't go after the Imaia here, we risk them digging in, making their position stronger."

Kojatere grinned at that.

"And you trust that Phantom isn't the one trying to eliminate us?"

Aiteperit snorted.

"Honestly? No. I trust those he works for, though."

Kojatere cocked her head, "You gonna elaborate on that, sir?"

Aiteperit sighed, "There are certain things I can't share with you or Suulehep, Kojatere. No matter how much easier it would make things on me."

He took a step closer, "Know this, though. Phantom's goal is to complete the mission. My goal is to keep you all alive while doing it. Just don't call him an asshole next time. No matter how much you think he deserves it."

Kojatere nodded, and Aiteperit straightened, reaching behind him and opened the door, "Good. Now, we need to go over every detail you remember about the Juusaran estate from your tour. We can use as many orangenodes as you need to get everything just right. I have a plan."

Darkness.

Exodus countdown: 19 days, 6 hours, 8 minutes

Done that? What was it trying to do?

Even Ynuukwidas doesn't understand the Aathal. I don't think Skadaatha does either.

White, red and gold.

C. 30 years, 3 months, 18 days before the Destruction of Yrmuunthal

Shards of broken, frozen rock and soiled, dark snow rained down on Kojatere as a battery hit the outcrop just above where she and Suule pressed themselves against the cliff wall, trying to avoid enemy fire from the estate at the top.

Fortress is more like it.

Phantom's photos had only told half the story. Once the Juusara guards had discovered her team's presence, they'd revealed even more men and weaponry. The manor was a military installation disguised as a rustic, if lavish, country retreat.

And it was snowing.

Normally, Kojatere would have enjoyed the snow. Here, it was a nightmare that obscured cracks and smaller rocks and made scaling the treacherous cliffside even more deadly. Their camo fatigues helped them blend in, but that wasn't much comfort when the enemy had the high walls.

There aren't even any oruu.

She'd seen a few on the way over, but they're disappeared once the fighting started. The spirits hated violence.

Darkside's eternal night made the situation even worse. Kojatere had never really noticed how much more difficult it was fighting here than on Lightside. She could see better here, with or without a mask, but a dark sky against dark rock and dark, angular architecture and the occasional dark clouds of powdersmoke all blended together to cloud Kojatere's vision and make her uncertain of exactly what she was seeing.

At a momentary pause in the falling rocks, Suulehep popped out from his place beside her and fired a few rounds up at the wall. He shouldered the rifle, using a single arm to aim and fire it—a falling shard of rock had sliced open his shoulder. He'd said he was fine, but he always said that.

As her brother distracted the defenders, Kojatere leaned away from the cliff and twisted. She brightened her clearnodes, aimed at one of the gun barrels that poked down over the battlements, and flared her violet nodes before pressing herself back against the cliff.

She heard someone curse as metal crunched and screamed, and grinned just before dimming her clearnodes.

The batteries started again, and more rocks and snow rained down on her and Suule.

He pulled himself closer to her, "Nice shot."

He had to yell for her to hear him over the attack from above.

Kojatere sighed beneath her mask. It was hot and sweaty. Its filter did little to block the bite of sweat and powder.

"I don't know if we'll be able to get the team out of here, much less complete the mission," she roared over the gunfire, "How did they get so much rotary gun tech over here without anyone noticing? That shouldn't have even gotten through the twilight band much less to a private manor like this."

Suule shrugged, "These old houses have deep pockets. That puts them above pretty much every law until they piss off another house with even more money to throw around. The Imaia seems to like using people like that, for all they talk about eliminating those same people in their own territory."

Kojatere gritted her teeth. More and more, she had begun to despise those who hoarded wealth. No good ever came of it. Even those who made big displays of spending their money to help people usually only did so to draw attention away from how they were hurting someone else at the same time. The Imaia had that part right, at least.

"Any ideas?" her brother asked.

Kojatere thought for a moment, then frowned. She had one, but Suule wouldn't like it.

"Hold here," she said, "I'm gonna see how Aiteperit and the others are doing. Watch for a signal to give them hell. You know it when you see it."

"Will I? There's a lot going on, if you haven't noticed."

"You'll know."

They waited for another pause, and this time, Suule threw a few coldflashes toward the battlements as she brightened her rednodes and conjured a darklight shield above her. The darkness blotted out the dim light of the stars, and Kojatere nearly tripped over a loose stone before her vision adjusted.

It didn't take long for her to reach another divot in the cliff where

Akna, Hambruus, and Mnene had taken cover. Hambruus was dead—propped up against the cliff wall between the two others, a dark spot on his shoulder between his helmet and shoulder armor.

Kojatere took a deep breath, praying for him, then looked to Mnene. "Where's the captain?"

She had to yell again for him to acknowledge her.

"Further up," he yelled, pointing toward the switchbacks Phantom had originally wanted them to take toward the fortress, "I think the rest of the unit is with him."

Kojatere nodded, "I'm going on to him. Suule is back the way I came. Bring him over here, then work on getting back with the rest of the unit."

Mnene saluted, and Kojatere brightened her rednodes again. She brightened her greynodes and greennodes, too, using them to leap around the rocky cliffside, taking larger strides and pushing and pulling on the ice and snow when she slipped or there was enough packed down for her to do so.

She breathed in the cold, thin air as she did. It made the heat under her mask a bit easier to bear, but made the sweat and grime feel worse, making her itch to shower or jump in a river.

When the rest of the team came in sight, Kojatere brightened her clearnodes, then cursed and hurried toward them.

Asuuri and Luujyndama knelt on the ground on either side of Aiteperit under a large outcrop. Samuuka, Ngonda and Yende pressed themselves against the cliffside, firing their rifles up at the battlements and filling the air with powder smoke. Rykard sat against the rock wall with bandages around his calf and thigh, holding splints to both. His had his mask tilted up. He was alive, but his expression was distant.

Kojatere forced herself to look back to Aiteperit, and knelt down next to Asuuri, forcing down her bile at what she saw.

Aiteperit's right arm was gone. He had the shoulder and half the bicep, and that was bleeding out fast despite the makeshift tourniquet someone had tied just above it.

Somehow, he hadn't passed out, and wasn't screaming in pain, though his eyes were squeezed shut.

"What happened?" Kojatere asked, looking to Asuuri.

She shook her head, "I don't know. A new weapon of some kind, but

I've never seen anything that could do this with a single shot. They definitely have some secret Imaia tech up there that even Phantom doesn't know about."

Kojatere ground her teeth.

"That's probably why he sent us here despite it being such a freezing death trap."

None of this was supposed to happen. After the Cabal's attempted coup, hiring and maintaining private armies had been made illegal. Even before that, it had been frowned upon. Members of the church had historically been the only ones allowed to fight, after the tradition of Kweshrima's Knights.

Taking a deep breath and shaking herself back to the present, Kojatere pushed Asuuri aside and took her commander's face with one hand.

"Aiteperit, look at me."

He opened one eye and looked at her, "Yes, Kojatere?"

"I don't think you're getting that arm back," she said, "And I can't burn it, but I can make sure you don't bleed out. It won't be fun."

His jaw bunched, but he nodded, "Do it."

Kojatere looked to Asuuri and Luujyndama, "Hold him down."

Asuuri moved behind him, holding down his shoulders, while Luujyndama moved over his legs, pressing down on his hips with her hands and using the rest of her body to pin his legs.

Kojatere unslung her rifle and held the leather strap out Aiteperit, near his mouth. He glanced between her and it for a moment, then took it between his teeth and nodded at her. She took a deep breath, then held her hand up to the bleeding stump of his arm and flared her violetnodes.

Aiteperit screamed through the leather in his mouth, thrashing beneath Asuuri and Luujyndama , but after a few seconds, no more blood flowed from his arm.

Kojatere hadn't unleashed a full coldflash—that would have been too hard to control, and could have done more harm than good—but she'd flash frozen any and all nerves and blood vessels in the exposed part of Aiteperit's arm, cauterizing them as well as any flame or hot metal would have.

Aiteperit stopped thrashing after a few seconds, going tense, and for a moment Kojatere worried he would seize or go into shock from the pain.

Then he opened his eyes and spat out the leather strap.

"Light, that stings," he hissed. He looked to Kojatere then glanced between Asuuri and Luujyndama, "That's no longer necessary, soldiers."

Both of them nodded and released him. Aiteperit drew in a deep breath, then sat up, though he winced.

Kojatere gaped at him beneath her mask, "How are you even conscious, right now?"

"Trust me, I've been in worse situations."

Aiteperit clutched at his shoulder with his hand and winced as he looked around, "Though not by much."

He looked back to her, "What's your plan, Lieutenant? I take it you didn't come here just to keep me from bleeding out."

Kojatere shook her head, and walked over to the edge of the small, sheltered area, taking a look around herself.

This was much higher than she and Suule had managed, and from here, Kojatere had a decent view of the surrounding area.

She could see the long rise that led down to the town in the distance —one that didn't even come close to matching the opulence of the estate. She saw the river that flowed by the estate and cut through the plains common in this part of Nimikadeka lands, often referred to as the breadbasket of the region. Patches of trees grew around the estate, growing into a few small copses between here and the town, and then a larger forest beyond at the foot of the mountains.

Kojatere turned back to Asuuri, "Keep that river in sight for any surprise reinforcements. We're going to need to get everyone to the evac zone, soon. Suule and the others should be coming up here soon, but they might be pinned down. They'll need someone with rednodes to help get them out if they are."

Aiteperit blinked at that, "You have a plan to get us out?"

Kojatere nodded, "I'm going to draw their fire by completing the mission."

Aiteperit gazed at her, eyes wide, "You're not serious."

She couldn't help but grin, "I know, usually that's your job."

"Lieutenant—"

"You never like my ideas. That doesn't make them bad ideas!"

"Kojatere! Think this through. We have no idea where the girl is, and it's a maze in there."

"I have thought it through," Kojatere hissed, leaning in close, "I know my way around this place better than anyone else."

"No. The plan was to clear it floor by floor, room by room and interrogate those we found along the way. You can't do that on your own."

"I think the pain is getting to you, sir," she said, "You're worrying too much. Interrogation won't be a problem. I'll just kill anyone who gets into my way."

"He's right, 'Tere," Asuuri said, "We need to retreat. The mission is lost. If a few of us go around to lure out the defenders—"

"No," Kojatere barked. She glared between the two of them, though she knew neither could see her eyes through her mask.

"I am going in to get the girl. By myself. I need a few of you to cover me and cause a distraction to draw fire, but that's it. I'll be more maneuverable on my own. Less noticeable. If any of you come after me, you'll only give me more to worry about. Got it?"

Asuuri held her gaze for a moment, frowning, but nodded. Kojatere looked ot Aiteperit.

"Are you sure?" he asked.

She nodded, wobbling her head, "I'm not going to miss out on the opportunity to fuck up this house for what these people have done."

Aiteperit nodded, "Fine. Do it. Go in there and complete the mission.

Kojatere blinked. She'd expected him to object again.

"Alright," she said, looking to Asuuri and Luumyndama, "On my signal. Suule should join in, too."

Both nodded.

"What's the signal?" Luumyndama asked.

Asuuri snorted, "We'll know."

Kojatere smirked, wobbling her head. She primed her rednodes, then flared her greynodes and leapt over the outcrop toward the Juusaran walls.

Black, violet and blue.

Exodus countdown: 19 days, 6 hours, 7 minutes

Heart pounding, Kojatere managed to look up. Off to the side of the dark room, she could see Koruuksi and Estingai frozen against the wall, eyes wide. They—

Light.

C. 30 years, 3 months, 18 days before the Destruction of Yrmuunthal

"If you're transferring, I'm going with you."

Kojatere started, whipping around to see who was behind her.

"Captain?" she breathed.

She and Suule were at the side of his cot in a moment. He looked between them, and glared at Suule when he tried to get Aiteperit to lay down.

Their captain had propped himself up in a sitting position. The scrapes and scratches on his torso told of a shirt ripped to shreds, and while his left arm had few marks on it, a large, messy bandage covered the stump of his right arm.

"How bad did you hit him?" Aiteperit asked her.

Kojatere swallowed, and realized she was blushing.

Aiteperit snorted, which just made it worse.

"That bad, huh?"

Kojatere sighed, "I think he'll only be seeing out of one eye from now on."

Aiteperit blinked, "I'm surprised you landed a hit on him. Seems too paranoid to allow that to happen."

Kojatere blushed again, "I had my amber brightened."

Aiteperit rolled his eyes, "Of course, you did. Still, don't worry about court-martials or anything like that. Phantom is technically outside the chain of command. If I sanitize the report and say we completed the mission due to his intel, we'll be fine. We might have trouble finding promotions or the work we want unless we're extremely visible and vocal, but I've become a bit better at that."

Kojatere frowned, clenching her fists.

"His intel fucked you and Rykard. Hambruus—"

"Wouldn't want us thrown in a pit," Aiteperit said, voice stern, but quiet, "We will remember him. That's all that matters."

Kojatere frowned, folding her arms over her chest.

"Would you come with us?"

Kojatere blinked, realizing Aiteperit was talking to her.

"What?"

"If all three of us leave," Aiteperit said, "It will be a blow to Phantom. Maybe not justice, but it will show those he answers to that his leadership abilities should be questioned. Aside from that, though...I'd like you to come with us."

For some reason, Aiteperit's words made a strange warmth blossom inside Kojatere. It wasn't something she recognized.

"You'd really just leave?" she asked, looking between the two of them. Both nodded.

"This isn't what we signed up for," Aiteperit said, "We're not giving up, but...we will if we fight under these circumstances too many more times, and we can do more good elsewhere. *If* we work together."

Kojatere looked between the two of them, then nodded.

"Alright. Let's do it."

The three of them shared a smile. Then Kojatere's gaze fell to where Aiteperit's hand should have been.

"What about your arm?" She asked.

Aiteperit frowned, looking at the stump.

"That will make things a bit more difficult," he said, "Normally, I'd probably be discharged or relegated to a desk job where I wouldn't be in combat. However..."

Kojatere frowned as he trailed off, then blinked as the rednodes on his chest grew bright, and golden hardlight extended from his stump.

It took roughly the shape of an arm and hand. Very roughly.

Aiteperit played with it for about a minute, then dimmed his rednodes and dismissed the construct.

To Kojatere's surprise, he was grinning.

"Well, not great," he said, "But with some practice and an extra gembrace or two on hand, that shouldn't be much of a problem for too long. I don't need a good-looking hand to carry a rifle, after—"

"Teach me."

Kojatere blushed as Aiteperit and Suule studied her.

She took a deep breath, meeting Aiteperit's gaze. He'd dimmed his rednodes, dismissing the hardlight.

"You were amazing back at the estate," she breathed, "And what you did right now—I've never seen anyone use hardlight that way. I need you to teach me. It will give you practice for using it as your arm."

Aiteperit held her gaze for a long moment. Then he smiled.

Darkness consumed her.

Exodus countdown: 19 days, 6 hours, 7 minutes

Othaashle couldn't remember what she'd been thinking about. She was still Othaashle. She had to be. If she was Kojatere—

No. No, I can't be her.

Her heart thundered in her chest. Would the power that overwhelmed her, flooding her mind with these visions, protect her from cardiac arrest? She didn't want to find out.

I can't be her. I can't—

White, red and gold.

C. 27 years, 4 months, 35 days before the Destruction of Yrmuunthal

"You may know him better as the Flame Swordsman."

The murmurs rose in volume. Normally, Kojatere would have tried to hear what people thought. Right now, she couldn't take her eyes off the massive Natari.

Matsanga. The Flame Swordsman. If this was really him, the man on the dais had lived for centuries, living through the Iron Empire and predating the Imaia itself.

"We brought you here to help counter the Imaia's expansion," the Tuumari woman continued, "And in doing so, serve all Efrumani instead of a single nation or people. It will be hard work. Any sense of normalcy you—"

She cut off as Matsanga stepped forward and gently pushed her aside.

"You are all the best in your respective fields, as we are," Matsanga said, "Here, we'll make you better. You'll need that against Skadaatha and the Imaia."

He gestured behind him, "We've served the people of Efruumani—both Lightside and Dark—for centuries. It's because of us, the Cabal failed. Though we had some help in that from House Tuumari. We called ourselves the Children of the Night, but we haven't been enough. When we're done with you, you won't be Children, but Knights."

Kojatere blinked at that.

As in Kweshrima's Knights?

That would explain all the religious imagery.

Matsanga stepped back then, and nodded to the Tuumari woman, who looked out over those gathered.

"As Matsanga said—our aim is to combat the Imaia's expansion and the destabilization it often causes to make that easier. Our organization will continue to work alongside the Union in a complementary manner toward goals of achieving naval supremacy in Darkside as a deterrent, as well as exploring the extensions and possibilities of auroramancy and georaurals, and their combination with mundane technology—"

"What makes you any different than the Imaia?" Kojatere asked, raising her voice as she stepped forward, "Or the Cabal, for that matter? Don't they both think they're working toward the good of all Efrumani? What makes your Knights any different?"

The Tuumari woman's golden eyes burned at the perceived insult. Just past her, however, Kojatere thought she saw Matsanga grin.

Darkness.

Exodus countdown: 19 days, 6 hours, 8 minutes

If she was Kojatere, that meant she'd betrayed those she loved. Didn't it? Why did she only see Koruuksi and Estingai here?

Where is Aite? Where is Suule? Where is my Svemakuu?

Dark. Light. Red. Violet. Black. White. Gold. Blue.

The colors flashed and swirled, yanking her between past and present. Between the realm of the mind, and that of the body. Between what was and what is…and what would be.

THE VISIONS PULLED KOJATERE, Othaashle—whoever she was—in a thousand directions at once as they poured into her mind. They did not take her and force her to live each one in real time, but rather washed over her before taking purchase in her mind, more like memories than visions.

She fought on a battlefield, a storm of Auroramancy. Important people—Phantom, the elusive Nevisi, even Matsanga himself—told her she was special, that she could be even greater than they. She tasted victory time and time again. Then defeat, her first experience with it, at the hands of fanatics and a powerful warrior, strong and unmovable as a mountain, who seemed neither Samjati nor Natari and wielded a blade reminiscent of Ilkwalerva.

She lay in bed with her husband, taking comfort in his embrace and his love. She spoke to Matsanga, confided in him about the burdens of leadership. She laughed with her family, held her children, those she'd birthed, and those she'd adopted.

Kweshrima bestowed great power upon her. She fought the strange warrior again. This time she emerged as the victor. She made a mistake. One that cost her the incredible power and status she had grown accustomed to and taken for granted. She nearly succumbed to self-pity. She humbled herself before Kweshrima and vowed to be better than she was. Kweshrima had a plan. Kojatere had power again, even greater than before.

It wasn't enough. Ynuukwidas defeated her. Aiteperit tried to save her. He wounded Ynuukwidas. The God King struck him down.

She exploded with pain, body and soul. It wouldn't stop. Something rent her soul in a blinding flash of pain.

Then it stopped.

She became Othaashle. She held Ilkwalerva for the first time. She killed with it. She and Ynuukwidas raised the first of the Redeemed after her. The world, the very fabric of existence trembled as the auroras vanished, and Yrmuunthal perished in a blinding flash of light. Yndlova and Itese flanked her at a High Command meeting. She killed one of the Remnant's leaders and exposed Kweshrima's treacherous betrayal. Ilkwalerva consumed the souls of the last of the Remnant leaders.

Then the visions changed. She knew now that most of the visions, the flashes and impressions of knowledge and sensation were memories.

Others, however, made no sense to her, and slipped away even as she tried to decipher what they could be.

A shining, ancient city lay in peace, hiding under Lightside's sun. A massive war—an invasion—tied three disparate worlds together. A strange, magnificent tree illuminated a sheltered Vale, cut off from the rest of the world. Worlds, hundreds of them, blossomed into being before Othaashle. They spread out among the stars, yet all connected. Massive vessels ventured between them, transporting people, goods, and weapons of war.

Massive, scaled creatures reminiscent of draakon soared above burning landscapes, belching forth fire to add to the conflagration.

A woman rode across a sea of endless grass alongside her wife.

An unlikely couple traveled from world to world to make sure they were always where they were needed.

Myriad peoples ventured to the stars.

A lion and a wolf fought each other when they should have fought together. A tortured warrior succumbed to darkness. It became *his* darkness.

Gods faded away just as a man who had rejected the mantle for so long, finally reached for it.

Men clashed against warriors of storm and stone even as a darkness —an all-consuming void—crept toward them unchallenged.

A massive explosion sent city-sized vessels hurtling through time and space.

Three brothers wielding three distinct blades swore an oath.

Souls forever linked were reborn so they could find each other once more.

A vast shadow in the shape of a man drew seven shining lights toward him.

A haunted man gave himself over to darkness in the hope that he might one day defeat it.

Giants opened paths between worlds, seeking a place to call home.

The Imaia spanned across the stars, yet another empire spread even farther.

Three great forces massed for a war that would spread across entire worlds, while one remained on the edge, undecided.

Colors swirled.

It was too much.

She saw Boaathal burn, Mjatafa Mwonga ravaged. She saw an all-consuming blackness, felt the cold nothingness that made Kweshrima's power seem a thing of light.

She saw a world where assassins deterred leaders from war to keep the peace.

She saw seven warriors journeying throughout the stars, together at first, then broken apart one by one. One of them fell to that black nothingness, another to something else.

She saw a world remade, then shattered to shelter the last of a chosen people.

A man, broken and ravaged, fought for that world against a shadow wielding a blade of darkness.

She saw Skadaatha in combat with a man armored in darkness. His light was almost gone. Almost.

She saw redemption, second chances, unity. Even a sense of... ending...

Light flashed.

No.

The defiant thought broke through even as the visions pulled Othaashle this way and that.

No!

She couldn't deny it. No matter how much she wanted to. All the memories focused on a single person.

Kojatere.

Dark. Light. Red. Violet. Black. White. Gold. Blue.

Light flashed. Colors swirled. Darkness consumed everything.

Othaashle's mind broke beneath the storm.

19

It Wasn't Her Fault

"Though zidanio and aikanuum are so incredibly rare, the amounts gathered near Mount Saanad and Vizier Skadaatha's notions that both may be found elsewhere in Aioa give me great hope for what the Imaia will be able to accomplish with such resources."

Exodus countdown: 19 days, 6 hours, 5 minutes

thaashle...
  No...
Kojatere...
No...
A ragged gasp escaped her lips.
Who...who am I?
She lay sprawled on a surface black as the Darkside sky. It even had its own twinkling stars.
And it was cold.
Against her cheek, against her fingertips as she tried to push herself up. Like the ice nearest Darkside's pole that had never known warmth to make it melt.
She wiped spittle from her jaw, pushing herself up on trembling arms.
"No."

The voice was ragged.

Tears flowed freely down her cheeks, stinging her eyes.

"That can't have been me. It can't!"

But which 'her' do I mean? Which one of them am I?

Two people still warred within her.

Othaashle: Kyfrytari, Deathknight, Mestari, Champion and Supreme Commander of the Golden Imaia. Wielder of Ilkwalerva. A warrior with no equal. Leader and First of the Redeemed.

Kojatere: Champion of Kweshrima's Knights Reborn and the Darkside Union, a warrior with no equal. Mother, sister, and wife.

Mother.

She latched onto that thought. Whoever she was.

I am a mother. Yes. I can do that. I can be that person.

"What did you do?"

Othaashle—Kojatere?—gasped as a strong hands grabbed her by the shoulder, flipping her onto her back. She hit the stone floor hard and choked, gasping for air and blinking through teary eyes at the woman above her.

Estingai. I know her.

Her son's—Svemakuu's—wife.

But, those eyes...why?

The woman seemed on the edge of panic and murder all at once.

"What did you do?" she shouted again. Estingai moved as if to grab Kojatere—Othaashle?—by her coat, but then Koruuksi was there, holding her back.

Koruuksi.

The sight of him made warmth blossom within her.

My son.

That was Kojatere's thought. But...

Didn't Othaashle experience something familiar?

She knew that warmth. That sense of respect and pride in the young man.

There was something else, too. Some other part of her that knew Koruuksi and regarded him similarly. Something more... ancient.

Kweshrima?

No... just her power.

The goddess was...

"Gone," Kojatere gasped. Yes, Kojatere. That part of her felt more real, more natural.

"She's gone."

"What do you mean, 'she's gone'?" Estingai demanded. "Who is gone? What did you do? Something feels different in here."

The woman had begun with ferocity in her words, but by the end, that emotion had morphed into fear.

"Did it work?"

Kojatere looked up at Koruuksi's—at her son's—words. She met those golden eyes—so familiar; they brought even more tears to her eyes —and somehow knew what he asked.

What he'd planned all along.

Kojatere slowly pushed herself to her feet. Her body wasn't weak. Rather, it was still growing accustomed to the incredible power now contained within it.

This form was meant to use such power to its full potential, if never so much of it at once.

As she steadied herself, Kojatere felt her mind expanding once more. Not to the point it had when she'd fallen prey to Kweshrima's trap, but enough that she understood what the goddess had done to her, and that not all she'd seen had been in the past. Much of what she'd seen had made no sense to her, focusing on strange and unfamiliar beings and worlds.

That... void.

Kojatere shivered. She now knew Skadaatha's 'Enemy' that she had created the Imaia to fight. After seeing, experiencing that...she found it hard to blame Skadaatha for all the terrible things the woman had done.

Remembering Koruuksi's question, Kojatere forced a shaky smile to her features.

"It did," she confirmed.

My son.

She turned that smile on a stunned, confused Estingai.

My daughter.

If not in blood, then in every other sense.

"How did you know it would work?" Kojatere asked, turning back to her son.

"What?" Estingai demanded. "If what would work?"

The woman tore herself from Koruuksi's gasp and glared between the two of them. That glare held unbridled hatred as she turned it on Kojatere.

She dropped back to her knees: She was Kojatere again, but she had been Othaashle as well. That woman was still a part of her.

Strangely, some parts of her memory were blurred, both Othaashle's and Kojatere's memories. Reflexively, she tried brightening her orangen-odes, but that did nothing to clear the fog. That still left more than enough memory of what Othaashle had done—what she had done as Othaashle—to make Kojatere want to vomit.

"Kweshrima," she gasped, a cold knot in her stomach. "The goddess stripped away the block on my memory that Ynuukwidas creates when he makes the Re—" She stopped, unable to voice that term and give it even the smallest sense of validity. "When he makes the Lightforged. The souls he turns into Lightforged are broken by their bodies' deaths, held from moving on by a thread. That creates an opening for him to insert a fragment of his power, his very being, into them. The cost of doing so—I don't know if it is something he chose, or an unavoidable part of the process—is that the soul doesn't remember who it once was. It also makes them more like him—more how he sees himself, at least."

She had to keep talking. Talking would keep even her expanded mind from thinking.

"How did you know?" she asked, looking again to Koruuksi.

My son.

He blinked at the question, expression unreadable.

"I... I didn't," he said. "It seemed like the best—" He cut off as his voice caught. His eyes shimmered. "Is it really you?"

Kojatere raised a hand to her mouth as a sob slipped out. Even so, she smiled, nodding.

Focus on him. That will keep everything else at bay.

She rose to her feet and stepped toward him, reaching out. "Koruuksi, my son. I—"

Estingai slapped her hand away, moving between Kojatere and Koruuksi. She was tense, ready for a fight.

"You do *not* get to call him that," she growled, "You left him. You left *us!* You lost that right a hundred times over."

Again, Kojatere found herself on her knees. She clutched her head, shaking it back and forth.

"No," she murmured as all the pain and suffering she'd caused washed over her. "No. It can't be real. I didn't do that."

Yet she knew she had. There were holes in her memory still, blurred patches her mind could grasp at, anything concrete slipping through its fingers. Many, however, were all too clear.

Kojatere remembered leading armies, slaughtering Union soldiers as they tried to rebuff her with near-comical futility. She remembered assassinations, terrorizing refugees while disguised as part of a Union force to make them see the Imaia as their only salvation, throwing the dissidents and those too dangerous to imprison yet too valuable to kill, into Makala.

Auroras, Makala! How could I have ever allowed something like that?

Before, those acts had been justified. They had been missions carried out for the greater good. A part of her still saw them that way. But now she saw the other, darker side as well, the cruelty and cold cunning with which such evil deeds were planned and carried out.

And I led nearly all of them.

Kojatere looked up. She met Estingai's gaze, saw the cold rage and pain there, and knew she deserved it.

What did I take from her? Is that one of the holes in my memory? Or are there simply too many horrible acts to sort through?

"You know it is," Estingai said, her voice like ice. "You know why the mere thought of touching a creature like you should disgust any decent person. Every horrible thing you can remember doing ruined countless lives."

She did.

Why, then? Why did Kweshrima sacrifice herself to return these memories to me instead of just ending me? Was it a final punishment for someone she trusted, who failed her again and again?

Kojatere didn't even know why the goddess had done it. There were vague impressions and ideas, but nothing solid. Nothing concrete for destroying the world she'd been charged with protecting.

She felt herself breaking. She couldn't do this.

"It wasn't her fault, Estingai," Koruuksi said. "Ynuukwidas killed her. Everyone knows that. What we didn't know was that he then twisted her soul. He made her into the monster that happily did all those awful things, just like he does with all the others."

Koruuksi's words were like the light of a single candle floating on an ocean of darkness. Kojatere clung to that light with desperation.

He made me do it. It was my hand wielding the sword, but I never would have done those things if he hadn't forced me to.

Even Skadaatha had been unable to stand against Ynuukwidas. What chance had she had?

Kojatere rose to her feet again. Her legs did not shake this time. Her body had adjusted to the power that burgeoned within it, and she no longer had to fight her own thoughts.

"He is right," Kojatere said, cheeks still wet with tears. "Ynuukwidas twisted me into an extension of his will when he killed me and prevented my soul from moving on. Kweshrima sacrificed herself to strip me of his touch. I failed her, and the two of you, once. I will not do so again."

Koruuksi grinned, pushing past Estingai.

Kojatere pulled her son into her arms, squeezing him.

Her heart caught in her throat for a moment, eyes burning with tears as she pressed her forehead to his.

"My son," she whispered, "I am so sorry. I will make this right."

"Thank you... for coming back to me."

"And how exactly do you propose to do that?"

With a deep breath, Kojatere looked up from her son to her daughter. Such pain.

Kojatere had seen the look before. In the eyes of citizens and soldiers of the Imaia whose families had died at the hands of the Union or the Remnant, and in the eyes of those thrown into Makala. She didn't know if there was anything she could do to ease it.

But I will try. It's the least I can do.

"Your escape plan was failing from the start," she said letting go of

Koruuksi, "but not without merit. I can still make it work and give the two of you and the rest of the Remnant a chance at a home and life worth living rather than one where you merely cling to survival, wandering the stars in search of a home. If you'll let me, that is."

Estingai met Kojatere's gaze, searching. Kojatere let her. She had a plan. She just hoped she could pull it off.

Finally, Estingai gave the barest nod, eyes hard and cold as ice.

"If you betray us, I will end you," she grated, "no matter what you call yourself."

Epilogue 1

Natsoje

Exodus countdown: 19 days, 5 hours, 11 minutes

As Natsoje pushed through the doors to her residential complex, she felt the day's stress start to fall from her shoulders. The first floor was emptier than usual, though Natsoje had caught the first train just as it had left her stop, beating the traffic of those whose shifts coincided with her own.

Still, as she walked down the broad hall toward the lifts at the center of the large building, Natsoje glimpsed a few familiar faces. They were all out in the two atriums that flanked the four halls leading to the center, of course, enjoying the day. Yet when they saw her through the galleried halls, they waved and called to her. She wasn't the only soldier living in the residence, yet the uniform of a lieutenant in the Imaia's Urban Corp., with its blue and yellow stripes running down each pant leg and the red and white armband with the black double-axe and scarlet sun of the Imaia, made her recognizable enough. She had taken her cap off, letting her multitude of thick black braids hang down her back. Between waving at her neighbors and smiling at the children playing hide and seek or catch under their parents' watchful eyes, Natsoje felt herself begin to relax.

When she reached the central spire of the complex, Natsoje headed for the stairs, as usual—she and her family lived on the fifth floor, but she never felt right taking the lifts unless she was carrying a heavy load, even at the end of a long day like today—when she caught a glimpse of Akarna, the building's manager, waiting for one of the lifts. Natsoje had been hoping to catch her before she got home to Myndir and the children.

As she altered her path, Natsoje raised a hand to wave to the woman. "Akarna, do you have a moment?"

The woman bobbed her head as she approached Natsoje, the Samjati equivalent of a smile when wearing their masks. Samjati were a relatively uncommon sight in the main areas of Mjatafa Mwonga, even after the mass migrations. Most stuck to certain areas made to shield their sensitive skin from the sun's constant light. Akarna often had to crouch or bend down to fit her antlers through certain doorways. Natsoje had never seen the woman without her gold and black armband that signified her husband's death in service to the Imaia, however.

"Of course, Lieutenant, what did you need?" the woman asked as the lift door opened.

They shared a look, Natsoje smiling at the couple that stepped out but did not engage in conversation. Retema and Kynde were dressed in very fine clothing reminiscent of the traditional Imbaa style, and the entire building knew they were courting by now.

Best not to keep them from their excursion.

"How many times have I told you to call me Natsoje, Akarna?" Natsoje asked with a raised eyebrow as she and the older woman stepped into the lift, selecting the proper button for their floor. "Honestly, you've known me since long before my promotion."

Akarna flashed a sly smile. "That just means I know how hard you worked for that promotion, Lieutenant. My Vilam tried to downplay things whenever he received a promotion or commendation, but I could always tell how proud it made him feel. He always stood a little straighter when people addressed him by his rank, just like you. Now, what did you wish to talk about?"

Natsoje shifted her shoulders, feeling her cheeks color. She didn't do that. Did she?

"I just wanted to see how the repairs were going, if anyone needs any help, that sort of thing." She softened her voice a little and met the woman's gaze. "How is your son doing?"

Akarna bobbed her head, then waved in an offhand gesture. "Oh, Koryn is fine, dear, you're so sweet. They let him go to work this morning but want him back this evening just to make sure he eats enough. As far as the building goes, there's still a bit of work that needs to be done, but things are going on schedule. Your Myndir was a great help today, actually."

Natsoje raised an eyebrow. "Myndir? What was he doing home?"

Akarna shrugged. The woman was much warmer and more emotive than many other Samjati Natsoje had met. "He said he'd made sure to finish as many orders as he could yesterday and this morning so he could be here to help. If I ever decide to start looking again, you'll have to tell me how you found him—he seems quite wonderful."

Natsoje smiled, feeling a familiar warmth spread through her as she thought of her husband, "He is."

The lift came to a halt and the doors opening a moment later. Natsoje blinked when Akarna stepped out with her, then looked up and realized where the woman must have been going.

Natsoje felt cold as her eyes fixed on the rough hole at the end of the hall. The fighter's blast had torn right through her neighbor Djata's room and into the hall.

A few men and women in rough, practical clothing worked to clear the rubble and scrub away what char and ash they could. Natsoje felt her entire body about to break out in a cold sweat as she remembered the panic she'd felt upon seeing the terrorists' fighters fly over residential areas. Over *her* district.

Years of training allowed Natsoje to take hold of herself and restore calm, though the hand not holding her briefcase rose halfway to the scar at her jawline before she caught herself. She realized Akarna had said something.

"Forgive me," she said, turning her attention away from the wound to her home and focusing on Akarna. "My mind was elsewhere. What was that?"

"Oh, nothing dear. I had just said that I should go see if the workmen need anything. Scarlet Light shine on you."

Natsoje smiled, returning the greeting, and looked after Akarna for a moment as she walked off.

People like her were what had driven Natsoje to enlist and gain the skills and clearances needed to help protect the Imaia and its people. A blow had been dealt to her home, yet if Akarna felt any bitterness, she did not show it. She simply went about her business, helping those who came to assist in the repairs, and making everyone else feel at ease with her calm demeanor. That was something worth fighting for.

Intellectually, Natsoje knew that many of the common folk who had resisted the Imaia in the past had done so out of either desperation or a misguided pride. Soldiering had been better pay than working on a farm or in a factory, or their leaders had crafted some dire reason to get men and women to enlist. Yet it still baffled Natsoje that people would fight over land and resources. The Imaia had fought to spread truth and enlightenment in an effort to free the common people from the yoke their masters held them with. Now they fought to protect the wonderful cooperative society they had created. The last beacon of light on this dying world.

And soon we will fight for freedom itself.

Though Natsoje hoped her children would never have to know the strife and terror of true war, she hoped she would live long enough to one day strike a blow against the Enemy. For now, however, she headed down one of the other hallways. Toward her family.

Natsoje and her husband both did quite well for themselves, yet not as well as some. Therefore, their apartment sat along one of the inner halls rather than around the building's perimeter. From this height, that would have given them a wonderful view of Mjatafa Mwonga's inner district. Natsoje worked toward one day being able to afford such niceties for herself and her family, as all in Imaia did, yet she rarely envied her neighbors who lived in such apartments. With the attack... Natsoje had found new things to appreciate about her current home.

As she opened the door to her apartment, the savory aromas of cooking meat and a blend of spices met her nose, while soft music from the stereo met her ears.

Such a wondrous invention.

Natsoje smiled even before she saw Myndir in the kitchen working with an unfamiliar arrangement of ingredients.

He must be working on one of his experiments.

Her children, Anar and Ykana, sat at the dining room's main table, cards in their hands and set on the table in mostly precise arrangements.

Natsoje hung up her hat, uniform coat, and briefcase on the pegs by the door, closing it behind her, then strode over to embrace her husband from behind as he worked. She settled her hands atop each other over his stomach as she brushed her lips over the spot on his neck she knew he liked.

"I missed you too, dear."

Natsoje smiled. She could hear the grin in his warm, resonant tenor.

Though she was the soldier, and he a tailor, Natsoje always felt more secure when around her husband. She still hadn't figured out if it was the way he towered over her like a redbear, or simply her love for him and that which he expressed in return. He kept himself fit and healthy as all good Imaia citizens did—not to the point which she and her fellow soldiers were required to do so—yet he had always been a larger man, carrying more bulk than the majority of those he cut cloth for. That was part of why he'd gone into the profession—out of a desire to make sure those who were larger or smaller in one way or another than the average citizen were able to find properly-tailored clothing, or get the necessary alterations made by someone who knew exactly what to look for. Myndir could talk for hours on the secrets of making clothing fit just right, or more specifically, the questions most did not know to ask their tailor. And he always informed his customers of what they should ask so that they would know if they ever decided to find a different tailor.

Few had ever needed to.

Natsoje ran her hands up husband's torso, resting them on his massive shoulders. Even with Myndir's skills, they strained at the fabric. He claimed there was only so much one could do with clothing for a man his size, yet Natsoje believed it a feature rather than an annoyance. Myndir knew very well how attractive she found his shoulders.

"I heard you took the day off work," she said, looking past him at the ingredients he worked with. He surprised her with a quick, yet deep kiss, then took advantage of her momentary breathlessness after to shoo her back.

"No peeking," he chided, "I want to see if Anar and Ykana can guess where this dish comes from, and you'll give it away to them if you have any clue what's in it. I only took half the day off. I'm ahead on my work, so I came back to help clear out the damaged apartments and clean what hadn't been damaged."

Natsoje smiled and kissed her husband again before turning to her children.

"I'm deciding that you two are merely so engrossed in your game that you didn't hear me come home, as I would hate to think you simply chose to ignore your mother," she said pointedly as she strode over to the table, resting her hand on the back of Ykana's chair. She heard Myndir chuckle from behind her and couldn't help the smile that spread across her lips.

She schooled herself immediately, however, adopting a firm expression as her children straightened, eyes darting toward her—though Ykana's had to twist.

"Of course not, Aitiba," they said in unison. Ykana began to rise, but Natsoje let herself smile again and raised a hand. She bent down to embrace her daughter, feeling her smile broaden as the little girl gave her a tight hug. She kissed the top of her head, then crossed the table and embraced her son. Anar's hug wasn't as enthusiastic as Ykana's, but Natsoje knew she couldn't expect a child's barely contained enthusiasm for everything in life from the young adult.

"How was school?" she asked, leaning on the high back of Anar's chair.

Ykana looked to her older brother, then up at her, frowning. "Duukebe said that the Night Mother and her Union are going to come get us in their sleep."

"That's stupid," Anar said before Natsoje could respond to her daughter, a bit of the occasional older-sibling contempt in his voice.

Natsoje frowned, tapping her son's shoulder, and Anar hunched his shoulders a bit.

"Sorry," he murmured. Then, "Sorry, Ykana."

Natsoje smiled to herself.

"You don't need to worry about that, Ykana," she said, crossing over to squat next to her daughter. She took one of the girl's small—though not as tiny as they had seemed such a short time ago—hands in hers. "The Night Mother destroyed herself when she destroyed Yrmuunthal, and the Union is no more. The Mestari herself saw to that. The people who attacked us were from a small group of bad people that want to hurt us because the Night Mother lied to them and convinced them to do terrible things before she destroyed herself."

Ykana smiled at her reassurance, then frowned again. "Why did Duukebe say that, then?"

Natsoje shrugged, squeezing her daughter's hand. "Some children do things for their own amusement instead of out of a sense of community and brotherhood. When you're young, doing things like that can seem fun, yet those who do so find that the fun disappears as they grow older. You don't need to worry about that, though. Just keep playing with your brother."

She glanced at the board, noticing the layout of the cards. "You lost the toss, then, or were you taking turns?"

This time when Ykana frowned, it was one of her more adorable lopsided ones—those she used when trying to gain sympathy from others. "I lost the toss."

"That's okay," Natsoje kissed her on the cheek, then looked to Anar. "Because next time your sister will get to be light, won't she?"

Anar rolled his eyes, but nodded, and Natsoje smiled as she straightened.

"Do you know when the repairs will be done, Mother?" Her son asked. "Or when everyone will be able to come back? I miss Demba and Ashjon."

Myndir chuckled. "I think he also misses Hovase, doesn't he?"

Natsoje laughed as her son's face went violet, eyes bulging.

"The repairs will be done three days from now." Myndir said/ "Akarna was able to bring in a greyarm to help out"

"What?" Ykana exclaimed. Anar perked up.

Natsoje glanced at her husband. "She didn't tell me that."

Auroramancers were far from uncommon among the Imaia's ranks, yet those who had not been convinced to enlist in one way or another were few and far between. If the greyarm had been a military man, Natsoje likely would have heard about it or even had to approve some of the paperwork.

Myndir nodded, eyes still trained on the meal he was preparing. "A friend's sister, apparently. It was amazing to watch her work. And quite humbling."

Natsoje glanced over at her son. Anar's face was no longer deep violet, but he was still flushed and trying to hide his face. Natsoje glanced at Ykana and rolled her eyes. Her daughter's broad, dopey grin wasn't helping with her older brother's embarrassment. She rested a hand on her son's shoulder. "I'll see if we can visit Hovase tomorrow. Maybe we'll bring him some treats or a gift."

Anar smiled up at her, face still a bit violet. "That sounds nice."

Natsoje smiled down at her son. Though she worried that if Anar ever wished to raise a child he would need to apply for adoption, that was outweighed by the lack of discrimination Anar would face for who he chose to love. Before the Imaia, many cultures—even those that had held up couples such as Mbara and Meresti as examples to young women and points of cultural pride—had expressed disdain or even hate for those who loved members of their own gender. Though the Imaia encouraged a family and community-oriented way of life, it also encouraged acceptance and inclusion rather than the varying bigotries that had once been widespread throughout the world. The Urban Corps were allowed to be heavy-handed in punishing such social injustices when they occurred, but such instances were rare. Merely living among people from different cultures and ways did most of the work, opening one's eyes to the fact that despite different clothing, features or background, they were all people of the same world.

Only those who committed violence against the Imaia and its citizens did not share in that acceptance. They were simply pitied for their misguided ways.

The children put their game on hold as their father brought the food over, though Ykana just piled up the cards rather than setting them aside so they could pick up where they left off. Natsoje grinned when Anar rolled his eyes at his sister's not-so-subtle ploy to restart the game with different suits. Once he sat down, Myndir had them each try a bite, then guess. Natsoje and her children provided no shortage of guesses, but Natsoje had yet to meet someone with as sophisticated a palate as Myndir. Or someone who also possessed the historical and cultural knowledge to pair with it.

As she savored another bite of Myndir's delicious cooking, Natsoje noticed Anar just pushing his food around the plate, eyes unfocused as he stared down at it. Natsoje reached out to touch her son's arm. "Is everything alright, dear?"

Anar started a bit. "Yes. I..." He paused, looking to his father, then to Natsoje. "What if the terrorists do come again? What if... what if this time, it's our home that they hit, or if they do something during Exodus? And instead of things most don't even need a doctor for..."

Natsoje let her utensils fall to her plate and pulled Anar into a hug as her son's voice wavered. The worry in her son's words—that her child even felt the need to ask such a question—broke Natsoje's heart. Across the table, Ykana looked between her and Myndir, eyes wide with worry. Myndir stroked his daughter's hair comfortingly. Natsoje met her husband's gaze and saw the same concern and compassion she felt. She gave him a faint smile, feeling a bit better as she looked into those loving eyes, drawing strength from his mere presence.

"Why do they want to hurt us?" Anar asked, his voice small and strained. "We didn't do anything to them."

Natsoje caught her husband's gaze and sighed. How did one explain fanaticism, the desire to murder and hate certain people without question, to ones so young and innocent without being patronizing?

As Natsoje mulled the question over in her mind, the neatly stacked deck of cards caught her gaze. She drew a few of the cards and placed one of dark and one of light down on the table between their plates.

"The point of the game is balance," she said. "It was meant to teach strategy, but also to show that one must have balance in all they do not only to succeed in life, but to be at peace with those around them. The terrorists are people who have fallen out of balance, taking their devotion to the Night Mother to such an extreme that either they overlook all the wrong she has done, or they think that the destruction she caused was right, so they seek to do the same. People like that unfortunately don't have any reason for doing what they do, dear. Not in a way where it would be possible to simply convince them to stop at least."

"I think I understand..." Anar said, nodding slowly, but his downcast expression pained Natsoje.

She squeezed her son's hand, smiling. "You don't need to worry about them, though. Othaashle herself followed after the one insurgent that got away to deal with them personally and make sure they won't harm us again. And I learned today that Skadaatha went out to join her in secret yesterday, returning earlier today, so they must be on to something."

Natsoje had also learned that Adjunct Yndlova, Othaashle's second in command, had rounded up a few spies in connection with the attack, but that was not for sharing. Nor was the fact that she was scheduled to help assist in the interrogations starting tomorrow. Even had she been allowed to share such information; she knew it would only worry her family further. Natsoje desperately hoped that those spies were the last remaining within Mjatafa Mwonga, yet she knew that was likely not the case.

Natsoje glanced at her family. The news of Othaashle and Skadaatha seemed to have raised her children's spirits. Regardless of what actions the leadership took with the captured spies, Natsoje planned on pursuing her own investigation. She would not let anything threaten her family again.

 With that decided, Natsoje took a few plates as she rose, she smiled down at her children. She wanted to keep their spirits lifted. "Now, who wants to hear the story of Meresti and Mbara?"

Ykana lit up at the prospect of a story, but Anar just shrugged. Natsoje knew her son preferred reading to himself all curled up in the garden, but that was less communal.

Before Natsoje could say anything, however, Myndir grinned, directing the expression at their son. "Come on, Anar. You might learn a thing or two for your visit with Hovase."

Laughter bubbled forth from Natsoje and her husband at the shade of Anar's face.

"Father!"

Epilogue 2

Nevisi

Exodus countdown: 19 days, 5 hours, 22 minutes

Nevisi pulled her fur-lined cloak tight around her as she picked her way down the edge of the ruined Vale with careful steps. Even with her violetnodes and her natural resilience to the freezing temperatures of Darkside, the top of the world could get cold at times. It didn't matter. She had a task to complete, and not even freezing temperatures that had made life nearly impossible for anything else would stand in her way.

Despite this place's fall from what it had once been and the destruction that marred its once great beauty, Nevisi had not been able to simply bring herself into the center of the Vale. As before, she could only travel to the edge, then make the rest of the journey on foot, slowly. Even with use of her greynodes to propel her over the ice and her other not inconsiderable abilities, the trek to this side of the mountains had taken Nevisi a day and a half.

As she continued down the steep slopes—the switchbacks that once led safely down into the Vale ruined when the Vale's heart had been destroyed—Nevisi remembered what had once been. When her old master Ki'aite had taken her here what seemed like a lifetime ago, the auroras overhead had shone brightly enough for both of them to require veils over their faces, and clothing that covered their skin entirely. Without his teachings, she wouldn't have been able to survive in this area for more than a few minutes. The destruction here had done something to Efruumani's atmosphere, though at the time not everyone had had an adequate understanding of planetary science to put it in such terms. The air was too thin, temperatures too cold. The auroras still lit the sky above Nevisi, colors dancing over the icy rocks around her, yet she could not bring herself to look up, for she knew she would feel only disappointment and pain for the lost wonder and beauty of this sacred place. Beyond that, Nevisi now knew the auroras themselves had not been solely caused by Efruumani's Aathal. She believed looking up at the shining lights would diminish her memory of this place.

Though she missed Ki'aite, she was glad he had lived a normal lifespan, rather than living to see what had become of Efruumani. Nevisi wished for his help and guidance, yet now she questioned if the old man's presence would have made any difference.

Even their god had not been enough to stop the destruction.

Ki'aite would have only experienced pain and sorrow had he lived to see that—the kind people like him should be sheltered from simply because of how good they were, and how they looked upon the world. Especially this place.

Nevisi looked up at what lay before her and felt a chill that had nothing to do with the icy breeze that came down over the Vale's mountain walls. Such a sight would have broken Ki'aite's heart.

Where once an impossibly tall and colorful tree had risen, branches reaching out almost far enough to touch the Vale walls, roots descending into the earth like massive, twisted columns, now only a large fissure remained. Where lush, snow-white grass had once sprouted up from the green-grey soil to spread out over the ground and even up the low slopes of the mountains like a thick carpet, now only bare earth remained. It was as though no life had ever existed in this Vale.

A few large, crumbling rock formations rose up near the Vale's heart, some on the edge of the fissure, others standing alone. Nevisi shivered when she realized the resemblance, they bore to Yrmuunthal's roots. She brightened her orangenodes, looking into the past of the area before her.

Tears stung her eyes and her chest tightened at seeing the Vale in all its glory, now lost forever. The memory confirmed it.

Dimming her orangenodes with more effort than she'd expected, Nevisi dropped to her knees, shuddering as she pulled her cloak tight around her. A small part of her wondered at the implications of that, but she shoved such tangential thoughts away. She had a purpose in coming here, beyond viewing the destruction Kweshrima had caused.

If she did not do what she had come here for, it would mean that Kweshrima had destroyed the Aathal for nothing.

"It was the only way," the goddess had told Nevisi when giving her this task, "I needed to distract Ynuukwidas, otherwise more than Efruumani would suffer for what he has done."

The goddess's words had sounded of prophecy to Nevisi, a dangerous thing. However, she could understand the dire situation the goddess had found herself in, even if she did not agree with the goddess's actions.

Nevisi had been tempted to flare her ambernodes and opalnodes and look into the future herself. She'd eventually decided against such an attempt. Knowledge of the future could corrupt as easily and silently as power. Her true motivation would not be curiosity or a desire to know she was doing good, but twin needs within her: to be able to condemn Kweshrima for what she had done with certainty and authority, and to know that the goddess had indeed been right in what she had done, restoring Nevisi's faith.

Neither of those were worth the risk. It felt wrong, anyway. The inherent need to know something was not the way of the Samjati. There was a reason Kweshrima's Throne had often been referred to as the Throne of Secrets—a far more apt title than the Throne of Darkness. Such a mindset had been largely foreign to Nevisi's people before they had made contact with the peoples of the South. Before that, she and many others had been able to accept that there were things they either could not know or were not meant to know. Most—what little remained of Samjati blood, at least—still held to such beliefs. Yet in this, Nevisi had to constantly remind herself that she did not need to know everything.

When Nevisi finally reached the Vale floor, she fell to her knees and squeezed her eyes shut. She had somehow been able to keep herself strong until this point. Seeing the destruction and emptiness from above... somehow Nevisi had been able to convince herself there had to be something of that wonder left down here. As Nevisi knelt against the cold, harsh stone, the only life in this place—the only life that *could* be here—she could no longer deny this emptiness.

Nevisi wept.

Her tears turned to slush between the frigid temperature of the Vale and the warmth of her body, trudging down her cheeks and stinging her eyes. They stuck when she tried to wipe them from her face. Nevisi couldn't find it in herself to care.

Ki'aite had shown her the Music of Efruumani. At first, she had seen it merely as a way to enhance her powers and perform marvels that no one else could. As the decades and even centuries had passed, however, Nevisi had come to understand the true gift Ki'aite had given her in teaching her to hear and understand the Music of the world. She had learned to hear the Music in all things, and through that find a connection with them. That connection with everything around her had brought Nevisi unparalleled joy and wonder for so long, yet when Yrmuunthal had been destroyed, the sense of wrongness and pain that flowed through that connection from Efruumani had overwhelmed Nevisi, leaving her in a catatonic state for days. What had followed upon her awakening... Nevisi did not like to think about those dark years of her life.

Here in the Vale, Nevisi no longer felt that same pain. Instead, she simply felt an emptiness and a lack of Music. That in itself was a more horrid perversion than anything Ynuukwidas or his Imaia had wrought so far.

Setting her jaw, Nevisi straightened and relaxed her mind, focusing on the world around her. Kweshrima had convinced Nevisi to undertake this task months ago as a last request, but Nevisi had seen it as a hopeless one until eight days ago. The faint pulse of energy, followed by an echoing, far off melody, had directed Nevisi here. It had been different than anything she'd heard before, almost alien. So far, she had kept herself from hope. Hope was dangerous to the person she had become. Yet she could not hold back the desperation to find the source of that melody. If she could find it, so much loss would not all be for nothing, and someone, at least, might have a chance against the Imaia.

Channeling that desperation, Nevisi opened her senses up to the ruined world around her, and let her mind search, listening intently for even a hint of that unfamiliar melody. She needed to hurry. Something had happened on Lightside a few hours ago. Nevisi sensed she would be needed there soon.

THE END

Continue reading for a chance to sign up for my mailing list and receive a free short story, and an exclusive free novella: Cleareye.

Awakening the Lightforged Book 2: Sanctuary:

Three Cities. One Doom.
The Empire took the Estingai's family. Now she leads the surviving rebels.
The God King's Champion has offered her a deal that will ensure her people's way off this dying world. Estingai does not trust it, yet has no choice but to accept.
Desperately searching for other options, Estingai sends her brother and sister to locate a group of magic-wielding refugees.
But Estingai has a secret mission of her own...
Could salvation lie in the forgotten hero who once forged the empire, then fought to destroy it?

An apocalyptic science-fantasy combining the best of *Star Wars* and *The 100* with elements of Brandon Sanderson and Fonda Lee. Fans of M.L. Wang, Pierce Brown, and Christopher Ruocchio will love this epic trilogy.

"Wow. This was absolutely amazing...Astounding Character development." —Starred Reviewer
"The story is engaging, the world building is detailed, and relationships between the characters are explored in depth." —Starred Reviewer

THANK YOU SO MUCH! PLEASE KEEP READING!

After years of writing, rewriting, learning about story, creating fictional languages, worlds, and cultures, drawing maps, and more rewriting, *Awakening the Lightforged* is finally here. Your journey into Aioa has begun.

I can't properly express how much it means to me that you read this book. Without readers, stories cannot truly live. I can write all this out, wrap it in a beautiful package, and put it out into the world, but only when someone picks it up and starts reading, do these characters and this world come alive. Thank you so much for supporting me and making it possible for me and other writers like myself to practice this craft that we love so much.

If you gotten to this point, I assume you enjoyed it on some level. If that is the case, I highly recommend picking up *The Last Knight*, as—in my opinion—it is my best written work so far. It begins immediately after the prologue of this book, and can give a bit more insight into the Remnant, and Estingai, Koruuksi, and Uuchantuu specifically. If you enjoyed this, please consider rating and reviewing it on Amazon and/or talking about it on other platforms. It makes such a huge difference. Hundreds of thousands of authors fight for a place in your heart, in your eReader, or on your bookshelf every day. Leaving a review for an author you love is one of the single most powerful things you can do as a reader to help readers find their books, and authors find their readers. Reviews are what help our books stand out from the sea of millions of books that grows larger every day.

This is my passion. I am going to keep doing it until the day I die, and I want to be able to spend as much time as I possibly can writing and working on creating wonderful stories for you to read. I would love it if you could help make that dream a reality.

I promise to make sure that this is the worst book of mine you ever read, because I will never stop writing, learning and nerding out about prose and story, and improving my craft. The stories will only get better from here.

Spencer Russell Smith

GET AN EXCLUSIVE, FREE SHORT STORY AND MORE EFRUUMANI CONTENT

Building a relationship with my readers is one of the best things about writing. I occasionally send newsletters with details on new releases, special offers, and other bits of news relating to the Awakening the Light-forged Trilogy and upcoming projects.

If you sign up to my mailing list, I'll send you a copy of my exclusive novella, *Cleareye* which is not available for purchase anywhere. The story travels far back into Efruumani's history, when the Samjati and Natari peoples had only just become aware of one another. You'll also receive links to my free short story *Music of the Lights* to learn a bit more about the mysterious Nevisi.

You can get both the short story and the exclusive novella **for free** by signing up at spencerrussellsmith.com/freenovella

ABOUT THE AUTHOR

Hi, I'm Spencer Russell Smith!

Everyone writes for different reasons. I started writing out of boredom in class. Then I realized I had stories in my head I needed to get out. Then I realized how reading shaped who I am as a person, and that crafting stories of a quality that could one day do the same for someone else.

I love writing about magical worlds that reflect or enhance the wonders of our own universe, and exploring the incredible complexity of humanity. Writing Space Opera, Epic Fantasy, and blends of the two allows me to do that in a unique way.

I've also made suits of armor, composed music, and love to dive deep into history and the cultures of the world in my research. It's my hope that you will get lost in the worlds I create, be filled with awe at the epic scale of the stories I write, and cling to the intimate character moments that give them a reason to be told.

I make my online home at www.spencerrussellsmith.com. If you like my books, or just want to talk about other people's books, follow me and reach out on Facebook, Instagram, or TikTok, listen to my music at https://soundcloud.com/spencersmithcomposer, and send me an email at mail@spencerrussellsmith.com if the mood strikes you!

facebook.com/spencerrussellsmithauthor

instagram.com/spencerrussellsmithauthor

tiktok.com/@spencersmithauthor

youtube.com/@SpencerRussellSmithAuthor

ACKNOWLEDGMENTS

There are a lot of people who helped me on this journey, either directly or indirectly.

Jonothan Oliver provided me with professional feedback and criticism of my novel, as well as some much-needed confidence and insight into the industry.

Stuart Bache crafted the incredible cover for this book, making it feel more real, and then whipped up another one when I realized I was marketing to the wrong genre.

I owe a lot to my mother and father and the rest of my friends and family for supporting me and believing me since I started this journey in high school.

Brandon Sanderson is a godsend for posting his lectures online, showing me Fantasy that breaks from tradition and encompasses incredible, expansive worlds, and reminding me to enjoy the journey rather than focusing on the destination.

I also owe a lot to Christopher Paolini for inspiring me and showing me the reality of a teenager who could be a published author.

My wonderful wife, Marissa Botticelli-Smith, put up with my constant ramblings and questions and gave me such detailed feedback on my book that I believe she is a large reason why Mr. Oliver found editing my work so enjoyable.

I have to thank my best friend Keshav Dasu for telling me to stop procrastinating and focus, for letting me call him up whenever to talk about story and magic and characters, for pushing me to have a better grasp on my craft, and for the incredible chapter header illustrations he provided.

Lastly, I owe more to J. R. R. Tolkien creating Middle Earth, and to

Peter Jackson and his team for creating the films of the Lord of the Rings Trilogy, than they can ever imagine. Watching those films changed my life, and revealed to me exactly what I wanted to do with my life—something I have come to learn more and more is incredibly rare—at age twelve. I actually wrote my college essay on that subject.

Thank you all so much. Even though you may not know it, you helped this book come to life, and it means the world to me.

NOTEBOOK OF VYSLA MODIBODJARA

Though the Ministry of Science has been so far unable to run any tests on the Champion's blade, Ilkwalerva, a survey of reports referencing the blade has gathered the following information: The blade is able to cut through any substance, organic or inorganic, and grants its owner even greater Auroramantic abilities than afforded the Redeemed. There is also its supposed ability to create more Redeemed.

Vizier Skadaatha believes that while the blade is certainly involved in the process of creating new Redeemed, it is not wholly responsible for such an incredible feat. As to the blade's origins, she believes that it is at least partially a physical manifestation of Lord Ynuukwidas' power, similar to the gold markings many Redeemed bear upon their bodies. Her other thoughts about the blade's origins are quite...unsettling, and should not be recorded into anything that might become a matter of scientific record at this time.

Georaural technology allows for simple storage of extra investment, though an artificial crest would be far more practical for such things. If I am to construct a weapon that can hope to match Ilkwalerva in both power and convenience, much more complex and precise design is required. At the present time, many components needed for such a feat are unavailable due to Exodus. Even then, I would be stretching georaural technology to its limits, if not for the discovery of zidanio.

In this first, limited design, zidanio plays a critical part, found both in the georaural framework, and integrated into the weapon itself, particularly the grip. I have constructed six interlinked georaural frameworks, integrating three into the guard, and three into the pommel. Not all Auroramantic functions will be critical to this weapon's use, and keeping economy of space in mind, I have been very precise in my selection of which functions to include.

As this weapon will be handled exclusively by Vizier Skadaatha, I decided to include a single amethyst setting to allow for the production of lightning, the regulation of temperature and the production of fire or freezing temperatures for an Auroramancer that can call on both polarizations of each biogem.

Similarly, I decided not to include an aquamarine setting, as manipulation of fire and ice has proven terribly cumbersome when performed with georaural technology in comparison with practiced Auroramantic abilities. I believe the presence of zidanio will increase the innate alertness provided by aquanodes far beyond what a georaural could accomplish.

The ability to push and pull on water and volcanic rock seems unsuited to a weapon of this sort, but I have included two emerald settings for healing. Though the effect is negligible and unsuited for use in battle under normal circumstances, I believe zidanio will amplify the effect to the point where it may be of use. I pray, however, that Skadaatha will never need to test this effect save under controlled circumstances.

As I know of nothing that can reliably reproduce Ilkwalerva's ability to cut through any substance, I have included six settings of moonstone divided equally between two of the frameworks. They should increase the durability of both the blade and the hilt, and a bit of extra strength and speed could provide a useful edge on top of the reserves already available to Skadaatha.

Diamond's ability to increase the senses is useful, but does not affect the weapon in any manner that warrants its inclusion. I have included opal settings with each structure as a last resort, though I must admit, I am somewhat frightened of what a zidanio-enhanced power flare could produce in the hands of someone like Skadaatha.

Topaz settings were an obvious inclusion, and a matter of tradition to bless the weapon and its owner with good luck during battle. After some deliberation, I have also decided to include a single sunstone setting as part of one of the frameworks. While its facilitation with viewing past events is unneeded, I am curious to see if the memory enhancement will extend to muscle-memory when combined with zidanio's effects.

Ruby settings took up half of each twelve-setting framework. With Miss Kwangeta's breakthrough in hardlight technology and zidanio's unique properties, I believe that this weapon will not only produce a hardlight blade that can maintain a cutting edge, but that the edge will resist any attempts at deformation and cut through whatever surface it encounters. I used only one setting to assist with quickened reflexes.

An abundance of sapphire settings were also necessary, as Skadaatha insisted on testing the weapon's ability to function as a power siphon. I believe the inclusion of three sapphires per framework in my design will allow it to both siphon power from another's gemcrests and transfer the stored power to her own when needed. I declined to include any sapphire settings calibrated to affect aging.

Lastly, I included one amber setting and one onyx setting for an added edge with premonitions and investment interference respectively. Amber's ability for foresight is best kept to an Auroramancer, as are onyx's abilities to detect and shroud Auroramantic signatures, though if the chance arises, an onyx sensor may be an acceptable inclusion, and aikanuum could react with amber in a very advantageous manner if my suspicions are correct.

For now it will need to be handled with bare hands, or at least bare palms, though I have several theories about surpassing that barrier in later tests. The zidanio increases the power of one's Auroramancy, but that same power does not translate to the georaural technology. Aikanuum, however, has proven quite useful in recent tests as an alternative.

Test of the blade against darklight and other hardlight surfaces proved successful. Each impact placed the device under great strain, however, and required great strength from handler even with zidanio's enhancements, especially during prolonged periods of contact.

After Vizier Skadaatha's feedback gained from an extraordinary field test, I have polarized half of the ruby settings. The framework is one of several designs that I produced with help from Miss Kwangeta, though for the moment, they are purely theoretical. The Vizier's notion of combining darklight and hardlight to allow the blade to flex as one made of steel seems so obvious that the only reason I can find for not originally attempting it is that I have no clue if it is even possible.

Given how the blade overloaded, I have lengthened the hilt and hollowed it out to an extent. This allowed me to include more moonstone and sapphire settings in order to both keep the blade and weapon together, and allow for greater storage of power.

After days of testing, Miss Kwangeta and I have finally managed a blade of layered hardlight and darklight that allows for a razor edge as well as strength and flexibility. I cannot sufficiently test the durability and power storage, unfortunately, but these modifications should do for now.

Though zidanio and aikanuum are so incredibly rare, the amounts gathered near Mount Saanad and Vizier Skadaatha's notions that both may be found elsewhere in Aioa give me great hope for what the Imaia will be able to accomplish with such resources.

IMAIA ANTHEM: BY YOUR LIGHT

"There, out in the darkness,
A threat waits, lurking
Enemy of life
Enemy of peace
Ynuukwidas witness,
We never shall yield
Till freedom reigns
Until freedom reigns

We go to fight the true fight
We who refuse to be slaves
Millions look on the axe with hope,
Millions of hearts beat as one
And if one falls as Matsanga fell
The flame, the Axe

We shall spread through the stars
Braving all dangers
Fighting the darkness with order and light
We shall be the sentinels
Forged in battle
Keeping watch for the night
Keeping watch for the Night

We know our place in Aioa
We hold to justice and truth
And We weep for the fallen both friend and foe
But we cannot turn aside
And those who fall as Kweshrima fell,
Will fall in Flame

And so it must be
Arise the Imaia
Raise your golden banners high
The fallen march with us in spirit
And in the Light

Lord bring us our enemy
So that we may all know your justice and peace
So that our deaths are not in vain
We will never rest
Until your light shines unhindered
This we swear by your Light"

GLOSSARY

GEMCRESTS

Every living creature on Efruumani, both flora and fauna, is born with a gemcrest of biogems, or "nodes" as they are often referred to in conjuction with their specific color, but other than the legendary Draakon, which have unfortunately passed into extinction, only the sentient races of the Natari and Samjati are able to use those gemcrests as a focus for the abilities commonly known as auroramancy. On plants and animals, the placements of these gemcrests vary widely, but they are more consistent on the sentient races, forming over the brow on Samjati, and at the clavicle on Natari. Each gemcrest is made up of twenty-four individual biogems that are smooth and rounded to the touch, capable of holding brilliant auroralight for up to nine days if the individual uses no auroramantic abilities during that time. If these biogems are cracked, they will still function, but will leak auroralight, depleting the individuals store of auroralight at a faster rate.

THE AURORAS AND LIGHTLESSNESS

Efruumani is defined by its auroras. The tidally locked world would contain no life on either side if not for the strong magnetic field that gives life to these magical auroras, and the power they give all life on Efruumani to adapt to its otherwise harsh environments. Though solar flares constantly and erratically hit the habitable moon's magnetosphere, the auroras dance constantly at both the anti-solar and sub-solar poles, and every six days, they spread out over the skies, dancing through the atmosphere like a massive net and showering Efruumani with their light, converging on the twilight band, where they linger before returning to the poles. When these auroras light the skies, every biogem, whether in a living creature's gemcrest, or harvested from one, fills with auroralight. Though the gemcrests vary by size, all hold enough auroralight to last from six to nine days on Efruumani, during which they experience the latent benefits of those gemcrests. Auroramancers are the exception to this, as their abilities use up auroralight at a faster rate. If they use up their reserves and are unable to replenish their auroralight from a harvested biogem, they will become lightless.

Lightlessness is the absence of auroralight in one's system. It manifests differently depending on the color of an individual's gemcrest, but in general it is a sort of physical and mental depression brought on by a lack of auroralight flowing through one's body. To deprive someone—even an animal—of auroralight intentionally is considered torture, and those with auroralight to spare will offer it to someone who is lightless or on the verge of being so without a second thought. Long-term effects of lightlessness have rarely been studied, and though there do not appear to be any permanent effects, recovery after an extended period of lightlessness is a long and arduous process. There have been individuals able to function with some sense of normalcy while lightless, but those individuals exhibit a strength of will far beyond that of the average person.

AURORABORN, FIREBORN, ICEBORN, AND GENETICS

Auroramancy is a genetic ability, and at the same time, not. Two auroramancers, or even one auroramancer and a non-auroramancer will have a better chance at producing an auroramancer child than two non-auroramancers, yet it is not an exact science. It is estimated that at any given time, twelve percent of the world's population are auroramancers, and of that fraction, one twenty-fourth are full auroraborn, with access to all twelve auroramantic abilities. It is estimated that another twenty-fourth have opalescent gemcrests, which are effectively useless both in auroramancy and in any latent abilities they pass on, and that the other eleven auroramantic abilities are divided equally among the remaining auroramancer population.

There are two sides to every auroramantic ability, reflecting both the climate and Throne of the side of the world that each race inhabits the majority of. Natari auroramancers can use one set of abilities, for which they are often referred to as "fireborn" or sometimes "lightborn", and Samjati auroramancers are similarly referred to as "iceborn" or "shadow-born" for their abilities. When the two mix, and the union produces an auroramancer, that auroramancer either has one set of abilities or the other, never one of each. For the most part, Samjati and Natari experience the same latent effects of a given gemcrest, with the exception of grey and violet gemcrests.

ORIGINS OF THE POWERS AND LEGENDS

Gemcrests and auroramancy have been around as long as Efruumani itself, with the Draakon likely earning their places as the original auroramancers. It is speculated that at one point, there were only six auroramantic abilities for either race, with this perspective pushed by those who have engaged in the study of history and the study of the mystical Thrones of power, but there is little evidence to corroborate sub arguments.

INDIVIDUAL ABILITIES & BASIC MECHANICS

All life on Efruumani is constantly using auroralight. This is coloquially referred to as "burning" auroralight, likening it to a candle or oil lantern. To use one's abilities, an auroramancer can "brighten" their gemcrests or "nodes", "flare" them for bursts of power, and "dim" them to stop using their abilities or even suppress the latent effects they receive from their gemcrests. Very skilled auroramancers can even brighten and dim their gemcrests node-by-node. This is part of the trade-off that full auroraborn experience when using their powers, as they must learn to control their abilities by individual node, or at least by each pair of colored nodes.

Through great discipline and concentration, non-auroramancers can slightly dim or brighten their gemcrests to achieve augmented or diminished latent effects. The benefit is often not considered worth the intense training, but for those with moonstone or emerald gemcrests, the difference could be between winning or losing a fight or athletic event, or even between life and death.

Because auroramancers use up their auroralight at a faster pace more often than not, they experience a compounding effect of the latent abilities, especially while using their abilities.

Violet or Amethyst

Those with an amethyst gemcrest have the latent ability of temperature regulation inverse to their auroramantic ability. Samjati are able to produce cold sensations or even ice if there is enough water in the air around them, while they tend to run warm to better adapt to their native environment. Natari can produce heat and fire, while they tend to run cool, giving them a break from the humidity and constant heat of their environment.

Since cold is merely the absence of heat, the Samjati amethyst ability is not as straightforward as its Natari counterpart. While the Natari can heat objects with a touch, or even the air around them, as well as produce directional fire or even lightning if they flare their abilities, heating up that air until it becomes fire or plasma, the Samjati instead siphon the heat from the air around them or the object they are holding. As such, while Natari can "shoot" and direct fire or lightning from a starting point to an end point, Samjati, more often than not must choose an endpoint or space in the air. They can freeze the air around someone, but cannot imitate Natari by throwing columns of ice or darts, unless they form those darts and then physically throw them. The one exception is when Samjati flare this ability. A flare can power freezing the air far away from the auroramancer, or it can power what is colloquially referred to as an "ice beam" or "cold shock". This connects the auroramancer to a point in the distance and supercools the air in a thin line from one point to the other, leaving whatever is on the receiving ends supercooled and flash frozen. It also creates a flash of light and a screech due to the sudden localized drop in temperature.

Aqua or Aquamarine

Those with an aquamarine gemcrest sleep more soundly anyone else, yet wake more easily and are either more refreshed or alert when they do so. They also tend to be more alert and focused in general when awake. The auroramantic ability allows manipulation of the races' respective elements. Natari are able to manipulate fire, lightning or energy, and molten lava up to a certain distance and volume. They are also able to cool lava, but that requires a flare of their powers. Samjati are able to manipulate ice, water and mist up to a certain volume and distance, though changing phases requires them to flare their powers. Each race is able to shape its respective element and move it through space. The more they manipulate and the farther the distance from them, the more difficult it is, and the more auroralight it uses up.

Green or Emerald

Those with an emerald gemcrest tend to have better constitutions than anyone else. They are more resistant to disease, muscle aches, stomach aches, never have allergies, and heal at a noticeably faster rate than anyone else. Emerald gemcrests grant the ability to push and pull on the races' respective elements with the focal point as one's center of gravity. This does not allow for the same freedom of movement that those with aquamarine gemcrests command, but it does have its advantages. Samjati are able to push and pull on ice and water, and can form a bubble around themselves with great practice, while Natari can do the same with molten lava or volcanic rock. The greatest advantage both hold is a semblance of flight and fast movement. Both can hover over either element and push themselves in great arcs to travel large distances at a great speed. One observation made by Samjati that have ventured to lightside is that the warmer the water, the more effort and auroralight it takes to push or pull. Those particularly skilled in balancing their pushes and pulls are able to achieve incredibly graceful, almost dance-like movements in the air.

Grey or Moonstone

Those with moonstone gemcrests have their latent abilities split by race. Those of Natari heritage tend to move faster and be more agile with incredible balance, stamina and flexibility, while those of Samjati heritage tend to be stronger, have stronger bones and ligaments, have an easier time building muscle, are harder to cut or scrape, and have more control over and awareness of their individual muscles. The auroramantic abilities are similarly divided. Samjati auroramancers can brighten their gemcrests to achieve greater strength and durability, as well as bursts of it, and the Natari can do the same with physical speed and endurance. Both can achieve a semblance of the other's ability to a certain degree. Natari can move their limbs faster to harness more power in certain movements, and Samjati can use their strength to run faster or control their muscles to move faster in short bursts. Moonstone nodes use up auroralight at a faster rate than most other colors

Clear, White, or Diamond

Those with diamond gemcrests have more acute senses than those around them, are more sensitive to touch, can distinguish color and tone quality and flavor a bit better, and experience greater and more frequent arousal, both sexual and flight or fight, so they tend to be more perceived as more passionate, erratic, or emotional. The auroramantic ability allows for senses that are enhanced even further. Flaring their abilities can give great temporary bursts of pain and clarity depending on the sensory input. All senses are enhanced at once and though the auroramancer cannot pick and choose, those who are especially skilled can tune out the other senses.

Multicolored or Opal

An opal gemcrest is often considered the most useless gemcrest. To this day, it has no known latent effects, and its auroramantic ability is only useful in conjunction with other abilities. An auroramancer with opal biogems can flare their auroramantic abilities far beyond that of a normal flare, to the point where it will deplete anywhere from an entire biogem to a pair.

The only way in which the opal gemcrest has been deemed useful by itself is that those with one who have experienced lightlessness seem to feel less of a depression, as though by not losing access to any latent abilities, the effects of lightlessness are muted.

Orange or Sunstone

Individuals with a sunstone gemcrest have extremely good memories. Often, they have some sort of eidetic memory of some sort, whether it is visual, audio, or some other sort of mnemonic assisting. The ability it grants is that to see into the past. The more auroralight expended, the father into the past one can see, and the longer an expanse of time they can view. This sort of past-sight is localized, however. A person on one side of the world would not be able to view the past of someone sitting on the other side of the world, or even down the street from them. Some have reported occasionally being able to touch a person or object and see their past beyond the current location, but that is an area requiring further study.

Yellow or Topaz

Those born with a topaz gemcrest are either born lucky or unlucky. The degree of that good or bad luck varies, but the distribution tends to lilt toward moderately lucky, though that luck does not always manifest in the ways one would expect. Some believe that these individuals have a greater connection to Fortune rather than simply being lucky, or are maybe more aware of their place in events.

As such, auroramancers with a topaz gemcrest are able to manipulate luck, chance, and coincidence in a localized manner. They can further manipulate their own luck, or do so for everyone or a few individuals in a room they occupy. Theoretically, an unlucky topaz auroramancer could constantly expend auroralight reversing their luck, but this would require many spare biogems, as topaz biogems use up auroralight even more quickly than moonstone biogems.

Red or Ruby

Ruby gemcrests bestow quicker and more deft reflexes on individuals. The auroramantic abilities they bestow are again similar, yet divided between the races. Natari have the ability to create and manipulate hardlight, while Samjati have the ability to create and manipulate darklight. Both of these can act as solid constructs, though while hardlight is more angular and solid, darklight tends to form in more rounded or circular constructs with wispy edges. While auroralight is necessary to maintain both, one's will is what defines the shape. Ruby auroramancers are often seen as masters of their thoughts due to the control they must exert to keep their constructs in a given shape. Recent study has discovered that both hardlight and darklight are a sort of magnetic forcefield capable of keeping air and pressure in or out of a given area. Though hardlight and darklight are often used as armor, shields, or blunt weapons, it is almost impossible to use either to create an edged weapon due to how fine that edge would need to be in order to cut as well as a metal or even wood edge.

Blue or Sapphire

Those with sapphire gemcrests will age slower than others and in general look younger once reaching maturity. This includes their skin aging less easily, and Samjati with sapphire gemcrests experience sunburns less frequently to a point. All with sapphire gemcrests have younger, more child-like features in general even after maturity.

The sapphire gemcrest offers auroramancers the ability to transfer power. Samjati can take auroralight from others, while Natari can give their auroralight to others. This is easier to do with animals or non-auroramancers, but even then, if the person is aware and resisting, it can be difficult. Though this can be done without touching the target, it is extremely difficult. If one's gemcrest is full, the recipient gains a burst of energy that can affect them in strange ways, and experiences a concentrated, sustained boost of the corresponding latent ability of the gemcrest they have taken their energy from.

For auroramancers, many believe that they can only steal enough to fuel a single pair of biogems, and while this is easiest, it is not impossible to use auroralight from another single-color gemcrest to fuel an entire auroramancer's gemcrest.

Samjati are stigmatized for this while Natari are praised, and most Samjati with sapphire gemcrests have an unspoken rule that they will never steal enough to make another lightless, and try to only do it in dire situations.

Amber

Amber gemcrests give individuals a certain amount of foresight. The feeling is like a premonition or gut-feeling, but more solid. Auroramancers can use an extension of this that allows them to see a short time into the future, and speeds up their mental processing in order to act on this information in a timely manner. This ability burns through auroralight more quickly than any other and makes these individuals particularly dangerous, as one on a battlefield or in a fight could take down countless opponents even without much skill.

Though gifts of foretelling and prophecy are rare, they do occur almost exclusively in full auroraborn and those with amber gemcrests.

Black or Onyx

Onyx gemcrests make an individual more aware of the auroramancy being used around them, and interfere to a small degree with others' abilities to detect power being used in their immediate vicinity. They allow Samjati auroramancers to hide their own use of power or create a fog around them, and allow Natari to detect uses of power. Skilled onyx Natari auroramancers are able to pick out exactly what auroramantic abilities are being used, and even sense auroralight being burned at a resting rate. They say there is a certain music that defines each one, but nothing they can latch onto enough to replicate.

Full Auroraborn

Full auroraborn have twelve pairs of each color biogem. Their ability to use all twelve powers of a given set makes them extremely dangerous. There have been no recorded instances of individuals with a full gemcrest who were not auroramancers, but auroraborn do experience a mix of those same latent effects, just to a lesser degree. Similarly, the tradeoff for their abilities is economy of auroralight. While some skilled auroraborn have figured out how to transfer auroralight between their different pairs of biogems, they can only burn two biogems's worth of one color at a given time—though this can be offset by their opal flares —and they must choose which abilities to expend their auroralight on. Due to this, auroraborn often use up their auroralight faster than any other auroramancers, and they cannot always be burning at faster rate like many single-color auroramancers do.

SUBSTANCES OF INTEREST

Silver

Silver has demonstrated the ability to pierce pure investment, such as aurora or Efruumani's spirits, the oruu. Some primitive cultures who feared the oruu used to capture and pierce the spirits in rituals. While many of these old practices were barbaric, their study led to our modern, far more ethical methods of corralling the oruu and manipulating them for our purposes. Though there have never been tests to confirm, it has been theorized by Vizier Skadaatha that if a god such as Lord Ynuukwidas, or his avatar, at least, is made of pure investment, silver could potentially harm a god in ways that other materials cannot. Though no credible evidence has been found, it is rumored that Lord Ynuukwidas created a weapon of silver for Othaashle Mestari to use against Kweshrima if necessary, though that point is now moot. It has been theorized that Type-Two Lightforged, the Unbound Redeemed, are more affected by silver than other metals, but Othaashle Mestari has not allowed tests to confirm. She did, however, confirm the rumors that all Redeemed armor is plated or lined with silver depending on the function. She would not elaborate on why.

Aluminum

Aluminum possesses the remarkable ability to disrupt abilities fueled by investment (auroralight), so far including both georaural technology and Auroramancy. Tests are still being run to measure the exact parameters of this disruption, but it has proven invaluable in military use, engineering, and integration into georaural technology. In georaural technology, aluminum plating and wire can be used to direct the effect of a given georaural, or even one of its smaller components. Its most common application is shielding. The lightweight metal can disrupt the fire conjured by a violet-crest Fireborn, but it will not do anything special or unusual against fire or magma manipulated and directed by a Fireborn. If someone uses Auroramancy within a room lined with aluminum, a black-crest Fireborn will be unable to sense the activity. Similarly, a black-crest Fireborn inside an aluminum-lined room will be unable to sense any Auroramantic activity outside the room.

Iron

For whatever reason, iron causes severe injuries and illness to both Natari and Samjati. While other metals will simply cut and lacerate, iron burns to the touch. This does not apply to any other species on Efruumani, however. Any animals or plants cut with an iron blade experience the same effects as when cut with any other edge, metal or otherwise.

Causes harm to Natari and Samjati

Zidanio

Zidanio somehow increases the power, strength or potency of whatever it touches exponentially. This extends to physical strength, latent biogem abilities, and use of auroramancy, though not to georaural technology. The metal itself cannot be used as a battery, but can be used in concert with one to great effect in increasing output. Measurements are still being recorded to test the effects of greater and lesser quantities of metal with a given device or auroramancer. The Redeemed would be perfect test subjects, but for political reasons, that could cause unneeded issues. Tests such as heat treatment and the creation of alloys are forthcoming pending the discovery and mining of greater quantities of this ore, as the current supply is too low and too precious to accidentally waste. Studies of myths and folk heroes on both lightside and darkside suggest that

Zidanio has been used in the past without knowledge of its exact properties to create supposedly holy talismans and arms of great power that granted their owners incredible abilities, physical strength most common among them.

When applied to georaural technology, the metals do not impart power to the device, but instead act as a power converter, an even greater breakthrough. This allows georaural technology, previously only capable of being powered by auroralight, to be powered by other forms of energy such as electricity. It was this breakthrough that allowed the Imaia's scientists and engineers to make such incredible breakthroughs in spacefaring technology so quickly, and is largely what will allow project Exodus to work as planned. While the widespread application of such technology could be revolutionary, catapulting even the most average citizens of the Imaia years into the future, the limited supply of the material has led to its existence being classified, as its applications must be carefully weighed and applied where they will most benefit the Imaia as a whole.

Aikanuum

Aikanuum somehow increases the physical speed of whatever it touches, or rather, increases the capacity for physical speed. Reactions and reflexes are most uniformly affected, while the act of walking or running or conscious movement seems more easily regulated. Its touch seems to grant a sense of what is going to happen, but this is hard to measure, especially in comparison to the increased speed. Myths and folklore imply that like Zidanio, this metal may have been unknowingly used in the past, allowing for individuals to move and react at great speeds, as well as premonitions. Other folktales of impossibly lucky individuals, even when compared to yellow-crests, fortune tellers, and prophecies suggest that this metal may have more properties, but how to test and quantify these properties remains a mystery.

When used with georaural technology, Aikanuum increases the "battery-life" so to speak, of a given device. It both takes longer for the device to use up its stored power, and seems to almost entirely eliminate decay when not in use. Flares and functions that take increasing amounts of energy still use more energy than the base functions, but at a proportional rate.

THE REDEEMED

The Redeemed, or "Lightforged," as they are referred to by enemies of the Imaia or those uncomfortable with the Redeemed, are the Imaia's elite warriors, led by their champion Othaashle, the first of the Redeemed. Not much is known about the Redeemed outside of their own numbers and the leaders of the Imaia's priesthood and armed forces. The public is told that the Redeemed are warriors that fell in battle on one side or the other, who Ynuukwidas, Lord of the Imaia, judged worthy of Redemption and a second chance at life to fight for the Imaia. They are supposedly immortal warriors who always wear masks to hide the identity of those they once were from themselves and others. They have no memory of their past lives, and are seen as a symbol or Ynuukwidas' power and the might of the Imaia. They fight the battles of the Imaia so that fewer of the Imaia's citizens need give their lives in service of their neighbors.

Though "Redeemed" is the official term used to refer to these soldiers, in scientific terms, they are referred to as lightforged invested entities, either Type-One or Type-Two. The type-one entities are what are most commonly referred to as Redeemed, whereas type-two are often referred to as "Unbound Redeemed." Though the preferred term refers to their physical state, type refers to the manner of their creation.

All Redeemed are created by snatching a soul before it passes on through the Gates of Death. That soul can be held for a thus-far indeterminate amount of time, though it is theorized that the soul will start to deteriorate after a certain point. Upon "resurrection," the soul is restored to the physical realm by tying it to something physical with power, and then using that same power to fill any cracks or wounds the soul sustained at the time of death or during its previous life. It has not been conclusively proven, but theorized, that the more a soul suffered in life, and the more traumatic its death, the greater power it would wield as a Redeemed, or at the very least it would possess a greater affinity for the use of its powers. Upon resurrection, the soul is granted the abilities of a Natari Auroraborn in addition to their previous Auroramantic abilities.

Type-One entities are resurrected by re-attaching their soul to a physical body, usually the soul's original body. When this happens, the body's skin turns a pale white-grey, and markings of shining, solid gold that feel like metal to the touch form over its body. These do not appear to form any sort of uniform markings, though they close over open wounds in stylized manners, and there is at least one grouping on either side of the torso, each limb, and the face. The irises turn a silver, gold-flecked color and glow. If the body is Samjati, the antlers turn silver and become as hard as steel, forming sharp edges and points. If the body is Natari, any markings such as stripes or spots turn gold. They also grow a second gemcrest. If Natari, they grow it out of their brow, and if Samjati, out of their clavicle. The newer gemcrest seems to have tiny gold flecks at the edge of each individual biogem on the gemcrest, but since these are usually covered by a mask or armor, little formal study has been performed. Most Redeemed also experience some sort of growth in height or musculature upon resurrection. This is theorized to happen because their primary duty is that of intimidating warriors.

Type-Two entities are souls whose physical bodies could not be retrieved, either because they were lost on the battlefield or too far gone upon death to be restored. These souls are given bodies constructed of hardlight, with accents of the same gold that the Type-One entities receive. Though their bodies are slightly transparent, they appear to function normally, though somehow, these individuals seem to grow back the gemcrest their old soul maintained. Something fascinating, but not properly researched at this point.

The cost of this resurrection for both types of Redeemed is the lost of who they once were. When they awaken, they have no memory of the person they once were. It is assumed they somehow retain certain general knowledge incongruous with true amnesia, as well as honed reflexes and skills, as though the lightforged train, the only sort of "basic training" they are known to receive is a formal education in Auroramantic abilities and the use and application of newer technologies. Lord Ynuukwidas has explained that he scours the Redeemed of who they once were, so that their loyalties to the Imaia will not be tested, and they will not need to worry about discrimination based on who they were before their redemption. Because of this, all type-one entities wear masks to hide their faces, and most wear either a uniform or full armor at all times. Type-two entities have facial features that move like a normal face when they speak or look around, but the features emulate that of the masks of the Redeemed, and betray very little emotion.

Though it is not known exactly how Lord Ynuukwidas catches these souls before they pass through the Gates of Death, it is believed that the sword, Ilkwalerva, wielded by Othaashle, is the mechanism through which this is performed, as in battle, she often sought out the most dangerous enemy Auroramancers, and reports have confirmed that the other Redeemed did not begin to appear until after Othaashle began using Ilkwalerva in battle much more frequently rather than simply relying on her Auroramantic prowess.

ARGILEON
ENTERTAINMENT